Roak Garfield came like a
curse into people's lives...leaving
them branded like cattle!

In place of conscience he had cold-
blooded ambition—and his trademark
was murder and deceit.

As he pursued his ruthless quest for
power and money, three women were
drawn under his strange spell. And
each suffered with an intense and
painful pleasure.

But most men loathed Roak Garfield.
Two in particular. One swore to
kill him. The other had more
elaborate plans—*to make Roak
Garfield suffer until he killed himself!*

**THE
GARFIELD
HONOR**
was originally published by
The Dial Press at $3.95.

THE
GARFIELD
HONOR

———◆———

FRANK YERBY

A GIANT CARDINAL EDITION published by
POCKET BOOKS, INC. • NEW YORK

THE GARFIELD HONOR

Dial Press edition published September, 1961
Giant Cardinal edition published December, 1962
1st printing........October, 1962

This *Giant Cardinal*** edition includes every word contained in the
original, higher-priced edition. It is printed from brand-new
plates made from completely reset, clear, easy-to-read type.
Giant Cardinal editions are published by Pocket Books, Inc., and
are printed and distributed in the U.S.A. by Affiliated Publishers,
a division of Pocket Books, Inc., 630 Fifth Avenue, New York 20, N.Y.
*Trademark registered in the United States and other countries.
**Trademark of Pocket Books, Inc., 630 Fifth
Avenue, New York 20, N.Y., in the United States
and other countries.

L

THE
GARFIELD
HONOR

Chapter One

"YOU KNOW anybody in Arizona?" the doctor said.

"No," Roak Garfield said.

"Texas?"

"Yes," Roak said.

"Who? How long? Well enough to write and ask him . . . ?"

Roak looked at the doctor.

"That bad, Doc?" he said.

"That bad. Another winter in New York will finish you. I'll stake my professional reputation on that. If you weren't a tough little hickory limb, you'd be dead by now. Walking around with that hunk of lead in your lung. . . ."

"They was scared to take it out. Heard 'em talking. They thought I was out, but I wasn't. They'd run out of opium the day before. Always fresh out of something you need rightly bad in a war. . . ."

"Especially the brains and guts it takes to find some other way to settle disputes besides murder in the first place," the doctor said. "Get on with it, Roak. Whom do you know down there?"

"Friend of my pa's. Man named Furniss—Jess Furniss. Funny thing, they was war buddies, too, him and Pa. Different war, though—the Mexican one. Pa saved Mr. Furniss's life at Buena Vista. Always seemed rightly grateful. Said if there was ever anything he could do—"

"Write him," the doctor said. "Right now. Tonight. You'd be fine down there. Hot, dry climate where you wouldn't catch cold would keep that scar tissue from bursting loose. Inside of six months, you could forget you had that Rebel souvenir in you. A twinge or two once in a great while, but nothing worse. Get this prescription filled. It's to keep you from coughing. That's all I can do for you, boy. What you need is air—and sun."

Roak picked up his shirt and put it back on. His fingers were long, deft, powerful. They seemed not to match his small hands.

"What did you do before?" the doctor asked.

"Farm boy," Roak said. "Can't you tell?"

"No. Funny thing, too. Usually I can spot an ex-plow-hand the minute I look at his fingers. Plowing thickens them. Twists them, too, sometimes. But on you it doesn't show. You've the hands of a violinist."

Or of a killer, Roak thought. Aloud, he said:

"Never was any great shakes on the farm. Pa used to take a square yard off my hide every time he saw how I'd done what he'd told me to do. . . ."

"Which is why you left. Had a bellyful, eh? No more sod busting for you. Big City. Lights, wine, women, song—"

"You a mind reader or something, Doc?" Roak said.

"No. I've seen a hundred like you. And you're wrong, every mother's son of you! Farming's hard work, lonely work; but it's a good life. What have you got here, boy? Tell me: what have you got?"

Roak looked at him again. A long time.

"Nothing," he said.

He groped in his pocket for the money.

"No," the doctor said. "The visit's on me, boy. Hang on to your money. Heard Mike kicked you out because you were sick too much. You'll need it—"

"I can pay," Roak began.

"Oh, don't be a fool!" the doctor said. "Just you write that letter."

"All right, Doc," Roak said, and turned to go.

"Roak," the doctor said.

"Yes, Doc?"

"Merry Christmas, boy," the doctor said.

Roak stood there.

"Christmas," he said. "It is, ain't it?" He put out his hand. The doctor took it.

"Merry Christmas, Doc," Roak said. The two of them shook hands, gripping hard, like old friends. Roak let go of the doctor's hand and moved toward the doorway. In it, he turned.

"You know, Doc," he said, "you're the first human creature I've shook hands with in more than a year. . . ."

Then he was gone through that door with a speed and silence befitting the catlike grace of him.

"Damn it," the doctor said. "Oh, damn it all!"

It was still snowing. The snow muffled the sound of Roak's footsteps, so he could hear the drivers of the horsecars on Broadway, two blocks away, cracking their whips and swearing. So now it was Christmas, 1867; and the War had been over two years for everybody else, and three years for him. Three years of being half-alive, and that half on borrowed time. He thought about how he had got this way. For a long time it had been a good thing to think about; but it wasn't any more. Because he had believed that maybe he had been saved for something. Now it looked like what he had been saved for was to die like a rat in a furnished room on 23rd Street, choking to death from his sick lung, instead of dying like a man before Nashville on that cold, crisp 15th of November, 1864, with the dry leaves crunching under his horse's hooves and the white powder smoke rising under the trees gone red and gold with autumn. He was riding in the vanguard of Wilson's Cavalry, pounding down on Chalmer's troops entrenched before Nashville, when a Reb sniper had knocked him out of the saddle with a minie ball in his right lung. He had lain there coughing up blood, staining the autumn leaves redder than they already were. He hadn't wanted to die. He had been twenty-six years old then; and no man's dying is an acceptable thing when he is that young and the longing and the lust and the dreaming are in him still. No man's dying is ever an acceptable thing. He knew that now, even though he was twenty-nine years old and tired and sick and alone and without prospects, friends or even hope. Still, it would have been better to have died that day. A hell of a lot better. Because a man would have died then. A soldier. But what was it that was dying now?

He opened the street door and started climbing the stairs. There were five flights, and he had to stop on every landing to get his breath back and to keep from coughing. He opened the door with his key. It creaked as he pushed it open. The room was cold. As cold as the tomb.

He struck a match and lit the lamp. Then he saw the white square of the envelope lying inside the room where the opening door had swept it. He stood there and stared at it. He knew who it was from. Fanny. His sweetheart. Maybe. Even his fiancée. Again, maybe. He even knew what it was going to say.

He knelt down clumsily and picked it up. He took out his jackknife and slit the envelope. He tried to read it, but it was too dark, even with the lamp lit. He moved over to the lamp, and held the letter inches from the flame. Then he read:

"Just heard you lost the job at Mike's, just like you lost the other one. I'm sorry, Roak; but it's quits between us, now. I can't wait forever for you to straighten up and make your way. Besides, sickly like you be, don't give a girl no real prospects. I didn't mean to tell you so soon, but I've been walking out with another gentleman friend for quite some time now. He's got him a good job, driv-

ing the delivery wagon for Kramer's Brewery. Fine figure
of a man, too. Strong as an ox. So you see. . . ."

He saw, all right. He saw it was Christmas night and
that he was sitting in an ice-cold room trying not to cough
because the next time he coughed he might bring up blood.
He was sitting there like that, knowing that if he lit the
fire he wouldn't have coal enough to last 'til New Year's;
and if he bought more coal, in a couple of weeks anyhow,
he wouldn't have the money to buy the one meal a day he
was down to eating now. He saw all that very clearly. That
and the fact that there wasn't a soul in all that great sprawling mass of the city he could truly call friend. The doc,
maybe. Yes, surely the doc. And now his girl—such as she
was—was gone, too.

He sat there, gazing at the dead fire, fighting the choking sensation in his lungs. He sat there a very long time,
while the chill climbed up his small, thin, curiously graceful body, that never in his life had been outdone in feats of
skill (the little fellow's painfully acquired compensation
for his lack of height and strength) until at Nashville he
had come to the end of the youth, the skill, and now even
the hope and the dreaming.

He got up then, slowly. As he dug in the drawer where
he kept the Army Colt, he saw how slim and sure his
hands were. The doc was right: they were the hands of a
violinist—or an artist. Only he couldn't play a note; and
his sole artistry consisted in a gut-twisting love for and
skill with cold steel. He was a damned fine shot; but there
was a thing in him a blade appealed to—an icy, rat-bastard meanness, he reckoned, that was mightily pleasured
by the silent, glittering thrust; the sudden horror in his
victim's eyes; the thick, ropy spurt of blood. . . .

It had put a barrier between him and his fellows. Or
wasn't he putting the cart before the horse? Hadn't the
frozen vein of cruelty in him sunk deep because of the
barrier already there, shutting him away from the warmth

of companionship, of love? His mother, Hilda Garfeldt, had died giving birth to him, and try as he would, his father, Otto Garfeldt, could never forgive his last-born that. How many times had he seen his pa looking at him with eyes like frost and flint? How many times had he run to the man who should have been his refuge and his strength only to have Otto push him away, none too gently, and say, his voice coming out grim and quiet: "Run along, boy, and play. I've got things to do. . . ."

"Run along, boy." His father and his brothers—always that phrase. Or, "For Pete's sake, Roakie, quit tagging along! Go play with kids your own age. . . ."

And he, growing older, knew why. Because of the beloved wife he had cost his father, because he didn't measure up to the standards unconsciously applied by all Garfeldts, was too little, too delicate, too dreamy, maybe even too poetic. But his keen eyes missed nothing. He saw the Humboldt boys, the same age as his own brothers, patiently taking little Willi Humboldt—even younger than he—everywhere with them, cutting whistles for him out of the reeds down by the creek, teaching Willi how to swim, how to fish, how to hold a gun—all the things that big brothers were there to teach, but which his brothers never bothered to teach him. He knew blamed well that that big oaf Phil Pfeifer never picked on Willi. Johann and Martin Humboldt would have taken him apart if he'd dared. Oh, no, Willi was never left to come crying home, one eye swollen shut and purpling, his nose streaming blood, which was how *he* arrived at the Garfeldt farm every time Phil could catch him. Then what? Then Hansel and Manny stood there laughing at him and calling him a cowardly ninny who couldn't even fight. . . .

Well, he'd learned to take care of himself soon enough. He'd learned that a well-honed jackknife could throw a sick quaver of fear into the biggest, especially when it was used the way he'd taught himself to use one. His pa had striped him all over the time that Officer Schmidt had brought him home after he'd slashed Phil Pfeifer across the back of his right, his punching hand, leaving it so Phil could never hit hard with it again, thus ending his career as a bully forever. Oh, yes, Otto had called his youngest Absalom that day; had sworn the mark of Cain was visible on his forehead. Otto Garfeldt had been a God-fearing, Bible-reading man. . . .

Only, Roak thought bitterly, you didn't read the Scriptures right, Pa—or else you'd have known that Absalom had his pa's love. You might have realized that Cain turned killer because his brother, Abel, was the favored one. And me—I had two favored ones to buck: Hans and Manfred. Big like you, Pa. Good-looking. Nobody ever called *them* "Runt" Garfeldt. Nobody ever pounded the living daylights out of them. And the girls—blushing when Hansel and Manny eyed 'em; going peony-faced, soft-eyed, dreamy. . . . But when I looked at a female, what did she do? Laugh, that's what! "Puny li'l feller, that Ruarch Garfeldt!"

He thought about that. About all the girls he'd been in love with. "Puppy love," his brothers would have called it, if he had dared confide in them, which, of course, he hadn't. Millicent Steiner. Olga Fischer. Irmagarde Zauber. But why go on? The list was endless. And the response of his adored, calico-clad, blonde-curled goddesses almost invariable. In fact, the girls of Meeker, Ohio, confronted with Ruarch Garfeldt's teen-age ardors, had had only two reactions: outraged scorn at his presumption, or attacks of near-hysterical laughter.

That, like everything else in life, had a why to it. Had reasons that later he realized, instinctively understood. He had been terribly timid, absurdly gauche, stammering, awkward—like the vast majority of boys of his age. But timidity and awkwardness can be charming in big, good-looking oafs like his brothers—because, granted good looks, physical strength, stature, promise, they take upon themselves the sympathetic coloring of modesty. But when a fellow was little, skinny, runty, unimpressive—timidity and awkwardness (of speech, of manner, because he was never awkward physically; but too graceful, if anything, so that, in him, even that attractive characteristic became suspect) fitted him too well, subtracted from the sum total of what he had to offer—did not seem, as these negative qualities seemed in Hansel and Manny, a genial pretense. Only what good did it do to understand a thing you could neither cure nor help? A thing that marked you to such an extent that, growing up, becoming a man, you always sought out the undesirable, even the faintly repugnant, the Fannys of this world, because you still didn't dare risk the scorn of a true woman or the competition of other men?

Yes, that was it—a goodly part of it, anyhow. He'd been little Ruarch Garfeldt with his red hair and his body like a ballet dancer's, born out of his time and place among a race of farmers. Clodhoppers. Sodbusters. Poor dumb plowpushers who didn't understand the ache in him, the itch, the glory hunger. Nope. That hadn't been good enough for him. He had to be Mr. Roak Garfield of New York City and maybe marry a banker's daughter. Now look. He was Roak Garfield, all right. Who couldn't even keep a job tending saloon because he wasn't strong enough to push a nickel beer mug across a greasy bar. Who couldn't even marry a flighty little dime-store counter jumper, because he wasn't good enough for the likes of her now.

He drew the gun out. He sat down again, holding it in his hand. Then he cleaned and loaded it. That took him quite a time because a model 1860 Colt Army revolver was a cap-and-ball pistol manufactured while the Smith & Wesson people's patents kept anybody else from putting a hand gun chambered to take metallic cartridges on sale. He hadn't cleaned the lamp in two months so it didn't give enough light for him to see that the paper cartridges he bit the ends off of and poured the black powder out of into each of the six chambers were damp and moldy. Anyhow, they were the only ammunition he had. He rammed the .44-caliber balls home with the loading lever, and began to fit the six copper percussion caps to the nipples at the back of the cylinder. The caps were green with corrosion, but he didn't notice that either.

He hefted the big Colt. It was heavy. But at the last moment, as he pointed the muzzle straight at his right temple, he smiled.

It wasn't a good smile. Fanny, he knew, was going to have herself a time, bragging about how a man blew his brains out over her. And the funny part about it was she was right. Right for all the wrong reasons. Write her a note, maybe, saying: "Critter not good enough for a cheap little counter-jumping tart like you ain't even fitten to live. . . ." No. Leave her brag. He wouldn't be around to hear it. Nor her damnfool giddy talk; nor to be gutsickened by the airs she put on. Good to leave all that: Fanny whose virtue lasted through the third glass of whisky, then dissolved into a breathy spurting of words thrust into a man's ear like so many oxgoads—and for the same reason. Words he kept wondering where the devil she'd ever learned, and that left the afterward—instead of a good, warm tiredness —a sickness. A cold, deadly coiling in his middle, puking sick like a starving man who has been forced to eat swill to end his hunger. Because a man had to be starving to take Fanny. No more now. Forever and ever no more amen. No more Fanny. No more tiredness. No more being cold, being sick. . . . No more—

The hammer clicked down on the dead cap over the damp powder. Roak lowered the revolver and stared at it. He felt something stirring in him, something dim and deep. He raised the Colt again, bringing it up fast. He had to do it now, before the thing in him got too strong. He eared the hammer back again. Pulled the trigger. Another click, and—silence.

He sat there, looking at the big Colt. He remembered all the times it had saved his life. Like that time they'd run into Nat Forrest and those Cracker horsemen of his who could do things with their bony nags and their home-made Dance revolvers that nothing human ought to have been able to do; but then, maybe there was more than a mite of truth in the Union Cavalry's belief that Nat's ma had run into the devil down by Bitter Creek some nine months before Nat was born. Roak had shot his way out of that one and with this same gun. It had never missed firing before, not even once. He was sweating now, cold as it was.

"Third strike's out," he said aloud; and jammed the muzzle against his temple. The hammer stroke of the third misfire jarred his eye teeth. He jerked up from his chair and crossed to the window. He opened it and stood there. He was shaking all over, but he wasn't cold any more. He pointed the Colt upward. He cocked the hammer and pulled the trigger three more times. On the last shot, the percussion cap fired; but even its blast, striking through the touch hole of the nipple into the chamber, couldn't make that damp powder go off.

And Roak Garfield threw back his head and laughed aloud.

He turned then, and crossed the room to the fireplace. He laid a fire in the grate. He struck the match, lit the fire, and stood back. The flames licked up through the kindling. It caught and the sound that it made was like laughter, too. He felt a draft on the back of his neck from the window he had left open. He went and closed it, then came back to the fire. The coals began to catch now, and the knife edge went out of the chill. The glow of the fire was a cheerful thing. He drew up his chair and spread out his slim, deft hands to its warmth.

It reminded him of home. They'd had a big open fire-place in the Ohio farmhouse where he had been born. He remembered how, at Christmas time, his father and his brothers used to gather around the fire and sing together in German, "Silent Night, Holy Night. . . ." That was the one thing they never left him out of. He'd had a good voice then, a choirboy's soprano, already dropping into an alto. . . .

He began to sing it now, in a hoarse baritone. But he stopped it almost at once. It brought Manny's and Hansel's faces too clearly to mind. They had both been bigger than he by far; strong, square-built German-American farm-boys with the kind of faces that always got a fellow named "Dutch" or "Squarehead." Quiet boys, not given to mouthing life over. Quiet forever now, since Shiloh Church, since Spotsylvania, since "Butcher" Grant, having learned he couldn't outthink Bob Lee, set out to smash him, steam-roller over him by sheer weight of numbers, cost what it might. What it cost was five thousand men in the first five minutes; five thousand anonymous corpses—anonymous except to those who had known and loved them, fought with them, swum the creek with them in the golden, lazy Ohio summers, hitched plow teams with them, broken sod —called them brothers.

The fire blurred before his eyes. He shook his head angrily. Not that. All right, he'd loved them—loved his brothers with what had seemed to him an unrequited love. Gone on loving them even after he'd thought he was over giving a damn for anybody or anything. Maybe that was why he had done the thing that put the slow, dull ache of shame into him every time he thought about it. Like now. He tried to force it from his mind, but he couldn't. So now, deliberately, he thought about that, too. Concen-trated on it. Tried to see what meaning he could drag up out of the ugliest of all the many ugly things he'd done.

He had come home on leave in the spring of Sixty-

Three. After Shiloh Church. Before Spotsylvania. He had come back. To find that Otto Garfeldt had brought Hansel's body home before him. Had journeyed all the way to Shiloh to do it. Spent very nearly every penny he had so that Hansel Garfeldt could lie in familiar earth, under the trees he had so loved.

And Roak Garfield—for already then Ruarch Garfeldt was dead and buried, more profoundly dead and deeper buried than Hansel would ever be—went, driven by the wild mourning in his heart, by the hurt all the more anguished because Hansel had never known, wanted, accepted the worship little Ruarch had felt for the broad giants of his clan, to kneel beside his brother's grave, to say a prayer to the God he scarcely believed in any more, to—even that—to shed a tear, to weep for what might have been.

When he walked into that cemetery under the trees, the birds were singing. It was very cool and quiet and peaceful in there. Dying didn't seem so bad when you could sleep in this good earth under these big oaks with the birds singing to you. Even if you couldn't hear them. But then, who knew? Maybe you could. Far off and faint—like echoes. And maybe the memories of the good life you'd had came back to you like a kind of dreaming. . . .

He moved down the rows between the headstones, reading the old familiar names: Meeker, Humboldt, Zimmer, Zauber, Schickel, Miller, Kopfer—Garfeldt. . . .

He stood there staring at his mother's headstone, big enough for two graves, with his father's name already carved on it, only that one place for the final date left blank. His eyes blurred a little. For the sounds that rode in upon him cut through his half-formed thoughts like a knife.

A woman was crying. Crying in the same way that

some of the Rebel women who came out on the battlefields after the fight was over to look for their dead had cried. It wasn't a thing a body could stand listening to very long. Not if there was anything like pity left inside him.

He took a step forward. Then he saw her. She had laid a spray of roses on Hansel's grave. She knelt, with her bright blonde head pressed against the headstone, and cried like that, so that in every note of it, juddering up from that throat (swan-slender, white as milk, he noted even then), he heard how much she had loved his oldest brother, how much she missed him, how she was dying on the inside in that peculiar way that good and true women have, from wanting and needing him so.

Roak came over to her. He put out his slim, smooth hand, and touched her shoulder.

"Please, ma'am," he said, "don't cry. Not like that. For the Lord's sake, ma'am, don't cry. . . ."

She whirled, faced him. Then all the color went out of her face. She knelt there, looking at him. Her lips moved, but he didn't hear what she said. He couldn't, because nothing came out. Nothing at all.

"Please, ma'am," he pleaded, "I loved him, too. He was the best brother a fellow ever had. . . ." He heard his own voice going on, telling those cold, deliberate lies. Or were they? Weren't they perhaps a part of his dream, his need, his anguish? "Him 'n' Manny, too. But 'specially him. He used to cut whistles for me out of the reeds down by the creek when I was too little to do it for myself. He taught me how to fish, how to hold a gun—I was the baby, you see. That's why I'm asking you not to cry. He wouldn't want you to. And I—doggone it, ma'am, I just plain can't stand it!"

"Why—why," she whispered, "you're crying, too! I'm sorry. You're Ruarch, aren't you? The one who ran away?"

"Yes'm," Roak said. "Can I help you up now, ma'am?"

"Yes," she said.

He helped her to her feet. She was a small girl. Her blue eyes had to look up even to meet his, short as he was. Her lips moving were like—like wild rose petals, he reckoned, the palest kind of pink. And she wasn't thick-set, or broad-hipped, or sturdy like most German-American farm girls. She was willow-slim, sweet-curving, graceful.

"What's your name, ma'am?" he said.

"Gwendolyn. Gwendolyn Heindrichs. I—was your brother's intended. . . ."

"I figured that much. Hope I didn't frighten you, Miss Heindrichs. But I just couldn't let you cry like that. Was scairt I was going to bust out and bawl myself. . . ."

She smiled at him. Her smile was tender. He stopped breathing, looking at her.

"You did," she said. "And you know what, Mr. Garfeldt?"

"No, ma'am, I don't know what—"

"I'm glad you did. Only a good man cries for his loved ones."

He thought: Good? You Dresden china baby doll, if you knew what I'm thinking right now!

"And I'm glad you're good," Gwendolyn went on. "You did frighten me at first. It was like seeing a—a ghost. You are so like Hansel! So very like—a little shorter, and much, much slimmer; but your face is exactly the same. . . ."

He stopped then, and looked at her.

"Is that a point in my favor, Miss Heindrichs?" he said.

She looked back at him. A long time, and very slowly.

"Yes," she said; "it very definitely is a point in your favor, Mr. Garfeldt."

He felt a sudden surge of icy, exultant joy. But nothing else. None of the other things another man in his place might have felt: neither love, nor tenderness—nor even shame. Nor, if the truth were told, did he feel so healthy a thing as lust. He didn't desire her slender, graceful body particularly. What he did desire, he couldn't have put into words: to prove something; to humiliate by proxy the entire sex who had so often humiliated him, to demonstrate to his own deep self-loathing, his profound and festering doubt, that he was at long last, and truly, a man.

"Can you walk with me a little while, Miss Heindrichs?" he asked.

"As long as you like, Mr. Garfeldt. I have nothing to do. . . ."

"Lord, but you do talk fine!" he said.

"I'm a schoolteacher, Mr. Garfeldt. It would be a disgrace if I couldn't talk reasonably well."

They walked on, arm in arm, through the shady lane. Roak found himself, he who had never been a talker, telling her everything, judiciously embroidered with lies: why he ran away, his adventures in Cleveland, the War. . . . When he got to the story of how he had been hit before Vicksburg, her fingers dug convulsively into his arm. He smiled at her, sure now, very sure.

"So I lay there in the mud," he lied grandly, "not able to move. That night it turned cold. And I plumb froze to the ground. The stretcher bearers had to chop me loose with picks when they found me that next morning. That's why I limp, sometimes—"

"Oh," she breathed, "how awful! But you know, I hadn't even noticed that you limp. . . ."

"I don't, most of the time. Only when the weather's bad. You—you don't mind, do you?"

She gazed at him. Her blue eyes were very soft.

"I don't mind what, Mr. Garfeldt?"

"The limp. Some girls has plain got a horror of a cripple. . . ."

".Why, Mr. Garfeldt! What do you think I am? A girl who'd turn her back on a man injured in the service of his country is not fit to speak to! Your limp is a grand thing, a badge of honor. I like you better for it."

Which took care of that nonexistent limp. They walked on. Roak found words, found eloquence. It was a long time before he noticed he was having trouble seeing her face. When he did, he played it smart.

"Lord God!" he said. "It's after dark! What are your folks going to say?"

"I haven't any folks, Mr. Garfeldt, except my brother Fritz, and his farm is way over on the other side of Bellefontaine," Gwendolyn said. "I live at Mrs. Meeker's boarding house. And," she laughed gaily, mischievously, "you don't have to worry about what Mrs. Meeker will say. I became the town's fallen woman half an hour ago as far as she is concerned. . . ."

"Lord, Miss Heindrichs, ma'am, I'm sorry! I'll take you home right now!"

"You don't have to hurry, Mr. Garfeldt. I don't care about Mrs. Meeker. Besides, I'm enjoying your company. . . ."

Which, though true, was the wrong thing to say to Roak Garfield. A bad choice of words to use to a man with a black devil in him, gnawing at his guts. To little Runt Garfeldt who had a hell of a lot to pay the whole race of womankind back for.

Gwen Heindrichs was a good girl. Prim, proper, a mite strait-laced. But she had fallen into the hands of a man who could sit beside her and say to himself: All right, you miserable rat-bastard, you no-good puking polecat, what are you going to try next?

To Gwen's credit, nothing worked. Nothing at all until the night before he left. He rented a buggy. There was a moon. And he had all the diabolical skill of the heartless. An hour later, she was weeping in his arms.

"I'm so ashamed!" she sobbed. "Oh, Roak, I want to die!"

He kissed her then. A long time, and very thoroughly. And Gwen Heindrichs discovered she didn't want to die after all. Found, to her pained astonishment, that what she actually wanted to do was repeat the offense.

"Take me home!" she stormed.

"No," Roak said, and kissed her again.

And that was that, not only then, but every night of the week he overstayed his leave.

She saw him off. Her blue eyes were flooded, blind.

"Come back to me, Roak!" she wept.

"Of course, Gwen, darling," he lied.

But he had gone back, after the wound he'd got at Nashville had healed enough to permit him to travel. Not out of any goodness or nobility of soul. Because he figured that the way he was now, he needed a woman to take care of him. And Gwen was already his. Hell of a lot less trouble than starting a new courtship. Or so he thought.

Only it hadn't turned out like that. Gwen wasn't there any more. Only their stillborn child was, buried in the Garfeldt plot by that stern, God-fearing man, his father.

He remembered his return. Because it had begun at once to go bad in a way so peculiar that it was hard for him to say why it was bad at all. Put it this way, maybe: all the good people, all the folks he truly admired and respected in Meeker, his home town, the place where he had been born, stood back looking at him with faces that were both questioning and yet already shut tight against any explanation he could possibly give them. So he got his back up, and wouldn't give any at all, simply asking word of Gwen, trying to find out where she had gone—to which they replied that they didn't know. But what got to him maybe even a little more than the attitude of Meeker's first citizens was the fact that every raffish good-for-nothing, every worthless idler, every drunken sot in town found occasion to come sidling up to him, lick slack and lecherous lips, dig an elbow into his ribs, wink, and say:

"Must have been mighty fine, Roakie! High-toned missy like that one—tell a fellow, won't you—how was it?"

And he feeling his big gut knot with sudden sickness went into Blocher's Saloon to try to drown that sickness—that one and a couple of others—shame, maybe, and a slow, dim hurt at not being able to find Gwen that was as near an acknowledgment of the perhaps unrecognized way he had come to feel about her by then as he was capable of at that stage in his life. Inside the saloon, it was worse. All the tipplers surrounded him, slapping him on the back, laughing, shouting:

"Hail, the conquering hero comes!"

"Hero? 'S the truth! Don't know how many Rebs he laid out, but when it comes to pushing over uppity schoolmarms. . . ."

"On me, Roakie! Have one on me—to celebrate yer vict'ries. Show us your trophies, boy! One busted hoop from a crinoline, one pair of torn, lacy—"

Trembling a little from the unexpected rage he felt and from the bitter knowledge that he was in no shape to whip even one of them, Roak downed his rye, clapped a coin on the bar, and walked out of there.

But when he came out into the street, he saw why he should have left town two days earlier, instead of hanging around trying to trace Gwen. Because when he pushed open those swinging doors, her brother, Fritz, was there.

Surrounded by a crowd that within minutes was reinforced by all the men who had been in that saloon. A nine-foot leaded muleskinner's whip in his hand. He flipped it out in the dust sinuously, uncoiling it like a blacksnake. And Roak, looking from face to face greedy for his blood, from eye to hard, glittering eye, to lips drawn tight over wolfish teeth, knew at last what his father had meant when he said that the mark of Cain was on his forehead. What entered him then was not fear, but rage; the bottomless cold, feral rage of the outcast; the ravenous fury of the pariah dog he was.

He took a step toward them. His hand went inside his coat where he had a double scabbard hung on a shoulder sling. With his knives in it. With those knives he could shave with; that he loved and trusted in a way he'd never love and trust a gun.

Fritz Heindrichs's arm came back, back, snaking that whip out behind him—out, out, prolonging that moment, savoring it. And Roak's hand came out from under his coat with a speed that blurred sight, so fast that they saw only the glitter, saw silver leap the intervening space between the small, catlike man and big Fritz Heindrichs, saw a bolt of lightning flipping end over end. . . .

They saw Fritz drop the whip. Clutch at his arm. Saw Roak Garfield cross to him slowly, ignoring them as though they weren't there. Saw his hand flash out, closing, tugging, and the blade slipping free, thickred and dripping.

Roak stood there.

"That'll hold you for now," he said. "Only it won't show. You'll forget, maybe. You and the rest of these yellow-livered bastards. So I reckon I'd better leave you a reminder. . . ."

Then his hand came up. Fast. Whipped in, once, twice, three times. And Fritz Heindrichs no longer had a tip to his nose. Both of his earlobes were deep-notched, like a sow's.

"There, now," Roak said. "And if any of you gentlemen want to be decorated for free—just start toward me. . . ."

Then he marched through them, seeing with cold delight the fear in their eyes.

Which didn't last, of course. Within a half-hour their individual shame at having had their individual cowardice witnessed by half a hundred men had found a collective fury stronger than their fear.

Roak was at the railroad station by then, waiting for the eastbound train. He saw them coming, equipped with ropes, tar, feathers, pitchforks, a shotgun or two. Led by Will Meeker on horseback. On a nervous gray gelding who was fighting the bit.

Roak stood there waiting until they were close enough. Then he drew his big Colt and powderburned the nag—shooting so close that the gun blast branded the gray though Roak threw deliberately wide. The gray went back on his haunches, pawing the air. Will Meeker, who was nobody's horseman, slipped over the beast's back, hit the ground, lay there. The gray gelding whirled, plunged into the crowd, scattering them. They hung there a moment longer, until Roak pumped three more bullets into the dirt as close to their feet as he could put them, which was plenty close. That did it.

Ten minutes later when the train pulled in, not even the stationmaster was around to wave Roak Garfield good-by. . . .

What meaning did it have? What meaning did anything have? Was there some significance in the fact that all the Garfeldts—his pa, Hansel, Manny, big, fine, strapping men—were dead now, and he, a dirty little rat-bastard, was left alive?

Alive and likely to go on living. All Doc Turner had said was that his lung was dangerously weak. A year or two in a hot, dry climate like Texas would make a new man of him. Pa had always raved about Texas since that trip he took to visit his old friend, Mr. Furniss. . . .

He'd have to write that letter now. Jesse Furniss was a good man. He'd do anything for one of Otto Garfeldt's sons. And seeing that this one last Garfeldt had taken a minie ball through the lung and come out of it walking, and his own .44 had plain upped and quit before it would kill him, maybe all the things that had happened to him meant there was somebody, after all, who was keeping him alive—for something.

Yep, it meant that. Maybe. Or more likely that the world belonged to rat-bastards, since there were so many of them. Or that God didn't give a hoot up a hollow stump for mankind and all its works, and maybe wasn't even there.

All of which added up to the same thing: he, Roak Garfield, was going to make it, by whatever means that making it required. He'd play it straight, if that looked effective. But if dirty fighting was necessary, the world would find it was facing a past master.

He turned to the table, and picked up the steel-tipped pen.

"Thank you, good Lord," he said mockingly, and began to write.

Chapter Two

WHEN HE had finished the letter, he got up at once to go and mail it. Then he remembered that it was Christmas Day and that the post office was closed. He stood there, thinking. Heck, it was Christmas, dagnabit; and he had something to celebrate after all. Being alive was suddenly an important thing, a wonderful thing. Nothing had changed: he was still cold, sick, alone: but all the same it was good to be alive and to even have the chance to stop being cold, sick and alone. He'd celebrate that. He'd go down to Mike's and pour himself a snootful . . .

He got back into his old Army greatcoat and went down the stairs. It was only two blocks to Mike's. But now the air—the same snow-filled, wet, miserable air—was like wine in his nostrils. He pushed open the door of the saloon. It was jampacked. He had never seen so many people in it in the whole year and a half he had worked there. He wormed his way up to the bar. He plunked down a silver dollar. "Gimme a snort, Mike," he said.

Mike glared at him.

"Git that gawddamned coat off and yuh apron on, damn ye!" he growled. "Can't you see it's swamped I am?"

"You fired me," Roak said.

"Well, I just rehired ye," Mike said. "Damn it, man—come on!"

He mailed the letter the day after Christmas. And while he was waiting for the answer, he managed, by pampering himself outrageously, not to get sick again. He saved his money. With it he bought himself a good suit and a serviceable pair of boots. Then, remembering all the stories he had heard and read about the West, he took the Colt to a gunsmith and had the cylinder bored straight through so that it would take .44-caliber rim-fire metallic cartridges. The gunsmith knew his business. He took off the loading lever, and added in its place a side-mounted ejector rod to punch out the empties and a loading gate hinged to swing out in the right-hand recoil shield. This was one Colt that wasn't going to misfire any more. Roak was sure of that.

He was sure of a lot of things, though for the life of him he couldn't have told why. Afterwards, he used to look back on the time and money he had spent getting ready for a trip he had no proof that he was ever going to make with a kind of wonder. "Fool thing," he said, "but all the same I was certain sure. . . ."

The answer came the last of February. It was cordial and kind. Jesse Furniss invited his old friend's son to make the Bar F his home—for life, if need be. As for the job Roak had asked about in his letter, time enough to talk about that when the Texas sun had cured him.

On March 1st, 1868, Roak Garfield was on the train bound for St. Louis. Six days later, he got off a big river packet in New Orleans. He felt great. The leisurely trip downriver, reposing in a comfortable cabin, had done wonders for him. Before he even looked for lodgings for the night, he had reserved passage on a Gulf steamer bound for Brownsville. But in Brownsville the nineteenth century's mechanical marvels ran out on him. To go the rest of the way, he had to take a stagecoach.

Roak climbed down from the stage and stood there, squinting into the light. It was the kind of light you had to squint into to see anything. He had the feeling that if he opened his eyes wide just once, that glare would leave him stone blind.

He looked up at the stage driver.

"How far did you say it was to the Furniss ranch?" he asked.

" 'Bout thirty-five, forty miles, south 'n' west," the driver said. "Didn't you let them Bar F folks know you was a-coming?"

"Yes," Roak said.

"Reckon they'll be along to fetch you, then. You just go right on into the station and wait."

"But," Roak said, "I sent 'em a telegram from New Orleans that I'd be in this week. Only I didn't tell 'em what day. Couldn't. Didn't know myself."

"Don't make no nevermind. 'Course, a telegram's a mite slower out here than back East. Nearest station's Brownsville. So they had to send a rider out to the Bar F to deliver it. Anyhow, it was plumb bound to get out to the ranch afore yore boat docked. 'Sides, ain't but two stage days, Mondays and Fridays. Case they came to fetch you Monday, they'll know it'll be today, 'cause you warn't on the Monday stage."

"What if they didn't come Monday?" Roak said.

"If they got yore wire, friend," the driver said, "they come. Cap'n Jess is the widest-spreading man in the whole blamed state. Ain't nobody ever outdone when it comes to hospitality. Don't worry yourself none a-tall. You're in Texas, now. Down here we just plain knows how to treat folks right."

"Thanks," Roak said.

"Don't mention it, friend. You'll find grub in there, you be hongry. Soap 'n' water, too, if you wants to freshen up a mite. . . ."

Roak looked down at his suit. It was—or had been—black broadcloth, just about the worst color he could have chosen. Now it was yellow gray from the alkali dust. He couldn't change. It was the only suit he had. In his lone carpetbag were only shirts, socks and underwear. Besides, changing wouldn't have made sense anyhow, what with another forty miles to go through the same dust and heat.

"Some country you've got down here," he said.

"You betcha," the driver said. "Folks say the devil owned all this section hereabouts, but after spending one summer in the brush down Nueces way, he plumb lit out for hell to cool off and turned this here spread over to the Greasers. Staying long?"

"Don't know," Roak said. "That depends."

"Sure know how to hobble your lip, don't you, friend? Good habit. Folks down here don't take kindly to windies. Be seeing you, now. . . ."

"Be seeing you," Roak said.

The stage station was made of adobe. There was nobody inside except the stationmaster, because the hostlers had gone outside to change the horses for the next run. The stationmaster was a lean, sun-browned man with his mouth clamped shut.

"Howdy," Roak said.

The stationmaster nodded. Roak put his carpetbag down, took off his coat, hung it on the steer-horn rack, and roved over to the tin basin in the corner. He poured some water into it from the pail underneath, and scooped up a little of the soft soap from the dish alongside. He had all he could do to keep from letting out a howl when that soap bit into the skin of his face. It was pure lye. But it got the dirt off, pronto. Roak had the feeling it had taken the skin off along with the dirt. He stretched out his hands toward the roller towel. Then he stopped. The towel had been hanging there since General Santa Anna had cleaned his boots with it before retreating into Mexico in 1848. After that, it must have been put to the daily use of wiping the grease off stage axles. He groped in his pockets and came out with his handkerchief. He managed to dry himself with that after a fashion.

He looked into the mirror. Somebody had put a bullet through the exact middle of it, so that the cracks radiated out from the hole in every direction like a spider's web. But there was enough left for him to see that his reddish-blond beard had sprouted during the stage ride. He looked like an angry porcupine. He didn't know whether Mr. Furniss had a wife or daughters, but he figured it wasn't smart to get there looking like a tramp. He opened his carpetbag and took out his razor, shaving soap, strop and brush. He managed to remove the whiskers without cutting himself fatally, in spite of that mirror.

Then he went back outside and slapped enough Texas dust out of his clothes to start a small farm. He combed his hair with his own comb because the stage station's offering, suspended from a nail on a rawhide thong, had long since lost the last tooth it had.

"Any place around here to get something to eat?" he asked.

The stationmaster jerked his head toward an inner door. "In there," he said.

Roak went through the door. Inside the eating shack, the air was blue with flies. A fat Mexican hunched over the counter. He was fast asleep. Roak didn't wake him. The food in this frontier Delmonico wouldn't be calculated to whet a man's appetite. He was sure of that.

He came back into the station.

"Thought you was hongry," the stationmaster said.

"I *was*," Roak said.

"Well, this ain't the Astor House," the stationmaster said, "but we can rustle up enough bait to fill a gut. You want me to wake th' Mex up?"

"No," Roak said. "I'll wait and eat at the Bar F."

He didn't have to wait long. In a shade under a half-hour, he saw the buckboard coming up the draw. He stood up, squinting into the light. The buckboard came up to the station, and the man driving it climbed down. He was something to see. He was a hair over six feet tall, with shoulders he needed to turn sidewise to go through any door. But his waist and hips were slimmer than a stripling's. He had on tight-fitting levis, boots, spurs, a broad-brimmed hat, a kerchief around his neck. But no gunbelt; no six-gun. His eyes were black with the squint built in. There was a sprinkle of gray in his black hair. His face was the color of old saddle leather. Hot as it was, he was wearing gloves.

"Howdy," he said. "You Mr. Garfield?"

"Yes," Roak said, putting out his hand. "And you?"

"The handle's Nevis. Bart Nevis. I'm Cap'n Furniss's range boss."

"Pleased to meet you," Roak said.

"Likewise," Bart Nevis said. He didn't take off his gloves even to shake hands.

"Where's your plunder?" he asked. "I'll store it so we can get moving. Miss Hannah's waiting supper for you."

"Miss Hannah?" Roak said.

"Cap'n's daughter," Bart Nevis said. Then he added, very quietly, "And my intended."

"Oh," Roak said, "I didn't know."

"Well, now you do," Bart Nevis said. "This your whole outfit?"

"Yes. Didn't think I'd need much stuff out here. Besides, I figured that whatever I'd pick to bring would be most likely wrong. . . ."

"Smart reckoning. Starting with that shooting iron. If I was you, I'd store it in the bag. The Cap'n don't take kindly to gun-packing."

Roak unfastened his gunbelt.

"Why?" he asked. "I thought that out here a man strapped on a Colt before he put on his boots."

"You thought wrong," Bart said. "But then Eastern folks most generally do."

He stood there waiting while Roak wrapped the gun-belt around the holster and stored the Colt in the bottom of the bag. All the time his black eyes were measuring Roak, inch by careful inch.

Rock picked up the carpetbag and put it in the spring-bed of the buckboard. Bart climbed in again and took the reins.

"All right," he said. "Reckon we'll mosey along, Mr. Pilgrim. . . ."

Roak climbed up beside him. Bart Nevis didn't open his mouth for the first five miles. Then he said, "You ride?"

"Some," Roak said.

Again that black, measuring gaze.

"Cap'n and Miss Hannah both give orders to stake out a cayuse for you that's plumb lady-broke," Bart said, "but I'm reckoning you can handle more hoss that that."

"Could be," Roak said. "Anyhow, I'll manage. . . ."

Bart Nevis looked at him.

"Reckon you will at that. Funny thing, you don't look like no greenhorn."

"Don't I?" Roak said. "Thanks."

"And you don't even talk like one. Besides, you never got that way of handling yourself jumping counters. I'll eat my boots with the spurs still on 'em if you're an Easterner at all."

"I'm not. Ohio. Farm boy, to tell the truth. I didn't even see the East 'til after the War."

"Figures," Bart Nevis said. He measured Roak again with a long look. "You fight in the big fuss?"

"Yes," Roak said. "Are you going to hold it against me?"

"Hmm," Bart said. "Ex-blue belly, eh? You just keep that part quiet, and you'll do. Mighty heap of boys down here who haven't been reconstructed yet. 'Specially don't

go jawing about your war record with the Yankee Army
around Miss Hannah. She had the command instead of
Lee, the War wouldn't be over 'til come next branding
time."

"But you don't feel that way about it?" Roak asked.

"No. You see, I fought against you fellows. Reckon if
I learned anything in the big fuss, it was that a man's a
man, no matter where he hails from. . . ."

"Thanks," Roak said. "Hope I can qualify."

Bart studied him openly.

"Kind of think you will. Looks like to me you've got
the makings of a mighty good hand once you're in shape
and have learned a thing or two. Don't even reckon it'll be
hard to teach you. Well, appears to me we've jawed enough
for now. It's a fair stretch out to the Bar F. . . ."

Roak had never imagined there was anything like the
country they were driving through. There couldn't be this
much emptiness in the whole world. There were no real
trees, only chaparral, mesquite and cholla cactus. He tried
to pick out a single plant that didn't have thorns on it.
After a while he gave it up. There weren't any. He was
so tired his bones hurt. The stage had been bad enough;
but it at least had springs. The buckboard, jolting over
the solidified lava of the *malpaís,* the badlands, jarred his
eyeteeth. He closed his eyes against the sun glare. At once
he was asleep, sunk down into a slumber as profound as
death.

He was awakened by Bart's heavy hand on his shoulder. The black eyes were friendlier now.

"Here we be," Bart Nevis said.

Roak felt the evening coolness. He knew then he had
been asleep for hours. He stared at the adobe-walled enclosure. Inside was a cool, whitewashed Mexican *casa
grande,* a chapel with its cross and bell, a scattering of dun-
colored adobe outbuildings.

"Looks Spanish," he said.

" 'Tis," Bart said. "Mex, anyhow. Cap'n bought it off a Spik family named Martínez. Fine folks, not like the usual run of pepper guts. Only Texas folks is plumb death on Greasers, even good, educated folks like the Martínezes. Made it so rough for 'em they had to sell out. Cap'n stuck up for 'em all he could. Paid 'em a fair price when he bought, 'stead o' taking advantage like he could of. They moved back 'cross the river. Cap'n still visits with 'em from time to time. In fact, he's down there now."

"I see," Roak said. "When is he coming back?"

"Today. Long 'bout first dark, I reckon. Said he'd get here in time to welcome you in person . . ."

A Mexican vaquero threw open the big gates for them.

"*Hola,* Señores!" he said.

"*Hola,* yourself," Bart said. "Miss Hannah at home?"

"*Sí* Señor Bart," the Mexican said. "She is waiting for you and thees *caballero.* She is also mad. She says the *comida* will be burnt if you do not arrive *pronto.* Ay, but she is much woman, the señorita!"

"A sight too much at times, eh, Pepe?" Bart laughed. "I'll just go up there 'n' gentle her a mite. . . ."

They rode up to the *casa grande.* She was waiting on the patio, under the cottonwood trees Jesse Furniss had set out for shade. And every bit of the bone-deep tiredness drained out of Roak Garfield, vanishing as though it had never been.

She was tall for a woman. Her blue eyes met his dead level. They were something. All of her was something, from the taffy-colored mass of hair piled high on her head and the mouth that was compressed into a pale pink line to the pointed toe of her riding boot tapping an angry drumroll beneath her ankle-length skirt. More than something. As Pepe had said: much woman.

"Han, honey," Bart began; but she cut him off.

"Later, Bart. This is Mr. Garfield?"

"Yes'm," Roak said quietly.

She put out her hand. "I welcome you in behalf of my father," she said.

Roak took her hand. He stood there looking at her.

"But not on your own, Miss Furniss?" he said.

The blue eyes were very still.

"I had two brothers, Mr. Garfield," she said. "They rode away to defend their country against the people who were invading it. Your people, Mr. Garfield. And they didn't come back, neither of them. You wore—that uniform, my father tells me. Under those circumstances, you can hardly expect my welcome to be—exuberant, can you, Mr. Garfield?"

Roak turned loose her hand.

"No," he said. "And I'm sorry, ma'am. You don't know how sorry I am."

She bowed her head the barest fraction of an inch.

"I'll have Josefina show you to your room," she said. "Supper will be served in a quarter of an hour."

"But," Roak said, "I came here to work, Miss Furniss. Reckon my place is in the cowboys' quarters—"

"The bunkhouse," Bart corrected him.

"No," Hannah said, "you are my father's guest. The Captain is more generous than I. He, at least, is looking forward to meeting you."

As he followed the Mexican maid up the stairs, Roak could hear Bart Nevis's deep rumble.

"Appears to me you were a mite hard on him, honey. Looks square enough to me. . . ."

Whatever Hannah answered, Roak couldn't make out. She kept her voice too low.

Jesse Furniss got back in time for supper. He was a big man, taller even that Bart Nevis. He wore his iron-gray hair long, and was full-bearded. His voice, even at its quietest, made the windows rattle.

The supper was good. There was fried chicken, barbecued beef, red beans, greens, potatoes, cornbread, apple pie and gallons of coffee. But most of Roak's appetite was gone. Hannah's blue eyes, resting on him with all the warmth of a prairie blizzard, made the food stick in his throat. But Roak saw that Captain Furniss was eating considerably less than he did, even, from time to time, putting a hand to his middle while his eyes darkened with pain.

"Father," Hannah said, "your stomach isn't getting any better. If you don't send for Doctor Murray soon, I will!"

"Waited too long to get married," Captain Furniss said. "Gut was already too worn out for even your ma's cooking to save it. Nothing to worry over. Let me see—what was I talking about?"

"The Mexican War," Roak said.

"Yep. Your pa couldn't even speak English so good in those days; but he was one hell of a man in a fight. I remember—"

"Father," Hannah said, "isn't there anything else you can talk about besides fighting and killing?"

"Sorry, baby," Jesse said fondly. "Forgot what a sore subject that is with you. I'll drop it, right now. . . ." He turned back to Roak. "How're your brothers?" he asked. "Otto brought the oldest one down here when he visited us that time. Fine boy. Three of you youngsters, weren't there? All boys, if I remember right. You were the youngest—"

"Yes," Roak said; "I was the youngest. . . ."

Hannah's eyes were on his face now. She was a woman and things like the note of pain breaking through a man's voice got over to her. Roak had the feeling that she almost knew what he had to say.

"How are they faring?" Jesse said.

Roak bowed his head. A fly buzzed across the table. The noise it made was loud in the silence.

Roak looked up. He was very careful not to meet Hannah's eyes.

"They're dead, Mr. Furniss," he said. "I don't know

how Hansel died, except that it was at Shiloh. But Manny, I do know. He was with General Grant at Spotsylvania. He was in the first wave that was ordered out to reduce the Bloody Angle. He didn't make it, sir. Nobody in the first wave did."

"Goddammit, son," Jesse began; but the scrape of Hannah's chair drowned his words. She stood up, already whirling, her riding boots hammering out a staccato beat as she ran from the room. The three men stared after her. Bart Nevis got to his feet.

"Better leave her be, Bart," Jesse growled. He turned back to Roak. "You hit her on a raw spot, son. Reckon you didn't know about—my boys?"

"Yes, sir," Roak said. "She told me. I was trying like the dickens to avoid that subject, but I couldn't think up any answer to what you asked me but the truth. Anyhow, reckon it's time we let our dead rest in peace—on both sides, sir. . . ."

"Amen," Jesse Furniss said. "Reckon you better go turn in, son. You look all stove up. I'll show you about the place tomorrow."

"Thank you, sir," Roak said. Then to Bart: "Be seeing you, Mr. Nevis."

"Bart to you, boy," Bart Nevis said.

Roak lay on the bed staring at the ceiling. He had known he wouldn't be able to sleep. He thought about Fanny and all the miles and centuries of difference between her and Hannah Furniss. Then he stopped that. Brought himself up short. Threw a checkrein on his dreaming. Because falling in love wasn't in the cards he'd dealt himself. To go where he meant to go required a clear head and a cool one. Go soft on this *malpaís* rose, and he just might miss that obscure fork in the road that leads on to fortune. Which wouldn't do. Which wouldn't do at all.

He was lying there like that, half-lost in one of her

late brothers' nightshirts, when he heard the knock. It was so light he thought at first he had imagined it. But it came again, stronger.

"Come in!" he said.

The door opened. Roak jackknifed up in the bed. He sat there staring at her. He hadn't even blown out the lamp, so he could see that she had been crying.

"I came to tell you," she got out, "to say. . . ."

"What, Miss Furniss?" Roak said.

"That I'm sorry. I was rotten to you. Of course, I didn't know; but that's no excuse. You—you loved them, didn't you?"

"Yes," Roak said.

"Like I loved mine. Funny. We're both alone—and for the same reason. Roak—"

"Yes—Han?" Roak said.

"Will you forgive me? I never even thought about the other side—that way. Not as people who died, and left folks to grieve over them. It—it makes it worse. More terrible, somehow. People, country people, just like us speaking the same language, worshiping the same God— will you forgive me, Roak?"

"No," Roak said.

She opened her eyes very wide.

"No," Roak said again. " 'Cause for that I don't have to forgive you. I never even took offense. And for the other there just ain't no way for me to. . . ."

"What—other?" she whispered.

"For being you," Roak said. "For tangling a man's breath up inside his gullet every time he looks at you. For being so pretty it hurts; and so good a fellow wants to go down on his knees and plain thank the good Lord for the luck of just being around in the same time and the same place where you are. But most of all for being so close and so doggoned far out of reach at the same time. No

Han; don't reckon I'll ever be able to forgive you for all that. . . ."

Hannah stood there, looking at him.

"So you can talk, when you want to," she said.

"Yes," Roak said. "Fat lot of good it does me, though."

There was a silence between them. It went on and on and on up to the rim edges of forever. Roak felt like he was strangling. Then he realized he had been holding his breath all that time.

Hannah's blue eyes darkened until they were sage purple; and beyond that to the color of the sky between sunset and first dark. When she spoke, her voice was queer.

"You—you know I'm spoken for?" she said.

"Yes," Roak said. "And I don't mean to lift a hand. But if ever—"

"That 'ever' will never come, Roak," Hannah said.

Roak smiled at her. Because he was certain sure it would. Only he'd have to go slow now. The stakes were higher. What this slim blonde she-critter represented was the damnedest spread of land in West Texas, lying there outside his window under the stars, stretching itself out cool and velvety in the moonlight, touched now with night magic, in itself a little world. He reckoned that he could keep tight enough rein on the kind of green-sapling kid stuff that made a fellow fall in love with a bit of fluff— even a prairie flower as lovely as this one. But he danged sure could fall in love with a sweep of earth like this. In fact, he already had.

He made sheep's eyes at her. Dragged that smile out, making it slow, warm, tender.

"I'll wait just the same, Han," he said.

Chapter Three

WHEN THE man came into his office, the last of his patients had gone home, and Doctor Turner was sitting there, staring at nothing, waiting for the tiredness to subside a little so that he could get up and go to bed. He wasn't even thinking, because it was summer now, and the heat lay over the city like a blanket. A sticky, humid blanket.

Wearily he got up, reached for his bag. And it was then that he heard his receptionist, Nelly, give a muffled shriek. Doctor Turner started toward the waiting room, but the man was already there, in the doorway of his office, blocking his path.

"I know it's late, Doc, but—" he began.

"What the devil did you do to Nell?" Doctor Turner demanded.

"Nell? Oh, the girl out front? Nothing, Doc. Reckon my face kind of frightened her," the man said.

Doctor Turner turned to the oil lamp on his desk. He took off the shade, turned up the wick, lit it, put the shade back on. Then he held it up so that he could see the man's face.

"I see," he said. "This is what you came to see me about? I can't do anything about this, son. Don't believe the finest surgeon on earth could repair that damage. Looks deliberate. Indians?"

"No," the man said.

"I'm sorry," the doctor said, "but—"

"Didn't come to see you about my face, Doc. I know

that can't be fixed. I'm trying to trace a feller. Name of Roak Garfield. Heard you knew him. . . ."

"I did," the doctor said. "What do you want to trace him for?"

The man laughed quietly. So quietly that Doctor Turner wasn't sure it was laughter. A low, gurgling sound that came over to him, faintly. It was singularly unpleasant.

"I owe him something," the man said. "Don't like having debts. Mind telling me where he is?"

Doctor Turner stared at his visitor. This man had been big once. The doctor could tell that. But now all he had left was bones. He towered there, lean and cadaverous, peering at the doctor out of that horror that also once had been a face.

"Roak Garfield do that?" Doctor Turner said.

Again that throat deep, almost soundless gurgle.

"I'm asking the questions, Doc," the man said. "C'mon, now, tell me where he is."

"In Texas," Doctor Turner said. "Beyond that, I don't know. Went down there to go into cattle raising. But I never heard him say what town, or even the name of the ranch."

"Kind o' fond of him, ain't you, Doc?" the man said.

"Yes," Doctor Turner said; "and you?"

"Well, now, I reckon I'm not too fond of anybody now, Doc. A mug like this doesn't cement human fellowship. Wife left me two years after it happened. Sister's gone, too; but I know where she is. . . ."

"And where's that?" Doctor Turner said.

"St. Louis," the man said, as though he were discussing the weather, "in a whorehouse. Sure you don't know any more than just Texas? Mighty big state, Texas—"

"No," Doctor Turner said; "that's all I know. . . ."

"Thanks, Doc," the man with the butchered face said. "So long. Be seeing you. . . ."

"Good-by—friend," Doctor Turner said.

But the tall man had gone through the door by then, vanishing out of that segment of space, of time he had temporarily occupied as though he had never been. As perhaps he hadn't. Not really.

Seized by a sudden impulse, the doctor ran after him through the empty waiting room—for Nelly had gone by then, too—but the man wasn't in the waiting room or in the corridor and no footsteps sounded from the stair. Doctor Turner put his hand to his forehead. Been working too hard, he thought. Then he heard it: sourceless and remote, coming from no direction, no place, perhaps even from no time—that felt palpitation of nothing, that soundless flesh crawl, chalk scrape, induced unease—

That laughter.

Chapter Four

THE FIRST thing that Roak saw as he came up to the corral the next morning with Hannah and the Captain was that horse. The second was that the top rail of the corral fence was covered with squatting cowboys.

"Looks like the op'ra house is plumb sold out," Captain Furniss grinned.

"Opera house?" Roak said.

"Top rail of the corral fence," Hannah said. "They always squat there to talk, or to watch things like breaking a mustang. . . ."

"Or seeing a greenhorn thrown," Roak said.

"That's what they're waiting for," Hannah said. Her voice was grim. "Father, couldn't you—"

"No," Roak said. "Thank you, Miss Hannah; but I wouldn't want to spoil their fun."

He strode up to the sway-back gelding that stood before the corral, not even hitched to the rail, just standing there trailing his reins in the dirt, head drooping, fast asleep. He walked all around the animal, staring at it.

"Is it alive?" he said.

A roar of laughter went up from the opera house. A bewhiskered old cowhand reached down and poked Roak on the shoulder.

"Now, looka here, son," he said, "don't let that there cayuse fool you. He's just plumb setting there storing up energy. Wake him up, and he's purely a woollywhyow, a natch'l cross betwixt a wouser 'n' a catamount. Thet there hoss knows more movements than a bandleader. He kin sunfish, pump handle, walkin' beam, kettle, jackknife, crawfish—"

"That's enough, Will," Hannah said. "Don't believe him, Roak. I picked this one out myself because I know he's gentle."

"I still think he's dead," Roak said. "And, begging your pardon mighty humbly, Miss Hannah, I'd rather not ride him." He turned to the old cowhand. "You mind moving over a bit, friend?" he said.

Will moved over. Roak put his two hands on the top rail and hoisted himself up with one easy pull. The pain in his chest stabbed deep from the effort, but he ignored it. He braced himself there, staring at the horses. Then he dropped back down again.

"If you don't mind, Captain," he said. "I'd like to try that spotted one—"

"Oh, Roak, no!" Hannah said.

From his place on the top rail, Bart stared at her. His dark face tightened a little.

"Now, look, son," Jesse Furniss said, "that there paint is a mite frisky. More'n a mite. I know you've done forked a hoss up there in Ohio; but a farm hoss and a Texas bronc ain't the same breed o' cuss a-tall."

"You ever ride him, Captain?" Roak asked.

"Sure, son; but I was born with spurs on my heels, and—"

"You, Miss Hannah?" Roak said.

"Hell, son, that don't make no nevermind," the Captain said. "Han can stick on damn nigh any critter that I can."

"Still," Roak said peacefully, "I'd like to try him. He's not a wild horse. He's been ridden. I'm sure I can manage him."

"Now, look, Roak," Hannah said, "it's fine to be game, but—"

Bart Nevis eased his big frame down from the top rail.

"Let him try, Cap'n," he said. "That pinto ain't *that* wild."

Hannah stared at Bart. Her boot toe started its drum-roll against the hard-packed earth.

"Bart, I told you that I wouldn't have any greenhorn hazing!" she said. "Mr. Garfield is our guest; and breaking his neck is no way to show hospitality! I tell you—"

"Neither is refusing the gentleman's request," Bart said blandly. "If I'd have picked out that Calico for him, you would have had grounds for complaint, Miss Hannah. But he chose it himself. And you and the Captain have gone and warned him. So now it appears to me that keeping it up is plumb downright insulting to Mr. Garfield. You and the Captain are treating him like he wasn't weaned yet. He thinks he can fork the paint. And you know what, Miss Hannah?" Bart added solemnly. "I think he can, too."

"Bart," Hannah began.

"Please, Miss Hannah," Roak said, "I don't break easy."

"All right," Hannah said, "it's your neck, Roak. Will, you and Angelo saddle the paint. . . ."

The old cowhand and the young Mexican dropped into the corral. Angelo swung the rope. The loop whirled about his head. He threw, the loop snaking out, rising. It dropped perfectly over the head and shoulders of the pinto pony. At its touch, the pinto went back on his haunches, pawing the sky. The rope whistled through the *honda,* the slip-knot, tightening around the horse's neck. They brought the black-and-white splotched pony down again. Angelo moved up the rope until he was close to the pinto. Then he slipped a rawhide halter over his head, and led him from the corral.

A dozen hands jumped down to help saddle the pinto.

"No," Roak said; "I'd like to do it myself. Get him used to me. I want to go on riding him, if he doesn't belong to anyone else."

"Hell, no," Will growled. "Paints you kin have, partner. They's just too damn much trouble. Hammerheaded as the dickens; never kin learn 'em nothing. . . ."

The hands fell back, staring at Roak. Bart handed him the bridle. Roak walked up to the painted pony. Then quietly, easily, expertly, he went about the business of saddling and bridling the mount. He knew that his skill was a dead giveaway, but he didn't care. Time somebody took these wild and woolly cowhands down a peg, he thought.

When he had finished tightening the two cinches that ran under the horse's belly to hold the saddle on, he turned to the others.

"All right," he said, "turn him loose—"

"Don't you want me to hold him," Will asked, "leastwise 'til you gits up there?"

"No," Roak said. "Want to see if I can handle him myself. . . ."

"You," Hannah said, "know one heck of a lot about horses, Roak."

"A little," Roak said. Then he cheeked the paint, catching the cheek strap just above the bit and yanking the pony's head around until it was almost touching the saddle, which was the right way to do it with an unknown mount. That way the pinto couldn't even start to go into action until Roak was in the saddle. He put his left foot in the stirrup and swung his right leg over, mounting easily, beautifully, perfectly. The pony danced briefly. Roak barely touched the reins, and the dancing stopped.

"Well," he said to Hannah and the Captain, "shall we go?"

"I'll be damned!" the Captain said. "I'll be double damned and blown away by a blue norther!"

"If thet," Old Will said sorrowfully, "is a greener, I'm a hen wrangler. We's been brace dealt!"

"You can ride," Bart Nevis said. "Cavalry, wasn't you?"

"Wilson's," Roak said.

"Figures," Bart said. "Say, Cap'n, can I come along? Like to size up your friend. Looks to me like this here fake pilgrim's got the makings of a top hand."

"Sure, Bart," the Captain said.

Hannah didn't say anything.

The four of them moved out of the gate. Hannah, like every decent woman in the West, rode sidesaddle. Her riding skirt had lead shot sewn into the hem to keep it down and preserve her modesty. Being a horsewoman in that country was quite a trick, Roak thought. He would hate to have to ride like that.

Hannah touched her mount with a spur, and brought it up alongside Roak.

"Well," she said, "now that you've taken the pins out from under us, would you mind telling me where you learned to ride like that?"

"Cavalry," Roak said. "Nearly four years of it. My job was to bust the wild ones. That is, before I got promoted—"

"And what," Hannah asked, "did you get promoted to?"

Roak grinned at her.

"Always heard Western folks didn't poke questions at a fellow," he said. "Why don't we just forget that fuss, and settle down to being friends?"

Hannah stared at him.

"You sure are a maverick if I ever saw one," she said. "All right, Mr. Close-Mouth, I apologize. You're right. I have been prying too much. Don't know why. I'm not that interested."

"Aren't you?" Roak said.

"Say, Roak," Bart called out, "you know how to rope, too?"

"No," Roak said. "I'd be mighty grateful if you'd get somebody to break me in on it, though, Bart."

"I'll turn you over to Old Will," Bart said. "He can

snatch a cow out of brush so thick you can't even see the horns. Start you off tomorrow."

"Thanks," Roak said.

Ahead of them, a jack rabbit broke cover out of the cholla cactus.

"Doggone it," the Captain said, "wish I was packing a shotgun. That jack would make mighty fine eating. . . ."

"You want him?" Roak said. He didn't even wait for the Captain to answer. He just clapped spurs to the pinto and thundered off after the rabbit. The jack gathered speed, weaving, changing course every half-minute. But with the lightest touch of knees, reins, spurs, Roak kept the pinto right on top of him.

"You see what I see, Bart?" the Captain growled. "You ever see a paint that made a halfway decent cattle-working horse?"

"Nope," Bart said. "Don't know why, but you never can keep those spotted critters in close enough to a steer to cut it out of the herd. But danged if this fancy pilgrim isn't teaching him to peg all four feet into the ground, stop dead in his tracks, and get moving in another direction without losing time. . . ."

"A real peg pony, eh?" the Captain said. "They're rare in any kind of horse, but paints—"

"Unheard of," Bart said, "but he's doing it, all right. See there! Again! He keeps this up, and you'll have yourself a natural wonder, Cap'n: a pinto who's a cutting horse and peg pony combined."

"Look at him, Bart!" Hannah laughed exultantly. "He's turning that paint on a biscuit and not even cutting the crust! Still think you're the best rider on the Bar F's range?"

The jack rabbit was tiring rapidly now. He was making the mistake of running straight for longer stretches. Roak took his left foot out of the stirrup. Then he swept down, hooking the toe of his left boot behind the cantle and holding on to the saddle horn with his left hand, riding like that, with his face not much more than a foot from the ground, he swung his free right hand out and caught the jack rabbit by the ears. Smoothly, easily, he pulled himself back upright in the saddle, thrust his left foot into the stirrup again without even groping, swung the pinto into a tight circle with one hand, and came galloping back toward where he'd left the others.

He gave Hannah the rabbit.

"Present for a pretty lady," he said.

"The last man I ever seen who could ride all over a bronc like that," the Captain said, "was a Comanche. And he put twenty-seven arrows in my pony's hide in less than three minutes."

"Thanks, Roak," Hannah said. Her voice was very soft. Bart Nevis stared at her. But he didn't say anything.

They rode on. Roak kept looking for the cattle, but he didn't see any. Finally, when they were close to the Nueces River, Captain Furniss pulled up his horse.

"This here," he said, pointing with his quirt, "is where my south spread starts. It ends down on the Rio Grande. Reckon you been wondering why you ain't seen a cow yet, ain't you?"

"Yes," Roak said.

"That's because we've been skirting the edges of the *brasada,* the brush country. The cows get into that chaparral and plain disappear. And getting them out isn't any fun, I can tell you. 'Cause you can't skirt the brush and hope to catch one of those old mosshorn with a college degree and four or five letters behind his name. You've got to hit those thorn thickets center, flat, on the run, and tear a hole in them. Now, what I'm figuring is that a man who can ride all over a horse the way you can would make a fine brush hand. Riding like that, and keeping your eyes open, you'd stand a chance to keep at least part of your hide."

"Father," Hannah said sharply, "he's sick, remember."

Bart spoke then. His voice came out flat, slow-toned, even.

" 'Pears to me you're taking mighty good care of the dude, Han," he said.

Hannah looked at him.

"Just what do you mean by that, Bart?" she asked.

"*I* don't mean anything," Bart drawled; "it's up to you to put the trimmings on it, Han."

"Now look, you two," Jesse growled, "this is no time for a lovers' spat." He turned back to Roak. "Just wanted to say that you're perfectly welcome to stay here 'til your lung is sound, and then go back East. But if you mean to take up this life, you ought to know what you're doing. It's not so bad while you're working—that is, if you've got a cast-iron lining to your big gut so range cooks won't ruin your stomach the way they've ruined mine—but in slack seasons it's the lonesomest existence a man ever hung onto himself. Some men can't live without women; but a cow hand has just plain got to. There aren't any out here to speak of. Of course, you can send back East for your *dulce* after you get set—if you've got one . . ."

"If by dool-say, you mean a girl," Roak said, "no, sir, I haven't."

Bart Nevis's black eyes rested on him, then, like a brand.

"Better like that," Jesse rumbled. "Most town-bred fillies just can't stand the life, anyhow. But I want to tell you one thing: in dang nigh forty years of ranching, you're the first pilgrim I've ever seen who was actually fitted to make a top hand from the outset. Like Bart, here, says Old Will can teach you enough betwixt now and fall branding time for any outfit on the range to take you on with pleasure. What I can see looks sixteen hands high, son—"

"Thank you, sir," Roak said.

"But what I can't see bothers me. Can you lay up in a bunkhouse and count the flies on the ceiling without going plumb out o' your mind? What'll happen the first time you gets caught in a blue norther 'n' the herd starts to drift? Can you hold your likker? Got bottom enough to ride the river 'n' not panic? Hoss sense enough for me to trust you with a six-gun whilst you're line riding 'n' not let some gunslick crowd you into drawing?"

"Suppose you try me, sir," Roak said. "I don't even know what you mean by half the things you said. All I know is, it's a pretty poor man what'll live off another man's charity. I aim to work for what I get—without favor. If, come fall, I don't measure up, you just say the word, sir, and I'll be off—"

"Spoken like a man," Jesse said. "Here's my hand on it, son. You ride with Ol' Will tomorrow."

But that next day was another thing he hadn't figured on. He nor Doctor Turner either. Because when the good doc had insisted upon Roak's going to live in a hot, dry climate, there was one characteristic of that kind of country that the medico hadn't taken into consideration: the dust. What happened was a matter of simon-pure bad luck —combined and compounded with Bar F hospitality. Since they all knew he wasn't ready to ride the thorn thickets of the brush country, Old Will took him out on the open range.

And a dust storm blew up.

The cattle started drifting before it, so that all the old hands had their work cut out for them inside of two minutes flat. Roak tried to keep up with them, but his paint was new to the task, largely because of the stubborn range superstition that spotted ponies didn't make good cattle-working mounts; so instead of moving in close the way a trained cutting horse would have done whether his rider was guiding him or no, the paint swung wide. Another two minutes and both he and Roak were as lost as only a greenhorn and a half-broke calico pony could possibly get, increasing that lostness every minute as they drifted before that dry storm, because by then Old Will and the others had the cattle heading homeward, moving in the direction directly opposite from the one Roak took. In two hours, Roak was ten miles into the *malpais* and twenty from the others, since in that same two hours they had moved ten miles more or less from the spot they and Roak had started at.

Which would have been a small matter to a well man with sound lungs. But for Roak Garfield, it came within inches of being fatal. He had sense enough, of course, to pull his bandana up over his mouth and nose. But that flour-fine grit went through the pores of the kerchief as though it weren't there. Roak knew he was going to cough. He also knew that if he did, he wasn't going to be able to stop. On top of that he piled the grim certainty that if he couldn't stop coughing within a reasonable length of time he was going to hemorrhage, and if he hemorrhaged, he was going to die. It was as simple as that. And as inevitable.

He doubled over when it hit him, fighting to stay in the saddle. But after that wracking torture had gone on for five full minutes, he saw he wasn't going to be able to do that, either. So he climbed down slowly, and with great dignity, because it seemed to him an insupportable ignominy to fall. He lay on the ground beside the painted pony and shielded his face as best he could with his Stetson. Within minutes, it was full of blood. He was strangling, choking, going out on a red tide. Then, abruptly, the wind stopped dead.

Which did him a fat lot of good. Because, by then, he was too weak to get up, had lost too much blood, was not really conscious. He lay there—a black spot stretched out in the badlands with the lonely figure of his paint standing beside him under the vast sky. It was hot. A turkey buzzard tightened his arc against that white-blue, sun-stricken emptiness. Another. Another. Soon they were making concentric rings above him, cutting them sharper, smaller, dropping lower.

It was this that caught the Mexican boy's attention as he pushed his ugly, hammerheaded cayuse up out of the draw. He kicked the beast into a gallop. Got there, dismounted.

A gringo, he thought; a pig of a gringo who has been shot and left to die. Fitting food for the buzzards; still—

Still, he was Ramón Benevides Camargo. That name went back centuries. Benevides had ridden down from Castile to wreck the Moors' last hopes at Granada. Benevides had planted the sword and the cross over half the New World. And though he did not know it, the Aztec blood which gave his skin its coppery tint was older, and as proud.

To leave this man to die like this—member though he was of the race that had despoiled the Benevides of their lands, run off their cattle, killed in cold blood Ramón's father and elder brother, and, beyond that, robbed his country of half its territory in an utterly unjust war—was a thing that Ramón Benevides was simply incapable of. Sighing, he lifted Roak up and laid him across the paint with his head and arms dangling over one side and his legs and feet over the other.

Then he headed south toward the Rio Grande, leading the paint with its burden behind him. There was nothing else to do. If he had sought help for their fellow countryman from the gringos, they would have shot him on sight and asked questions later.

He brought Roak to his own house, an adobe *casita* on the edge of the village twelve miles south of the border —that village which Captain Furniss's friends, the Martínezes, dominated, owned. Once the Benevides had been richer than the Martínezes; and the Camargos, his mother's family, richer still. But they had been fighters instead of diplomats like the Martínezes. So they were dead, all the Camargos, and all the Benevides except him and his sister Belén, while the Martínezes lived, and enjoyed the friendship and protection of the biggest gringo in all Texas.

"Belén!" he called. "Little sister, come, for God!"

Belén came out of the house. She wasn't his *hermanita* his little sister, as he called her. She was nineteen years old three years older than he. But he called her little sister for all that. It made him feel more a man.

Belén stood there staring at what appeared to be a dead gringo. Her face twisted in horror.

"You shot him?" she whispered. "Oh, Ramón!"

"No," Ramón said tiredly; "I did not shoot this gringo I found him like this. And I—I could not leave him there lying in the *malpaís* with the buzzards already circling above him. I do not know why, *hermanita mía,* but I could not."

"Because," Belén said softly, "thou art a Benevides *mi hermano*. And throughout history we have died for our foolish *caballerosidad,* our sense of honor. Still, it is no to be helped. Come, let us take him into the house. Then you go in search of Doctor Arjona—"

"Perhaps," Ramón whispered, "the doctor will be drunk—"

"No matter," Belén said. "Drunk or sober, he is the finest doctor in all México. . . ."

Which was debatable. Benito Arjona Bermúdez was five feet two inches tall, and weighed two hundred pounds His capacity for tequila was legendary, as was his reputed skill with the scalpel. Both with much justice. Doctor Arjona's knowledge of *materia medica* had vast and windy gaps; but he was one damned fine surgeon. And like mos surgeons, knife-happy, purely loving to cut.

He bent over the patient. The tequila on his breath

was enough to provide Roak with all the anesthesia he
needed. The good, fat doctor was drunk as usual. No,
drunker than usual. Which turned out to be Roak's great
good fortune. For Benito Arjona was too drunk to have
the cautious second thoughts that even he would have had
if he'd been sober. The tequila swimming in his big gut
didn't allow him to reflect that to go into a man's lung
in that heat in search of a ball that was resting in a four-
year-old cocoon of scar tissue was as close to deliberate
murder as it was possible to get.

No. Benito Arjona didn't reflect. He simply opened
Roak Garfield up, and took that ball out of him—using,
by very nearly direct divine intervention, instruments that
Belén had scrubbed with hot water and soap, not because
she knew anything about sterilization, but because, as she
told Benito wrathfully, it would have been shameful to
use knives as dirty as that to cut a piece of beef, not to
mention a human being.

And Roak Garfield compounded the felony of profane
and drunken miracle-working—by living. Topped even
that by recovering. By rising from that bed of pain practically as sound as he had been before the War.

But, before that, there was time. Time to exchange that
old hurt for a new one beyond Doctor Arjona's skill. Beyond anybody's skill. Anyone's at all.

He opened his eyes—having dropped three whole weeks
right out of the middle of his life without missing them,
not knowing they had been—and saw her sitting by the
bed. He never had been much with words, and for this
one there maybe weren't any words, anyhow. None that
suited, fitted, made sense. Say her hair was black, and what
had he said? Nothing. Black was nothing, night was nothing, wingfeathers of a raincrow, pitch, jet, the bottom pit
of a Pennsylvania coal mine—say all that and he wasn't

even close. Say, maybe, an older thing, find the ancient, majestic words to catch the quality of that blackness—the darkness of the deep, before God spoke, and light was. That, maybe. Then what? There were still her eyes. Blacker even than that. Making heat lightning in an August sky as they moved. With all the stars plumb plunged into them—and drowned. So that only the shimmering was left. Only firefly flicker; afterglow rising to the surface now and again like a spray of diamonds on black velvet.

Arch of throat, swan-slender. Only swans were white. Or black. They weren't—golden? Coppery? Bronzed? No. There were no words for that, either. No single, simple words. Dusk rose. Yep, start with that. Dusk rose underneath. And on top of that a wash of prairie sunlight, so pale golden that you could see that rose pink under it, through it, deepening about her cheekbones as she felt his eyes.

He looked at her mouth, and quit cold. No point in even making the attempt. Because any words that came to mind were a profanation. Her mouth wasn't to be described. It was there to be clung to and cherished. He had a feeling that the sweet sighing, the soft tremble, the warmth of it would put a spring thaw into the ice-cold misery of living that would carry a man through to his dying day, banishing the frost forever.

"My God!" he said.

"You will please not to talk," Belén said in English.

"Don't want to," Roak whispered. "Not talk—pray!"

"Good," Belén said; "I shall send for the padre."

"Don't need a padre," Roak croaked. "Can say it myself: dear Lord, thank You!"

"Amen," Belén said softly. Then: "You have, perhaps, hunger?"

"No'm," Roak said. "Thirsty, though. . . ."

She brought him the water in a gourd dipper. It strangled him a little, going down.

"There," she said gravely. "You will be all right now, I think."

"Baby," Roak grinned weakly, "I have never been better!"

"You do not mind being alone for a little while?" Belén asked, "I have a thing to do. . . ."

"Being alone," Roak said, feeling the strength creeping back into him, "no. Letting you out of my sight, yes. . . ."

She stared at him.

"You will please to be good," she said evenly, "and not to entertain ideas. I am neither a chile pepper nor a hot tamale, which are what you gringos are so fond of calling girls of my race. I have nursed you for three weeks now, which was not pleasant. It is for that that I go: to put you in other hands. . . ."

He could feel her words across his face like a whip.

"Don't reckon you're being fair, ma'am," he said; "I didn't ask the good Lord to make me a gringo. . . ."

"There are good gringos," Belén said quietly. *"El Capitán* Furniss, for example. I should not especially hold being a gringo against you, despite all your people have done to mine. It is just that—"

"Just what?" Roak whispered.

"It does not matter. You are my guest. It should be discourteous of me to—"

Roak held her with his eyes. She could see the pain moving there.

"Say it!" he croaked. "Tell me—why you—hate me. . . ."

She could have lied, then. Denied his words. But she did not. She said, very simply:

"You raved. And since the delirious tell always the truth, I think you are a most unpleasant man—more so, even, than most gringos. I am sorry, but you asked me."

He lay there, looking at her.

"What—what is it—you don't like?" he got out.

"That you love no one. That you are incapable of—of *ternura*—I do not know the word in English—"

"Tenderness?" Roak guessed.

"Ternura—tenderness. . . . Yes, that is it. You have done a most shameful thing with *la novia* of your brother who is dead—which you regret, but not for the right reasons. You have not shame of your sin, but only sorrow that you could not profit from it. You plan to use *la hija*—the daughter—of *el Capitán* Furniss in order to inherit the lands that should be mine—"

"Yours?" Roak said.

"Yes. After my father, Don Manuel Benevides Motijo, and my brother Timoteo were killed by the gringos, the Martínez produced papers signed by my father giving them title. Papers of which Ramón and I knew nothing, had never heard our father mention. In a night Ramón and I were reduced from *hacendados* to something less than peons. Capitán Furniss bought those lands from the Martínez, which is why I hold him blameless. He knew not what went before. . . ."

"And now?" Roak said.

"Nada. Nothing. I have become a *costurera,* a seamstress, making pretty dresses for Carmen Martínez who is a quarter-kilo of bones and who cannot even show them off due to the flatness of her chest. . . ."

"Which," Roak grinned, "is a thing nobody can say about you, baby!"

"Please not to call me *bebé,"* Belén said. "My name is Belén Benevides Camargo, Señor Garfield. And now, I go."

"No, wait!" Roak said. "I—I'm sorry I'm—a most unpleasant man, Belén—"

"And I," Belén said. "Since my brother had to risk his life to save yours, it would have been better for him to risk it for someone worth saving, I think. Yet, *tal vez,* it has served for something. Perhaps he has granted you time enough to learn that any man who believes that life *can* be lived any other way but honorably, that the possibility of perpetually outsmarting everyone even exists, Señor, is —a fool. But I must go now, truly—"

"Where?" Roak whispered.

"To the *casa grande,* to the house of the Señores Martínez to tell them that you are awake and can talk to them. It is a grave thing to have a wounded gringo among us. It could cause trouble. You will please to be still until I return. I shall not be long. . . ."

After she had gone, Roak lay there, staring out of the window. He saw a youngster ride up, driving a small herd. He watched the boy idly; then something about those cattle struck him. He narrowed his gaze. Sure as shooting, that was the Bar F brand!

Only it had been altered, the F crudely changed into a P by a line connecting the two horizontal bars. But the new burns were so fresh that he could make out the original brand under them, even from where he lay. This kid was a cattle thief, a rustler. He fixed the boy's face in mind. Such knowledge could come in handy to a man trying to advance himself.

Then he saw the boy had dismounted, was striding toward the house. On the threshold, the youngster stopped.

"Belén!" he called. "Where art thou, little sister?"

Then he saw Roak's opened eyes.

"Buenos días, Señor Garfield," he said politely. *"Me alegro de verlo con vida de nuevo—"*

"Don't you—" Roak got out, "speak English."

"Sí. Of course. I said that I am happy to see you with life once more, señor. And my sister? Where is she?"

"At the Martínez'," Roak said. "You—you're the one who saved me?"

"Sí, señor. I, and Doctor Arjona, and, *tal vez,* even God. When did Belén say she would come back?"

"Shortly," Roak whispered. "I—I want to thank you, boy—"

"*Por nada*," Ramón said. "It was nothing, Señor Garfield. Absolutely nothing at all."

Chapter Five

IT WAS hopeless, and they knew it. Every one of them had heard of, and even seen, cases where a man had let his pony drift before a dry storm, and plumb disappeared. And what happened after that was a matter of time. If you found him within the first day or two, there was a chance. But after that, in the badlands, the heat got him. The sun struck him down. Then you could find him handily enough: all you had to do was to ride to the spot the buzzards were circling over. Only by then, it called for a cast-iron stomach to even look at him, and you had to shove a couple of bandanas up over your nose while you put him to bed with a pick and shovel.

Everybody knew that—except Miss Hannah. She'd kept them scouring the *malpaís* for more than three weeks now. Most of the time she rode with them, her face burning and peeling, her blue eyes bright with—pain. Stark, naked pain. Plumb shamed a hombre to look at her. The way she felt about that there fancy pilgrim sure Lord showed.

And it sure Lord wasn't helping Bart Nevis's disposition none a-tall.

"I 'members one time," Old Will said, watching her out of the corner of his eye, "a dude got lost on the old Flying U range. Well, we found him, all right. One thighbone. Took that home for proof—"

"Will—" Bart growled warningly.

"But ol' Matt Parks—he owned th' Flying U, back in them days, y' know—wasn't having none of that. Sent us back to find the rest of the dude. Took us from fall branding time 'til Christmas. Them coyotes had done scattered him from—"

"Will!" Hannah's voice was a quirt slash. "You stop it!"

"Yes'm," Will said mournfully. "I was jes' talkin' to pass th' time . . ."

And it was then that they saw the riders pounding toward them.

Bart let his hand drop toward the butt of his gun. Then he took it away. Even from that distance he'd recognized the Martínez' chestnut horses.

They waited. The Mexicans came up to them. At the sight of Miss Hannah, they all swept off their sombreros, grandly.

"Buenos días, Doña 'Annah!" they chorused.

"Hola," Hannah said shortly. "What can we do for you boys?"

"Nada," their leader grinned; "nothing. But we 'ave done a thing for the señorita, I think. Don Manolo sent us to inform the Señorita that we 'ave one small dude at the *casa grande—"*

"What!" Hannah got out. "Then why on earth haven't you notified us before now?"

"Because we could not, señorita. You see, he was unconscious 'til yesterday so it was impossible to demand of him his name or his *paradero.* But when he told us he was stopping with *el Capitán,* we came at once—"

"Thank you," Hannah said softly. "Come on, boys, let's ride!"

"Han," Bart said; "where d'you think you're going?"

"To the Martínez'," she said; "where else?"

Roak was in the guest bedroom of the Martínez *casa grande* when she came. They had moved him there as soon as they'd found out he was a friend of Captain Furniss's. Which made all the difference in the world. Because, when Hannah got there, she didn't see Belén Benevides. Nor did anyone think to mention Belén or even Ramón by name. Not even Roak. He had a sneaking suspicion that Hannah's clear and apparent liking for him wouldn't be helped much by the reflection that he'd spent three weeks under the same roof with a girl who looked like Belén. So he kept his trap shut.

Which, as it turned out, did him no good at all.

He lay two months abed. During that time, as little given to talking as they all were, he found out several things: the efforts Captain Furniss had made to find him after he'd disappeared had been major—and nobody had dared even come close to Hannah in all that time. Not even Bart. From what her maidservant Josefina told Roak, Hannah had been almost out of her mind.

He didn't find all that out, of course, until after he was back at the Bar F being nursed by Hannah herself. Because Doctor Arjona wouldn't let them move him from the Martínez' until more than a month after Hannah's first visit. During that month, she'd visited him twice weekly, and would have ridden those twenty-four miles down there and back home daily if the Captain hadn't succinctly pointed out to her that she was making enough of a spectacle of herself already. Roak could have guessed most of it for himself by the way Hannah fussed and fretted over him; but Josefina, her maid, put it into so many words:

"Vaya, hombre! Any *idiota* can see that the Señorita is *loco* for you!"

Which should have pleased him no end. But he kept remembering Belén's words, the cold dislike in her tone when she said: "I think you are a most unpleasant man— more so, even, than most gringos. . . ." And: "You love no one. You are incapable of tenderness. . . ."

Damned little Greaser wench! he snarled inside his mind; but the words were meaningless, made no sense. No words made sense applied to Belén except maybe the words born of that tenderness she said he didn't have.

He got up from his bed two weeks before the fall branding of the half-grown calves they'd missed during the spring cowhunts. He rode, exercised, strengthened himself. He felt great and told the Captain so. But the Captain wouldn't let him go to work until his own personal physician, brought all the way from Houston at great expense, had checked Roak over.

The doctor pronounced him fit, completely cured. Said: "Man who survived a job of butchery like that one is operating under a special dispensation from on high, Cap'n. And a feller who was *cured* by it—well, all I can say is he ought to be hung up in the church as proof of the fact that miracles still happen. Far as I can tell, he's good as new. . . ."

And that was the beginning of it. Of a life that was nothing like anything Roak had ever dreamed of. Having seen him ride, the hands accepted him almost as one of themselves. They accepted him even more when he refused to be taken in by any of the tricks they always played on greenhorns: the circular story that ended on the same line it began with so that the teller would be halfway through it a second time before the usual greener caught on; or their invitation to go on a wouser hunt—a wouser being an animal which combined the worst qualities of a grizzly, a mountain lion and a loco wolf—and a complete figment of their unbridled imaginations. But the night he cleaned the whole bunkhouse with the murderous brand of cutthroat poker he'd learned in the Army, their acceptance became complete. After that, he was one of the bunch.

He practiced with the lariat from dawn to sundown. After two weeks, he could bust a steer nearly every time he threw. He learned to keep his loop small because there wasn't any room in the chaparral. He learned to get almost on top of a steer before throwing, going over the withers whenever that was possible; if not, hitting just back of the horns with the *honda* to make a figure eight to pick up the forefeet as well as the neck; but most of all, heeling—catching the brush cows by the hind feet, which was the most convenient way to rope an animal in the *brasada*. At least he could do these things most of the time.

At the end of the month, Old Will was saying proudly of his pupil: "He don't waste a loop much now, Bart—only oncet in a while. You kin take him out after them strays y'all missed in the calf roundup any time you wants to. He's plumb nigh ready."

"All right," Bart said; "outfit him in a *brasadero* rig, and I'll take him out tomorrow."

That next morning, Roak put on the *brasadero* rig. He was sorry he didn't have a mirror to see how he looked. He was proud of his new clothes, but he had the feeling they were a little less than elegant. He was right. *Brasadero* clothes were designed to keep as much hide on the rider and off the thorn thickets as possible. The hat was small, unlike the broad-brimmed sombrero of the plains, because a big hat would catch in the low-hanging branches of the chaparral. The *barboquejo,* or chin strap, was made of the lightest, weakest rawhide thong possible, so that it would break if the hat did get hung up instead of strangling the rider as the plainsman's much stronger chin cord would have in the brush. He wore a stout leather jacket with extra hide at the elbows so he could fend off the mesquite by throwing his bent arms out. Levis, of course, but over them chaps, cut in the narrow Cheyenne leg style instead of the range riders' batwings which would have hung up sure as hell. His big Mexican spurs had been filed down to blunt their rowels, since no cowboy ever wanted to cut up his horse. And his lasso was very short and tied to his saddle horn.

Bart looked him over and grunted.

"You'll do," he said. "Where's your hogleg?"

Roak had learned a good bit of range talk by then.

"Thought you said the Cap'n didn't take kindly to gun packing," he said.

"He doesn't," Bart said, "when it isn't necessary. Such as around the ranch, riding into town and such. Boot hill is full of good hands who cashed in their chips because they had a shooting iron on them. Cap'n thinks they would have hobbled their lips and kept their danders down if they hadn't been heeled. He's right."

"But right now, I ought to have a side arm," Roak said. "Why?"

"Because you're going into the brush. Or out on the range. A fellow needs his iron under those circumstances. Sidewinders, for one thing. This country is crawling with snakes. Then, when you're line riding, you can run into anything: rustlers, or even a bunch of Comanches, once in a while. Or you get thrown and break a leg. Three shots'll bring you help, pronto. A six-gun's a right handy thing, used right. It's using it wrong the Cap'n objects to."

"By wrong, he means gunning a man down in a stupid quarrel? Makes sense. What I don't see is why they don't just scrap with their fists and get it over with," Roak said.

Bart stared at him.

"Dressed like that, and riding like you do, I forget you're a greenhorn, most of the time—at least until you open your mouth. Listen, pilgrim, there's one thing a cowhand doesn't do, not *ever,* and that's fight with his hands. Down here we say that if the good Lord had meant for us to fight like dogs, He'd have given us longer teeth, and claws. The fuss isn't serious enough to reach and draw over, it's not worth the risk of breaking a pair of good roping and branding hands against some randy cuss's hard head. So we forget it. And we try hard not to give offense, nor to take any, when it wasn't intended. Hot-tempered boys don't live long down here. But go get your artillery. You just might need it where we're going. . . ."

They rode out together, followed by Old Will and Angelo. Will and the Mexican were to brand the strays that had been missed in the spring roundup. In the brush country, it was easy to miss more than a few calves. And if the Bar F hands didn't get a brand on the little fellows pronto, they became easy pickings for some slick-working rustler practicing his artistry with a running iron.

Roak looked at Bart Nevis, riding a little ahead of him. He was dead sure that Bart didn't take kindly to his friendship with Hannah. But not by word or gesture did the big cowboy show it. Roak figured that Bart had settled down by now, been reassured, wasn't even worried. The Bar F's range boss was bigger, stronger, and handsomer than Roak in every way. Besides, ever since Roak had moved to the bunkhouse with the other hands, he had seen Hannah very, very seldom. Too blamed seldom. He'd sworn he'd never lift a hand, and yet. . . .

The brush was ahead of them now. Roak wasn't riding the paint. When he saw that brush he was glad of it. His spotted pony was far too pretty to get all torn up like this. The mount he had now was a grulla brush pony, ugly as all hell with hips that sloped like a mule's. Its color was a mousy blue-gray, which was what the word *grulla* meant. Its chest, neck and forelegs were a mass of thorn scars; but that slope-hipped cayuse headed straight for the chaparral without shying.

Ahead now, Bart pushed his hat down over his forehead and clapped spurs to the big dun he was riding. Roak and the others followed him. The dun hit the brush flat out, making a hole in it big enough for the others to get through. They worked their way through the mesquite cautiously. Two hours went by before Roak got a chance to rope a calf. They spotted dozens of the little fellows following their mothers; but when they worked in close, they saw they'd all been branded in the spring cowhunt. Looking for the ones that had been missed was some job.

But when they did find one, Bart waved Roak forward. Roak made his throw underhanded without swinging his loop and hindfooted the calf. He was off the grulla in half a second, the rawhide thongs used to tie the calf down, which the hands called "piggin' strings," ready in his hands. The mousy gray squatted on his haunches holding the rope taut. In spite of his looks, he was one fine roping horse.

Roak hogtied the calf under Bart's critical gaze.

"Calf on the ground!" he called.

"You'll do," Bart said. "A mite slow, but the speed will come; roping's not at all bad for a learner, at that, I'll take the next one to show you how."

Angelo and Will made a fire to heat the branding irons. Bart and Roak moved off to hunt down more calves. Roak saw now why Captain Furniss had called brush work "cow hunting." It was just that. In here, the word *roundup* made no sense at all.

Bart put his string on the next one with a *peal* that snaked out under the branches of the chaparral and picked up each of the calf's hind feet in a single loop of a figure eight. Roak had learned enough by now to see how beautiful that throw was.

"Lord!" he said. "Think I'll ever learn to rope like that?"

"Yep," Bart said; "in about seven years."

"Seven years?" Roak said.

"Just about. That's how long it took me to make top hand with a rope. You're as good as I was at the beginning; maybe even a mite better. But a champion roper never quits practicing. Goes stale if he lays off long as a week. Git down, Roak. I want you to see something."

Roak got down, letting his reins trail. He walked over to the calf. He saw at once that this one had been branded.

Then he saw at second glance that there was something wrong with that brand.

"See anything funny?" Bart said.

"Yep. The brand's been altered."

"You're a smart 'un," Bart said. "Know what that means?"

"Rustlers?" Roak said.

"Right ag'in. More likely one rustler—and a amateur. That's the poorest specimen of running-iron work I seen in a coon's age. Mex, I bet. Done it with a cinch ring held between two sticks. Closed up the back bars of the F to make a P." He grinned suddenly. "That's a good 'un. The Bar P!"

"Why?" Roak said.

"In Spik that could mean the Bar Whore Ranch. Th' word begins with a P in Spanish. Reckon that pepper gut had a sense o' humor. C'mon now, we better git this li'l feller back to Ol' Will. Take him home tonight to show to the Cap'n—"

"Then what happens?" Roak said.

"Organize a posse likely and find this iron artist."

"And then?"

"We'll decorate a cottonwood with him, natcher'ly. What else can you do with a rustler?"

"You mean you hang a man for trying to steal a cow?" Roak said.

"Why, sure. If them chili-eating *pelados* from south of the border didn't see a crop o' human fruit swinging there to remind 'em oncet in a while, we'd never be able to keep a critter on the whole blamed range. C'mon, now."

By nightfall, they had flushed six unbranded calves out of the brush. Even riding all over the horse, ducking, dodging, using his elbows, Roak's face looked like he had tangled with a half-dozen bad-tempered wildcats by the time the sun went down. And they had found three more worked-over brands. Like the first one, they were botched jobs.

"Some fool Spik kid," Bart said.

Roak sat there, looking at him. He hoped they wouldn't send him out on that posse. Because even if he had been a polecat puppy most of his days, helping them to hang the boy who had saved his life was a cut below even him. And when the fact that that boy was Belén's brother was piled on top of that. . . . Besides, somehow Belén had taken the fun out of the smart dealing he'd taken so much pride in before. She'd planted the seeds of a couple of entirely new ideas: that maybe it wasn't so dumb to play it straight, after all; that maybe it was even—smart. . . .

He thought about that as they rode back to the bunkhouse. He thought about it a long time and very clearly. By the time they got there, he knew what he was going to do. Bart had told him they'd probably start out after the rustler at dawn, giving him time to gather up his string of altered strays, so they could catch him with the goods. That gave Roak all night. He was dog-tired; but he had gone without sleep before. Besides, that Houston doc was right: he wasn't sick any more. He wasn't sick at all.

He lay down on his bunk with his boots on. He waited until Bart had gone up to the *casa grande* to report. Then he went out to the corral and roped a fresh mount from the *remuda*. He saddled it, mounted and headed back for the *brasada*.

It was a moonlight night. The chaparral was washed in silver. A perfect night for a running-iron artist to get his string onto a calf with not much more trouble than by day. He worked his sorrel through the brush carefully. He lost only a little more skin off his face. He rode in wide zigzags, spooking the steers out of the mesquite as seldom as possible. He kept moving south, toward the Rio Grande.

It was around midnight when he saw a glow. Somebody

down there close to the river had made a fire. You could do a lot of things with a fire. Among them was heating a hot running iron.

He reached down and unlimbered his Colt. He had to make sure. It might not be the kid. And a real rustler was likely to be gunsharp, too, one of those hombres who wore it low, tied down, and pulled it smoking, as old moss-horn Will put it. He couldn't draw faster than a gunny, so he didn't propose to try. He worked the sorrel in, moving it through the brush like an Indian pony—stepping pigeon-toed, daintily, quietly.

He pulled the sorrel up in the last clump of chaparral. He sat there unmoving, looking at the calf tied down and the skinny Mexican kid, looking not a day over sixteen years old, who was holding a cinch ring between two green sticks, heating it cherry red over the fire. His guess had been perfect. It was Ramón Benevides, all right.

He got down. He didn't so much as rustle the brush. On scouting expeditions during the Tennessee campaign, he'd learned to move like that on nights when even a twig crackling underfoot would have brought a sentry's ball. He moved in a circular direction until he was facing the kid. Then he walked out into the little clearing, hold-ing the Colt pointed toward the ground.

"*Hola,*" he said quietly.

The kid dropped the cinch ring, reached. Roak brought the Colt level.

"Wouldn't do that if I was you," he said.

The kid crouched there, licking bone-dry lips.

"Stand up," Roak said.

Ramón got to his feet.

"Loosen your gunbelt 'n' let it drop," Roak said.

The kid dropped the gunbelt around his feet.

"Now kick it toward me."

The heavy gunbelt scraped toward Roak. He bent down, his own gun still level, and picked it up. He drew the kid's revolver and stuck it in his belt. Then, quietly, he holstered his own.

"Now we can talk," he said peacefully. "You can still speak English, can't you, son?"

"Yes," Ramón said. His voice quavered.

"Know what I'm s'posed to do with you?" Roak said.

"*Sí,*" the boy whispered. "Turn me over to the sheriff."

"And then?"

"They hang me, Señor Garfield," the boy said.

"Aren't you scared, son?" Roak said.

"*Sí,* señor—terribly. But I am a man; and *los hombres no lloran*—men do not cry."

"Sit down," Roak said. "Build yourself a smoke, if you want to."

"And you, Señor Garfield?" the boy asked politely.

"Don't smoke. Tell me, Ramón, what am I going to do with you?"

The boy stared at him.

"I do not know," he said bitterly; "what a gringo does is beyond my comprehension. I suppose you're going to turn me in. . . ."

"I know. Figured you'd reckon that. Only you're wrong. I aim to take you home and have a little talk with your sister. Tell me, where's your horse?"

"Over there," the boy said.

"Let's go get him, son," Roak said.

Only when they were both mounted and headed for the river did hope flame in the boy's eyes. They reached the Rio Grande and nudged their ponies into it. It was shallow enough where they were to walk their mounts across.

Standing there on Mexican soil, Roak held out the gun-belt to the boy.

"Here," he said, "put it back on. Do I have to unload your six-gun before I give it back to you, or can I trust you?"

"You, señor," the boy said, "are—rare. But you can trust me. I do not shoot a man who had my life between his hands and gave it back to me."

"Me neither," Roak grunted. "Here."

Ramón holstered the big, old-fashioned Walker Colt.

"Now," he said, "we are quits, Señor Garfield. My life for yours, no?"

"Not quite. Tell me one thing, though: you're neither a peon nor a *vaquero*. What made you try rustling?"

The boy stiffened in the saddle.

"I am not a thief," he said. "I only take back my own. All that land over there belonged to my father. *Los gringos* forced him out. He sold, for practically nothing, to a family called Martínez. Afterwards, the gringos forced them out, too."

"I see," Roak said. "Come on. I still want to talk to your sister."

They rode until they came to the pueblo. The sky was clearing now. Going gray, fading out the stars. They dismounted before a house painted blue.

"Belén!" Ramón called out quietly.

"*Eres tú*, Ramón? Is it thou?" the voice came back. It was low and husky with sleep.

"Yes, little sister mine," Ramón said, "but—"

"Come," the voice said, "enough of talking, little one. I have sleepiness still. Come."

Ramón shrugged and entered. Roak followed him. From pure ignorance. Not knowing the enormity of that offense in the eyes of any Latin-born.

She was lying there in bed, covered to the waist by an embroidered spread. She had on a white night dress. Against her coppery skin, it was like snow. It clung to her. Roak knew he shouldn't look at that roundness, that swell, seam-straining and proud, even, curiously, under his hard gaze, that quite visible thrust, lift, pucker. He tore away his gaze, met her eyes. He was sure all over again that he had never seen eyes like those before. Black—yet luminous. He stared into them. A long time. A very long time, feeling his good resolutions sinking down; and in their place. . . .

Stark, naked lust rising up. A gut hunger for her in him now, hotter and crueler than a brand.

Which, though he didn't stop to think about it, was a new thing in him. Maybe even a better thing. He had wanted women before, had taken them when he could; but he had never wanted a woman as he wanted Belén now, with absolutely no desire to humiliate her, shame her, degrade her, take vengeance upon her because she knew, could see, understood that he hadn't been born six feet tall with shoulders like an oak tree's spread. He just wanted her the way a man should want a woman, except that he still hadn't quite achieved the grace of accompanying tenderness; and maybe even that would come with time.

"So," she said, "you came back. Why?"

"Don't know," Roak said, "except that I couldn't stay away. And to ask you mighty kindly to keep this fool kid on this side of the river before somebody decorates a cottonwood with him."

She turned questioning eyes upon her brother. Ramón launched into swift, lyrical Spanish. She lay there, listening to him. Then, very slowly, she sat up in bed.

"For your life," she said softly, "you give back a life. Very well, Señor Garfield. Now we are quits."

"No," Roak said, and she could hear the pain in his voice like a scrape, like a strangling; "we purely aren't quits, ma'am. For what's life to a man when all the sweetness has been taken out of it, all the savor?"

She stared at him. Her lips did not move; but her eyes went darker, softer still.

"And what is it," she said, "that has taken away the sweetness and the savor of your days, señor?"

Roak looked at her.

"You," he said.

Ramón whirled upon him.

"This I will not support, señor!" he said. "In this of saving me, you have done no more than put things equal, so—"

"So," Belén said quietly, "you will have the favor to shut up, my little brother. And both of you will now march yourselves from here while I get up and dress. Then *el señor rubiecito* and I will talk; for truly, brother mine, I find him—rare. . . ."

She rode back with Roak to the river, Ramón trailing with sullen discretion a few yards behind them. Her voice was light, gay, mocking. Clearly she was enjoying herself, pleased to have him so visibly in her power, take her small, deadly, feline vengeance upon him for all the hated gringos' sins.

"You are trying to say, then, Don Roak" (she pronounced it Don Roo-ak, making music of it, flutes and cymbals) "that you love me?"

"Yes," Roak said, realizing as he spoke that this was getting to be quite a bit less than a lie, while falling still a trifle short of truth.

"How?" she said coolly. "How do you love me, Don Roak?"

"How?" he said. "I don't think I really understand that question, ma'am."

"Do not call me 'ma'am,' " she mocked. "If we are going to be *novios*—engaged ones, no?—you must call me Belén, or my dearest, or my life, my soul, my love—"

He was neither insensitive nor a fool. He caught the deadly mockery of her tone.

"Please, Belén," he said, "you aren't being fair—"

"*Alal!* But I am!" she said. "It is entirely fair of me to ask you *how* you love me. What is not fair is that you do not answer. . . ."

"If I truly knew what you were getting at—" he began.

"At this," she said sharply. "Do you wish to marry me, Don Roak?"

He sidestepped that one.

"And if I did want to," he said, "would you?"

"Alal!" she laughed. "You are a *pelin*—a smart one, no? I am not to be caught this way. Answer first my question, and I will answer yours, which is fair. Do you, Don Roak?"

Roak knew better than to lie. He had the feeling that those black eyes were peering into his sacred heart, reading his miserable history in his soul.

"I don't know," he said quietly; "I don't know you well enough to tell that yet, Belén. What I do know is that I've never seen another girl on God's green earth who could hold a candle to you, Belén. . . ."

"Not even Hannah Furniss?" Belén asked.

"Not even her," Roak said truthfully.

"I see," Belén said; "then you are willing to leave her for my sake, Don Roak?"

"Well—" Roak said; "heck, Belén, I don't know. All I know right now is that when it comes to crowding a fellow into corners, you sure Lord are an expert!"

"Thank you," Belén smiled. "It is just that when dealing with tricksters, one has to be precise and define one's position down to the smallest details. And so, once again I ask you: are you willing to throw away your chances with the daughter of the greatest landowner in Texas in order to engage in some sort of as yet unexplained relationship with a poor Mexican seamstress?"

Roak stared at her. The hard part about her questions was that he didn't know the answers himself. Here and now, looking at her, there was an ache in him, a strangling. A sickness like sunstroke, his eyes blinded, his head dizzy, all his breath a tangle in his lungs, his middle gone weak and hollow. Here and now, the need in him, the wanting, effortlessly overruled the cold, insistent promptings of his brain. He'd give up Hannah for her. Hell, yes! Hannah and the whole blasted state of Texas, only—

Only he waited too long to say this thought, to spill out in words the way he really felt.

"Don't bother," she said calmly, almost kindly. "I know what you are thinking, and it is not strange. I have met your kind before. You are strangely transparent, you blond ones—"

"And what am I thinking?" he said.

"You were—how do you say *explorando las posibilidades* in English? It is almost the same, but it does not come to me—"

"Exploring the possibilities," Roak supplied; "go on, Belén—"

"You were exploring the possibilities of doing both. Of marrying your ice-cold *rubia* for convenience, and—also for convenience—keeping this little *morena* hot tamale, this brunette chili pepper south of the border to thaw out the chill she will have put into you. Is it not thus that you thought, Don Roak?"

Roak looked at her.

"Yes," he said.

She leaned over and patted his cheek as though he were a small boy. A rather naughty small boy, caught out by his mother.

"That is better," she said gently, "much better. Now, occasionally, you even tell the truth. . . ."

"Then you—you're not offended?" Roak said.

She let her nightshade gaze linger coolly on his face. Then she said:

"Of course not. Only those we care about can offend us. Since what you want does not interest me, and the possibility of your accomplishing it is nonexistent, I am not at all offended, Don Roak. What *is* strange is that I am beginning to like you. I think that you were forced into being a trickster. I have for you, most oddly, *lástima y piedad*—

both sorrow and pity; because you have been flawed, it seems to me, and what you could have been can still be seen in you, twisted and distorted, but there—"

"And what could I have been?" Roak asked humbly.

"A man," Belén said.

"Then what am I now?" Roak said.

"Un granuja, y un sin vergüenza, which go not easily into English. Say—a small-sized crooked one, and one without shame. . . ."

"I see," Roak said. "Tell me, how do you say 'I love you' in Spik?"

"Te quiero," Belén said softly; "and it is Spanish, not Spik!"

"Te quiero," Roak said. "You think you're so little woman you couldn't teach me to say it with my heart? That you couldn't make me forget Hannah, the Bar F and whatever else there is between us? That, having done that, you might not change me, even, making the penny-ante trickster go away, taking the no-regrets sharpster with him, and leaving only—the man?"

She smiled at him. And then, quite suddenly, that smile took the place of the Reb sniper's ball. It made a small and dreadful wound that was going to bleed forever.

"I *know* I could," she said peacefully, "but why on earth do you imagine I should want to, Don Roak?"

He bowed his head, then. And the pain in him was very deep. She could see it silhouetted against the pale golden wash of dawning, see the shoulder sag, the tightening, the old accustomed gestures of one who had been hurt many times before.

"You win, Belén," he said tiredly; "reckon there's no way of getting around that one. . . ."

She put her hand out suddenly, let it rest upon his arm.

"No," she said softly, "I do not win, and you have gotten around it. Day after tomorrow is fiesta. A very appropriate fiesta: that of Nuestra Señora de la Merced—

Our Lady of Mercy. Will you come, Don Roak—as my guest?"

He stared at her in astonishment, in dawning hope.

"Gladly," he said. "But would you mind telling me—why?"

"Because I am a woman," she said. "Is this not answer enough, Don Roak?"

He got back in time to join the posse that was beating the brush for the rustler. He sat there straight-faced and solemn and Old Will pointed out the tracks of the two horses going into the river.

"Two of 'em, eh?" Bart said. "Well, we'll be a-laying for them next time."

On Saturday, Roak carefully brushed off his one good suit and polished his boots. He brought out a ruffled white shirt and a string tie. Old Will watched him solemnly.

"Going gallin'?" he asked.

Roak stared at him.

"Daggum it, I have to explain ever' little thing to you, dude!" the old man growled. "Gallin' means visiting yore gal. . . ."

"I don't have a girl," Roak said.

"If you don't, I'm laying odds you'll have one soon. You got the look of a hombre what's riding herd on a filly. Who is she, son?"

Roak grinned at him.

"Don't you wish you knew?" he said.

"Daggum it!" Will began, but the clatter of hooves and the creaking of harness cut him off. The two of them looked up. The Captain's buggy rolled past. The Captain and Hannah were in it. They waved at Will and Roak. With them were four outriders: Bart, Angelo, Pepe and Enrique.

"Where're they going?" Roak asked.

"Down to that Mex fiesta. Cap'n's Spik friends, the Martínez, invited 'em—what's the matter with you, dude? You havin' a fit o' sumpin'?"

"No," Roak whispered. When he straightened up, there was a light in his eyes. Maybe this was a part of his luck, too. Belén was something. Like nightsmoke, like flame, like the heart of a rose. When Hannah saw that, it was going to be either the end—or the beginning. He wasn't sure which. But one of the two it was going to be.

Chapter Six

ROAK GOT the tickets *en sombra*, the shady side of the bull ring, as Belén had told him to.

"En sol," she said, "the sun is in one's eyes and that makes much *molestias* and also pains in the head. One sees better *en sombra*. . . ."

"If I can see you any better than I do right now, you're going to have to rope and hogtie me, Belén," Roak said.

"Oh!" she laughed; "I like it when you call me Bellain, like that, Roak! It is so *anglo*. But sweet. You are sweet, I think. Now I am flirting with you outrageously. Do you like it, *rubiecito mío?*"

"Very much. What does *rubiecito mío* mean?"

"My little blond one. Because you are blond and you are not very big. In fact, for a gringo, you are almost an *enano*—like the seven *enanos* of Blanca Nieves. . . ."

"One of the seven dwarfs, you mean? All right, I'm properly insulted. Now, come on! We're going to be late. . . ."

They were late. As they raced for the bull ring, Roak was surprised to note that Belén's stride was a trifle unsteady. Apparently even the relatively small quantity of wine they had consumed in celebrating the preliminaries of the fiesta was more than she was accustomed to. But she was not too tipsy to carefully straighten her mantilla of centuries-old white lace, darkened by the years to the color of cream. Framing her black hair, that lace was something. Her fiesta dress was white, too. It was tight in the bodice

77

above a full ruffled skirt. The part of her that the bodice outlined was a pure glory.

They moved down the row towards their seats. When they were a few feet away from Hannah, the noise of people rising to let them pass caught her attention. She rose, and stared straight into Roak's face, then into Belén's. Roak stopped dead, transfixed upon that look as upon a sword. He was aware of a vast and murmurous silence in which the music, the voices of the spectators, the rustle of cloth, of fans, died out of time and mind. The blade in his heart was like death, but whether from an excess of grief or joy he did not know.

Belén's lips, as she leaned forward, brushed against his ear. They were scalding.

"So truly, thou art a swine, my Roak," she said almost without moving them, "when I am to be used to make thy *rubia* jealous. Very well; if it is comedy you wish—"

She caught him by the arm, tugged him half-around, her mouth soft and open, inches from his own. Her voice, speaking, was low, lazy, slumberous, as sensual as a long, long kiss. She spoke in Spanish, knowing that Hannah had been bilingual from babyhood and that it did not matter that Roak understood no single syllable.

"Porqué esperas, mi amor?" she said. *"Ven, cariño mío, ven—"* "Why do you wait, my love? Come, my dearest, come—"

Roak moved forward like a sleepwalker. His booted feet weighed tons.

" 'Scuse me, Miss Hannah," he muttered; " 'scuse me, Bart. Beg your pardon, Captain. Pardon me, señores—"

Captain Furniss grinned at him.

"Sure Lord throws yourself a wide loop, don't you, son?" he said.

"Father!" Hannah said. "You mind your own business, please!"

Bart looked at her.

"You real sure you're minding yours, Han?" he said.

"Oh!" Hannah gasped. "Oh—" Then she turned her face away from Roak. But not fast enough. The tears had been there in her eyes for several seconds before she realized it.

"*Alal!*" Belén whispered. "*La pobrecita!* The poor, poor thing! She is dying of love for you!"

"You," Roak said glumly, "have too much imagination, Belén. She's engaged to that big hunk of beef she's sitting next to—"

"Ah, so?" Belén said. "Your voice tells me you do not entirely like the idea. . . ."

"My voice tells you too blamed much," Roak said.

"I know. *Alal,* but this is diverting! Not only do I have the bony Carmen to kill with jealousy, but this, thy *gringa rubia,* also—which is why you brought me, is it not, my Roak?"

"One," Roak said grimly, "*you* invited *me,* remember? Two, you changed those tickets so we'd be sitting here. Three, I didn't even know Hannah was going to be here. Folks up at the big house ain't in the habit of letting cowhands in on their plans."

"Why," Belén said impishly, "I have the strangest feeling that you are speaking the truth—which makes it more diverting, still. Watch her, Roak—I will make her bite herself in the lips 'til she draws blood!"

She caught his arm to her, snuggled her lace-clad head against his shoulder. Her lips parted. The rustle of her breathing stirred against his face.

"You little witch," Roak grinned. He was beginning to enjoy himself now.

"A weech?" Belén said. "What is this—a weech?"

"A woman who can work hexes on folks. Cast spells—puts 'em in her power. . . ."

"Ah, *una bruja!* Of course I am *una bruja!* I shall en-chant you, and make your pale *rubiecita* sick at the same time."

"Don't know about making her sick," Roak said, "but when it comes to enchanting me, you're doing just fine. . . ."

He cast a sidelong glance toward the others. The Martínez were staring at them openly. The Captain was watching the parade of the bullfighters. Bart Nevis sat there like a man carved of brown granite. Roak couldn't see Hannah because Bart's bulk hid her. But at the last moment, she leaned forward and looked in his direction. Her face was very pale. She met his gaze and jerked backward so he could no longer see her.

And Roak Garfield became the first man in history to sit through a bullfight without seeing it at all.

The dancing was in the public square under a full moon that filled half the sky. Roak was nobody's dancer, but the wine helped. He whirled Belén around and around. She clung to him, her face hidden against his throat. He was aware that Hannah was watching him, but he took a kind of cruel satisfaction from that fact. That "ever" would never come, she had said. But the grief in her face was naked. He gloried in that grief.

A *charro,* splendid in gold-embroidered sombrero and filigree-worked riding suit, bowed over Belén's hand with an inquiring glance toward Roak. Belén started to shake her head, but Roak said quickly, "Ah, dance with him, sweetheart."

She got up sinuously, serpentine, boneless in her grace. Roak waited until the *charro* had whirled her away, then marched over to where Hannah sat with Bart.

"Do you mind, Bart?" he asked; and took Hannah's hand.

She came up at once, her eyes night sapphires. Bart growled something, but neither of them heard him.

"Roak. . . ." Hannah breathed.

"Yes, Han?"

"That—that girl. Are you—in love with her?"

"More questions, Han?" Roak said.

"I'm sorry. I know I haven't any right, but—"

"But what, Han?"

"Oh, Roak, why are you making it so hard for me?"

"Am I?" Roak said.

"Oh, take me back!" Hannah said. "I don't feel like dancing any more!"

"All right, Han," Roak said.

He led her back to where Bart sat, his hard, tanned face gone blacker than a thundercloud as he watched them approaching. But Roak didn't give the big cowboy a chance to say anything. He bowed quickly over Hannah's hand, and was gone.

He found Belén sitting at the table alone, waiting for him.

"Roak," she said, "have the favor to order some more wine, please. . . ."

"Now look, baby," Roak said, "don't you think you've had enough?"

"No. It is all gone, the fumes of the other I drank before. I am quite sober, and I am beginning to be sad. Please, Roak . . ."

Roak signaled to the waiter.

"Más vino, por favor," he said. He'd heard that one phrase repeated enough that afternoon to learn it very well. Then he turned back to Belén.

"Why are you sad?" he said.

"Because—*porqué*—oh, I do not know!"

"Más grande que una casa," Roak said. He'd got that phrase from her. She said it very often.

"Sí," she said, "you are right. It is a lie bigger than a house. I do know why I am sad. The reasons are various. And complicated. I'm not sure I could explain them cor-

rectly. And I am more than secure that I should not explain some of them at all. . . ."

Roak grinned at her.

"Start with those," he said.

"Start with what?"

"With the reasons you're certain sure you oughtn't to explain to me. These sound mighty interesting, *mi amor*—"

"*Mi amor*," she said morosely; "how nicely you say it. If only—"

"If only what, Belén?"

"Nothing," she said. "Ah, *gracias á Dios,* here is the wine!"

He watched her downing cup after cup. And matched her. Because a sadness was in him, too. A hurting. The beginnings of anger.

"Belén," he said, "why do you drink?"

"I—I don't know," she said. "I never have before. Not to excess. But tonight—there is this sadness in me like a weight of darkness, and—"

"And what?" Roak said.

"I have been lonely too long, I think. The boys whom now I can marry due to my poverty cannot even speak my language in a sense. So I have refused to sally forth with *vaqueros, pistoleros,* half-peons. *Hidalgos,* sons of somebodies, are few, and those few looking for fat dowries. I am speaking so frankly because I have had too much wine and I am sad and you are nothing to me, so it does not matter. . . ."

"What you mean," Roak said, "is that you're sad because being with a gringo pig isn't so Lord-awful after all."

"Precisely," Belén mocked, her black eyes resting on him like a brand. "I hope you are sufficiently proud!"

Roak looked at her, his blue eyes grave and still.

"Proud? No, Belén. The boot's on the other foot, it

appears to me. Let me tell you how it is—the truth. I found out that Hannah was coming down here an hour before I left. A whole hour. Plenty of time to back out, not to come at all. Because, if you knew Hannah, you'd know that flaunting another female, especially one so goddamned, heartbreakingly pretty as you, in her face, is just about the very worst tactics I could have ever dreamed up. Too crude. All she'll say is, 'That's what you want, Roak? Then have it!' So I knew that by coming down here I was tossing my chances with Han, my hopes of owning the Bar F one day, right out of the window. But I came anyhow, knowing that. Because I couldn't stay away. Listen to it, baby, and be proud. I threw away my chances with Hannah to be with a girl who thinks I'm a small-sized crook, and a man without shame. Laugh, Belén. Go on, laugh!"

She stretched out her hand and let it rest upon his arm.

"No, Roak. This is a thing for tears, rather than for laughter. Do you really want to know what it was that made me sad?"

"Yes," he said.

"Because you danced with her," Belén said softly.

He turned, staring at her.

"Truly. I was dancing with Antonio who is a marvelous dancer, and I could not keep step because all I could see was the way she was devouring you with her eyes. She still is. Look!"

"No," Roak said. "Get on with it, Belén."

"I realized then that if it were your plan to make her jealous of me, you had succeeded better that you knew, because I wanted to go to you, snatch you from her arms, slap her face, pull her hair, and scratch out her eyes! For the first time in my life I had envy to be the daughter of a peon so I could be allowed to behave so badly. So now, Don Roak, it is your turn to laugh. Why don't you?"

"Belén," he said, "what are we going to do?"

"Drink!" she laughed. "What else? You are a poor gringo cowboy, and I am a poor Mexican seamstress. And while we *Méxicanas* are the most romantic girls on earth, we are also the most realistic. We know that hunger is the worst enemy of love. And you, my Roak, have this night made other enemies: that too-big *novio* of Miss Furniss, and perhaps even she herself out of her hurt at being scorned. I think that Texas is going to become a very unhealthy climate for you. So, since our romance ends before it begins, let us drink and be gay!"

"Right," Roak said.

But halfway through the third bottle, she quit.

"Take me home, Roak," she said.

"Lord, it is late, isn't it?" he said. "That kid brother of yours is gonna be fit to be tied!"

"No," she said tipsily, "Ramón has gone to Nogales to another fiesta. He will not be home for days. . . ."

Which was a mistake. She shouldn't have said that. Because Roak Garfield was only half-drunk. Maybe not even half.

As they left the *baile,* Roak saw Hannah looking at them. And what was in her eyes was another sword. A different sword this time. The one of fire the angel held up before the gates of Eden to prevent the sons of men from ever entering there. Only it wasn't enough. By then all the heavenly hosts wouldn't have been.

Hannah was watching him. Hannah who hadn't a poker face, nor a feminine wile to her name, nor even a nodding acquaintace with deceit, watched him with her whole heart showing in her eyes. But instead of deterring Roak Garfield, it spurred him on. He threw back his head and laughed aloud.

When they got to Belén's door, she turned to him.

"Good night, Roak," she whispered.

He grinned at her crookedly.

"Not even a little old measly kiss, baby?" he said.

She stood there, staring at him. Her eyes vanquished the night, drowned even the light of the stars.

Then, very quietly, she slipped into his arms, tilted her face to meet his mouth.

Which was her second mistake, and her final one.

He picked her up as though she were weightless. Shouldered open the door, and went through it, into the dark.

First in the waning moonlight, as he lay sleeping, she saw that scabbard he took off only to sleep or to make love and not always even then. He had hooked the thin black leather of the straps that looped over his left shoulder, and crossed his chest to hold the scabbard flat and ready, around the bedpost, and she could see the twin hilts of his throwing knives nestling there together. She put out a tentative hand, her fingers trembling, inching toward one of those hilts, touching it, closing. She jerked it out of the scabbard, lifted it high.

He opened his eyes, stared up at her. At the cool glitter of death in her hand. She held that blade there, searching his eyes.

"You want to, baby?" he said. "Then go ahead."

She turned her face, looked at the knife as though she were seeing it for the first time. Then she threw it wildly away from her. It clattered to the floor. She buried her face in the hollow of his throat. He could feel her shaking. Quivering like a birch sapling in a high wind.

"Oh, Roak, I love you so!" she wept.

"I know. And baby—"

"Yes, Roak?"

"You'd be a lot more comfortable if you got out of the rest of your things. Fine as that was, making love with your clothes on is like taking a bath the same way—"

"Oh, Roak, I am so ashamed!" Belén wailed.

He lifted his hand, stroked her black hair.

"Kind of late in the day for shame now, baby. C'mon now, get out of your things," he said.

Before it was light, he mounted the paint and rode back to the river, dancing the stars above his head in slow and stately measure to the clipclopping of the pinto's hooves. Ahead of him now, the stars grayed out, and the first thin, washed-out yellow of the morning appeared above the prairie rim. He moved on, riding quietly, gently, wrapped in a mantle of peace bigger than the encircling sky.

He came up to the bunkhouse in the full light of day. Went in, changed into his working clothes, came out ready to ride. A shadow fell across him. He looked up. Saw Bart Nevis sitting there on a big dun gelding, looking down at him.

"Roll your bed and drift, dude," Bart said.

"You mean you're firing me?" Roak said.

"No. I'm just plain running you off the place. Half an hour from now, I want to see empty space where you're at."

"Captain tell you to put me off?" Roak asked.

"Nope. I'm putting you off, personal. You still around in half 'n hour, you better know how to handle that there six-gun you got hanging on you."

"No," Roak said.

"No, what?"

"Not either one. I'm not leaving unless the Captain puts me off himself. And I won't go gunning for you. I can shoot, Bart; only I don't hold with killing. 'Specially not over whatever wrong-headed, tomfool idea you've got in your head." He turned to Will. "Old-timer," he said, "here's my gun. I want you to keep it 'til I ask for it. So if anybody finds me perforated, it'll be plain murder and an invitation to hanging. . . ."

"You," Bart said contemptuously, "are as yellow as mustard without the bite."

"I don't think so. What's more, you don't think so, either. Now, get out of my way, Bart; I got work to do."

He walked straight toward the dun. Bart's hand dropped toward the butt of his Colt. It hesitated there, came away empty.

"Damn you!" he swore. "Goddamn you to hell 'n' Pecos, dude!"

Roak didn't answer him. He swung himself aboard the painted pony and rode away. Not even once did he look back.

He was riding the open range that week, checking on strays. He had got far out when he saw that horse coming toward him at a gallop. He groped for his gun, then remembered. So he sat there, like that, waiting. Then he saw that the rider was mounted sidesaddle. Han, he thought; Lord God!

She came up to him. Her face was white. Her teeth chattered in spite of the heat.

"Will told me," she got out, "that Bart—that Bart—"

"Gentle down, honey," Roak said.

"That Bart's out gunning for you! Oh, Roak, I—"

"Don't fret over it, Han, honey," Roak said. "Reckon I cooled him off a mite a while back."

"I know. Only he's drinking now! He just might shoot you even if you're not packing a gun! And then I'd—I'd—"

"You'd what, honeychild?" Roak said.

"I'd die!" Hannah wailed.

Roak grinned at her.

"Why?" he asked. "Because I'd cashed in my chips or because they'd likely make that big range bull guest o' honor at a necktie party?"

"Oh, I wish he would shoot you! You're meaner than a sidewinder! Sitting there forcing me to say—"

"What, Han?" Roak said.

"That I love you! As if you didn't know it already! Flaunting your hot tamale in front of my face! Gloating over how I was making a fool out of myself! I cried, Roak! Didn't you see that? Right before everybody. Father's fit to be roped and hogtied! I'm afraid he's going to put you off the place. . . ."

"Don't worry about it, honey," Roak said. "Maybe it'd be better all around if I put a lot of territory between me and Texas. . . ."

She stared at him.

"Oh, Roak—no!" she breathed.

"Why not, Han?" Roak said. "What have I to offer you? No job, no money, no prospects—"

"Shut up!" she flared. "I don't care about that! You drift, I drift, too! You think I'm going to let that little chile pepper get her hooks on you again, you're— Come here, Roak."

He danced the pinto over to her.

"Kiss me," Hannah whispered.

He bent to her, found her mouth. It was warm, soft, trembling, salt with tears. He straightened up. Then a thousand skyrockets burst inside his head, as her gloved hand exploded across his face like a pistol shot. He reeled back away from her. She sat there smiling at him, her eyes starry.

"The kiss," she said, "was because I love you. That slap was for what I know blamed well you did last night! From now on, Roak Garfield, you're mine. You understand that? You ride back across the border just one more time, and I'll use my quirt!"

Roak sat there, holding his jaw and grinning at her.

"You," he said, "sure pack a mean wallop, Han!"

"That was just a sample, Roak. You heard what I said?"

"Yes'm," Roak said; "yes, ma'am, Miss Boss Lady, ma'am!"

"Oh, quit clowning! I don't want to boss you around. I want a man, not a bawling yearling. Roak—"

"Yes, Han?"

"What are we going to do?"

He sat there, looking at her. His eyes were very peaceful, very sure.

"Wait," he said. "Love is just fine, hon; but it don't flourish on a empty belly no better than anything else. I'm going to quit here. Let me have my say, baby, and you'll see I'm talking sense. I'm going to quit because staying here won't lead to nothing but trouble. They'll say that Bart run me off with my tail dragging, that I was down in my boots, gun-shy, yellower'n mustard. Let 'em. There's more than one way of being brave. Never seen Bart handle a gun, but I'm certain sure I can do anything he can do with a shooting iron and maybe more. Only I won't. The way I figure it is I got the simple guts not to be crowded into killing a man because I'm scared of what folks think of me. I just don't give a damn what they think. And anyhow, I kind of like that big, stupid hunk of beef. . . ."

"You sure you aren't taking into consideration the fact that he might make wolf meat of you?" Hannah asked dryly.

Roak smiled.

"Yes'm," he said, "I'm taking that into consideration too. 'Cause I got a lot to live for now. Only I don't worry about that side of it too much. For four long years I had to take that into consideration every day, 'til I got plumb used to it. I had a whole hour to mull over the idea from ever' which a way whilst I was lying on a pile o' dead leaves in front o' Nashville and coughing up blood every time I opened my mouth. So it don't cut much ice with me, Han —not any more. We all owe the good Lord a dying, sooner or later, and the only thing what counts is how we manage it—"

"Oh, Roak!" she said. "I'm sorry! I didn't mean to—"

"Don't worry your pretty taffy-colored head none a-tall. The best thing for us to do is to wait. 'Til I've got a

stake, started a little homestead. 'Til the range bull tumbles
to the fact that there ain't no way to keep a filly on the
home range who's bent on straying—not even with a gun.
So now, you just ride down there and tell the Captain to
send a rider out to relieve me. I aim to hold a little get-
together with him today. . . ."

Hannah moved her mount over until she was very
close to him.

"All right, Roak," she whispered, and put out her
arms to him. When she pulled away from him at last, her
blue eyes were dancing with mischief.

"Do I kiss better than your chile pepper?" she asked.

Roak looked at her solemnly.

"Never was in the habit of comparing lip brands," he
said. "Besides that isn't the important part. What I aim
to find out is what else you do better—"

"Oh, you!" Hannah gasped, and yanked her pony's
head around.

Watching her pounding away, Roak realized the one
great advantage he had over Bart Nevis. He wasn't afraid
of decent women. And Bart, like every cowboy born, was.

Sitting in Captain Furniss's office, Roak Garfield was
the calmest man in Texas. The Captain, on the other hand,
was visibly troubled.

"I was going to tell you to roll your bedding, son," he
said gravely, "but you got ahead of me. Not because I
have anything against you, but because whether you mean
to be or not, you're a troublemaker. A mite too handy
with the fillies, it appears to me. Been understood since
they were kids that Han and Bart were to wed. Bart's the
son of a friend of mine. Good stock, cowfolks from way
back. . . ."

Roak sat there listening. He didn't interrupt.

"Besides, he's the most valuable man I have in the
outfit. While you—though you've learned more in less

time than any greener I've ever seen—have years to go before you'll be worth as much as he is. Another thing. To tell the strict truth, I'm dead set against a match between you and Han. You've a bum lung, no money, and a hell of a lot to learn before you can even get started. That is, if you ever do get started. . . ."

"You ever asked Miss Hannah what she thinks about all this?"

"Yep. She thinks you came right off the top of the Christmas tree, as you know damned well by now. Only I don't care for filly reasoning, because I know she'll get over it. Now, here's what I mean to do. Rod Cameron has a nice spread north of the Nueces. I'm going to write him a letter—you take it to him—to tell him the truth: that you're a sight less green than grass, but not much. On the other hand, you can ride, and you can learn. He'll take you on because he's shorthanded and as a favor to me. All I want from you is your promise that you won't ride down here looking for my daughter."

Roak considered the matter.

"All right," he said; "it's your spread, Captain—and your daughter. I'll stay north of the Nueces—at least long enough to see whether you can change Han's mind. If you can, I don't want her. But I don't think you can."

"You've gravel in your gizzard, haven't you, son? Talking to me like that! All right, you just sit there while I write the letter—"

"Captain," Roak said, "one more thing—"

"Yes, son?"

"Will you lend me the paint and a saddle to get over to the Cameron spread?"

"I'll do better'n that," the Captain said. "I'll make you a gift of 'em. Write out a bill of sale right now, putting in 'for due 'n' proper considerations—' "

"Thank you, Captain," Roak said; "that's mighty white of you."

"Don't mention it. Wish I could do more. And son—"

"Yes, Captain?"

"I'm sorry it turned out this way. Sorrier'n old hell. . . ."

"Me, too. Captain," Roak said.

As he rode away from the Bar F, he saw Bart Nevis coming toward him at the head of a band of cowhands, on a long slant calculated to cut off his path. When they had him blocked, Bart pulled up the big dun and waited. Roak came on at an easy lope, straight toward them. When he was close enough, Bart looked at his waist, and spat into the dust.

"Where's yore gun?" he asked.

"In my saddle roll," Roak said; "didn't figure to run into nothing real dangerous today."

Bart grinned at him mockingly.

"Shore got cold feet for such a hot country, ain't you, dude?" he said.

Roak looked at him.

"Feet's warm enough," he said; "just didn't aim to stay 'til my cinch was frayed. . . ."

"It's plumb ragged now," Bart growled. "You're 'bout as welcome as a polecat in church. Only you're moving mightly slow. Let's see if you can git some speed out o' that *cuitado* paint—"

"I can," Roak said peacefully, "but I don't aim to. Got a long ride in front o' me, and I don't believe in mistreating horseflesh—"

Bart didn't answer him. He raised his arm suddenly, and slashed down with his quirt against the pinto's hips. The pony gave a leap and dug in, running. Roak gave him his head, and let him go. Then he heard laughter behind him. He pulled the pinto up, turned him, and loped back quietly.

"Bart," he said, "I don't hold with killing, and any-how I promised Miss Hannah. But if you'll get down off that cayuse and put your fists up, I'll be rightly willing to oblige you."

Bart looked at him, his sunbrowned face darker than ever.

"Told you I don't dog fight," he said; "you think I want to bust the finest pair o' roping paws in Texas on your hard head?"

"Reckon not," Roak said, "but don't quirt my pony no more, or I'll drag you off and clear five acres clean o' brush with your stupid hide. Any punk can be brave with a gun. Takes a man to have grit without one."

Bart sat there, looking at him.

"You git going, pilgrim, afore I forgets you ain't heeled," he said.

"You won't forget it," Roak said; "even if you have been bored for the hollow horn, you got more sense than that."

Then he turned the calico pony again, and moved off at a slow trot. This time, only silence followed him.

Chapter Seven

THAT 5th of January, 1869, three months after he had left the Furnisses', Roak lay on his back in the bunkhouse of the Flying U, Rod Cameron's ranch, counting the bullet holes in the ceiling. They had been put there by bored cowhands shooting at flies. When he got to two thousand, he quit. It was too hard a chore. The trouble was he could never make out which bullet hole he'd started with, so he wasn't sure he hadn't counted the same one over twice or even three times.

"There's 3,266 by my reckoning," the cowboy in the next bunk said.

"Good Lord," Roak said, "haven't they anything else to do?"

"Not much, come wintertime. Listen to those two old wranglers over there."

"Of peaches this here can contains," one of the wranglers was intoning, "a full eight ounces, packed in their natural juices with nothing added but sugar. . . ."

"This here can contains the finest French beans," the other old mosshorn took up the chant, "twelve ounces net, b'iled in pure creek water with nothing added save four grams of phosphate to presarve the color. . . ."

"They crazy or something?" Roak said.

"Nope. That is, not quite. They're trying to keep from being. So they're holding a memorizing contest to see which one can remember the most labels on air-tights. I was you, I'd quit, dude, while I still had more sense than a little nigger with a big belly button. Stay on, you get to be as loco as the rest of us."

"But why?" Roak asked. "I don't see—"

"It's the lonesomeness that gets you," the cowboy said. "Hell, I haven't seen a decent woman since old Miz' Cameron died. And that's what she died of, too—lonesomeness. Only white woman in three hard days' riding. And when that boy of theirs, Rod junior, run away back East and married that actress, it plumb finished her. Didn't even live long enough to find out she had a grandson, Rod three. Reckon they named him that to get on the good side of the old man. No good, though; old Rod blames 'em for the old woman's death. Heard tell he's cut his boy and the poor little maverick off in his will. Going to leave the place to Hank Flynn—"

"Look," Roak said, "you think you ought to be telling me, or anybody, for that matter, all that? Seems to me the boss's family troubles are a private matter. . . ."

"You're right. You see? That's another thing. It even gets to you that way, diarrhea of the jawbone, talking too damned much. Oh, Lord, if I could even see a likely filly. They tell me that Cap'n Furniss has a mighty pretty daughter, but I can't figure out an excuse to ride over there. . . ."

"Yes," Roak said, "Miss Furniss is very attractive—"

"You've seen her? Lord God, dude—what's she like?"

"Well," Roak began; but he never got the words out. At the far end of the bunkhouse, two cowhands were on their feet facing each other.

"Draw, damn you!" one of them roared. "Ain't no mangy polecat gonna call me a cowpuncher and get away with it!"

The range boss, Hank Flynn, got up slowly.

"All right, you two," he said, "just hand me over those six-guns. We don't need any crow bait this time of year."

"But Hank, he called me a cowpoke! And he wasn't joking, neither!"

"And if you don't both quit it," Hank drawled, "I'm going to call you both a couple of sheepherders and make it stick. You boys are just winter-locoed. Forget it and shake hands."

The cowboys shook hands grudgingly, and sat back down to their card game.

From the other bunks the endless arguments went on:

"That there mule-hipped cayuse o' yourn couldn't outrun his own shadow. And when it comes to cuttin'—"

"Don't tell me about that *cuitado* Navaho pony you forks; why—"

"Tell me," Roak said, "What's so bad about being called a cowpuncher?"

"A cowpuncher or a cowpoke," the cowboy explained, "is one of them tramps the railroads hires to punch the steers with poles to get 'em into the cattle cars, and afterwards to poke 'em ever' time they tires to lie down whilest they's loading, or the other critters piling into the car behind 'em would stamp 'em to death. Now, oncet in a while a cowhand down on his luck will take the job, but you ain't never gonna hear one admit it out loud. Hit's plumb nigh the lowest work they is next to herding woolies. Hank hadn't been here, that could of come to shootin' . . ."

"So," an old mosshorn in another bunk cackled, "he ups 'n' sends for this here heart 'n' hand woman from the matrimonial agency. When she comes, he finds out that the picher she sent him was took twenty years and a hundred pounds afore. Couldn't see no way to back out, so he ups 'n' marries her. 'N' on their wedding night, she straps his spurs to her bare heels— Brother! That wuz one bronc peeler what got hisself peeled, I tell you!"

"Say, dude," the cowboy said, "you going to the shindig? From what you just said, you know Miss Furniss."

"No," Roak said; "I dance like one of those wooden Indians they set up in front of cigar stores back home."

"That's good enough. Heard tell there'll be all of five or six fillies there."

"And how many cowhands?" Roak asked.

"About two hundred. But then we'll heifer brand the half of 'em—"

"Heifer brand?" Roak said.

"Tie a bandana to their right arms. Then they have to dance lady-style. Never enough females to go around."

"I'll be damned if I want to dance with anything in pants, bandana or not," Roak began; "Why, I'd rather—"

That was as far as he got. The door opened, crashing against the wall. It looked like the cowboy in the doorway was trying to tear it loose from its hinges. He gazed around the bunkhouse. His eyes reminded Roak of those of a hammerheaded mustang who'd been feeding on loco weeds for a month.

"Dude!" he called out. "Dude!"

"Yes?" Roak said.

"There's the prettiest little palomino filly out here asking for you! Lord God, dude, tell me how you do it! Come here and let me touch you—maybe some of the luck'll rub off!"

"Tell her to wait a minute, won't you, Red?" Roak said. "Be there soon as I get my boots on. . . ."

Every hand in the bunkhouse was on his feet. They stood there, staring at Roak. Lee, the cowboy he'd been talking to, came over and touched Roak's face. Then he stared at his fingers.

"Grease 'n' dirt," he said solemnly, "jes' like he was human!"

Two of the hands started for the door. The range boss held up his hand.

"Give the dude a minute o' privacy, anyhow," he said. "Could be he wants to buss his bunny a good 'un."

"Thanks, Hank," Roak said. Then he went through the door.

Hannah stood there beside her gray gelding. Red was holding the horse. And staring at Hannah.

"All right, Red," Roak said, "make tracks, boy. . . ."

Red went back into the bunkhouse. Roak took Hannah in his arms. Gently. Like she was made of cut glass, and he was afraid she was going to break. She hung back, staring at him. Her boot toe started its warring drumroll against the frozen earth.

"Well," she said, "do I hit you first or kiss you first this time, Roak?"

Roak grinned at her. Then he bent down and kissed her. A long time. A very long time. Hannah wrenched her mouth away from his. "Roak!" she said. She sounded like she was strangling. Then she buried her face against the hollow of his throat.

And all hell broke loose from the bunkhouse.

The Flying U hands burst out of the door, falling all over each other as they came.

"Yeee-owww!" they screeched. "Yeeee-hi-yowww! Brand 'er, dude! And us calling him a shorthorn!"

Hannah smiled at them.

"Now, boys," she said, "is that any way to greet a lady on her first visit to the outfit?"

"You'll have to excuse them, ma'am," Hank Flynn said. "They are all a bunch of strays their mothers left out on the prairie. But just like the nester's wife said, when her little boy asked her if cowhands eat grass, 'Nope, Willie, they're part human. . . .' "

"I know," Hannah laughed; "I've lived on a ranch all my life. In fact, I'm a neighbor of yours—"

"Then you're Miss Furniss?" Lee, the cowboy who'd been talking to Roak, said. "No wonder this human clam said he knew you!"

"He doesn't talk much, does he?" Hannah said. "I call that a good trait."

"Ma'am," one of the younger hands said wistfully, "won't you come in 'n' visit with us for a while? You can ride herd on th' dude a little later. You just plain don't know how long it's been since anybody in this here bunch o' longhorns seen a real honest to God fem-i-nine lady. Shore would pleasure us all a mighty heap. . . ."

"Why, I'd be glad to, friend," Hannah said.

"Lord God!" Red said. "That there bunkhouse ain't fitten for no lady's sight! C'mon, you mosshorns, let's go curry up th' place!"

Half a dozen cowhands raced back into the bunkhouse. Three minutes later they came out grinning. "Come in, ma'am," they said.

Roak took Hannah's arm. He had never seen the bunkhouse so clean. Then he looked downward. All they had done was to throw or sweep their plunder under the bunks.

"Cookie," Hank said, "make some coffee for th' li'l lady."

"Coming up," the range cook said.

They all stared at him. Range cooks, as every good hand knows, have a disposition like a rattlesnake with a sore belly. To see Cookie showing his fangs in a broad grin was something. "Pity they ain't no lady rangehands," Lee said.

Hank Flynn looked at Hannah. He frowned. He knew Captain Furniss very well. What's more, he knew Bart Nevis.

"Miss Furniss, ma'am, 'scuse me for being a inquisitive cuss," he said, "but does th' Cap'n know you're over here?"

Hannah faced him.

"No," she said.

"I see," Hank said.

"No, you don't see, Mr.—"

"Flynn, ma'am. Hank Flynn, at your service."

"Mr. Flynn. I'm afraid you don't see at all. My father doesn't know I'm over here because he's up in St. Louis trying to get those railroad people to run a spur line down into Texas. If he'd been here, I'd have asked him. And he'd have let me come."

"Alone, ma'am?"

Hannah flushed.

"Maybe he would have come with me himself," she said, "or sent a couple of outriders; but he wouldn't have refused to let me come, even though . . ."

"Even though what, ma'am?"

"Hank," Roak said, "don't you think you *are* asking a few too many questions?"

"Yep, dude," Hank said, "and I'm sorry, boy. But I have to ask 'em. I'm responsible for the welfare of this outfit, and straying fillies have been the cause of some mighty rough range wars. . . ."

"All right," Roak said. "That's fair, Hank. So I'll answer for Miss Hannah. The Captain doesn't approve of her marrying me. Nothing personal. His friendship with my pa dates back to the Mexican war. The Captain's reasons are good ones, and I respect them. I don't have two bits in Confederate money. I'm greener than grass in this business. And I have a bad lung as a souvenir from the War—though that seems to be all right now. Only I aim to change all those reasons, given a chance—"

"I see," Hank said; "it's just that the Bar F folks and we have always been rightly friendly. I'd like to keep it that way. . . ."

Hannah smiled.

"I don't think my father would start a fight over your offering a little hospitality to his daughter after a long, cold ride. All he's likely to do is to take a quirt to me . . ."

"Now, look here, Han!" Roak began.

"Shut up, dude," Hank said. "What about—Bart, ma'am?"

"We called it—quits, like good friends. Which was all we ever were, I reckon. Bart's a man, Mr. Flynn. He didn't like it; but I made him realize it wasn't the kind of thing he could arrange with a six-gun. . . ."

"Glad of that," Hank said gravely; "because even before you told me all that, I was a mite worried about the dude. Knew he was sparking some filly from the way he was always riding off two, three nights a week. I was afraid that being a Yank, not knowing our ways, he might borrow himself more trouble than he could handle. Only I didn't give him credit for having either the sense or the taste to pick—you, ma'am. . . ."

"Thank you," Hannah whispered. She was white to the lips. Her hand shook so her coffee cup clattered in the saucer. But she was a thoroughbred. She smiled at Roak.

"May I have another cup of coffee, please?" she said.

Roak and Hannah rode away from the bunkhouse together. He kept watching her, waiting for the explosion. Because Hank Flynn, with no intended malice, had given him away. He hadn't so much as set foot on the Bar F's range since the day he had quit his job there. But no explosion came. At least not then. When Hannah spoke at last, what she talked about was quite a different thing.

"Roak," she said, "about getting a start—I could ask father to stake you. He'd do it. He hasn't anything against you, personally. You know that—"

"No, baby," Roak said; "I can't be obligated to your father. Not to him, nor to any other man. My stake can come later. Right now, I've other things to do."

"Roak—" Hannah said. Her voice had a shake in it.

"Yes, Han?" Roak said.

"Why didn't you come to see me?"

"You know why. I promised your pa—"

"I know. But that wasn't why. You were testing me, weren't you?"

"Yes," Roak said.

"Satisfied, now?"

"Yes," Roak said.

She sat there, looking at him.

"Do I always have to beg you to kiss me, Roak?" she asked.

"No," Roak said; "God, no!"

"That's enough, Roak," she whispered. "You know, I —I'm human, too. . . ."

"Sorry, hon," Roak said.

"Don't be. I suppose all the things a decent girl is taught before she's married are exactly what she has to forget, afterwards. . . ."

Roak grinned at her.

"You figure that'll be a chore, honey?" he asked.

"No. What is a chore right now is not to forget them too soon. Oh, Roak, it's so hard to wait!"

"Oh, come off of it, doll baby," he teased; "It can't be that hard. . . ."

She stared at him. Her eyes brimmed, light-filled, crystalline.

"For you, I guess it's not," she said, her voice flat, twanging, calm, "seeing that you've no scruples against cheating, or against anything else, it seems. Two or three nights a week—that *was* what Mr. Flynn said, wasn't it? Down there—with her. Tell me, was she—fun? Did you enjoy yourself?"

"Now, just you wait a minute. I—"

"I told you I'd take my quirt to you, Roak. I told you."

He caught her wrist as she swung, twisted it cruelly. She dropped the quirt, though it still swung from her wrist by the loop in its handle.

"You—you're meaner than a sidewinder!" she sobbed. "You've fractured my wrist, I bet, and—oh, Roak!"

"Doll baby," Roak said solemnly, "you don't want a man so poor in spirit that his own woman can horsewhip him, do you?"

"No," she wept, and clung to him. "But neither do I want to play second fiddle to your chile pepper, either! Oh, Roak, I hate you sometimes; you hear me? I hate you! You've been down there every chance you could get, with that hot tamale, and you can't deny it, now, can you? Can you, you straying maverick?"

"No," Roak said peacefully, "truthfully, I can't."

"Ohhhh!" she wailed. "I could kill you! I really could!"

"No, you couldn't, doll," Roak said. "And anyhow it makes no sense to blame me for what's a goodly bit your fault, and the rest, the way I'm made. . . ."

"My fault! Roak Garfield, if you please!"

"It is, though. I lie up there in the bunkhouse, dreaming about you, and longing for you and wanting you, until in another minute I think I'm going to burst. So what do you want me to do? I haven't two red coppers to rub together so that we can get married right now; and I happen to have too much respect for you to ride over there and say: 'Now, look, Hannah, it's going to be a mighty long time before we can put on double harness, so how about a little free sampling of the goods beforehand to cool me off a bit, or else I'm going to tear loose and start to howl. . . .'"

"So," Hannah said, her blue eyes very wide, "because you can't have me, you hop across the border and bed down with that—that—"

"Let's skip the hard names, Han. Besides, you're putting it straight out and ugly. But something like that, yes—"

"And the only way I can stop you from straying would be to play the cowtown dove, and compete with her?"

"Well—" Roak grinned.

"Go to her," Hannah whispered. "I'm retiring from this rodeo, Roak. Because it's no contest. The whole thing's rigged; the game's brace dealt. I give in, and the next night you sashay over there to compare notes to see which one of your riding fillies has got the better gait. And I end up with a little unbranded maverick in my arms while you belly through the brush for parts unknown. . . ."

"Han!" Roak said. "You wouldn't! I—"

"I would, and I'm going to. Good-by, Mr. Pilgrim Garfield!"

She put out her hand to him. He took it, and with one long, smooth pull, drew her into his arms. When he turned her loose, finally, her eyes were starbranded, moonflooded, blind.

"All right," she sobbed, "you win. I—I can't give you up. But don't make me keep you on *that* basis, Roak. Please don't. Because I—I even might. To keep you—to stop her from having you—I just might. And then I'd never be able to look at my own face in the mirror again as long as I lived. . . ."

He looked at her, his face grave and tender, trying to sort out the confusion in his mind. He didn't need her for that. For that he had Belén, who was more than enough for any man. For that, and maybe for everything else a true man needed out of life. Only he wasn't true, and maybe he wasn't even a man. So he needed Hannah, too, for quite another thing: so he could stop playing nursemaid to a herd of cows. Live in the big house. Sleep in a big bed with soft white sheets and no lice. Have his food brought to the table and served hot. Have men look up to him, say: "That's Captain Garfield, owner of the Bar F. . . ."

That was it. It was all very simple. And he had it. All of it. Only—

Only he had run out of what it took to do it. He wasn't

that bitter any more. Shame had caught up with him. He knew suddenly and abruptly and completely what ought to be done to a man who could do a thing like that to a girl like Hannah. He ought to be shot. She was too good to be cheated, too sweet, too fine. Even, damn it, too pretty. What she deserved was—everything. All on earth a man had to give, not to be taken in loveless wedlock for her money. He couldn't do it. What he was doing to poor Belén was bad enough. But this would be worse, maybe even worse than what he'd done to Gwen.

But she was staring at him, heedless of the white-blazed streaks her tears made on her face in the moonlight. Then she said it, the right, the perfect thing, the words that released him, that made his road clear.

"Roak, can't you love me? At least a little? Can't you—even try?"

"Yes," he said, knowing that he spoke truly, and done that way, pledging his manhood to keep this, his solemn, his sacred oath, it would be all right, just, acceptable, good; "and more than a little. Only it's got to be square and straight and legal. I know the Captain objects to our getting married. But if we eloped, he'd have to accept it. You're of age, Han, and I'm getting overaged, if anything. We would keep it a secret a while, 'til I got my start, then announce it. . . ."

"Oh, Roak!" she breathed. "We couldn't! Father'd be fit to be tied!"

"I can manage even that, if necessary," Roak grinned.

Hannah stared at him, her eyes very clear.

"Roak," she said, "Father's going to be away for two whole weeks—"

"And there's a justice of the peace in Brownsville, isn't there?"

"Witnesses?" Hannah whispered.

"Couple of the hands from this outfit. Not Hank, though

—he's staying out of trouble to make sure he inherits the Flying U. Some of the younger fellows—"

"The ring?" Hannah asked softly.

"Got enough saved for that—and for a couple of days honeymooning at a first-class hotel to boot. Now, let's plan it sensibly: we go down there separately—"

"Oh, Roak!"

"Listen to me, honey. I want us on different stages. I want you down there two days ahead of me so's we can damn well prove I never spent five whole minutes alone with you afore the knot was tied. Don't want nothing about our wedding to smell of shotgun. A thing like this that a body only does once ought to be done right. What d'you say, Han?"

She didn't answer him. She stood there staring out over the cold prairie, ghostly and dim under the light of the moon. Then she turned to him.

"Roak—"

"Yes, baby?"

"You—you like big families?"

"Lord, Han, what a question! I'd like a whole platoon o' little hellions. Why?"

Hannah rested her head against his shoulder.

"Kids need—brothers, Roak," she said; "I found that out when I lost mine. . . ."

And it worked out just like they had planned it. The only thing that didn't go according to schedule was the first morning of their honeymoon, when, instead of sleeping late as they had intended to, they were awakened by gunfire. Roak leaped to the window in time to see the masked man come out of the bank across the street and leap into the saddle on a ratty-looking roan which belied his looks by getting out of there faster than any horse Roak had ever seen before.

Roak's head jerked toward the bedpost where ordinarily he would have hung the scabbard with the throwing knives; but Hannah had made him put them in his carpet-bag, because she didn't like seeing them there.

Could have got him, he thought, could have got him sure!

By then two or three men had come out on the street and were shooting at the rider, but all they had was six-guns, so the rider was as safe as if he was in church. Because to hit anything smaller than the side of a red-painted barn with a hand gun from more than twenty-five yards was danged nigh impossible. And when the target was barreling out of there hell for leather in a cloud of dust, the chances were less than that.

If I ever have to go gunning for somebody, Roak decided then and there, I'll take me a scattergun loaded with buck-shot—or a Henry rifle. Six-shooters ain't fitten for nothing but barroom brawls, 'n' Old Will says he's seen more than two gunnies shoot it out almost across a card table without neither one of 'em getting a scratch. . . .

He stood there, staring out the window.

Funny thing, he mused; I'd swear I'd seen that there bandit fellow somewheres before. . . .

"Roak!" Hannah said sharply. "What's happening? Somebody get shot?"

"Nope, doll," Roak said. "Fellow just stuck up the bank. But it looks like he got clean away. Reckon I'll slip on my pants and mosey down there to—"

"No, you don't, Roak Garfield! It's none of your business anyhow, and— Roak! You come away from that window! People can see you!"

"Well," Roak grinned, "if they ain't never seen a bow-legged cowhand in the altogether, they won't even know what they're looking at."

But as he turned away, the excited babble of voices came up to him: "It's him, all right! That there awful ugly

feller who was always laughing in a way you couldn't hear
him but you knowed he was laughing 'cause—"

Roak took a step toward the bed. Then he stopped,
because he could have sworn he'd heard his own name
spoken. Afterwards it seemed to him what he'd heard was,
"Come down here looking for a feller name of Roak Garfield, and I told him—" but that part of it wasn't guess-
work, he'd heard it, all right; "—and I told him the right
place to look for any Texas cowhand warn't Texas, but
Abilene, Kansas, 'cause sooner or later they all show up
there. . . ."

He stood there, frowning.

"Roak. . . ." Hannah stretched luxuriously, glorying in
her slim nakedness the way a woman always does when
her initiation into her own body's uses had been managed
by a top hand. "You come here!"

He came to her. She wound her white arms around his
neck.

"Roak," she said gravely, "I'm going to ask you a question and I want the truth: am I—better than—chile pepper?"

He thought about that one. About the answer. That
some creatures were built for speed, and others for strength.
And that this daughter of the northern fiords and snowy
wastes, however far removed in time and space from her
race's origins, couldn't expect to compare with—nightsmoke, flame, ecstasy like a murderous stab to the guts
of life, with the product of twenty centuries of Mediter-
ranean sunlight soaked in sweet and slow until it was em-
bedded in the bone's own marrow; the essence, the distillation of red wine, of guitar music even, of figs bursting ripe
until that mouth he could never describe had always the
taste of them.

No, comparison wasn't possible. Because, among other
things, in his pale blonde bride, even surrender had been
cerebral. She had consciously desired to compete, not

knowing that the thought of competition, contrast, comparison, or any kind of thought at all put the tenseness, the rigidity of anxiety in where even the anxiety to please wouldn't do, hobbling that sweet-soft, undulant bonelessness; quenching, if only a little, that flame that hollowed a man out at the last from his neckbone right down to his tight-curled toes.

But he didn't have to answer.

She stared at him. And her blue eyes filled up very slowly, brimmed, spilled.

"So," she whispered, "you're going to go on wanting her—go on—"

Then she came up from there. Clung her pale pink mouth that was made for singing lullabies, maybe, to his, lightly, softly, suspended upon a breath so that he sensed more than felt its quiver, tasted its tear salt, divined its anguished hurt. She raised her hands very slowly, put them behind his head, her ten fingers widespread and moving gently, gently through his hair. Then, without taking her mouth from his, she said it so that the words came out muffled:

"Love me, Roak. Enough to make yourself forget her. I don't care what you do, or how—but less than that, no. Please, Roak. Oh, please, please, please!"

Which was why he never did get around to asking whether or not he'd really heard his own name spoken, or find out what the bandit looked like, or whether they'd captured him, or anything. Because when he and his bride finally did come downstairs all such mundane considerations had flown from his weary mind.

Chapter Eight

IT WASN'T easy. It wasn't easy at all. Only the fact that as supposed fiancé, and hence heir presumptive to the Bar F, Bart Nevis had gone to St. Louis with Captain Furniss had made it possible for Hannah to get away from the ranch at all. But now both Bart and the Captain were home again. And Mrs. Roak Garfield became, to all intents and purposes, Miss Hannah Furniss once more.

There was no way for her to see Roak. The weather, that February of 1869, was hellish. One blue norther followed another. Hoarfrost whitened the chaparral; on the open ranges, there was even snow. No good for her to say: "Oh, I'm sick of the house! Think I'll go for a ride," because anybody who didn't have to ride out into the icy misting of rain that fell all winter long, and who insisted upon doing so, was obviously a fool or—up to something. And Captain Jesse was neither an idiot nor blind.

Looking at her father, Hannah saw the taut, drawn lines of worry in his face. Saw his hand go to his middle, the sudden grimace of pain. That was bad. She loved her father. She didn't want to hurt him. And yet. . . .

"Father," she said suddenly, "could I go visit Carmen for a while? It's a lot warmer down there, and at least I'd have a womenfolks to talk to. . . ."

Her father looked at her.

"You get a mite hungry for she-talk, don't you, honey?" he said. "Your mother was the same way. I can understand that. A female purely gets to pining for some chatter about frills and furbelows, and cooking and Lord knows what else that an old hardside like me can't even call to mind. All right. I'll send Enrique, Angelo, and Bart—"

"Not—Bart, father," Hannah said.

"Now look, baby," Captain Furniss said, "don't you think it's time you and Bart made up? All young folks have their spats; I had my share with your ma—beforehand, that is. Because after we were wed, we never even had one. I like Bart . . ."

"So do I, Father," Hannah said quietly, "very much. Bart's a fine man, as good as gold; only—"

"Only what, baby?"

"Only I don't love him. I love Roak Garfield."

"Oh, hell!" Captain Jesse said wearily. "All right, I'll send you down there so I don't have to listen to you saying that, if for no better reason. And I won't send Bart. Reckon you need to be by yourself a spell to think things out—"

"Thank you, Father," Hannah said. "Will you tell the boys to be ready tomorrow, early?"

"Sure, baby. You've been looking mighty peaky these last few days. Trip down there will do you good."

But it didn't.

Because the first morning she could get away, Hannah mounted and rode straight to Belén's house.

Ramón wasn't there. He never was any more. Now, despite his youth, he rode with Cortina's band. Belén knew why. She had been careful, never again allowing Roak to come to the house. They met in an abandoned hut that had belonged to a shepherd. The shepherd had run afoul of a Comanche war party six years earlier. Had died badly. Now no one would go near that hut. The peons held it accursed; and the *hacendados,* who had no reason to ride that way, shared, perhaps, in secret, their peons' superstitious fears. Only, Belén realized, her remarkable success in concealing her sin wasn't enough. To one who knew her as her brother did, it showed. It was upon her like a brand. It surrounded her like a glow. Shimmered upon her throat and mouth—moved like an unseen presence between them; cleaved them apart like a sword.

So Ramón had gone. Not out of fear of having to meet Roak Garfield, for that was a simple thing. Over the honor of a wronged house, two men always met; and one man always died. He could kill Roak, or Roak could kill him, and that, too, was meaningless. One died when one was sixteen or when one was eighty-six; and either stretch was a firefly flash in the dark night of time. No. He fled from having to ask Belén, from the intolerable anguish of hearing her say: "Yes, brother. I did this thing. I committed this unspeakable sin with this enemy of our people—yes."

Fled. Because, fleeing, he could preserve his faint, fond, foolish doubt; not have actually to know.

So Belén was alone when Hannah came.

Hannah sat there on her horse looking down at that face already martyred; at those eyes that did not so much reveal or experience love as suffer it; at quietness sunk beyond silence into quietude; at this woman enwrapped in calm, acceptance, peace, standing there—tearless by the grave of hope.

"Have the favor to dismount, Señorita Furniss," Belén said.

Why? Hannah thought wildly. To put myself on your level—at least physically? But I cannot reach your level, Belén: you've plunged to depths beyond my fathoming; or soared to heights above my spirit's grasp. One of the two. Maybe both.

Slowly she climbed down.

They stood there facing each other. The little house was on the very edge of the village. Beyond it was the desert— a hell of mesquite, chaparral, cactus, and sand. And, it seemed to Hannah Furniss then, that the desert moved in upon her, so that all her heart was vacant, empty, sore, burned dry; and thorns tore at the interstices of her mind.

"Would you like a chair?" Belén asked.

"No," Hannah whispered. Then she repeated it idiotically, her voice gone loud, dry, harsh: "No!"

"Very well," Belén said, and waited. Armored in that quietude. Hedged about and sure-girt with that acceptance.

"I—I guess I'd better go," Hannah said miserably. "There—there really isn't anything to be said, is there?"

"Nothing that would change anything," Belén said.

"Not even—if I told you I'd married him," Hannah said, "that I am his wife?"

Belén shrugged.

"Not even that—now," she said wearily. "It might have, before. But now, it's too late. . . ."

"I came to ask you to give him up," Hannah said, her voice rising, edging, "to ask you, don't you understand, Belén? Not to demand, because I can't. You want me to beg for my husband? For my own husband, before men and in the sight of God?"

The black eyes swept over her face. She could feel that gaze physically, like a touch; black velvet midnight moving on her flesh.

"Is he?" Belén said.

"You want me to show you the license," Hannah screamed at her, "the ring, the—"

"No," Belén said quietly; "I want you to show me his love."

Hannah took a backward step.

"What do you mean?"

"Nor for that are there words," Belén whispered.

"Try!" Hannah said. "Tell me. I want—I need to know!"

Belén smiled. But her eyes were turned inward, the smile secret, private, a remembering. Entirely without mockery. When she looked at Hannah again, her gaze was soft with pity.

"Forgive me," she said, "I do not wish to be cruel; but has he ever looked at you—afterwards—and said like this: 'My God!'?"

It was Roak's voice speaking suddenly, surprisingly, out of Belén's mouth. Hannah bowed her head.

"No," she said; and turned back to her horse.

So it was that when the first wave of sickness hit her, Hannah attributed it to grief. She rode on, clinging to the reins, torn and shaken by the poisonous green tide of nausea, until she came to the house. When she tried to dismount, she fainted. Fell, surprisingly, into the arms of Guillermo, the Martínez groom. He set up a cry:

"Ai-yi! Señora! Come here, for God! The Señorita is dying, I think!"

Both Carmen and Petra, her mother, came racing from the house.

"Bring her inside, Wili," Petra Martínez said to the groom. Petra was what the Mexicans call *una mujer brava,* a brave woman. The term is not entirely complimentary. When Latinos say a brave woman, what they mean is a hard one.

The groom carried Hannah into the guest bedroom, lay her down upon the bed, stood there staring at her, said:

"Alal, but she is sweet and soft, *la gringa*! And how nice she smells!"

"You get out of here, Wili!" Petra said.

Aided by Angeles, the maid, Petra applied cold compresses to Hannah's forehead. Carmen stood there wonderingly.

Hannah's eyes fluttered open. She gasped, turned her head, and vomited. Carmen stared at her American friend with astonishment; but Angeles and Petra looked at each other, their eyes very sure. Petra turned to her daughter, said, in the same words, in the same tone she had used toward the groom:

"You get out of here, Carmen!"

Carmen's dark eyes widened.

"But why, Mamacita?" she asked. "What passes with Hannah? Is it—something grave?"

"Of the gravest," Petra snapped. "You heard me, Carmen; go!"

"*Sí*, Mamacita," Carmen said.

"And do not listen at the door, my girl," Petra fired after her as she went, "for truly, this is not for thy ears!"

When she turned back to the bed, she saw Hannah's pale gaze resting on her face.

"What is it with me, Señora Martínez?" Hannah asked in Spanish. "You said it was *gravísimo*. Am I then likely to die?"

"Hardly," Petra said coldly. "Tell me something, foolish child; how long is it since it has been with thee after the manner of women?"

Hannah's eyes widened, widened. Then they softened, glowed; filled up with wonder, awe, even—joy. Then beyond joy into triumph. Let Belén talk as she likes now! Hannah exulted; I've won! I've won!

Petra's heavy face darkened into fury.

"Hast thou no word for shame in that harsh language of thine?" she stormed. "You come to my house, already *embarazada,* already with child, and put this thing upon us! What will I say to thy father? How can I tell this great and good man that his daughter has played the whore?"

"You don't have to, Señora," Hannah said calmly; "I shall."

"Oh!" Petra gasped. "But truly thou art a shameless one, with thy face of milk and thine eyes of an innocent child! How canst thou lie there so serenely and say that thou—"

"Will tell my father?" Hannah said. "Why not? I have

nothing to fear." She sat up then, swung her legs over the edge of the bed. Sitting there like that, facing Petra Martínez, she put her hand down the neck of her dress and drew out the gold chain of her necklace. On the end of it the ring hung. Hannah unfastened the clasp, held the heavy gold band reverently in her hand; then, with grave ceremony, she slipped it on her finger.

Petra stared at her.

"Thus wouldst thou arrange it?" she said. "Thinkest thou that thy father is a fool? A ring! *Alal!* What is a ring?"

"Angeles," Hannah said quietly to the maid, "have the goodness to give me my handbag."

The maid crossed the room lumpily, picked up Hannah's bag, came back and handed it to her. Hannah opened the bag, took out the stiff parchment, opened it, extended it to Petra.

"You," she said, "have little English, I know, Señora. But I ask you to call back Carmen to read this to you in Spanish, for you wouldn't trust my translation of it. And I ask you to pay special attention to the date so that you may have a beginning point for your reckoning."

Petra was staring at the heavy paper with its ribbons and seals.

"Thou art married, then?" she exclaimed, relief struggling with disappointment at having lost a scandal spicy enough to keep her neighbors' ears waggling for years.

"Yes," Hannah said, "I am, Señora. So in this of the child, I have nothing to fear, all the more so, since I, at least, know in what condition I came to my marriage bed."

Petra's expression changed once more. Hannah could see suspicion rising behind her eyes.

"Yet," she said, "there is here a thing that begs for explanation, child. You have your ring and your certificate of marriage, but both of these you have concealed, not only from me, it would appear, but from all the world. If this is a true marriage, and not a *trampa,* a fakery, I see not the necessity for this of the hiding. . . ."

Hannah sighed. Why the devil did I ever come down here? she thought.

"Yet it is necessary—or it was," she said. "And though it is not *cosa suya*—your affair—I will tell you. I have married against my father's wishes. . . . And my husband is—"

"The small *rubio* who was at the *corrida de toros* with Belén!" Petra finished the phrase for her triumphantly. "Securely! Who else could it be?"

"No one else," Hannah said quietly. "And now, if you will be so kind as to provide me with an escort, Señora, I had better go home. . . ."

"I think you had best repose yourself today," Petra said. "In your condition, this of riding can be overdone. Tomorrow I will send you home in the wagon. . . ."

"No," Hannah said; "I go today—and I ride."

Roak stood over the little fire of twigs. He had his oilskin slicker draped over his shoulders, and was trying to shield the fire with that. The rain came down in a slow, insistent drizzle that penetrated to a man's bones. Lifting his head, Roak looked out over the prairie, a gray world stretching out to the rim edges of forever and beyond. He could feel himself shrinking, diminishing to the dot of an *i,* set against that bigness, vanishing even to the nothing that a man and all his works were under that endless sky.

He was cold all the way through; and that sadness was in him like a weight. That bad sadness that came on him when he had to live alone too long, when there had been no escaping his nemesis, his loved and loathed adversary: himself. He thought: I'll head south. I just wasn't made to live like this! And if I can't ride up to the front door of the Bar F to see my own wife, I'll—

But the hoofbeats cut through his reverie. They were

close. Roak looked up and saw the man coming toward him, mounted on the big dun. Bart then. On the hunt, a hand gun cradled at his hip, and a Henry rifle in a scabbard on his saddle.

Roak didn't move. The loneliness of space was in him; the big loneliness that bled the will out of a man by slow inches, day by sullen day. There was nothing epic about the conflict of two pigmies under that big sky, beneath the vacant eye of emptiness, in a vastness where even the sound of gunfire would be lost; upon an earth already rain-soaked, which could not distinguish between the feel and texture of rain and blood. Two fire ants, circling each other warily, their stingers out. Two insects, belly-down crawling to deal a useless death under the rain. No. He waited with a curious sense of detachment, as though he were a spectator watching from without, a watcher privileged to witness his own death.

But Bart sat there looking at him a long time. Made no move toward either gun. Sat hunched forward in the saddle, under the rain's driving, his big frame diminishing too under the gray sweep of forever; his big, fine, well-muscled body slack in the abject lineaments of defeat.

"Mount your cayuse, Roak," he said. "You're wanted at the Bar F. Cap'n Jesse give orders to have you brung in. . . ."

"I," Jesse Furniss said tiredly, "ain't a-going to pretty up what I'm thinking, not even for my daughter's sake. I think you're a sidewinder, Roak Garfield, as crooked as a diamondback rattler, and with your tongue just as forked. When I met Hannah's ma, I didn't have a dime, either. But I waited, worked like a nigger until I could show her pa a spread, show him I was man enough to support my wife."

Roak sat there looking at his father-in-law. He didn't say anything. There wasn't anything to be said.

"I'd have this marriage annulled, if I could," Jess went on; "but Han's of age—and with child—"

Roak came up then, his eyes wide.

"Sit down!" Jesse said. "The only creditable thing about the whole randy mess is that my grandson is going to be born legal 'n' proper, nine months and more after the wedding date. And for that I know you aren't responsible. I brought my daughter up right—"

"You're wrong, Father," Hannah said crisply. "Roak could have had me any time he wanted, without a license or anything. It was he who wouldn't, and—"

"And who suggested the elopement," Jesse Furniss said.

"Yes," Hannah whispered.

"Figgers," her father said. "In his bunk, or in a haystack, you'd have been just another straying filly, Han. A hell of a lot less fun, likely, than his little Mex. This here maverick ain't even hungry, that way. But standing up before the preacher or the justice, you represented a hell of a lot more—walking title to the Bar F, once I'm gone. . . ."

Roak leaned forward then.

"All right," he said, "you just get your lawyer from Houston, Cap'n Furniss. Make yourself a brand new will. Call in Bart and Old Will to witness it. Word it like this: 'All my holdings, of all I die possessed, are bequeathed to the State of Texas, the proceeds wherewith to be used to found an orphan's home,' or a home for old, stove-up cowhands, or a university college, or what have you. Then I'll just take my wife who I married 'cause I love her, and for no other reason, and drift. We might have it hard for a year or two; but we'll make it. 'Cause Han is no hothouse plant, and I reckon I got guts in my middle enough to build myself a future same as you did, sir. And one thing more: I'd appreciate it if you kind of stored away the hard talk. Like it or not, I'm your son-in-law, and the father of the kid who's going to be your grandson. Those are facts —and we all have just got to accommodate 'em."

He stood up.

"So, now, Cap'n," he said peacefully, "since there really isn't anything else for us to talk about, reckon I'll go help Hannah pack and—"

"Sit down!" Captain Furniss roared at him.

Slowly Roak sank back down again.

Captain Furniss stared at him.

"Either you're damned good at play-acting," he said, "or else you got more grit in your craw than I was willing to believe. Which is one of the things I mean to find out, pronto. All right. Here's my proposition, son. I'm gathering a trail herd to drive to Kansas. Bart Nevis is going to be trail boss. I'm going to sell that herd, half to him and half to you, for one dollar and other valuable considerations. You and Bart'll pay me twelve dollars the head out of your profits. Anything above that, and your expenses on the trail, you can keep and divide between you fifty-fifty. Fair enough?"

"Too fair," Roak said dryly; "What's the catch?"

"That you ride with 'em," Jesse said, "under Bart's orders. That you show me once and for all you can measure up to the size and shape of a white man in this country. Because trail driving is rough. And Bart'll tell me if you're fit to ride the river with—"

Hannah was facing her father then, her face white. She even forgot to make her customary drumroll on the floor.

"What you mean is that to get rid of Roak, you'd be a party to murder, Father?" she said, her voice high, tight, edgy. "I'm not vain, but you know how many white women there are within two hundred miles? Maybe five. Reason enough for killing—and safe, too! The herd spooks for water while Roak's riding the drags, pounding him into bloody mush in the stampede. Or they get to milling in midstream on a river crossing, and Bart sends him in to straighten 'em out. Or a rattlesnake gets into his bedding by pure accident. Bart could leave his six-gun home, Father! He could—"

"Han," Roak said quietly, "you're plumb downright hysterical. Bart could do all those things. Only he won't. He won't because he's neither a sneak nor a coward; and the only way he'd feel right about getting rid of me would be to crowd me into drawing, which I just ain't fool enough to do. . . ."

He turned to Captain Furniss.

"All right, Cap'n; I accept your proposition," he said.

Chapter Nine

THE MAN they called Prince Parker in Abilene, Kansas, though his real name was Ned, finished honing the action of his Wells Fargo Colt, and started to put the revolver back together again. On first sight, it looked like a mighty puny weapon for a man over six feet tall, for the Wells Fargo Colt, so called because that express company had issued it to its guards, was a small, five-shot, .31-caliber percussion-cap revolver that the Colt Company had put out in 1848. In actual fact, the little hand gun wasn't much bigger than a lady's pistol. Which was why Prince favored it. Like most professional gamblers, he was a dandy when it came to dress, and he had no intention of weighing himself down with a gunbelt and side holster. Another point he'd taken into consideration was the fact that when a man has to draw while sitting with his legs under a card table, a shoulder-holstered revolver is a hell of a lot faster than a belt gun, as Prince had already proved on at least five occasions. To draw a model 1860 Army or Navy Colt, a Remington, a Star, a Dance, or any belt gun whatsoever under the special circumstances of a gambling fracas, you had to push back your chair, stand up, maybe kick over the table before you could reach. And if you tried doing all that against Prince Parker, before you got halfway through you were already dead.

Prince had had the little Colt bored through for metallic rim-fire cartridges, of course, like any man with sense whose life depended upon his gun. It had gone oversize, and come out as a .32-caliber, which wasn't a handy size in an age when most men favored big bores. But he managed to keep a supply of .32 cartridges on hand. And he didn't need too much ammunition anyhow. By now those who were willing to tangle with Prince Parker were few and far between.

As he fitted the last piece back into place, he heard a low, almost soundless chuckle coming from some indeterminable point somewhere above his head, and turning, looked up into the face of the new sheriff of Abilene. Looking into that face wasn't calculated to improve a body's appetite.

"Planning to shoot somebody, Prince?" the sheriff said.

"No," Prince said mildly; "just aim to discourage them as aims to perforate me, sheriff. Don't hold with gunslinging. You ever hear tell of me shooting a fellow who wasn't already reaching?"

"Don't reckon I ever did," the sheriff said, "which is why I've never had the pleasure of hanging you. But one of these fine days. . . ."

Prince stood up. He was something to see. His hair was black above a face that was as milk-white as a woman's, largely because Prince slept all day and worked at night. He was clean-shaven except for a thin black mustache. His brows were heavy and black so that they made his ice-blue eyes look even paler than they were. He was lath-thin, and the fact that his clothes were all as black as his hair gave him the appearance of being even thinner. Very slowly he shoved the little Colt into the box-fit holster that had been tallowed on the inside so that when he drew, the gun came snaking out from under his left armpit so fast it was already speaking its piece before anybody even saw it.

"What have you got against me, sheriff?" he drawled. "I can't help it 'cause I'm pretty. . . ."

The sheriff chuckled again. Prince didn't hear that sound. He felt it with the spine-crawling sensation that a body gets hearing a piece of chalk dragged across a blackboard, raising his hackles with sudden cold.

"Nothing," the sheriff said. "Nothing personal. Only I purely enjoy a hanging. And your looks don't matter. Now, come on. The Kansas Pacific is due long about now. And the telegraph operator up the line a piece let me know there's a woman on it. A real, live, female woman. Young. Good-looking. And getting off here."

"Why'd he do that?" Prince wanted to know.

"Asked him to. Any time trouble's heading into my bailiwick, he's got orders to give me word ahead of time. And than a filly there ain't no worse trouble. 'Specially if she's decent. But I can't figure why no decent woman would head for Abilene—can you?"

"Nope," Prince said; "but then neither have I ever heard tell of no cowtown dove traveling alone. They usually fly in flocks."

"I thought about the same thing," the sheriff said slowly, "which is why I'm gonna head the welcoming party. And I figured it won't hurt to have a pistol artist like you along to help me out if things get rough. You want me to deputize you, or you'll do it private?"

"Private," Prince grinned. "You want to ruin my reputation forever, sheriff?"

The two of them started out together, walking toward the station, but long before they got there the sheriff stopped, squinted into the prairie light, and gave a snort of pure disgust.

"Damn!" he said. "Here comes that train. Never been on time before in living memory; but today, naturally—"

Prince saw the plume of smoke far down the tracks. Then he saw another thing: the local telegrapher hadn't been able to keep his mouth shut. The street was black with men converging on the station. Five minutes before the train got there, the station was surrounded. It would have been anyhow, because except when the trail herds came in, there was never anything to do in Abilene. But today it was different. There were more men than usual standing there waiting. And the way they waited was different, too. They weren't cracking jokes, laughing or even talking. They waited in silence. In a funny kind of a silence that a body could feel. Like chills and fever. Like a galvanic current, running from man to man.

I reckon, Prince thought, that the West won't ever get to be a peaceful, law-abiding place 'til there's at least one woman to every man. We stay edgy because there just isn't any feminine influence to gentle us down except a few lonesome whores too ugly and too rough to make it back East. Hell, I'd just as soon bed down with my horse. Sooner. My cayuse is prettier and a damned sight more gentle . . . .

The train came snorting up to the siding, spitting a shower of sparks and resinous black pinewood smoke out of its huge bell stack. Before it had stopped moving the crowd was running toward it.

"All right, boys," the sheriff called out, "stand back there!"

They stood back. By then, they knew what their sheriff was like. More, they had seen what he could do with a gun. Most of them had been in Will's Saloon the night Loco Weed Peterson had drawn on him. The sheriff had stood in the doorway and waited until Weed had got off three shots, hammer-fanning, a gunny's trick that worked only across the width of a card table and sometimes not even then, before he'd slowly taken his Colt out of his hip pocket—where he carried it in defiance of and contempt for the gunman's tradition of a side holster tied down to the thigh for quick drawing—aimed it carefully and put a bullet between Weed's eyes.

Which was one of the reasons they had made him sheriff. The other was that nobody else wanted the job,

since all his predecessors had been hauled off to boot hill
feet first.

Prince Parker stood back with the rest. He could see
the woman passing through the car now toward the platform; but beyond the fact that she was young, he couldn't
make out much about her through the soot-grimed panes.
Then she came out on the platform, and he saw her. He
didn't even hear the hungry animal growl that went up
from the crowd. He stood there, jaw dropped, petrified,
pole-axed, done. Stood there staring at the small blonde
with the face of an angel, whose blue eyes were—

Frozen suddenly. Filled with—

Horror? Disgust? Fear? He didn't know. He half-turned
toward the sheriff. All right, the sheriff's face wasn't the
prettiest sight on earth; but it wasn't that bad. Then he
saw that ugly mask was moving, working, and—

The Sheriff strode past him, mounted those stairs onto
the platform.

Prince moved forward, without even thinking about it,
not out of curiosity or need to pry into what wasn't his
business anyhow; just following the sheriff automatically
and without thought. Then Prince heard him say:

"There's an eastbound train at midnight, Gwen. You're
going to be on it."

"No," she said quietly. "You've no control over me
now, Fritz. You lost all your rights when you let Roak
take you. I'm staying. . . ."

"Goddamnit, Gwen!" Fritz said miserably. "I'm sheriff
here now, and you—"

"They don't have to know," she said. "We're just old
friends, sheriff. Incidentally, I'm sorry about—your face.
You're right: it is bad. As bad as you wrote me it was.
Now, how about escorting me to a place called Tiger Lou's?
I'm to be an entertainer there. Singing, dancing, and—"

"Stop it!" Fritz spat. Then he turned and saw Prince
standing there. "All right," he said, the words a thick

strangle, "I'll take you to Tiger Lou's, Gwen. But the first time you crook—"

"Sheriff," Prince said, "you mind introducing me to his little lady?"

"Hell, yes, I mind," Fritz said flatly.

"All right," Prince said; "reckon you're within your rights. But first, you mind telling a fellow what's wrong?"

That chuckle came then, soundless almost, but different now. Hushed, choked bitterness distilled to its very essence.

"I wrote a letter," Fritz said. "The wrong letter, to the wrong person, to the wrong place, with the wrong information in it, that's all."

"Or the right information, to the right person, at the right place," the woman called Gwen said. "Since it was written to me, telling me where *he* was, and more especially, whom he was hunting for. Anyhow, since it seems that our good sheriff is in one of his usual boorish moods, I'll just have to introduce myself. I'm Gwen Hei—Henderson. And you?"

"Ned Prince Parker, at your service, ma'am," Prince said; "but you call me Prince."

"All right—Prince. It suits you," she said. But Fritz was snarling at her, then:

"Come on! I haven't time for you to stand here all day!"

Then he moved off, almost pushing her ahead of him. A few yards away, she turned and looked at Prince. Then, very slowly, she closed one eye in the most gorgeous wink that ever thawed a gambler's ice-cold heart.

Then the two of them rounded a corner and were gone.

That night, of course, Prince had a table all to himself, next to that cleared-away space in the middle of Tiger Lou's Concert Saloon where that fat, sweaty herd of girls pranced, always out of step, before the crowd. Afterwards, they'd sit with a fellow if he asked them nicely. And after he'd blown half his roll on watered-down drinks for them and gut-twisted poison for himself, they'd go upstairs with him if he asked them more nicely still and showed them the color of his money.

That part of the act was over now. But the girls weren' having too much luck tonight. Every randy pack-jack in the house was sitting there—waiting.

Then she came out, and the silence could be felt. She had on a black velvet dress that fitted her like a sheath except for the pert and provocative bustle bobbing behind it. Then she moved and bedlam broke loose. That black sheath had been slit hip-high up one side, so that each stride showed a black silk-stockinged leg, punctuated by a frilly lace garter, and above that a flash of thigh that disappeared again into black lace and ruffles and peeka-boo bows. The funny part about it was that the girls in the chorus had had on a lot less than that. But the effect wasn't the same. It wasn't the same at all.

Prince sat there trying to figure out why it wasn't. And why seeing her like that made him feel sick. But he couldn't figure it. He'd never had a sister and he'd never been married so he couldn't recognize that gut-deep shame a man feels at seeing flesh of his own flesh on exhibition before the goats and monkeys of this world.

The piano player struck up something having a dim resemblance to a tune. The piano was full of holes now from self-appointed music critics shooting at the piano player. But tonight nobody noticed that he was a little worse than usual, or, if they did, they forgave him for it, because by that time she had sat down on top of the piano and crossed those long legs of hers so that they could see the black silk and the ruffles and the laces and that sweet curving sweep of white.

She began to sing—a simple little song, sort of a nursery rhyme, really. She sang reasonably well in a high, sweet soprano that was absolutely true and right on pitch. The words of the song were a kind of infantile prattle, innocent to the point of inanity. But the way she sang them, the slight, expressive gestures she made with her hands and body, formed a contrast with the innocence of the words, with the sweet, true, Sunday school choirgirl's voice that added a new dimension to obscenity, and were shocking in the purest, most profound sense of that word.

She got down from the piano and began to dance. But not wildly, nor with abandon. Instead she danced dreamily, shyly, tugging at the slit-in skirt to hide, never quite successfully, her legs.

That, Prince thought hotly, meanly, is just plain—dirty. Don't know why, nor how; but dirt is what it is!

He looked around him. Every man's eye was beady, glittering; every mouth was slackwet, opened, panting. If this was what she'd wanted, she'd got it, all right. The works. A full house. A royal flush.

Then a big man got up from his seat. A teamster named Wolf Grogan. Six foot four of pure poison. He lumbered out into that cleared space. Stood there looking at Gwen. Then he reached out a huge paw and caught at her skirt. Jerked, ripping. And Gwen stood there in her bodice and those black lace trifles of ruffles and frills and peekaboo bows. The house went wild. They roared like range bulls in season. Pounded on the tables. Guffawed. All of them except one man. Except Prince Parker.

When he spoke his voice wasn't even loud, but it cut through the uproar like a knife.

"Reckon you better reach, Wolf," he said.

Wolf Grogan whirled, already slapping leather. Gwen saw that. Then she saw that Prince was sitting there holding that puny little five-shot .32 in his slim, delicate hand, and smoke was curling up out of its muzzle. She was conscious that no time had passed, no interval, not even half a heartbeat; but Wolf Grogan was buckling, going boneless, his yellow-gray eyes glassing over, all within that no-

time, intervalless continuation of right now, during which
even the sound of the shot hadn't registered because that,
too, had come too fast for her to hear it. The noise Wolf
made striking the floor was curiously dull. As unreal as
all the rest of it. When he hit, Gwen could see that his
revolver was still only halfway out of its holster.

Then Prince got up, stripped off his jacket. Wrapped
it around her, hiding her legs. Walked with her, like that,
up the stairs to her room.

Inside, she took his jacket off. Handed it back to him.

"I'm supposed to be grateful for that?" she said. "All
right. I'll drop you a curtsy, and thank you, Mr. Parker!
Thanks for preserving the modesty I haven't got—at the
price of a man's life. Oh, yes; thank you mighty kindly!"

That pale blue gaze was upon her then.

"No," he said; "not to preserve your modesty. To put
my brand on you, Gwen. In public. So they'd all know. So
none of them would get careless with my property, no
more."

"Your property!" she said. "Of all the arrogant sons
of bitches I've ever met, you—"

He put out his hand then, hooked it in the neck of
her bodice. Pulled it evenly and slowly and steadily out
out, out—until it ripped. Then he caught her to him,
ground his mouth into hers, until it broke under his
opened, parted; responding almost instantly to his prob
ing, and her hands, moving on him, were like silk.

She could feel him against her like a bar of iron, forc
ing her back, back. . . .

"No, not like that. Gently. What do you think I've go
to fight for, anyhow?" she said.

First in the morning, when Prince Parker woke up
he saw the woman standing by the window. Her hair fel
over her shoulders like a mist of silver, too pale in th
dawnlight for him to even see its wash of gold. She ha

on a silken robe that was made of cobwebs and fog and dew. And inside it her body was still as far beyond his imagination as it had been the night before. She was smoking a pencil-thin, ten-inch-long cigar, and looking out of the window into the empty street.

"Gwen—Gwen, baby," he groaned.

She turned to him. When she spoke her voice was deadly.

"Are you going to make this worth my while, Prince?"

He stared at her. Said:

"What do you mean?"

"You've ruined my business—rather effectively. Scared off the customers. So. . . ."

Slowly Prince stretched out his hand; took the roll of bills out of the hip pocket of his pants. Counted out five $100 bills.

"This enough?" he asked.

She put the cigar down, grinding it out against a saucer on the table. Then she came to him. Opened that robe of cobwebs and mist, and taking his two hands, held them against her.

"See how warm I am now, darling!" she said.

He bent then and kissed her, brutally, savagely, trying to hurt her. His hands swept over her upward cupping. And it was then he heard the sudden sharp intake of her breath.

Heard it and whirled to look into Fritz Heindrichs's eyes. In them, he saw his own dying, and the manner of it.

Gwen clawed that robe shut around her, for all the good it did.

"You might try knocking next time, Fritz!" she said.

"And you might try locking your door," Fritz said. He stood there looking at Prince Parker.

"Fritz," Prince said, "you could have the decency to tell me what there is between you and Gwen that—"

Slowly Fritz shook his head.

"There's nothing betwixt us now, boy," he said; "nothing at all. And buying what's for sale purely ain't a crime. So that way, you're safe. . . ."

He stood there a moment longer, and his scarred face twisted into a grin. He let that chuckle out, that *leitmotiv* for a fugue called death.

"Nope—I'll just have to think of something else," he said, and, turning, left them there, moving so quietly he made no sound at all.

Chapter Ten

AND SO it was done. Bart and Roak signed the papers, solemnly handed over one silver dollar each to Captain Jesse, sat there looking at each other a long, slow time. Then Bart said:

"Come on, Roak. Reckon we'd better start getting that herd together."

They went out then, but a constraint moved between them, a tension honed into plain edginess. But there was nothing to be done about that feeling now. It had to be endured.

So early in the spring that the frost was still on the chaparral, they ran the cattle through the chutes, road-branding them for the trail. That was necessary because by purchase, departure and sudden death of their original owners, Captain Jesse had acquired seven different brands by then. So, to make up the trail herd, they had to give them all a uniform brand, above and to the rear of all the Bar F's, Running W's, Arrow O's, and Circle C's the longhorns already wore. If they hadn't done that, the nesters who lived along the trail would cut out a cow or two from the herd, and with their own peace officers backing them up, stoutly maintain the animal was theirs.

When the roadbranding had been done, Bart and the hands rounded up the sixty-five horses of the *remuda,* outfitted the chuck wagon, and said their good-bys.

Which wasn't easy, either. Not every man who drove a trail herd north got back to his home range alive. Hannah clung to Roak and cried. Made, in her extremity, the mistake of asking him to keep his temper, to give way, and not provoke Bart Nevis. Would have, Roak knew with a shame that clawed at the roots of his maleness, begged Bart for his life had Bart not stayed away from her. There are many ways of killing a man; and Hannah was still too young to know that what she was doing to Roak now— out of love, out of fear—was as good as any. Maybe better.

Then Roak and Bart rode out under the stars to where the trail hands waited with the herd. Sat there, looking at them a while. Finally Bart said:

"Let's go, boy. . . ."

So they started out with Bart and Old Will, the most experienced men, leading the herd, riding ahead to search out the trail, which in that flat country was mostly a matter of choosing what stretch of prairie they wanted to cross, giving them plenty of leeway to avoid rough going and possible dangers. After them, about a hundred yards back, Roak rode the swing position on the right side of the herd, while a cowboy named Marvis Hart rode the same position on the left. Their job was to keep the herd from fanning out from the trail. And since once a trail herd was in motion it would string out for more than a mile, Angelo and a Negro cowboy called, for some unknown reason, Posey did the same job farther back, riding the flanks of the herd.

But the bunch who went through pure, undiluted bone-dry hell were the drag riders. They rode behind the herd to push on the stragglers and look out for the cows heavy with calf and the little fellows who would be dropped all along the trail. And since trail-driven cows had the dangest habit of getting into heat whether it was their season or not, the drag riders had to see that the three or four bulls always included didn't kill themselves from overwork. So the drag riders, Pepe, Enrique and Juan, had it rough.

Driving a mixed herd was a man-killing job. And it wasn't until well after 1870 that it finally dawned on cowmen that steers, castrated animals, made a heck of a lot more sense, eliminating nearly all of the drag riders' troubles except the inevitable ton and a half of trail dust they had to eat.

Two other hands completed the outfit: Coosie, as the hands called the cook, Tom Brinkley; and Little Joe, the horse wrangler, a sixteen-year-old kid who drove the *remuda* of the hands' extra mounts. The kid probably had had a name originally; but by now he'd almost forgot it himself, because the horse wrangler was always "Li'l Joe" to the hands no matter what moniker his folks had hung on him.

The first day they pushed the herd thirty-five miles north. On the second and the third they averaged twenty-five. After that, they slowed them down to ten, so they wouldn't get to Kansas looking like racks of bone covered with rawhide. Yet fast driving the first days was absolutely necessary. If you didn't get the old mosshorns far enough from the home range at the start, they'd light out for familiar territory the minute you made camp. But driven far enough the first day, they got confused enough not to try it; by the second, they were more uncertain; and by the third, they were lost. After that, they settled down into a real trail herd, and driving them became something a little less than hellish, though it was still bad enough.

Even so, Roak found he liked it. Driving a trail herd did something to a man. Drew him out of himself, maybe. Set him up on the rim edges of a prairie sky, which was about as close to forever as a man gets, living, with that river of tossing horns, that torrent of red bellowing between him and—God, kind of. Gave him time for thinking. At night, by the campfire, under the high, clear stars, he'd sit there and stare at the flames with his tin plate full of son-of-a-bitch stew growing cold in his hands because he'd forgot to eat it, trying to pin down the notions moving like a ghost herd steady and slow through his mind.

Like whether, actually, a man's disappointment and disgust could make him sick—not just sick of heart and in his mind's imagining, but really sick the way Captain Jesse Furniss had looked before they left. All right, maybe I do give him a bellyache, Roak thought; but did he have to put his hand to his middle and twist his face up like it was hurting him?

"You ain't a-eatin'," Old Will said accusingly.

"Not hungry," Roak said.

"Heck, son, wimmenfolks ain't in no real danger 'til birthing time," Will said, "and you'll be back afore then. 'Sides, Hannah ain't no flighty Eastern filly. She's a mite slim, but she's a thoroughbred. Sitting there moping over her ain't going to help nothing. Here, lemme git you some more stew what's hot. . . ."

"No, thanks, old-timer," Roak said, "I'll eat this. Don't like my victuals too hot anyhow. . . ."

He ate the stew, made of the brains, sweetbreads, and the choice cuts of a fresh-killed calf. It was good. In fact, it was delicious.

"What's in it?" he asked Will.

"Ever' living thing except the hair, horns, and holler," Will grinned. "You kin tell what's in a son-of-a-bitch stew, it ain't no good. Finish it up, 'n' I'll go git you some nigger in a blanket."

"All right," Roak said; "you win. I'll stick my neck out. What the hell is 'nigger in a blanket'?"

Old Will couldn't resist temptation. He leaned close.

"You ain't seen Posey this evening, have you?" he said.

Roak hadn't seen the black cowhand, but he knew why. Posey was standing the first night watch.

"Well," he said dryly, "if Posey's going to taste anything like this stew, I'll take a stab even at him. . . ."

Old Will got up, laughing. He came back with two heaping plates of nigger in a blanket. It turned out to be a kind of sweet dumpling made of dough with raisins in it.

Sitting there eating it, Roak stared into the fire. Natural enough for Old Will to think he was concerned about Hannah. As a matter of fact, he hadn't really thought about her at all. Not directly. Only as—a cause, somehow. As what lay back of the expression of pain in Captain Jesse's face. As what had him trapped. Standing between him and Belén. Because he wouldn't dare sunfish south for a good long time now. The risks were too great. After the kid came, maybe he could. Hannah would be mighty tied up with the little maverick. And then. . . .

No, he thought miserably, not even then. Because if Cap'n Jesse was to get wind of my straying, he just might change his will for a fact. . . .

He stood up, then, and headed toward the chuck wagon to get his bedding. But because he had been staring into the campfire, when he turned away from it he was as blind as a bat. He kicked a stack of dirty tin plates so hard that the noise it made was blast loud in the silence. Instantly Bart Nevis was on his feet.

"God damn it, dude!" he said, his voice low and harsh. "You still ain't got sense enough to light a shuck when you leave a campfire? You spook that son-of-a-bitching herd and we won't git 'em rounded up 'til Christmas—if they don't mash us all two feet into the prairie when they lights out!"

Roak stood there, trembling a little. The rebuke was just and he knew it. Longhorns were just about the most skittish creatures the good Lord ever blew breath into. And every cowboy knew enough to light a corn shuck when he left a campfire, thus giving himself a little light that lasted long enough to accustom his eyes to the dark. Only he had forgot, because he'd been thinking about other things. But the fact that Bart was dead right didn't take the sting out of the situation. Made it worse, if anything.

"Sorry, Bart," he said gruffly, and started to move on.

"Don't move!" Bart snapped. "Just stand there, Roak,

'til they settle down. 'Cause longhorns only jump twice—first jump's to their feet, 'n' the second is to hell. . . ."

Roak stood there listening. He could hear the cattle stirring where they lay. He and all the rest of the hands held their breath. Because if that herd spooked and stampeded through the camp with most of the hands afoot and their mounts unsaddled and hobbled for the night, a good many of the men could wind up dead. Messily dead. Pounded into shredded meat and powdered bone under five thousand sets of hooves. Slowly the cattle settled down again. The hands let out their collective breath in one long, drawn-out sigh.

"All right," Bart said quietly; "now you can get your bed roll, Roak."

"Bart," Roak said again, "I'm plumb, downright sorry, I—"

"Don't be sorry," Bart said; "just be grateful you aren't crowbait by now. And move quiet around longhorns. That's all. . . ."

Roak moved off, feeling like a fool. Worse even than like a fool. Like a child, dressed down by a man. Which was a hell of a way to feel, especially when the man was Bart Nevis.

They pushed the longhorns on, covering their ten miles every day. At night they bedded them down, circling around them tighter and tighter until they had that wild bunch in a mass so compact they had to stop moving. And when longhorns stop moving at night, some instinct tells them to lie down. At least until eleven o'clock, when they'd all get up and then lie down in another position. Then the hands drew lots for the four watches: first dark 'til ten o'clock, ten to midnight, midnight to two, and two 'til dawning. Soon as the stars were out, they pointed the tongue of the chuck wagon at the pole star so they'd know which way north was by daylight the next morning.

After supper a man slept, or tried to. For Roak, that was the hard part, especially if he was going to have to stand one of the later watches. Lying there in his tarpaulin sack with all his clothes on except his hat, gunbelt and boots, he'd wait to be called, and—think. Not even his weariness could stop that. Lying there under the high stars, the thoughts would go pounding through his head steady and slow:

Your luck? Damned sure of that, aren't you? You've got Han, who maybe you don't even really want; got the Bar F, if not now—soon. But put your money on one thing, Roak Garfield: it won't pan out. Nothing built on that kind of a foundation ever can. Look at it, boy. Remember—Gwen? Remember when you went back to look for her, because you'd learned to love her by then, as much that as because you needed her, maybe more, she wasn't there? Only a new grave was. A little new grave of the kid who would have been the son you'd have been proud of. That and Fritz Heindrichs waiting in the middle of all the folks who used to be your friends, and who were just tingling all over at the prospect of seeing you get yours. . . . Belén, now. Why that? Why didn't I go on and marry her? Because she's—foreign? Because her skin's not white enough? Dirt-poor reasons, both of them. As a human being, it's she who's stooping, not you, boy. One more score against you. One more honest-to-God woman cut down to a dirtied rag doll for your pleasure. . . .

And now—another kid on the way. Likely to be born dead, too, and set Captain Jesse free to change his will. Lord God, why can't I play it straight? Haven't I had my nose shoved into the fact that straight is the only smart way to play it? But—

But playing it straight would have meant Belén, and halfbreed Mex kids catching hell all their lives from both sides. And a mighty long, hard row to hoe before I could have got started and—

"Roak," Marvis called, "your watch, boy. . . ."

Then again it was morning, and the last watch was singing out:

> "The bulls are in the pen!
> Arise and shine!
> Give God the glory!"

And he rolled out of his sack, got into his boots, limped to the campfire and poured hot, black Arbuckle's axle grease, as they called coffee, into his gullet until he felt human again. Going away from there stiff-legged, he roped a fresh bronc out of the *remuda,* and started the same old grind, endless, it looked like, going on forever, like that.

Like that. Until you came to the rivers. And that was another thing.

Because all the rivers ran east and west, crossing a northbound trail. So they had to cross them all, all the spring-swollen torrents: the Colorado, the Brazos, the Red, the Washita, the Canadian, both forks of it, the Cimarron and the Arkansas. And even on the smaller streams, like the Colorado and the Brazos, Roak found out exactly what a cowboy meant when he said a man was "fit to ride the river with."

There was nothing worse. Nothing at all. First they took the chuck wagon apart and floated it across piece by piece on rafts that were always too small for what they were trying to do, and half the time came apart in midstream. Then they swam the grub across, wrapped in their oilskin slickers and tied to the backs of the biggest horses in the *remuda.* After that they put the chuck wagon back together again, and helped Coosie make camp, build a fire, and start the grub cooking. Then, stark naked, with their gunbelts wrapped in oilskin and stuck inside their sombreros to keep them dry, they swam their mounts back across to where Bart and Old Will waited, ready to start crossing the devil's own stepchildren that those longhorns were. Bart and Old Will plunged their mounts into the river along with an old top sergeant of a lead steer. Whooping and beating their hats against their horses' flanks, the hands forced the rest of the herd into the river, riding in themselves, but not, as on land, on both sides of the cattle; that wasn't necessary. In the river they always had to swim their mounts downstream of the herd to keep those old mosshorns from drifting too far with the current and ending up facing steep cliffs so they couldn't climb out of the water; or milling around in midstream 'til they drowned; or, out of sheer perversity, turning completely around to come out on the same side of the river they'd started at. There were forty dozen things that could go wrong, and on every crossing, a sizable proportion of that forty dozen did.

But they'd got across all the rivers now except the Arkansas. They weren't too afraid of the Arkansas because it didn't have the reputation of being a poison-mean river to cross like the Red was. They had found five fresh graves on the banks of the Red when they got there; had read the rude inscriptions telling the names of the boys from a big outfit pushing another trail herd ahead of them who hadn't got across the Red. Maybe they had got across the Jordan. Or the Styx. Roak didn't know.

They got to the Arkansas at sundown, and made camp. They didn't talk about the crossing they were going to make first thing in the morning. They talked about the hell they were going to raise in Abilene, lying there waiting, only a week or two farther north once they'd crossed that one last river. Roak didn't talk. As usual, he sat on a log, staring into the campfire. Bart sat a little way off, looking at him.

"Say, dude," Marvis Hart said, "how come you wear that brace of toadstickers under your vest?"

"For protection," Roak said.

"Protection!" Marvis hooted. "You'd have six holes in you before you could get close enough to a fellow to do any good with a knife."

"Want to bet?" Roak said.

"Yep. I got five silver dollars right here what say I could curl you up six times over before you could get close enough to whittle me!"

"Done," Roak said. "Hold the bets, Bart?"

"Let Coosie hold 'em," Bart said; "that's customary. But before you two go too far with this, I want to know how either of you aim to prove a fool thing like that without anybody's getting hurt. Tell you right now I won't stand for bloodshed over a crazy bet."

"Easy," Marvis said. "I take all the bullets out of my gun. Posey'll stand by Roak over there, and Angelo by me. At the word go, Roak comes running towards me with his knife. If he can get to me before I've drawn and clicked my empty shooting iron at him six times the five smackeroos are his. If not, I win. Fair enough, Roak?"

"Fair enough," Roak said. "Only I want one other change. Posey, you cut two holes in this here hunk of planking and string a cord through 'em—"

"Why?" Bart asked.

"For Marvis's protection," Roak grinned. "His hogleg's going to be empty, but you can't unload a knife. I want him to hang this plank around his neck to cover his heart and other vitals. 'Cause even though he doesn't know it, I'm going to win this bet. . . ."

The Negro cowhand cut the holes through the planking, strung the cords through them, hung the plank around Marvis's neck.

"This damn thing gets in my way," Marvis complained.

"Don't take it off!" Roak warned. "Will, you call it."

"All right," Will said. "Count o' three, you jumps him. But I still think it's a fool trick to jump a man with a

shootin' iron in his hand with only a toadsticker in
yourn—"

"Just you count," Roak said.

"All right," Will said. "One!"

The two of them stood there, waiting.

"Two!"

Marvis's hand drifted down toward the butt of his revolver.

"Thr—"

They saw the blur. Saw lightning streaking silver across
the firelight. Heard that sodden plunk. And Marvis Hart
swayed there, staring at that knife that stood quivering
in the plank he wore around his neck. His fingers were
frozen around the butt of that gun he hadn't even had time
to draw.

"Lord God!" Old Will croaked.

Bart looked at Roak.

"Tell me something," he said. "The day I went gunning for you, and you wasn't packing your iron, did you
have that there gullet tickler under your coat?"

"And this one," Roak said; and they saw it flash. Then
it, too, stood quivering beside the other in the plank Marvis Hart wore.

"You ain't got no more of them things, have you?"
Marvis said plaintively.

"Nope," Roak grinned; "why?"

" 'Cause that there first one bit hide," Marvis whispered. "Angie, pull this damn thing out!"

They all crowded around him. The point of that knife
had gone a quarter of an inch into Marvis's flesh. The
wound was nothing much, but it bled like hell. Roak
could see Bart staring at him, and all the rest as well. With
the exception of the Mexicans, there was a new thing in
their eyes—the Westerner's cold distaste for the man who
favored a blade.

Fool trick, he thought. Should have known better than

that. Now they— Aloud, he said: "Keep your money, Marv. Wasn't a fair contest. You never had a chance—"

"No," Marvis said. "You won, Roak. Take your winnings. . . ."

The next morning they crossed the Arkansas, and by the time that was over, they'd forgot all about Roak's prowess with a blade.

It went off like clockwork at first. The current was strong enough, but they got the chuck wagon and the *remuda* across without any trouble at all. They were beginning to feel good about it now, because after the Arkansas there weren't any more rivers between them and Abilene. Once across, it would be a parade. They were thinking about Abilene itself as they worked, of that riproaring, rousing catamount of a town, where a body could really cut loose and howl. The bars that sold stuff that could sure as hell dissolve a gun barrel, the tinseled temptation in black silk stockings and knee-length skirts they meant to succumb to pronto. The faro banks, the green-covered card tables, the hotels where a feller could take a real honest-to-God bath and sleep on snow-white sheets like a white man. . . .

They were thinking like that as they swam their mounts back across to help Bart and Will get the longhorns moving. But once they were in position on the downstream side of the herd, they forgot about Abilene, because the Arkansas was still a river, and no river whatever was to be taken lightly. They were all naked except that they had their hats on, and inside their hats, wrapped in a piece of oilskin, their revolvers. That was because if a herd started milling in the river, you could sometimes stop them, get them headed into the long U curve cattle always swam in whether there was any current or not, until you got them to hit a decent landing place, by firing off your gun in front of the leaders' faces. Which meant you had to have your six-gun with you, even in the river, and that you had to keep it dry.

It started off just fine. The herd went into the river without any fuss. Started swimming across that broad golden surface, snaking out into their usual curve, swimming easily, powerfully, their broadhorned heads bobbing above the surface; and they, the hands, ice-cold and shivering, keeping their mounts crowded in so that the lead steer couldn't tighten that υ curve into the beginning of a circle, but beginning to feel good about it again because it was almost over now, and it the last one; when the ornery old bastard of a mosshorn that was leading the swimming herd turned fast and smooth as a screw-propeller steamboat and headed back toward where he'd come from.

Bart Nevis swam his mount in front of him to turn him, but the lead steer pushed the horse aside like a floating chip, tightening that υ into a c and that into the letter o, all the others behind him swimming in a full circle that in another minute was going to be a close-packed mass of cowflesh with the centre ones drowning. Bart tossed his flat-crowned black Stetson away and came out with his six-gun, forced his mount across where the leader swam to break that circle, firing off his gun in the air, turning them a little now, opening the circle out into a c and then into an s, when the crush of them bore down on him, and Roak, who was closest to him, saw his horse go over thrashing and come up again swimming strongly; but the saddle was empty.

Roak watched the spot where Bart had gone down, seeing out of that part of a man's eyes which takes in the space to the side of the direction where he is looking that everybody else was busy now pushing that herd shoreward; and that aside from him nobody had seen exactly what had happened, and that by the time it did occur to them that Bart hadn't come up, it would be too late. He thought:

Five thousand times $30 a head is $150,000 unsplit

and even with wages and expenses taken out that's money. . . .

Then, maybe because he thought that, maybe because he had spent too many nights staring into the campfire with those long, slow thoughts trailing through his mind, he took off his hat and threw it wide, gun and all, and dived, clawing for depth, beating his feet in a foaming rage against that wall of water gone solid, pulling downward with his arms with all his strength, so that he could get past that thresh and broil of hooves in time.

He opened his eyes in mud murk, dimlighted; and saw something white. He swam toward it on a long slant, praying his breath would last. It was Bart, all right. The trail boss lay on the river bottom with a tendril of redness rising up where his mount's iron-shod hoof had opened a six-inch gash in his head. Roak got to him, put his hand down, twisted his fingers into Bart's thick, graying hair, blood-slimed now, river-oozed—and jerked. Bart floated up like a thing made out of gray-white rubber, pliant, boneless; and Roak got his arm around the great bole of his chest and kicked upward, stroking, feeling the breath in his lungs like a hot tangle, the pressure behind his eyes becoming a fire, a sunburst, and then a darkness with that hoof thrash churning still above him, too far above him, and he, with the last of whatever it is in a human that makes him a man as distinguished from merely a male, put both his arms under Bart's armpits and shoved powerfully, seeing as the blackness roared in upon him, the choking, the sinking, that Bart was still going up, up, and he, while he could still think, shaping the words:

All right. I've paid back now. For everything.

And sank down very slowly into the dark.

He could feel something pressing on his chest. Hard. Then it came away. Pressed again. He heard Bart's voice, dimly, pain-edged and shrill.

"Keep it up, Posey! God damn it, don't quit! Can't let him die! Can't—"

And Angelo, saying:

"Let me, Posey. You're tired—"

And Posey, saying:

"Nope, Angie—I felt him breathe jes' now. Thah 'tis! Stand back, white folks, 'n' give him air!"

And he, Roak, turning over on his side and vomiting copiously, all the river murk, the green slime, and maybe even some of the black guilt and the shame.

He opened his eyes. Saw Bart standing naked above him, half his face blotted out with the thick red flow from the gash they hadn't even had time to bandage. He grinned feebly, said:

"Never would of believed that noggin of yours could crack, Bart. . . ."

The trail boss stood there. Then he put out his big, hard hand.

"And I never would of thought you was fit to ride the river with," he said.

Chapter Eleven

THE CATTLE buyers met them a few miles out of town. And because they hadn't pushed the herd too hard, most of the longhorns had gained weight on the trek for the very simple reason that the grazing along the northern half of the trail was a hell of a lot better than it ever was in Texas. So they sold the 4,953 head they had left after they had counted off the ones that had drowned crossing the rivers, the ones that had strayed, and the ones they themselves had eaten en route for $30 a head.

And that—by the time the sale prices of the horses of the *remuda* and the first string and the nine mules of the chuck wagon, and the $200 they got for the chuck wagon itself, had been added, and the money they owed Captain Jess for the cattle plus the wages and the expenses of the trip had been subtracted—meant that Bart and Roak were left with $35,444.50 each. Which was a lot of money for those days.

"The first thing I'm going to do," Bart said, "is to buy you a mighty handsome shooting iron to replace the one you lost in the river saving my fool hide."

"No," Roak said; "a six-gun I don't need, Bart. And I don't aim to ever need one again. I'm going to homestead now. Set Han up in a nice little house, and start out with a small herd. Got some ideas about that—mean to bring in some Eastern stock and crossbreed. Ever thought about the fact that longhorns are mighty poor beef animals? All horns, hide and hoof. Now, if they were crossed with some of the creatures we have up Ohio way—"

"They'd die. Texas is too rough for anything but long-horns. Eastern stock is used to eating regular, and grass— not weeds and thistles. But how do you figure to herd cattle without a six-gun to use for all the things a body needs a shooting iron for?"

"Don't mean to herd them myself. Going to start out with two or three hands. Like I told you, I mean to concentrate on scientific breeding. And since, in my case, the only thing I could use a six-gun for would be to kill people, I don't think I need one. When has killing ever settled anything, Bart? What do corpses call for except still more corpses, and blood more rivers of blood? We've soaked this land in it now, and are we really at peace? I had a belly-ful of killing during the War. God willing, I'd like to get the stink of death out of my nostrils forever more, boy. . . ."

They heard that sound then. That cross between a scrape and a gurgle. Or they felt it. Afterwards they could never be sure. They turned and looked into that face reduced into a gross caricature of humanity.

"Mighty noble sentiments, Roak," the sheriff said; "You're purely making my chores easier, boy. . . ."

Roak licked bone-dry lips. So that *had* been his name he had heard the morning of his honeymoon in Browns-ville. And the masked bandit had looked familiar with good reason. And the advice the stranger had given—"I told him that the right place to look for any Texas cow-hand warn't Texas, but Abilene, Kansas, 'cause sooner or later they all show up there"—had been followed to the letter. Maybe even beyond.

He wondered why he wasn't more surprised to find Fritz Heindrichs here. But the thing itself, that grim presence, ruled out surprise, brought with it, as man's fate always does, an element of prescience that linked itself effortlessly to all his nights of sleepless brooding beside the campfire, fulfilled his forebodings, carried with it its own brand of inevitability.

"What do you mean, Fritz?" he asked.

"When the good citizens of Abilene, Kansas, honored me with the post of sheriff," Fritz Heindrichs said, "I promised 'em I'd stop fellows from letting daylight through each other on purpose and through honest folks by accident. Likewise such fool tricks as making tenderfeet dance by shooting at their feet, and shooting up the town for the hell of it. So I passed a rule: any man who comes inside city limits has to check his iron in my office. I give him a receipt for it, and when he leaves town for good, I hand him back his gun. Town's been mighty peaceful since—"

"Makes sense," Bart said slowly. "As boss of this outfit, I'll tell you right now, sheriff, my boys will abide by the rule—"

"Thank you," Fritz said; "and you, Roak? Will you abide by it?"

"He's a part of this outfit," Bart began.

"I know. But I know him of old. So I got to ask him special. Will you, Roak?"

"Can't answer that," Roak said, "unless you answer me one first, Fritz: with all the mighty good, number-one, first-class reasons you have to hate my stinking guts, how do I know you won't gun me down?"

Bart stared at Roak, then at Fritz Heindrichs's butchered face.

"You do *that,* Roak?" he said.

"Yep," Roak said; "that and a few more things that don't even show. So I got to ask him: Fritz, as sheriff, with the legal right to bear arms at all times, what guarantee have I got you won't let daylight through me the first time we meet in town?"

Fritz chuckled softly.

"You got my word," he said.

"You mean," Roak said, "that you're willing to shake

hands and call it quits—in spite of all the puking polecat things I've done to you?"

"Nope," Fritz said; "I don't mean that, Roak. All I mean is that I don't mean to kill you. Not now. Not never."

"Why not?" Roak said. "Name of God, Fritz—why?"

Again that chalk-scrape, throat-gurgle, hackle-raising near soundlessness.

"Because," Fritz Heindrichs said, "for what you've done, Roak, dying's not fitting punishment. Look at it: I pull back on a inch-long hook of iron, and then there's a bang, a puff of smoke, a little flame, gone before you even see them good. A puny-looking round hole in you some-wheres. Blue—with a trickle of red oozing out. And that's all. That's it. You're gone. And at peace. Your troubles are clean over. Too damn easy, right?"

Bart was staring at the sheriff. You could read his thought on his face. Fritz answered it, even though it wasn't spoken.

"Nope, friend, I'm not crazy. Just got my own way of looking at things."

"So," Roak said, "you mean to keep me alive?"

"Yep. Up until the day you beg me to put you out of your misery, the time I'll have to watch you to keep you from doing it yourself—too soon. Because when these simple-minded Western folks get riled up and go gunning for a fellow they forget one thing—"

"And what's that?" Roak asked.

They could see Fritz Heindrichs's lips shaping that hor-rible copy of a grin. Heard or felt that soundless sound he made, issuing from between his teeth.

"That the dead don't cry," he said.

Bart Nevis snorted.

"So you want to see him cry," he said; "mighty child-ish way of getting even, if you ask me, mister," he said.

"I didn't ask you," Fritz said flatly. "But since you put your two bits' worth in, I'll answer that one, too. I want to see him cry, first. And second, I want to see him die—but only after he knows what it feels like to cry 'til your guts are torn to pieces and even your tears are blood. How the world looks when there ain't no more hope in it anywheres, when every living thing you've loved has been dirtied, snatched away, run off, dead and gone. Then I'll let him die—and by his own hand. Because the only real way to get even with a son of a bitch like Roak Garfield is to make him put a shotgun in his mouth, pull the trigger with his big toe and splatter his brains all over the ceiling. Then I'll know I've got him. I was only to perforate him, he might even die happy—and then I'd have to wait 'til my own time came and hunt him all over hell. . . ."

Roak stood there looking at him.

"You know I haven't got a gun, Fritz," he said. "You heard Bart trying to give me one. Mine got lost, it—"

"Yep," Fritz said. "A gun I'd almost let you keep, Roak Garfield. But you just hand me over them two Arkansas toothpicks you got under your coat. Don't know whether your friend here knows that you can do more with them gullet ticklers at any distance up to twenty-five feet than any gunslick ever born can do with a shooting iron—"

"Yes," Bart said; "I do know that; I've seen him. Hand 'em over, Roak."

"All right," Roak said, "since you've got other things 'sides killing me on your mind, Fritz—"

"Yep," Fritz said. "That there crossed circle is a road brand, ain't it? The original brand is Bar F—down Texas way, right?"

"Right," Roak said. "But why do you want to know?"

"Just so I'll know where you hang out, Roak," Fritz said.

"How do you know I won't drift?"

"I don't. But it don't matter. 'Cause wherever you drift to, I'll find you. You want a receipt for these here knives?"

"No," Roak said.

"All right. Be seeing you gentlemen," Fritz Heindrichs said.

Riding into town—since by general agreement, established ever since the first trail herds had reached Abilene in 1867, trail riders were allowed to keep their personal mounts even after they had sold them until the day they left for St. Louis by train—Bart and Roak didn't talk. Roak could see that Bart was struggling with himself, fighting his concern for Hannah's future, his simple curiosity. Finally Bart said:

"Wimmen trouble?"

"Yep," Roak said.

"His—wife?"

"Nope. His sister."

"And you—you wouldn't marry her?"

"Wrong word. I couldn't. I was home on leave when it happened. Didn't even know she was—like that—when I went back to my outfit. After the War I looked all over hell for her. Couldn't find her. Only Fritz wasn't in no mood to listen to explanations—"

"So you scarred him up like that?"

"To remind him not to be so hot-headed. Looks like it worked—"

Bart looked away over the prairie toward a little sod hut that lay ahead.

"Maybe," he said; "but I'd heap rather a feller come at me red hot than ice cold."

"Me too. But there's no help for it now," Roak said.

They were passing the sod hut, and Bart reined in suddenly. Roak pulled up his sorrel, too. Then he saw what had stopped Bart. She was sitting on a mound of dirt put there on purpose for people to sit on, and crying. The tears plowed white furrows through the grime on her face. Even from that distance, Roak could see that she was very pretty and delicate and maybe even refined. He could see all that in spite of the dirt. And he guessed that the reason she was crying was that a sod hut on a Kansas prairie was the last place on earth she wanted to be.

Bart had already climbed down by then. He had his hat in his hand.

" 'Scuse me, ma'am," he said, "I know it ain't none of my business, but is there anything I can do to help?"

She jerked her head upright, and Roak saw that though her hair was as black as Belén's, her eyes were the color of the sky come harvest time. Even with those tears in them, they were something. Then she spoke, and his guess was right. She talked like Gwen used to, like Hannah sometimes did when she felt like displaying her education.

"No, I—I'm afraid not. It's—it's kind of you to ask, Mr.—"

"Nevis. Bart Nevis, ma'am."

"—Mr. Nevis; but there isn't anything you can do. There isn't anything anyone could do—except maybe—God."

Bart smiled then. He had a good smile.

"I can listen, ma'am," he said; "I'm a mighty good listener. And nothing does wimmenfolks more good than talking things out, my ma always said."

The girl smiled then in her turn. Roak sat there on the sorrel looking at the two of them. He thought: Give him a chance, Good Lord. She looks pretty and sweet and I'd feel a heck of a lot better about things if old Bart was settled down and happy. So I'm asking you mighty kindly, Lord, give Bart a chance. . . .

"Your mother was right," she said. "Only you're a complete stranger, and—"

"Many's the man and woman what was complete strangers once, can count twenty-five grandchildren right now," Bart said. "Lord God! I plumb forgot the main thing! You —you ain't married, are you, ma'am?"

"No," the girl whispered.

"Look, Bart," Roak said then, "reckon I'll mosey on into town, and leave you and the little lady to talk private—"

"No!" the girl said sharply. "Please stay too, mister. My father'll be back any minute now. And it would look a lot better if I were talking to two strangers instead of just one."

"Bad-tempered hombre, your pa?" Roak said.

"No—not really. Just—disappointed. You see, he came out here with such high hopes. . . ."

"Then he just didn't know Kansas," Bart said.

"Nor did I," the girl said wistfully. "You see—"

But that was as far as she got. For the man came around the side of the sod house. Stopped dead. And snarled out in a voice that was like somebody strangling:

"Ruthie! I told you if I ever caught you even talking to one of them cowpunching varmints, I'd—"

"Now just you hold on a minute, mister," Bart said. "We don't punch cows. We drive them. Cowpunchers are another breed of cuss altogether. And I agree with you about them. But cattlemen, like us, can be gentlemen. Kind of reckon I can lay claim to the title. I'm range boss of the biggest ranch in Texas. And my intentions toward your daughter, before you ask me, are honorable. Last of all, my handle's Bart Nevis. What's yourn?"

The man stopped short. He, Roak saw, was fighting to maintain his pride. And he was going to lose that fight. Maybe because he was too used to losing it. There was a thing in the making of a man that when you had it, you took it as a matter of course, not realizing what it was like not to have it. But when a man didn't have it, it showed.

The man hung there, his anger dissolving into the sure, accustomed lineaments of defeat.

"Wilson," he muttered; "Harry Wilson. But I tell you, mister—"

"You," Bart said evenly, "don't tell me anything. You listen. This little lady is under my protection, now. And I don't want to never again hear tell of your doing anything to make her cry. You understand that, Mr. Wilson?"

"Why," Harry Wilson spluttered, "I never! I—"

"No," the girl said, "you've got it wrong, Mr. Nevis. My father's never been unkind to me. It's just that—that—"

"What—Ruth?" Bart said gently, making deep-toned music of her name.

Roak saw her response to hearing Bart say her name like that. Saw that aided by the loneliness and despair that living in a sod hut on that treeless hell where dust storms alternated with mud baths, Bart had already won. He realized that Bart would have won anyhow, being a mighty fine figure of a man; but that under other circumstances, it would have taken him longer.

"It's that—I was—lonely, Mr. Nevis," Ruth Wilson said. "I'm not really suited for this kind of life, nor is my father. Only—"

"Only," Bart said, "you'd better put on your best bib and tucker, and come have dinner with me and my friend, Mr. Garfield. That includes your pa, of course. Then we can talk. You and me, and afterwards, me and your pa—"

"And Mr. Garfield?" Ruth said with a flash of impish humor. "Who is he going to talk to?"

"Oh, him?" Bart said. "He can talk to his horse. Besides, he can save up all his talk for his missus once he gets back home—"

"Got that shot in fast, didn't you, Bart?" Roak said in mock anger. "I wasn't exactly aiming to tell a lady pretty as this one I'm already hitched, at least not right now. . . ."

"Well," Harry Wilson said, "it don't look right for us to accept no invitation from you gentlemen, seeing as how we just met and—"

"Wilson," Bart said, "you go hitch your hosses like a nice, sensible old party, and don't give me no trouble right now, will you please?"

Bart drove Ruth into town in the buggy, with her father, perched fearfully atop Bart's big roan, riding behind them with Roak. Harry Wilson eyed Roak speculatively. Roak knew what he was going to ask before he asked it.

" 'Scuse me, Mr. Garfield," he said, "but you known Mr. Nevis a long time?"

"Yep," Roak lied, "years."

"And he—he's got a good reputation? You understand, as a father, I—"

"The best," Roak said truthfully. "Bart Nevis is one of the most respected men in Texas."

"I see," Harry Wilson said; "but is he—I mean, has he—"

"Got any money?" Roak said. "Well, I reckon if you asked him mighty kindly, and he saw fit, he could count out more than $30,000 right this minute. Got it in his saddlebag. I seen it this morning. . . ."

He saw from the way Harry Wilson's eyes bugged out that Bart wasn't going to have any serious objections from that quarter. In fact, the quarter from which trouble actually came was one that nobody expected, he least of all.

He was sitting there with Ruth Wilson, because Bart had taken her father aside to discuss matters with him. En route to Abilene in the buggy, Bart had already had time enough to convince Ruth herself, putting it on the basis that he had to get back to Texas in a hurry, and the good Lord Himself only knew when he'd get back to Kansas again.

"I know," Bart told her, "that a girl's got a right to a long, sweet, slow courting. Only I ain't got the time, Ruth.

I only got me four days in Abilene before I got to head back home. And if you're going to say yes, you know it already. So it 'pears to me a lot more sensible for you to spend the next four days getting your trousseau together so we can have a real pretty weddin' in the church that we can both remember and treasure all our days, instead of making me spend all that time going through fool motions when you know right now what you're going to do. . . ."

"Bart," Ruth whispered, "you ever realized that a girl needs that long, slow, sweet courtship you mentioned? That it is—essential, maybe? So that she can get to know her man, be sure—"

"You," Bart said gruffly, "know me right now, Ruth —know me as good as you're ever going to. 'Cause I'm a simple, straightforward kind of a feller with no deceit in me. And you ain't going to be cheated out of your courting. 'Cause it's just starting, and it's never going to stop 'til the day they put me to bed with a shovel out on the prairie. Maybe not even then if there's anything to preacher talk—"

"Oh, Bart!" Ruth said. "I don't know what to say! I—"

"Then don't say anything—just pucker up and kiss me," Bart Nevis said.

And that had been that. Only now Bart had gone into the barroom of the hotel to discuss plans with Harry Wilson, which plans, Roak was dismally sure, were certainly going to include Bart's having his weak sister of a father-in-law on his back the rest of his life. But there was no hope for that, and maybe Ruth was even worth it.

"You're happy, Ruth?" Roak asked in order to make conversation.

"I—I don't know," Ruth said; "I—"

Then she stopped. His eyes stopped her. She turned, followed his gaze.

The woman in the doorway was blonde. She was dressed all in black. And she looked like an angel, except—except, Ruth decided, angels don't have the essence and distillation of hell in their eyes. She came toward them, smiling. And the way she smiled was another thing. Cold—feline. The smile of a great cat unsheathing her claws. Ruth heard the scrape of Roak's chair; then the woman was saying:

"No, Roak, darling—don't get up. No need to stand upon ceremony between old, old friends. The lady is— your wife?"

"No," Roak said. He sounded like he was choking. "Gwen, for God's sake!"

"A pity," Gwen said. "She's pretty. And good. One can tell. Your—fiancée, then?"

"No. My best friend's," Roak said.

"Trusting soul, to leave her with—you," Gwen said. She turned to Ruth. "Then, my dear," she said, "since you are neither sweetheart nor wife, you can't possibly have any objections if I—"

She bent swiftly. Locked both arms about Roak's neck. Kissed him slowly, carefully, with a sensuous relish that held Ruth rigid, frozen in her chair, watching that kiss that went on and on, the blonde woman trying, it seemed to her, to devour Roak Garfield living, until the door crashed open and Bart and her father stood there, their faces ludicrous with shock, and she, the blonde woman he had called Gwen, going on about the business of kissing Roak as though she meant to keep it up forever.

"Roak!" Bart said. "You mind telling me what the living hell you're doing? And right in front of my *dulce*, too! Why, God damn it, a body'd think—"

The blonde woman looked up then.

"*He* isn't doing anything," she said. "I was doing it all. A sample, Roak. An example of how far I've gone beyond your original lessons. I'm out of grade school now, darling. Don't you want to come home with me and find out how much more I know?"

"No," Roak said miserably; "you see, Gwen, I'm a married man now, and—"

Gwen laughed then. Her laughter was silvery.

"You mean that some irate father came home too soon? Or that dear daughter was showing such obvious signs of your tender affections that—"

"Ma'am," Bart Nevis said coldly, "you're in the presence of a decent girl. I'm sorry, but I have to ask you to watch your language or—leave."

Gwen stared at him.

"Now," she said wonderingly, "I've seen everything with the hide left on! For your information, mister, the man who can make me watch my language, or leave, or anything else just hasn't been born yet. Also for your private education—of the kind you need most of all—there's no such thing as a decent girl in the precise sense you mean. Any of us can be had. Ask Roak. There are women who are cold, and women who are scared; but decent women, no, friend. Every one of us goes right back on our little frilly bustles when the right man applies the push."

She turned to Roak.

"Are you coming quietly," she said, "or do I have to drag you feet first? I want to find out if you're as good as you used to be. Or whether it just seemed that way to me because you were my first and I didn't know any better—"

"Roak," Bart said grimly, "you better get her out of here!"

"That's what I like about you Southerners: you're so chivalrous," Gwen said. "Come on, darling. Your friend begins to bore me. And when I'm really bored, my behavior becomes unpredictable. I just might shoot him, or even stamp on his bunions. So you'd better—"

Roak took her arm.

"I'm sorry," he said; "my humblest apologies, Miss Ruth. I wouldn't have had something like this happen for nothing in the world. I—"

"Oh, shut up and come on, Roak Garfield!" Gwendolyn Heindrichs said.

Walking along beside her, Roak was trying to think of some way of getting out of it. Which, for him, consisted of thinking of some way to keep from wanting her. He dragged up the image of Hannah waiting for him, by now great with his child, but the vein of shame in him ran thin and shallow; and this taut, controlled, lying bundle of feline femininity at his side was too real, so that thinking about Hannah did no good at all, and thinking about Belén only a little. He knew he was going to give in, but he felt he owed it to himself to struggle a while, to display that hypocrisy which is vice's envious tribute to virtue.

But they had got to Tiger Lou's by then; and Gwen led him across the empty ballroom floor past the stacked-up tables and chairs and up the stairs to her room. She closed the door, locked it, and started to kiss him again.

Roak hung there, taking it, the sweat beading on his forehead, while she unbuttoned his shirt and put her two hands inside along the flesh of his ribs, running them over his body deftly, expertly, with such evident practice at the art of making a sucker halfway lose his mind that Roak Garfield, who was anything but a sucker, went cold on her, cold and sick.

She pulled her mouth away from his.

"What's wrong?"

"Nothing. Except you do that too well," Roak said. "Like you were forgetting something, Gwen. . . ."

"Forgetting what?" she said.

"That I ain't just a casual customer. I'm me—a man. A man who meant something to you once. Not just a hunk of male meat to be used, baby. So skip the routine, won't you? Throws me off my feed. Makes me druther just sit and talk. . . ."

"Oh," she laughed, "the talking can come later, if you still have strength enough to talk by then. . . ."

She moved into him. Curved, fitted. Moved back some time later. There was the whisper, the rustle of cloth, sinking down. Then the coolness. The perfumed warmth, slow writhing against him. Her fingers, deft upon the buttons of his clothing; fast, expert, sure. He reached for her, drew her down. Then he felt the hardness of metal against his chest.

He looked down, saw the snubnosed .41-caliber derringer she was holding against him. That mule-kick powerful little pistol that was a squat hand cannon, despite its size. That could blow a hole in a man at close range big enough to shove your fist into.

"Now," she said, "I'm going to have fun—my way. We'll just lie here—all cozy, like this, Roak, dear. And I'll kiss you, if you like. But you keep your hands off me, understand? A new experience for you, darling. Afterwards, knowing you, I'll bet you'll even brag about it, tell the boys, 'There I was with this fool woman stark, mothernaked in my arms, and—' "

"Nothing," Roak said; "that's it, isn't it, Gwen?"

"That's it. You've called it, darling," Gwen said.

"And I'm supposed to lie here and suffer?" Roak grinned. "Baby, I ain't the suffering kind. You just pull that there shooting iron back a couple of inches so it doesn't poke me so hard, and I'll treat you to the spectacle of a feller sleeping peaceful in your arms just like you was his mother—"

She jammed the muzzle of the derringer harder into his flesh.

"You won't sleep," she said. "I'll see to that!"

Then she kissed him, holding that gun against him. Ran her free hand over him. Moved in closer, until only the derringer separated them.

"Nice, isn't it?" she said.

"Kind of," Roak said.

She kissed him. Lay there looking into his eyes. Whispered:

"What are you, Roak Garfield? Besides human, I mean; 'cause that you aren't!"

"A man," he said quietly, "an ordinary kind of a man; but still—a man."

"Not a rat-bastard coward who got a girl with child and then deserted her?" she said.

"Give me your hand, Gwen," he said.

She put her left hand into his. He lifted it until her fingers touched that sixteen-inch-long ridge of scar tissue Benito Arjona had left when he went into his lung to dig out that ball. He felt her fingers slide along it slowly.

"My God!" she whispered. "You—you trying to say that's why you didn't come back?"

"No," Roak said; "I'm not trying to say anything. I don't have to try. I'm plain telling you what you'd know already if you'd stopped being mean mad and hurt long enough to ask somebody besides that crazy brother of yours."

"Go on," Gwen said.

"I did come back. The first think I did after I'd learned how to walk again was to come back. Only, for a fellow with a .50-caliber ball in his right lung, walking is quite a trick. Took me more than a year. By then it was too late. You were gone—"

"And you, I suppose, tried to find me."

"Ask Fritz. I raked up hell. Only you'd made damned sure that nobody knew where you were going. I asked everybody—all the good people who were looking at me and turning up their noses like I was something that smelled bad, and I asked all the good-for-nothings who kept clapping me on the back and trying to find out the dirty details—"

"Which, of course, you regaled them with at great length," Gwen said dryly.

"No," Roak said simply. "A wife's nakedness is her husband's, and I'd come back to marry you, Gwen. As quickly as I could under the circumstances. And from one hell of a long way—"

"A long way?" Gwen said. It seemed to him her tone was less hard now. That there was a falter in it. "Even if you were in Georgia or Carolina, it appears to me that you—"

"That's not what I mean," Roak said softly. "I came back from further than that, Gwen. From the valley of the shadow. From those filthy hospital beds where even the male nurses used to tie up their noses before they came close to a fellow who had a hole in his chest that kept bursting open every two or three days and spilling a quart and a half of pus out on the sheet. I came back, from that. From the fearing and the hurting and the wanting and the wondering whether it'd even be fair to ask you like I was then—"

"But—Fritz," she whispered; "what—you did to him—"

"He caught me wrong. Just when I was crying on the inside for what you and I could have had, for the kid we'd both lost, for the life I'd dreamed on until losing it was a kind of dying, he showed up and didn't even give me a chance to explain what couldn't be explained anyhow because a man just doesn't mouth over the most beautiful thing that ever happened to him in a public street in front of a bunch of drunks. So I scarred him. I went too far, and I'm sorry. Only I was out of my mind, really out of my mind because you weren't there like I'd hoped for and expected. So now you know. So now you've got your revenge. A hell of a lot better than that silly gun. Take your comfort from it, Gwen. From knowing that for every tear you shed, I let fall two. Or maybe five. Satisfied?"

He felt the muzzle of the derringer come away from

his side. Heard the sound it made striking the floor. Felt
her mouth slide along the slant of his jaw; and, turning to
her, found it ice-cold and trembling and salt with the taste
of tears.

"Roak," she whispered.

"Yes, Gwen?"

"Love me. Please, please love me. Because I want you.
And thought I was over wanting any man. . . ."

"You're just upset," he said.

"No. There. Feel. I'm on fire. There. Oh God, oh Lord,
oh Jesus, I—"

Then it was morning and the door opened very quietly
and Prince Parker stood in the doorway with his hand still
on his key, looking at them. They were sleeping very
quietly in that deep and profound slumber that comes
only with real completion and cannot be counterfeited.
Prince didn't move. He just stood there looking at them
a long time, and then he said:

"Gwen!"

She looked up, sleepily. Came up at once, her eyes wide.
Said:

"Me. Kill me, Prince, if you've got to kill somebody
over this. I brought him here. He didn't even know about
you. So let him go, Prince; please let him go!"

And Roak whirling to face the man, and saying, furiously:

"I won't have my life begged for, Gwen! I'll give your
husband satisfaction anywhere or any time if he's man
enough to wait 'til I've a gun in my hands, too—"

"I'm not her husband," Prince Parker said; "and I'll
wait, mainly because I don't want the whole town knowing
where and how I caught you. So I'll give you time to get
dressed. I'll be waiting downstairs—"

"Prince," Gwen said, "he hasn't got a gun. You know
the rules! Fritz took it off him, and—"

"Then I'll wait for him in front of Fritz's office. You tell him you're leaving on the twelve-oh-five, and he'll give you your iron, friend. Then you come out with it in your hand. I won't draw 'til I see you with it. Agreed?"

"Agreed," Roak Garfield said.

Walking away from Fritz Heindrichs's desk toward that door, Roak didn't feel anything at all. He stopped, staring at that doorway through which death waited for him. Then he looked at his empty hands. He turned back toward the sheriff.

"Fritz," he said, "you don't know what you're doing. I—"

Fritz Heindrichs chuckled. The sound was even more unpleasant than usual.

"I'll give you back them toadstickers, Roak," he said, "when I see you on that train. Hand 'em through the window. Know you too well, boy. Soon as you walked in that there door, I could see you was aiming to kill somebody. And knowing my no-good tramp of a sister even better than you do, it figgers that it's Prince Parker you're going after. So no dice, Roak. You don't need them knives, and you claims you lost your gun. Anyhow, you ain't got a damned thing to worry about. With all his faults, Prince Parker's a gentleman. Even if he caught you with Gwen, as from the look of you he likely did, he won't shoot unless you're heeled. So now you just get out of here and leave me in peace. I'll see you at train time."

Roak stood there. There were three things he could do. He could plead with Fritz Heindrichs. Or he could call out to Prince Parker that he still wasn't armed. Or he could walk out that door with his jaw clamped shut. In some ways, that was the easiest choice of all.

He moved toward the door step by slow step, not even wondering if Prince would hold off long enough to see his hands were empty. Just walking slowly toward that door driven by the vast and inexplicable melancholy that came upon him sometimes, that bone-crushing weight of sorrow, fatigue, and bad memories, his steps quickening now, becoming eager as he moved toward the end of having to think about—Hannah, the child coming, Captain Jesse's face, Belén's black eyes with that resignation he never could stand in them, even what he'd done last night, not lying, just twisting the truth a little, exaggerating it until it was worse than a lie, so that his chance encounter with Gwen had ended in an adultery that hadn't even the saving grace of being casual—all the things that put the black sickness at the back of his throat, the tangle in his gut, the nerve-crawling shame.

He went through that door. Heard the roar of Prince's short-barreled gun. Saw the splinters fly from the door jamb a foot from him because Prince's sawed-off Wells Fargo Colt just wasn't made for the kind of shooting he was trying to do with it now. Roak could have killed him after that first shot if he had had a gun. As it was, he had to stand there and let Prince miss him two more times, firing from across the street twenty feet away, slipshooting with his thumb in the way that had always worked in his across-the-card-table gun battles, but that wasn't worth a damn at a distance that required aiming and a gun with a barrel long enough to put a bullet reasonably close to the spot you were pointing at, until Fritz Heindrichs came out of his office, took in the situation at a glance, dragged his long-barreled Colt out of his pants pocket without haste, and shot Prince Parker dead.

Roak stood there, staring at the sheriff. At that face that he himself had reduced out of humanity.

"Why?" he said. "Name of God, Fritz, why?"

Fritz Heindrichs let that sound he made float up from his throat.

"As crowbait, you don't suit my purposes none a-tall, Roak. Told you that oncet," he said.

Chapter Twelve

ON THE train headed east to St. Louis, on the river packet butting downstream to New Orleans, on the coasting steamer to Brownsville, and on the stage that carried him as close as he could get to the Bar F—for that maddeningly roundabout route was the only way a body could get from Kansas to West Texas if he didn't backtrack the trail on horseback—Roak Garfield had all the time in the world to think about every one of the things he didn't want to think about at all. Especially after St. Louis, where he'd left Gwen Heindrichs clutching the five thousand dollars he'd given her between her two hands, and crying.

And that parting and the manner of it were maybe the worst things he had to think about.

The morning that Fritz Heindrichs had killed Prince Parker and saved his life—thereby breaking every rule of normal human behavior that Roak had ever heard of—he had walked or rather stumbled away from what had been in Abilene, Kansas, merely one more "corpse and cartridge occasion," but for him another signpost, another turning in the long trail he called his life. And among the mob of the curious who, as always, had come running toward the sound of the shots, he saw a little knot of men and one or two women bending over something on the ground.

"No'm," he heard one of the men say, "she ain't hit,

ma'am. Too far away from the shooting. 'Pears to me she just fainted."

Roak elbowed his way through the group, and saw Gwen lying there with a woman chafing her hands and another applying a handkerchief soaked in a nearby rain barrel to her forehead. He bent down, said softly:

"Gwen. Gwen, baby—I'm all right. . . ."

Her eyes fluttered open at the sound of his voice. Widened. Went lightfilled, flooded, blind. She put her arms up to him, wrapped them about his neck. Clung to him, crying.

He heard the men mutter:

"Prince Parker's woman. So that means—"

But they didn't say what it meant. And only one of them was bold enough to ask him:

"Say, partner—since it don't look like you's got a scratch on you, don't reckon there's no harm in axing you how Prince come out o' that powder-burning contest, is there?"

Roak lifted Gwen gently to her feet.

"Why don't you go ask *him?*" he said.

"Kin he answer?" the curious one persisted.

"No," Roak said. "Reckon he leaned a sight too hard on a bullet that was going past."

"Roak!" Gwen said. "You mean you—you—"

"Killed Prince? No, baby. Don't even own a shooting iron; and your dear brother wasn't even starting to give me back my throwing knives."

"But," Gwen said, "you said—"

"That Prince got his? He did. Fritz is a sight handier with a gun than I ever gave him credit for being. . . ."

Gwen stood there. The astonishment in her eyes was real.

"Fritz killed—Prince? Saved *your* life? *Yours,* Roak? God in heaven, why?"

"Reckon that's something you better ask him," Roak said. "C'mon now. You better go lie down. . . ."

But on the way back to her lodgings, Gwen figured it out. Only she figured it out woman fashion. Which is to say she oversimplified it tremendously as women always do when their feelings are involved.

"Roak," she said.

"Yes, Gwen?"

"Fritz—doesn't know you're married, does he?"

"No," Roak said; "leastwise I don't think he does. . . ."

"He doesn't," Gwen said firmly. "Or else he'd have killed you."

"I'll be damned if I see how you figure that, baby," Roak said.

"It's simple. But you men are thickheaded as always. Don't you see, Roak—even at this late date, Fritz is probably dreaming of forcing you to right matters by means of a shotgun wedding."

Roak didn't see anything of the kind, but he had sense enough not to say so.

"Gwen," he said, "I think you ought to quit speculating 'til after you've rested a bit. Here we are. I'll come back later and—"

"No, you don't, Roak Garfield! You're coming upstairs with me right now!"

Roak grinned at her crookedly.

"With or without benefit of derringer this time?" he asked.

"Without. And without anything else, either. I'm in no mood for—that, Roak. I just want to talk. A common feminine failing, which I seem not to have lost. Only thing I haven't, it appears. . . ."

"All right, Gwen," Roak said.

Upstairs in her room, Gwen took off her shoes and stockings and lay down on the bed.

"Come sit here, Roak," she said, "where I can see you.

Or else you'll lie to me, as usual. And right now, what we've got to settle is too important for lies. . . ."

"All right," Roak said.

"Roak. . . ." her eyes searched his, probing deep. "Do you—love your wife?"

"No," Roak said.

"Why'd you marry her, then? Because you had to?"

"No. I married her because she's just about the richest female in Texas, since you want it straight out and ugly, Gwen. And also because she's pretty, and good, and sweet. But I put the first reason first."

"I doubt the pretty part," Gwen said venomously. "I'll bet she's crosseyed, humpbacked, old, and—"

Roak put his hand in his pocket and came out with the tintype. It was very clear and the lighting was exquisite. The traveling photographer who had stopped at the various ranches in 1868 with his wagon laboratory had a-chieved an effect that his successors in later years with their vastly improved equipment were never going to be quite able to equal. Hannah's blonde hair made a halo; her eyes were lightfilled, dreamy, tender. Roak handed the tintype to Gwen.

She lay there, studying it. She didn't say anything for a long, long time. When she did, her voice was choked.

"No, Roak," she said, "you didn't put the first reason first. Any man who's not head over heels in love with a girl like this one is just plain out of his mind!"

"Well, I never was right bright," Roak said.

"But *that* stupid you aren't either," Gwen whispered. "Oh, Roak, she—she's just too damn lovely, and—"

"Don't cry, Gwen, baby," Roak groaned; "please don't cry."

"All right," Gwen said, "I won't. Crying's a waste of time, now, isn't it? And I have so little time—"

Something in her tone got over to him. Made him shiver as though from sudden cold.

"What do you mean by that, Gwen?" he asked.

"Not what you're thinking. I—I couldn't. I'm not brave enough, though I've thought about it often enough, God knows. . . ."

"But," Roak said, "what do you aim to do?"

"Not to waste time—this precious little time I have with you. So I'm going to stay right here where I am 'til to-morrow, which is when your outfit leaves. You're going to stay here with me. Since you're the only man alive, it seems, I can respond to; maybe because I'm a poor romantic fool who has to actually love a man at least a little to respond to him at all, you can do me that favor—"

"So," Roak mocked, "you love me only a little, and pleasuring myself with you is doing you a favor? Baby, if I could get insulted, I would be now!"

She put out her arms to him.

"It's not an insult, Roak," she said quietly; "rather, it's a compliment. And a hell of a bigger compliment than you deserve. I don't love you a little. I love you with all the capacity I have for loving, so much so that I try never to think about it, or examine it too closely, because what I feel for you is something on the general order of earth-quakes, hurricanes, and other such catastrophes of nature —utterly terrifying, even to me. And your loving me in your too-expert style—which is another thing I try never to think about because I don't want to mull over how you learned all that—*is* a favor. Say—I'm storing up warmth against the cold ahead; accumulating a stock of feeling before I go back to numbness—even, if you'll pardon the sentimentality, a few fond and foolish memories to cherish. So now, Mr. Roak Garfield, if you will be so kind!"

So there were that night and the morning after that until eleven o'clock to remember. Especially that morning when she clung to him wordlessly and cried until her eyes were two slits swollen shut in her pale face, and her mouth a wide bruise moving, moving against the hollow of his throat while the salt of her tears played all hell with the claw marks she had raked all over him, until he said:

"Get up and get dressed. I'm taking you to St. Louis with me. And when we get there, I'm going to buy you a dressmaking shop or a milliner's or something like that. . . ."

She tried to open her eyes, but she couldn't, so she whispered: "Why?"

"Because I don't want you to forget this," he said; "I don't want you to get it all blurred over in your mind by what came after it, for the wrong reasons like having to eat so you can go on living. And I want you to live respectably so when one day a really decent fellow, the kind you deserve, as completely different from me as possible, comes along, you can marry him and have a fine life from then on in—"

"No!" she said. "No! Not ever! I—"

"Shut up, Gwen," he said; "never is a long, long time."

Then, getting on the train, there were Bart Nevis and his bride in the same car, so that Roak, out of prudence, moved with Gwen to another car, feeling Bart's black eyes like augers boring holes in his back. But that didn't do any good because they had hardly settled in their new seats when Bart was towering over them.

"Roak," he said solemnly, "can I have a word with you in the smoking car, please?"

Roak looked at Gwen.

"Go with him," she said quietly; "you owe him an explanation, Roak—after the way we fouled up his wedding. Only—one thing, Roak. . . ."

"Yes, baby?"

"Tell him the truth. If you can. If you've got it in you. Please, Roak."

"Yes, Gwen," Roak said, "the truth it is."

"So that's how it is," Bart said heavily. "You're damned right. You are obligated to her. Maybe a mite too much. Lord God, I wouldn't like to be in the spot you're in now. Nor to have to carry your conscience around with me. . . ."

"It's no fun," Roak said.

"But," Bart said, "there are obligations and obligations. You know where your first one lies, boy?"

"Yes," Roak said. "With Hannah. With my kid."

"Right," Bart said. "So what do you aim to do?"

Roak told him.

"Hmm," Bart said, "a dressmaking shop, eh? Costing all of $5,000? Not a bad idea. But how are you going to explain the shortage to Hannah? She can figure to the penny how much money we ought to have made. Been in this business all her life, you know."

"Damned if I know, but I'll think of something," Roak said.

Suddenly, unexpectedly, Bart put out his hand. Roak took it.

"You're an off horse, Roak," he said, "but at bottom you're a white man. Now I got to go pacify Ruth. She thinks that hombres who cheat on their wives ought to be lynched. . . ."

Roak grinned at him.

"Maybe she's right," he said.

So he went back to where Gwen waited in the other car. And afterwards there was the hotel in St. Louis where, the fury burned out of her, she'd made what he was going to have to remember that much worse by being gentle tender. And St. Joe, where they'd gone to find the little shop, because nobody knew her there, and had found it; and again St. Louis where she'd insisted upon coming back with him and where she'd stood on the dock long after the old sternwheeler he was on had butted out of sight around

the bend, still clutching the money he'd given her to buy
the shop with between her two hands and crying.

So he got back to the Bar F more than a week after
Bart Nevis and his new wife. He had to ride all the way
out there from the stage station—with Pepe driving the
buckboard they'd sent to meet him, had been, in fact, sending to meet all the stages since the day that Bart and Ruth
arrived, because he, Roak, hadn't wired, in reality couldn't
wire them word of when he planned to arrive—not daring
to open his mouth to ask Pepe what he needed to know
most of all: whether either Bart or Ruth had let slip anything about what had happened in Abilene, or if Bart had
forgotten and told the Captain in Hannah's presence the
exact amount they'd got for the cattle, because having to
explain a shortage of $5,000 to her would be in itself
enough to start more fireworks than he felt up to handling
right now.

He doubted that Bart had said anything. But Ruth was
another matter. And if she and Hannah hit it off, more
than likely her pity for Hannah would show. Until one day
Hannah would be forced to ask her:

"Why do you look at me like that, Ruth?"

And out it would come.

He was thinking like that when they came up to the
house. By then it was already dark and the lamps were
lit. They spilled little yellow pools through the windows
upon the dark. And Roak stood there looking at them, a
stranger and alone.

"Aren't you going to go in, señor?" Pepe asked.

"Yes," Roak said, and went to the door. When he
pushed it open, he could see them sitting around the supper table: Hannah and Captain Furniss and Bart and
Ruth. Hannah had softened and rounded into a pre-
Raphaelite madonna though it was only August now and
her time wouldn't come until October. Bart looked serious,
a little puffed up and proud of himself like all new hus-

bands, while Ruth glowed with almost visible happiness and content.

But Captain Jesse looked like hell.

Something—a sound he made, maybe, an almost inaudible scrape of his booted foot—caught Ruth's attention. She turned; and the happiness, the glow, drained abruptly out of her eyes. Instead they spoke, silently, with words that Roak himself supplied out of his own imagination, out of his deep and festering guilt, for surely Ruth Nevis knew no such terms:

You miserable, cheating bastard. So you didn't stay with your whore. So you came back, after all. . . .

Hannah saw Ruth's glance, saw her frozen into that tension-stretched position, and following her new friend's gaze, hung there herself in the very core of that sudden silence that went on and on until the ticking of the clock on the mantel became hammerstrokes, thundercrash loud, jarring the very surface of Roak's brain. Then, very slowly, she came up from her chair, the motion dreamy; crossed that room like a sleepwalker, moving, Roak was sure, in a pool of light that accompanied her, her footsteps floating, as upon water, to the tune of music unheard.

And, in that moment, seeing her like that, rosy, and rounded into the lineaments of maternity, quite suddenly he loved her with a love that was sadness's self, offering her humbly and from afar what recompense he had to give, begging her with his eyes the lifetime of pardon that must forever be unvoiced, unsaid.

"Roak," she whispered tremulously; then: "Oh, Roak —oh, my darling! I thought you'd never come!"

He held her, kissed her as though she were a goblet of the most fragile crystal in this world, as though even a touch would shatter her. As they walked back toward the table, Bart got up, put out his big hand. And Roak recognized what was in his eyes: relief. Through Bart's gruff-voiced greeting: "Welcome home, partner; glad you made it safe . . . ," Roak's own thought ran, piping the high, discordant note of astonishment: Why, he thought I wasn't coming back! He thought I was going to take the $35,000 and run off with Gwen! And Bart continued in that slow, awkward tone of a man unaccustomed to lying:

"Told Han that spell o' sickness that laid you up in St. Louis wasn't nothing much, but she wouldn't believe me. . . ."

"Still less, now," Hannah said tartly, "seeing how fine he looks. Come on, Roak, take advantage of the fact that I'm in no state to quirt you, and tell me her name!"

"Which one," Roak said, "the redhead, the blonde or the brunette?"

"The brunette," Hannah said. "I know your tastes. . . ."

"You're right," Roak said, looking straight into Ruth's eyes that were blue ice now, frozen into complete contempt. "Only you already know her name, Han. I laid up in St. Louis a week, a-bawling my eyes out like a yearling calf 'cause she found out I was married and took Bart instead o' me. Think maybe we could arrange a swap, Bart?"

"Not on your life!" Bart said; then: " 'Scuse me, Hannah! I didn't mean that like it sounded—"

"I know, I know," Hannah wailed in mock anger; "now that I'm big and ugly and out of shape, nobody loves me!"

Ruth spoke up suddenly, then.

"I love you, Hannah," she said. "What's more, I envy you. I wish I were like you are right now!"

"Give me time, Ruthie," Bart grinned, "give me time!"

They all laughed then, and the tension went out of the air.

"How're you feeling, Cap'n Jess?" Roak asked.

"Rotten," Hannah's father said. "Got a pain in my big gut that's damn nigh killing me. . . ."

"Father, you should send for Doctor Murray!" Hannah said. "You've been complaining of that pain for months now, and—"

"Ate too much Mexican chili as a youngster," the Captain said. "Gut's plumb wore out. Ain't nothing serious. Well, boy, Bart tells me you held up your end nobly. Saved his life in the river. That took bottom—"

"No more than it took for Marvis Hart and Posey to save mine," Roak said. "An outfit plumb has to stick together on the trail, Cap'n."

"God's own truth. Still, I'm glad you made out all right. Talk about that later, in private. Got some plans for you, boy—"

"Thank you, sir," Roak said.

There was a silence. Roak broke it finally. He was afraid of silences now.

"And your pa," he said to Ruth, "he didn't come with you?"

"Nope," Bart said, "I thought I told you that. I set him up in the hardware business in St. Joe with that $5,000 I won from you in that there poker game. By the way, boy, I'd rightly like to pay you back. Playing poker for blood is all right 'twixt strangers, but—"

Bless you, Roak thought. You've covered me from every angle, haven't you? Aloud, he said:

"The heck you say! You trimmed me fair 'n' square, Bart. Call that there store my wedding present to you both."

Then he turned to Hannah.

"Honey, don't folks feed prodigal sons and returning husbands down Texas way?"

"Oh, Roak, I'm sorry!" Hannah said. "I'll have Josefina get you something right away. . . ."

"No, don't get up, Han," Ruth said; "I'll go call her."

"Yep," Bart said absently, "in St. Joe. Hope the old coot'll make it. 'Pears to me he ain't got much sand—"

It was then that it hit Roak. St. Joe—where he'd taken Gwen because nobody knew her there. That wooden-headed, whining weak sister that Ruth had for a pa—likewise in St. Joe, and knowing, because he had to know by now, because it wasn't human nature for Ruth not to have told him all about Gwen—if not all, a damned sight too much by anybody's reckoning. Well, the cards had a way of falling out like that, no matter how you shuffled 'em. And St. Joe was a mighty big town; maybe they wouldn't meet, maybe that silly old coot wouldn't remember Gwen, recognize her, or maybe he'd be gentleman enough not to say anything if he did. Maybe. And maybe the Mississippi would flow upstream, and a jack rabbit would spit into a coyote's eye.

Have to write Gwen, he thought, have to warn her. . . .

Then he felt his wife's hand on his arm.

"What ails you, darling?" Hannah said.

Chapter Thirteen

THE COLD came early that year. There was hoarfrost on the chaparral by the end of September, and the pinto's breath and his own made smoke. The rains came down steady and slow, dripping off the brim of his Stetson as he rode. He wasn't going anywhere in particular (does a man ever go anywhere in particular? Aren't the hoping, believing, planning so much breath fog on a cold day?), just making a show of line riding because he had to do something; because the waiting for his son to be born was getting to be a damned sight too much, because the bad, ugly pain always in Captain Jesse's eyes now wasn't a thing a body could sit around looking at.

He thought, as he did daily, almost hourly now, about Fritz Heindrichs. About what he'd do when Fritz came. Because Fritz would come, and nothing short of killing could stop him when he did.

Roak's stomach contracted, thinking that. He didn't want to kill Fritz Heindrichs. In fact, he couldn't. He knew the score now. All of it. Gwen had told him. And it added up: one scarred face, one sister lost, living, irrevocably lost. The baby Fritz's wife had aborted from the shock of seeing that face. The wife herself, first lost, now dead—of cold and hunger, Gwen had said, wandering the streets of Cincinnati, half-mad, seeking shelter, seeking bread.

He lifted his face to the rain. It was ice-tipped, made a stinging. He bent his head again and slouched in the saddle, slow riding, the drops dripping off his Stetson's brim and chasing one another down the yellow oilskin of his slicker.

No. He couldn't kill Fritz Heindrichs. Not on top of all that. While Fritz—meant to kill him. No—to drive him to his death. How? Dear Jesus, how? By striking at him through Hannah and the child? Fritz who had lost wife and child and sister through his fault?

Good thing I haven't got a sister too, Roak thought.

Yes, that was what Fritz would likely do. So now he'd have to be on the watch every minute. From now on. All the rest of his life, maybe.

But it was no good thinking about that, so he turned his pinto's head back toward the ranch house, moving steady and slow through the driving rain.

That night he saw Josefina heading toward Captain Jesse's room with the tray.

"Here," he said, "give me that, Josefina. I'll take it to the Cap'n. Got to talk to him anyhow."

He could see Josefina looking at him oddly, but he had no time to worry about what went on in the mind of a Mexican serving girl. He took the tray out of her hands and shouldered open the door to Captain Furniss's room with it in his arms.

"Howdy, son," the Captain said tiredly, "glad you come to see me. I've been meaning to have a little talk with you, but I just kept putting it off. Now's as good a time as any, I reckon. . . ."

"No," Roak said, "*after* you eat, Cap'n Jesse."

The Captain's smile was bitter.

"Son," he said, "I'm going to tell you the truth. I can't eat. I take some milk and whisky mixed. Nothing else will stay on my stomach. Beyond that is the other fact that I'm dying. I'll be gone afore Christmas, maybe even afore Thanksgiving time. . . ."

"Lord God, Captain Jess!" Roak began.

"Let me have my say, boy. Something's poisoning me—"

"Poisoning!" Roak said. "Who th' living hell—"

Then, in the pause during which the Captain drew in a long breath to speak, Roak heard the involuntary rattle of the door. He crossed to it in one long stride, jerked it open. Josefina almost fell into the room. Captain Jesse laughed feebly.

"Josie," he said, "how many times do I have to tell you that pressing 'em ag'in keyholes is going to ruin the shape of your ears?"

"*Pardóneme, Capitán!*" Josefina wailed. "But when I heard the señor husband of your daughter say *envenenado,* I—"

"You hear too damn much, Josie. Now, get out of here," the Captain said.

"Look, Captain," Roak said after the maid had scurried from the room, "*she* brings you your grub. And she *was* listening outside that door, and—"

"Nonsense," the Captain said; "Josie's as good as gold. Besides, you tell me something, Roak: what reason would *she* have for wanting me dead?"

"None," Roak said slowly. "The only folks on earth who would stand to benefit by your passing would be— Han, and maybe, through her—me. Hope you don't think I've been doctoring your victuals, sir—or paying somebody else to do it. . . ."

Captain Jesse looked at him.

"No," he said; "I don't think that, boy. I don't believe you're that impatient. Besides, I don't think somebody's poisoning me. Wasn't even what I said. I said 'something.' Something inside my body itself. I know you've got nothing to do with it, because it started nearly six months before you got here. And it's been getting worse, slowly, all the time. So, at the risk of making you impatient, I'll tell you right now what I've been a-meaning to: I'm leaving you and Han the place with the exception of that southern brush stretch, which I feel ought to go to Bart now that he's acquired himself such a sweet little missus. Compensation for all the years of loyal service he's given me. You don't object, do you?"

"Except for losing Bart's services as foreman," Roak said, "no, sir—not at all. But I'm telling you something, sir: first thing tomorrow morning, I'm going to ride to Brownsville and send Doctor Murray a wire. And if he can't come, or can't help much after he gets here, I'm going to round up every sawbones in these United States who ever specialized in stomach troubles and bring 'em down here, even if I have to drag 'em. That's how impatient I am. That's what I want, sir: you around to dandle your grandchildren on your knee. And not just this one— all four of the little wranglers Han and I are planning to have. . . ."

The Captain studied him, came to the only conclusion possible, because, for reasons he would have been hard put to even explain to himself, Roak Garfield was trembling, close to tears, and had never spoken with such utter sincerity before in all his life.

Slowly the sick man smiled.

"Thanks, son," he said gruffly. "Glad you feel like that. And I'm gladder still to see you mean it. All right, get Murray. Not because he'll do any good, because I'm beyond help now; but because you 'n' my baby both will feel better if you do, and it'll maybe stave off some ugly talk from folks who ought to know better, but won't. . . ."

"I never thought about that," Roak said slowly. "Come on now, sir; try to eat some of this here bait before it gets too cold. . . ."

But Roak didn't get Doctor Murray. He didn't get anybody. For at one o'clock that same night, Captain Jesse woke the whole house with his screaming. He went on screaming until, at four o'clock in the morning, he died.

Nobody would ever know who said it first. But it was evident on the very face of things that one of the Mexican vaqueros on the Bar F must have talked with Josefina and that he in his turn must have repeated that word *envenenado* to another and he to another until finally—but not slowly, because they hadn't even got Captain Jess under the prairie earth he had so loved before the riders were gathering—one of them must have said it in front of a white man who knew enough border Spanish to translate the *envenenado* back into the word "poisoned" that Josefina had heard in the first place. Which did not matter. Maybe they would have thought it up themselves without any outward stimulation, considered the fact of Roak Garfield's highly unorthodox marriage to the Captain's daughter, and the attendant circumstances of the Captain's visible and rapid decline coming hard upon the heels of an event that everybody who had ears to listen and an inclination to poke his nose into what didn't concern him, in short, everybody, knew the Captain had bitterly and violently opposed.

There was in their action a sort of rough justice. They sought out and found among the Captain's English-speaking hands the two who'd been called in to witness the new will. Then, the fact of there being a new will and the evidence that its contents, as any fool could plainly see, were motives enough for a fancy little Eastern dude to sort of hasten the good Captain's journey into the hereafter being established, they—all the men who had been neighbors and friends of Captain Furniss's except, of course, the Martínez, who, being Mexicans, naturally weren't invited, led by old Rod Cameron of the Flying U, seconded, more than a little reluctantly, by Hank Flynn, his range boss—rode down to the new 'dobe bungalow the Captain had had built on the edge of the brush country as a wedding present for Bart Nevis and his bride.

Bart came out at their call, stuffing his nightshirt into his recently donned pants.

"Well, friends?" he said.

Rod Cameron told him. Bart heard him out.

"I don't believe it," he said flatly. "Not that I think Roak Garfield is too good, but 'cause I think he's too smart. Why should he pizon the Cap'n to get what to all intents and purposes he's got already? With the Cap'n getting old, even the running of this place was going to have to go more and more his way. Don't make sense. On that basis, you could suspect me. The Cap'n left me these here brush ranges—"

"Don't nobody kill nobody over no thorn thickets," Rod Cameron said heavily, "but the rest of the Bar F spread is worth a mighty heap. And suppose he was scared of the Captain's finding out something that would make him change his will one more time?"

"There wasn't anything the Captain could have found out," Bart began; but from the darkness inside the still open door, Ruth's voice cut through his words.

"Wasn't there?" she said, her voice flat, twanging, cold. "Not even that your fine friend Roak Garfield was the kind of a skunk who would spend the whole time he was in Abilene in the arms of a—a fallen woman? And her, the woman, he himself caused to fall in the first place? And knowing that his own wife was in the family way when he left? And killing a man in a gunfight over his cowtown dove in spite of all that?"

"He did not!" Bart said. "The sheriff killed Prince Parker, and—"

"So," Hank Flynn said, "there's more than a mite of truth in what your missus is sayin, eh, Bart?"

"Enough," Bart said, "that I ought to take a quirt to her for saying it. And even more for what she's leaving out—"

"Like what?" John Farrell, another rancher, said.

"Like she's talking about the man who willingly of-fered up his own life for mine in the middle of the Arkan-sas River. So count me out. I won't go after the man who damned near died to save my life, and especially not over common gossip and silly suspicions. Or even 'cause Ruth's mad at Roak's getting the best ranges, which as the Cap'n's son-in-law he's entitled to. Besides, that filly in Abilene was two things: mighty fine, and out of that part of Roak's life before he even met Han. Without hanging any halo or wings on myself, I can say I know all you men daggoned well—and in that direction, as the good Lord Himself said, it purely appears to me that not a single one of us is rightly fittin' to chunk no rocks. . . ."

"All right," Rod Cameron said; "I'll accept that, Bart. But ain't no harm in us asking Mr. Pilgrim Garfield a few questions, appears to me. I'd appreciate it if you wouldn't warn him—'cause if he's as guilty as I damn well think he is, he'll go bellying through the willows so blame fast—"

Bart stood there, looking at them.

"All right," he said, "I won't. But on the condition that you fellows don't go off half-cocked. Leaving a woman who's heavy with child a widow ain't a thing to be under-taken lightly. Besides which, if you decorate a cottonwood with Roak and later on it turns out you were wrong, you'll have me to deal with—legal or otherwise."

"You threatening us, Bart?" Hank Flynn asked.

"Nope. Just telling you, Hank," Bart said. "And since the good Lord give us all a mighty short ration of breath, I don't mean to waste mine."

Then he turned and went back in the house.

He sat by the window for that long moment they ling-ered, worrying the thing over in their minds. After they had ridden away, he still sat there with his back turned toward his wife. Ruth came over to where he sat, and put her two hands on his shoulders. It was like touching stone.

"Bart—" she said.

He did not answer her.

"Bart!" she said again, her voice rising, edging. "Bart, please! You—you're angry with me. . . . We haven't been married two whole months and already—"

He stood up then, the bulk of him rising black against the blackness.

"Maybe," he said, "we've been married two months too long."

He went outside then, and stood there looking at the white dust rising against the night, far away now, where the riders went. After a time, Ruth came out and touched his arm.

"Here," she whispered; "here, Bart take this. . . ."

He turned then, looked down. She had his riding quirt in her hands.

"No," he said; "when things get to the stage that a body even thinks a thing like that is necessary, it's too late —already it's too late. . . ."

"Bart," she said, so low he had to bend to hear her, "you—you think it's too late between us now, don't you?"

He looked away from her toward that white dust rising. It was farther still, now, growing dim.

"And I promised not to warn him!" he said. "I promised. . . ."

She whirled then, ran back into the house. Came out again. She had on a dress over her nightgown. He could tell that because the nightgown was longer than the dress. She moved over to the corral fence.

"Nell!" she called, and the tame gray mare he'd given her came at once, nuzzling between the bars for her accustomed lump of sugar. Ruth opened the corral gate and led the gray out. Then she went about the business of saddling her.

Bart watched her without saying anything. But when she mounted, he caught the mare's bridle, said:

"Where the devil do you think you're going, Ruth?"

She sat there looking at him. It was too dark for him to see her tears. But when she spoke he heard them.

"Away," she said. "To the end of the night, Bart. To the edge of the sky. To find the place where it's never too late; because, maybe, it's always too soon. . . ."

"Now, look, Ruth," he began; "I—"

"If your pony broke his leg, you'd shoot him, wouldn't you, Bart?" she said. "Well, this hurts worse than that. Far, far worse—"

"Ruthie!" he said. "You wouldn't!"

"No," she said, finally, "I wouldn't, Bart. Only I need to be by myself a little—to—to think. To try to find out how—"

"What?" Bart said.

"To make you love me again," Ruth whispered. "Please, Bart, let me go, now. . . ."

He stood there. There was always a certain amount of danger involved in riding out on the prairie at night. She might meet a lone rustler, or even a gang of them. Or she might spook some ornery old cuss of a longhorn who knew just how to get up under a horse's belly and throw him over on his side. Or her mount might step in a gopher hole, or—any number of things that could happen but generally never did. There was a certain amount of danger, all right; but it was maybe less than the danger their marriage was in right now. Bart took the calculated risk. Turned the mare loose. Stood back.

"Thank you, darling," Ruth said.

He stood there, watching her ride off. Then he saw that she wasn't riding toward the open prairie but toward the *malpaís,* the badlands, where the ridges of frozen lava would cut her pony's hooves to ribbons in minutes if she didn't follow the narrow, crooked path he had shown her, the path that would bring her to Captain Jesse's *casa grande* in a shade over a half an hour instead of the two hours it was going to take those riders—who didn't know

about that pass and so, naturally, couldn't have taken it—
to skirt around the badlands.

He started to call out, ride after her, maybe, do something, anything; but then he stopped. He didn't *know* she
was going there. And he sure Lord didn't know what she
was going to do if she went there, because she didn't cotton
to Roak Garfield none a-tall. And as long as he didn't
actually know, nobody could say he had broken his word.

Roak was lying there beside Hannah with his two hands
under his head, staring at the ceiling. So now he was the
owner of the Bar F, and how did he feel? Like a pig. Almost like a murderer, because Captain Jesse's grief at the
way things had turned out had almost surely hastened his
end. Damned little sign of that respect he'd been counting on, either. The way folks had looked at him at the
Captain's funeral, a body would have thought—

The stone tinkled against the window pane. He lay
there, unmoving. Then the voice said:

"Roak!"

A woman's voice. Roak looked at Hannah to see if she
had heard. He might as well have saved himself the trouble.

"So!" Hannah hissed. "You haven't even any respect
for the way I am now, have you, Roak Garfield? Not to
mention my poor father's not even being cold in his grave!"

"Roak!" the voice came again; then it added: "Hannah!"

"Why," Hannah said, "why, it's Ruth!"

"Baby," Roak said, "you got a way of jumping to con-
clusions sometimes that—"

"Is usually right," Hannah said. "Go let her in, Roak
Garfield."

"Thanks, Ruth," Roak said; "I thank you mighty kindly
—the more so because I thought you couldn't stand the
sight of me. . . ."

Ruth stood there, looking at him.

"I still can't," she said. "Please forgive me, Hannah. He's your husband, but—"

"But he's an ornery breed of polecat," Hannah said. "I know that. You're perfectly right, Ruth. I can't stand him, either. Only it happens that I love him, which doesn't make sense; but there it is. Roak, what do you plan to do now?"

Roak stood there.

"Now, that depends," he said. "Han, do you think I slipped some loco weed in your old man's grub?"

"And if I did?" Hannah retorted.

"I'd wait right here," Roak said, "and receive your father's friends mighty kindly."

Hannah stared at him. Her hand crept up to the base of her throat, hung there.

"You mean it," Ruth said. "I can see you do. Hannah, tell him you don't believe that! There's no time!"

"No," Hannah said, "I don't believe you poisoned my father. And Roak—"

"Yes, Han?"

"I need you. My baby needs you. So don't—"

"Hannah, they'll be along any minute now!" Ruth said.

"—don't give way to that sadness you've had in you ever since you came back from Abilene," Hannah said. "I'll never ask you—about that. Because I don't want to know. Because I couldn't stand knowing. Now, go. Don't come back 'til I send for you."

"What d'you aim to do?" Roak said.

"Get Doctor Murray. Have my father exhumed, an autopsy performed. Prove to these suspicious fools what it was he died of. Which will take time. Go on, Roak!"

"Hannah," Roak said, "you can ask about that. And I'll tell you. Because I'm not ashamed, and because I even think you'd understand—"

"No!" Hannah said. "I don't want—"

But Ruth cut her off.

"Roak," she said, "will you accept my apologies, and then get the blazes out of here?"

"Your apologies?" Roak said.

"Yes. You aren't what I thought you were. Now, for God's sake, go!" Ruth said.

Roak went into the living room where the gun rack was. He put out his hand to take the Captain's Henry repeating rifle, but then he stopped. With that fifteen-shot rifle, he could stand off an army, pick off that would-be lynch mob one by one at distances their six-guns wouldn't even carry. Then what? What had killing ever settled? What good ever came out of powder smoke and blood?

He put the Henry back. Took instead that curious weapon the Captain had called his riot gun: a double-barreled shotgun with the barrels sawed off to a quarter of their original length and the stock cut down to a semipistol grip. Once when the Captain had been surrounded by Cormona's brigands, he'd fired this hand cannon twice and found himself alone, having dropped twelve men with two shots. If a body ever had to shoot his way out of a tight corner, the riot gun was the thing to do it with. Only. . . .

Only it still meant killing.

It's my life or theirs, Roak thought; then he saw the cartridges stacked up in boxes below the guns. All sizes, .38's, .45's, .44's, .50's; and the shotgun shells, buckshot, several grades of birdshot. . . . He put out his hand, took the cartridges loaded for quail, the lightest, finest shot of all, that couldn't possibly kill a man unless he caught them so close they hadn't had time to scatter, and not even then with a gun sawed off like this one. He broke open the box and dumped the shells into the pockets of his coat. Then he went out to the corral to saddle his pinto, but it came to him before he got there that he'd better ride a grulla brush pony who'd be a sight less visible than the paint.

Besides, since he'd likely have to hide out in the brush country, the paint wouldn't do. The thorns would ruin him forever. So he saddled the mule-hipped grulla and started away from there. But the minute he got clear of the ranch, he saw them converging on him from every direction. So he pulled up the mouse-gray cayuse and waited. He wanted them bunched. They were still too strung out for that hand cannon to get them all.

"Roak Garfield," Rod Cameron began, "you're under arrest—"

Roak eared those two hammers back.

"For what?" he said.

"For the murder of Cap'n Jesse Furniss!" Rod roared; and that was all. It was over then. Roak fired twice, shooting for the horses, and by the time they'd fought that screaming, shrilling broil of outraged horseflesh into something like a standstill, he was gone, only Hank Flynn having got off one wild shot before his pony reared. When they had their mounts under control—if control was even the word for the precarious balance they were maintaining atop horses stinging and dancing from the birdshot under their hides—they weren't even sure what direction he had taken.

"Goddamn him!" old Rod yelled. "The murdering little rat, he—"

"Hold on there, Mr. Cameron," Hank Flynn said; "you ever seen what a sawed-off scattergun can do when it's loaded buck 'n' ball and aimed at folks?"

"What th' devil d'you mean, Hank? He shot at us, didn't he?"

"And never hit a one of us, close as he was. Which was damn bad shooting, or damn good. I'm saying it was good shooting, sir. And you notice another thing?"

"What's that?" Canby Tyler, another of the riders, growled.

"Our broncs ain't even hurt bad. He used birdshot.

Which means he wasn't even aiming to kill nobody. Begging your pardon, Mr. Cameron, but this here makes me think. . . ."

"Makes you think what, Hank?" Rod Cameron asked.

"That Roak Garfield didn't kill Cap'n Jess. And that he's so sure he's going to be able to prove it that he wants to stay good neighbors with us. Be able to say, 'Now, look, boys, when I had y'all dead to rights, I only peppered your ponies a little. . . .' "

"You know what, Rod?" John Farrell said. " 'Pears to me Hank's making a mighty heap of sense."

"Yep, he is," Rod Cameron said slowly, "as far as he goes. Only how do we know that fancy little dude ain't trying to keep peace with us, not because he ain't guilty, but because he's so damned sure of pulling the wool over our eyes?"

"I vote we give him a chance to prove it one way or another," Canby Tyler said.

"Me, too," another of the riders threw in.

"He's long gone anyhow," old Rod said. "The best we can do is not to smoke him out of the chaparral. Give him a chance to come out himself. . . ."

He got down then, heavily, from his mount. Ran his fingers over the animal's hide. Found one of the lumps.

"Hank," he said, "hold this here cayuse for me, won't you?"

Hank got down, took the bridles of both his own and his employer's horse in his hands. Rod took out a penknife and dug deep under the pony's hide. The horse backed off, neighing shrilly.

"Hold still, damn it!" Cameron muttered. Then he held up the tiny pellet of lead. "Birdshot, all right. So we have to go along with Hank that he didn't aim to kill—this time. Reckon I better have a talk with that poor child tomorrow. Maybe she knows something that might— Oh, well. C'mon, boys, let's get along home. . . ."

Roak sat there on the grulla brush pony in the thickest part of the brush. During the War he'd been hit three times, twice lightly and the third time at Nashville, that ball through his lung that had finished the War for him and damned near finished him. But it wasn't a thing a man got used to. He could feel the strength draining out of him where Hank Flynn's wild chancy shot had gone into the upper part of his left arm. He was bleeding like a stuck pig, and any chance he'd had of hiding out in the *brasada* was gone forever. If he didn't get to something remotely resembling civilization pronto, he was going to bleed to death. Or if he didn't bleed to death, that arm was going to rot on him, go gangrenous, and they'd have to take it off before that dead blue color and that stink spread too far.

He knew all the possibilities of a gunshot wound and none of them were good. Even remembering how it felt to have somebody digging around inside you probing for a ball was enough to make the cold sweat pop out on his forehead. Each of the three times he had been hit before had been bad, and the ball he'd got in his thigh and the one that had dug a furrow along his ribs had caused him as much suffering as the one through his lung; maybe more, because from that one he'd been out most of the time. But this one was maybe the worst one of all, because in the War there had been medical corpsmen and doctors who, though they were ignorant butchers, were nevertheless better than nothing. And now he not only had nothing, but if he rode out of here to get help, he'd most likely end up trimming a tree long before Christmas.

He thought about all that. He thought about it all very slowly and carefully while he unwound his bandana from around his neck and stuffed one end of it into the hole in his arm. He should have done that a long time ago, but he hadn't thought about it. And now he was very weak and alone in the *brasada,* the brush country, with nothing but a slope-hipped grulla pony for company. In the end he did what he had to do now, the thing he'd sworn he'd never do because the risks were too great and the consequences unpredictable: he rode south. Crossed the Rio Grande.

When he came up to Belén's house, it was already morning. He was swaying in the saddle. He was dog sick and his left arm had stiffened into a log of firewood. Only logs didn't hurt like that. He climbed down. He was very clumsy and slow doing it, because getting off a horse isn't a thing a man does easily with only one hand. He went up to the door, knocked on it.

Belén opened the door, stood there looking at him.

"No," she said very quietly, "now it is different. Before what we did concerned only us and hurt nobody. But now you have a wife—a good woman who presumably loves you. So—no, Roak. You will please to go away. . . ."

He stood there. He was holding hard against the loosening, the give, the creeping black. He was afraid he was going to fall at her feet, and, as always, that seemed an ignominy to him. He didn't say anything to her because he was also afraid that if he opened his mouth what would come out would be a scream. So he turned back to his horse. He put his good hand onto the pommel of the saddle and tried to mount like that. Only he couldn't. He tried it three times with Belén standing there watching him, believing him drunk, her black eyes soft with pity, until he turned his face away from her so she wouldn't see the hot tears streaking the grime on his face, leaning there against the grulla pony, and crying.

Then he felt her hand on his arm, heard her voice saying:

"I will aid thee to mount, Roak, for this of the wine is a bad drunkenness that—" Her voice broke off abruptly, and turning, he saw her staring at her own hand, at the thick red that was stealing out between her fingers. *"Ai-yi!"*

she wailed. *"Maria Santísima, Madre de Dios!* Again he is killed, and I revile him for drunkenness!"

Then she slipped an arm under his shoulder and led him into the house. She eased him down upon the bed; then all the lights in the world went out at once, and even her voice came over to him dimly, saying: *"Madre mía, ten piedad! Te suplico, salvalo. El pecado era mío y sí requieres una vida, toma la mía, querida Madre de Dios! Te imploro! Te suplico! No lo dejes morir!"* But he didn't understand what she was saying, had no way of comprehending that she was begging the dear Mother of God for his life, offering her own in his stead, taking upon herself the full burden of their mutual sin. He didn't understand that. All he understood was that she was crying. So he said:

"Don't cry, Belén. Please, please, don't cry. I'm not worth. . . ." Then he stopped talking, for by then there was not even sound.

When he came back, Doctor Arjona was there, and the instruments were already boiling in a pot above the fire. The fat little doctor saw his eyes.

"Ah," he said, "have the favor to seek some tequila, Belén. Pour it into him until he is unconscious, for this is going to hurt with an insupportable badness, and—"

Roak grinned at him feebly.

"What the devil are you saying, Benito?" he said.

"I'm saying that you must drink a liter of tequila. Maybe more. Or that I should hit you over the head with a blunt instrument, because this is going to hurt. And you must not move or scream because where that ball is there are also some of the big nerves that control the motion of your arm. So if you do not want it dangling uselessly. . . ."

"No," Roak whispered; "no tequila. I won't scream. I promise you—"

"All right," Benito Arjona said. "Holy Mother of God, guide my hand!"

Belén stood there, holding him. Her eyes were very black and soft. She gripped his two hands very hard and held him, feeling his body going rigid as a bar of iron under that torture, seeing the sweat beading on his forehead, and she having no hand free to wipe it away, standing there holding him, watching helplessly while the sweat beads became streams, rivulets running down into his eyes, and his head going back, back, his mouth coming open under that intolerable anguish, and she, knowing that in another second he was going to scream, leaned forward swiftly and stopped his mouth with her own, absorbing that anguish so that Benito Arjona saw clearly the shudder and scrape of that soundlessness, that intaken cry quivering the soft flesh of her throat as she clung her mouth to his, and her tears in the lamplight were blood and fire.

Then the forceps came out with the ball. Doctor Arjona stood back looking at them. He sighed.

"You can turn him loose, Belén. He has no further need to cry," he said.

Roak lay in her arms with his head pillowed against her breasts. It was the third night he had lain like that, but the first two there was nothing he could do about it because the sickness and the fever were in him still. But now he knew that the weakness and the pain were no longer enough. He raised his head, said: "Belén. . . ."

"*Sí,*" she said simply; "for there is no way for us to stay apart, is there, my Roak? And I have envy of thee. *Te amo y te quiero.* I love thee and I want thee. I want thy body which is very fine. So now let us do quickly what we must before I remember the gravity of this sin or even that it is a sin. . . ."

He kissed her, then. A long time. A very long time.

"No—not quickly. Slowly and with savor," he said.

Chapter Fourteen

HE KNEW what the risks were. If you could call them risks. Because if he started back across the river tonight, what was going to happen to him was closer to a certainty. Risks involved chance. And there weren't any chances for Roak Garfield now. They'd all run out on him. On both sides of the river they'd run out on him. But all the same he was going back.

He had come home last night to his tender refuge to find the street before Belén's house filled with horsemen. Hard-eyed Mexican horsemen with double cartridge belts making white x's across their chests and backs. Armed with carbines, revolvers, and machetes. *Bandoleros;* surely Juan Nepomuceno Cortina's band.

He had seen them in time. Turned his grulla brush pony into an alley. Made a wide circle through the sleeping town. Dismounted in a street back of the house. Started toward it on foot, the riot gun cocked and ready, creeping in soundlessly, quieter than a breath, the way he'd learned to walk during dismounted actions in the War.

He came up to the back door. Stood there, hearing Belén's voice saying very, very quietly:

"If you kill him, Ramón, you kill me. For I shall push this knife into my heart before your eyes. And do not try to take it away from me. I have others. Knives are cheap. . . ."

Ramón's voice came over to him, grave and slow, much heavier than he remembered its being; but then, it had been a year since he had seen the boy.

"Thou art dead now, sister," Ramón said flatly, sadly, calmly, speaking, it seemed to Roak, without anger but with another thing that was absolute, and thus absolutely terrible: the certainty of being right. "When a Benevides is dead to honor, living on becomes an offense in the nostrils of God. I shall weep if you die; I shall have perpetual masses sung for the salvation of your soul—if that now is possible. But I shall not cease to seek Roak Garfield because of thy threat, *hermanita*. I shall kill him, not in anger, but out of a certain necessity. And if thou diest because of this, I shall sorrow; but such a sorrow is more supportable than the one I feel now, and a thousand times more bearable than my shame at what you do. . . ."

There was silence, vibrant as a violin note above the range of sound. Roak could feel that silence. It had terror in it, and the feel of death. Then he heard Belén's voice whispering:

"He—he is armed. What if he kills *you*, Ramón?"

It was too dark for him to see Ramón shrug; but he knew the boy had shrugged.

"I die," Ramón said flatly. "It is not I who have to answer that question, *hermana mía*, but you. If, when we meet, he kills me, then what of thee?"

Her voice faltered, shuddered, died. Rose up once more, dark-winged with pain.

"I shall leave him. And then go mad. What else? Oh, Ramón!"

"So," Ramón said, "either way I win. But now I go. There is a certain Señor Cameron of the *rancho* Flying U who has committed the grave error of kicking a Mexican vaquero on his place. Tonight we visit the old gringo. *Adíos*, Belén—think well what you do. There are always the *conventos religiosos* for broken lives like thine; this of the dying is not a necessity, and the laying of violent hands upon thyself is a mortal sin. Better the veil of a nun than that, sister, better the life-long repentance and the service of Our Lord. . . ."

"Ramón—*tú*—" her voice was all edges, jagged, splintering; "Ramón—my brother—thou—thou wilt not promise not—not to—"

"Kill him? No. No, María de Belén Benevides Camargo —I say all thy name so thou wilt remember *who* thou art —such a promise is not possible. If I were to give it, there would remain no living Benevides standing tall in honor. So I cannot promise thee this. Neither my life nor thine is worth that much. . . ."

There was a silence, the sound of a kiss. Then Roak heard the clatter of Ramón's booted feet against the tiles. Heard from the street the hoof dance as he mounted, the jingle, clipclop, armed clangor, growing softer, going on. But he did not enter the house to comfort Belén. He could not comfort her, being himself comfortless.

Because it had to be now. Last night, tonight, tomorrow, his son had been, would be born. Last night, tonight, tomorrow, Hannah had been, would be facing that very nearly ultimate anguish in sorrow, and alone. Because he, Roak, was a coward. Because he'd muddied the waters of his life so utterly that—

No. Tonight he'd go. Even if they caught him, they wouldn't hang him before he'd seen his son.

He eased the grulla into the water, swam him across. Came out into the brush ranges that belonged to Bart Nevis now. Only it wasn't late enough. And there was just too damned much moonlight. Wait then. In here where the mesquite was thickest. Rest a while, gather his strength.

He sat there thinking that the thing between him and Belén was over now. Inescapably over. Entering into a duel with Ramón, he was lost. Dead in his blood, or standing with smoking gun above her brother's body, he was lost. Just as lost either way.

Then suddenly, wildly, he clapped spurs to the grulla. Because it had come back to him. Thinking about Ramón had brought it back. If he got to the Flying U first, if he warned old Rod Cameron, maybe they'd see him in a new light then; maybe they'd give him a chance. Then he could double back home, and even if the baby had already been born, he'd have his acceptable proof to give Hannah, he'd have reasons she'd understand. . . .

He pounded on, thinking that, riding at a fast canter. He didn't dare gallop all that way because he might need the grulla to get the hell out of there. Wouldn't do to arrive with his pony done. Only he should have known better. For if there is any demonstrable characteristic of the laws of chance it is that they seldom work for good.

Chance. Pure chance. Compounded by all the things Roak didn't know. Such as old Rod's insomnia, the aging man's night-long wrestling with loneliness and grief. Remembering his good wife, dead in sorrow, his stiff-necked, unbending son back East, married to a woman who had shown her legs in an opera house, thinking about the grandson he'd never seen—who bore his name, too, Rod Cameron III, a sign maybe that his son was less stiff-necked than he was; yearning in his old and broken heart for his boy to make one sign, one small gesture that would have made reconciliation possible, enabled him to revoke his hotheaded act of willing the Flying U to Hank Flynn at his death, which now he could not in honor do, recognizing sadly that, flesh of his own iron flesh, bone of his stubborn bone, young Rod II was as incapable of such a gesture as he himself was—remembering, thinking all that, old Rod Cameron rode out nightly now to weary his body, rock-hard still at sixty-odd, into a state where, near morning, he could sleep.

Rode out and met—by chance, or by those mathematically exact workings of the forces governing man's fate that no people since the Greeks have truly understood—Ramón Benevides and his band.

By then, Roak was close enough to hear the shots. That close, and that far. For when he reached the old man's sorrel standing head and riderless, they were gone.

He climbed down, lifted that lionlike old head. Rod opened his eyes. They were clear. He rumbled:

"Roak! Glad you're back, boy. I was meaning to tell you—"

Then his words choked off in a rush of blood. He spat it out copiously, said:

"Got one of 'em. The young fellow who was leading 'em. They carried him off—"

But the red tide rose again, dark and stifling. Roak felt the old man sag. He bent, tried with all his strength to lift him up, but he could not. Old Rod weighed close to two hundred pounds. Roak stood back, considering what to do; but even in that on this night his timing was off, as it had been in everything else. For he heard the ball whistle, carbine bark before he heard the hoof thud, gallop pounding. Went up from there into the saddle like a winging thing, leaning forward on the grulla's neck flat against his mount, not shooting back because he had no time even for that and because he didn't want to kill one of the Flying U hands even by accident. The moonlight was as bright as day. He heard them shout:

"It's Roak! It's the dude! Come back and kilt the old man!"

Then he settled down to the business of riding. Their ponies were fresh while the grulla had done a lot of traveling by then. On the other hand he was lighter and smaller than any of them, he'd saved his mount all he could on the way there, and there was another thing, curiously freakish, as real things often are. The *brasada,* the brush country, was reaching out farther into the open ranges every year, threatening to devour them. The reason was simple: though

mesquite with all its thousands of seeds seldom takes root
in virgin soil, once those seeds have served as fodder,
passed through the bellies and guts of cows and horses,
and dropped to earth in their dung, gestation is infallible.
Men had come and brought the vast herds who ate the
mesquite seed, producing an explosion of brush where no
brush had grown before. So now, instead of having to ride
all the way back to Bart Nevis's place to find that protec-
tive screen, Roak had only to slant his ride westward across
one two-mile stretch and plunge into a long tongue of
mesquite that had crept from Bart Nevis's brush ranges
across a long, shallow valley in the Bar F's west section
and into the Flying U itself. Then he'd be safe. But two
miles were two miles.

What saved him was the fact that to hit anything from
the saddle while pounding at a gallop, you have to be close
enough to powderburn your man. And that the matchless
heart of that ugly, hammerhead, slope-hipped little mouse-
gray brush pony never let them get that close. Covered
with lather, foam-flecked, heaving, he plunged into the
thickets that were his home still full of fight after a ride
that would have killed any other mount Roak had ever
seen.

Even that didn't stop the Flying U's hands, but it de-
layed them enough. Roak could afford to slow the grulla
now, let him get his breath back, ride at a steady walk
through the thorn-covered brush head on and straight,
while their mounts shied and balked and had to go round,
until he came to the river, plunged in, swam across with
white geysers from the whanging, flat, trajectoried carbine
balls rising up all around him, knowing it wasn't his night
to die, that his luck wasn't yet that bad—or that good.

When he came out of the river, having lost them for
good, because with Juan Cortina now commanding the
Line of the Bravo, having ten thousand bandits he called
soldiers at his back, a gringo invasion which consisted of

only thirty men would have been suicide, he found Belén there. Mounted. Waiting for him. She wasn't even crying yet.

"I heard the shots," she said in that flat-toned utter calm that is hysteria's purest manifestation. "I was already looking for you, my Roak. You see, Ramón—"

"I know," he said; "I heard you talking to him. But that wasn't Ramón. Some gringo friends of mine. They want to play Santa Claus. Decorate a tree with me—"

Those black eyes widened, drowned the stars.

"Why?" she whispered.

"They think I killed a man. Don't worry; they're wrong. I didn't. Maybe they'll even find that out—though that'll be just as bad; because some of your brother's playmates did."

She bent her head.

"So that was why!" she whispered.

"So that was why what?" Roak asked tiredly.

"They took him away. He was so—so *pálido,* so pale, so sick, so hurt. But they wouldn't let him near me. And I heard one of the officers tell them that they were not to enter this *distrito* again within six months. He was a general, I think, this officer. That was in case the *yanquis* investigate, Roak! I understand it, now! That way General Cortina can tell *los gringos* that the ones who raided Texas tonight are not here. . . ."

"I see," Roak said; but he neither saw nor cared. He muttered, "Let's go home, baby—I'm plain worn out. . . ."

"Are you, Roak?" she said.

"Yes, Belén. Why do you ask me that? When a fellow's ridden eighteen miles with a bunch of idiots shooting at him all the way, he sure Lord needs rest."

Riding back to the house with her, he thought about his son who'd be grown before he saw him now, likely; and about poor old Rod Cameron, dead now, surely, gunned down like a dog because he'd lost his temper and kicked some lazy chili eater. And the only thing he had to be even a little glad about was old Rod had died without holding him any grudges, thus making the deceased the last white man in Texas he could have maybe called a friend.

Only he was wrong. Rod Cameron wasn't dead. He didn't die for fourteen more days and nights of utter anguish. And before he did, as soon as he was conscious, in fact, he cleared Roak Garfield's name. For the second time. For Doctor Thurston Murray of Houston, Texas, sent for by Hannah, had already cleared it once by taking his oath before witnesses that he had known Captain Jesse Furniss had had cancer of the stomach for years, and that he just hadn't had the heart to tell the bitter truth to the man who was both his patient and his friend.

Which didn't help the immediate situation much, because Roak Garfield didn't know any of those things, had to go on living in Mexico, a prisoner of his fears, until somebody told him. And that, with Cortina and his brigands growing stronger every day, was going to be quite a trick.

Nor did he know that at four o'clock in the morning after that night he'd outdistanced Hank Flynn and the Flying U hands, Hannah gave birth to a daughter. Alone, except for Josefina, just as he had thought. In bitter anguish because of that, also as he'd thought. She named the child Jessica after her father, as was fitting.

But Roak Garfield didn't know any of those things. He was too bone-weary, beaten, sad when he came up to the little blue house on the edge of the desert just before dawn. He opened the door. They went inside together. And then without hesitation or warning or even thought, Belén's lips were on his and they were scalding.

"Lord God, Belén, I——" he said, when he could.

"I need thee," she whispered, her voice a breath rustle against his throat. "You see there was no more time and it was finished and all night I have been thinking of thee and now there is time again and life has come back and we have six more months which is very little so I do not mean to waste an instant of them—"

"María," he said, calling her by her first name which he very seldom did except when he was truly moved; "María *mía,* did I ever tell thee that I love thee? Truly and with all my heart? But of verity I am very tired. . . ."

He said that in Spanish. He said it very badly and with an atrocious accent. But it wasn't a lie. He meant it. He truly loved her and he was really very tired. Only, as she should have known by then, and probably did, he was never that tired. Which made what he said untrue to a certain degree. But where the line of demarcation between truth and falsity lay that morning he couldn't have determined to save his soul. Which, maybe, was what he was trying to do. Because twelve miles from that place there was another woman screaming in awful pain right now maybe with only a fat, frightened Mexican maid to help her as she brought forth his continuation, his prolongation in time, his one chance at immortality, the little bundle of breath blood cells nerve bone and maybe even spirit that was the part of him that would go on after he died and even project some small surviving attribute of him, his good or his evil, maybe, his capacity to suffer pain, further into the future still. Against that now, even this matchless, stranger love became a blasphemy.

Only he couldn't say that. Not to Belén. He had hurt her enough now. And, he grinned wryly in bitter self-knowledge, in utter honesty, there was always tomorrow.

She drew back a little, looking at him. Sighed.

"All right, *cariño mío*—as thou wilt," she said.

Chapter Fifteen

THE SHAPE of that land was the shape of loneliness. Hannah knew that now. She sat by the window looking out at it, lying there under the moonwash, dim-silvered, endless. It was a very beautiful land, but it was also very cruel. It froze you in winter with its blue northers, drowned you in spring with its flash floods, parched you all summer, baked your skin into something that looked like an adobe wall, dried out your hair into strawy wisps. Most of all, it dwarfed you. It's skies were too high, its stars too far, the sweep of it too vast, so that even standing in your own doorway you were already lost, reduced in stature, becoming ant-sized under that sky, before that sweep, against that vastness. . . .

She had always loved it before, but now she hated it. All the things she saw in it, she had seen before; but now she saw them heightened, etched sharper, their outlines clearer: the bones of a steer white upon the wasteland; the dried clutch of feathers that had been a small bird impaled upon a Joshua tree; the tortoise lying helpless under the desert sun still living while the soldier ants ate out his eyes. The stiff-legged death dance between a roadrunner and a snake; the old longhorn gone lame in the *malpaís,* standing there, a rack of bones, head down, while around him, no longer even flying now, the buzzards sat, in obscene patience, waiting.

The shape of that land was loneliness. And cruelty. And death. And she was a dwarf thing, waiting against that vastness, not for her mate, for she knew where Roak was now, knew what he was doing, but for the careless fang slash, the too-long stretch of sun-dried earth and no drop clinging to a blade of grass to quench the burning in her; the sudden lift and scurry of a prairie wind to—blot her out, erase her tender flesh, bleach her into horror, sand-drifted, coyote-scattered, under a pitiless sky. . . .

From her crib on the far side of the bedroom, the child made a sleepy gurgle. Hannah got up at once and went to her. Jessica Garfield was six months old now, but she still had never seen her father. I am not being fair, Hannah thought; just as I sent Pepe down there to find out what I was already sure of, merely to confirm my suspicions, I could have sent him or another of the Mexican boys to tell Roak that he's free. They can come and go with impunity even if it is dangerous for us now. Roak doesn't know Mr. Cameron cleared him before he died, nor that Doctor Murray—

She bent above the sleeping child, seeing that she was all right, the sound she made only an involuntary breath gust made in turning.

"Cancer," Hannah murmured; "your grandfather died of cancer, Jessica. But what am I dying of, my pet? Loneliness. Jealousy. And grief. I pray God you never know them. . . ."

She crossed to the window again, stood there in her night dress, looking out at the sky. Then she turned, came back to her bed, that vast bed that both she and her daughter had been born in. She lay down upon it. And, after a time, though she had not believed she could, she slept.

When she awakened, the moon was gone, and the stars were pinpoints of fire in absolute black. She lay there very still, not daring even to breathe, trying to decide what made her so sure that she and the child were no longer alone in that room. But she had no physical evidence for that certainty. There was no sound at all, except the fear-quickened rustle of her own breathing, the sudden pounding of her heart.

"Roak . . . ?" she said tentatively.

Then that sound floated in upon her, that low, suppressed, almost soundless chuckle. But unlike everyone who had heard it before her, Hannah didn't feel her flesh pimple with sudden cold, or the small hairs at the back of her neck rising, or a shiver of distaste. Instead that sound drifted over her like a caress, lay along her flesh like the felt vibrations of music.

"No," the shadow said, "not Roak, ma'am. I take it he's not here?"

"Who're you?" Hannah said. But she did not raise her voice. And, she realized with calm wonder, she was not afraid.

Again that deep-toned, velvety almost-silence, like bells plunged in wind, their clangor drowned, so that what came over to her was the mind's reconstruction of remembered sounds, warm with associations, calling up not quite the memory but the feel of lost and pleasant days.

"What do you want?" she said sharply.

"Now, that depends," the shadow said. "Mind if I light the lamp? I'd like to see you. . . ."

"Not at all," Hannah whispered. She told herself she said that because the intruder sounded like a madman, and it was better to humor him; yet she was aware, even as she shaped the thought, that that was not the reason. But she didn't know what the reason was.

She heard the scrape, saw the blue spurt, the yellow flare. He cupped the match between his hands, pooling the light so his face floated upon the darkness, demonic, terrible. She could feel the scream rising to her throat, but she held hard against it. He found the lamp, took the shade off, lit it, turned it up. The warm yellow glow stole out, washing the room with light.

Then she saw that his face wasn't really demonic, saw

that it had been savagely, brutally, fiendishly mutilated; but that the mouth under those flaring, v-notched nostrils was sensitive, even maybe kind.

"Thank you, ma'am," he said.

"For what?" Hannah said.

"For not screaming. Women generally do the first time they see my face. . . ."

Hannah smiled.

"There's nothing wrong with your face," she said; "I —I find it rather handsome. . . ."

He stared at her. But there was no mockery in her voice.

"Your scars *are* ugly, yes," Hannah went on; "but since it's obvious that you didn't put them there yourself, I fail to see how you can be held responsible for them. Is that why you came through my window in the dark, instead of knocking on the door?"

"No'm," he said; "I'm plumb used to this mug by now. I don't try to hide it."

"Then why did you?" Hannah asked.

"Tell you that later, ma'am," the man with the butchered face said. "First you tell me one thing: just where is your husband?"

He saw her face tighten, saw the brief blaze in those blue eyes; saw pain, grief—all he needed to see, to know.

"I don't see what business that is of yours, Mr.—"

"Names don't rightly matter now, ma'am," he said. " 'Sides, you've done already answered my question, part of it, leastwise. Where does this filly live that Roak is with?"

She stared at him, her eyes widening.

"I ain't a mind reader," he said. "You see, ma'am, I've been knowing that there polecat you're married to one heck of a long time. . . ."

"Your face," she said. It wasn't even a question. Then she said: "Why?"

"Ancient history, ma'am," he said; "just you tell me—"

"Your wife, or your sister?" Hannah said.

"My sister. And afterwards, my wife left me because of my face. Only she's dead now. I just found that out a while back. . . ."

Hannah studied him.

"You want me to tell you where Roak is so you—"

"Can kill him? No'm. If I'd wanted to do that, I could have long ago. That's too easy. A damned sight too easy. What I want is to see him wallowing in the dirt, a-crying, first. And after that. . . ."

"After that, what?" Hannah whispered.

"I want him to do it—he, himself."

"Why?" Hannah said, her voice sinking further still. "What difference does it make? He'd be—dead either way. . . ."

"That way I'd know he'd felt the hurting and the grief like I've felt 'em, ma'am. Then we'd be even. So—"

"So," Hannah said, "when you came through that window, you—you meant to—to—"

"Yes'm," the stranger said. "Just what you're thinking, ma'am—and make him watch it. Only he crossed me up again. Without him here, it's different."

"Different," Hannah said, her voice sinking almost out of sound, "different how?"

"Less sporting. Maybe not even worth it. . . ."

He stood there looking at her. His mouth widened into a crooked grin.

"But then, maybe it is worth it," he said; "you're something mighty fine, ma'am—"

"I—I'll scream," Hannah whispered; "there're twenty-five cowboys—"

"Down in the bunkhouse, half a mile from here," the stranger said. "No, don't worry about it, ma'am. Like I said, I'm not even sure I want to— Why, glory be! This here is *his* kid? His and yours?"

"Yes." Hannah's lips shaped the word without sound.

The stranger bent over the crib and picked up the sleeping child. Jessica gurgled, stuck a thumb in her mouth, sucked at it contentedly. The stranger looked at the baby. When he turned back to Hannah, she saw, startled, the great, hot tears in his eyes.

"I had a kid like this, ma'am," he said solemnly; "or I would have had, if it hadn't been for your husband . . ."

"Oh, for God's sake!" Hannah flared. "Roak couldn't have—"

"Yes'm, he did. When I came home with my arm in a sling, and my face a bloody mess, my wife went into hysterics, lost the kid she was carrying. Then, two years after that, she left me. She was out of her mind, kind of. Heard she starved to death. . . ."

"Oh, dear God!" Hannah whimpered. "Mr.— whoever you are, give me my baby—put her down, please!"

"I was to catch her by the feet and swing this soft little head against the doorpost," the stranger whispered, "then he wouldn't have a kid either, would he?"

"Ohhhh!" Hannah wailed; then: "Put her down, mister! Please, please, put her down!"

"Be so easy," the stranger said; "she wouldn't feel it hardly at all, ma'am—"

"Stranger," Hannah said, her voice high, taut, breaking, "put my baby down and I'll—"

The stranger's awful grin widened.

"And you'll what, ma'am?" he said.

"I—I won't—scream," Hannah whispered; "I—won't even—fight. . . ."

He chuckled then, made that sound that men heard as a nail dragged across windowglass but to her was the warm flutter of rich velvet. Gently he lay the baby back in her crib.

"No," he said quietly. "Thank you very kindly, ma'am; but no."

Hannah stared at him.

"Of all the mavericks I've ever seen . . ." she whispered.

"I'm the oddest. Right. Only I'm not a baby killer, ma'am. I just haven't that much poison meanness in me. I wish I had. And I'm not in the mood for a woman tonight. Besides, you aren't the kind of female to be made sport of. In fact, you aren't even the kind I'd have expected him to marry. . . ."

"No," Hannah said, the edge coming through to him, the tension-tautening, the anger; "the kind you'd have expected him to marry is the one he's with right now."

"Then," the stranger said, "I guess I'd better pay a little call on them—wherever they are. . . ."

"No!" Hannah said; and her voice was a splintering, a crystal crash, jagged and fine. "Don't go! I. . . ."

He stood there, looking at her, seeing her eyes growing wider, darker; the glisten of moisture upon lips no longer shell pink, but deepening into rose, and at the base of her throat the flutter of hidden wings. He smiled. But his smile was a little sad, and when he spoke his voice deepened into what sounded to her a little too much like pity.

"Why not?" he said. "What can I do for you now, ma'am?"

"You—" Hannah whispered, "—can tell me the truth. Because I—I would have. To save my baby, I would have. So why?"

"Rather not, ma'am. Rather keep your friendship."

"I won't be angry," Hannah said slowly; "but if you know anything about women, you'd know—"

"That to turn them down, even when they don't want to, even when they're sacrificing themselves, is the worst thing a body can do to them. Maybe especially when they're sacrificing themselves. Cuts the ground out from under them. Makes them feel unwanted, kind of, and—cheap. And an ugly mug like me, to boot. Right, ma'am?"

"Right," Hannah said.

"All right. Begging your humble pardon in advance, you didn't count in this at all, ma'am. I only came to cut Roak Garfield down to size, to make him bellycrawl like a snake. And you don't serve for that. You, and maybe not this sweet little angel, either. Else he'd be here. Can't hit at a fellow through what doesn't matter to him, now, can I?"

"I see," Hannah whispered; "and you're right. Mind telling me your name now, pilgrim? Roak must know it already, so—"

"My name's Heindrichs, ma'am, Fritz Heindrichs," the stranger said.

"And was—was your sister called—Gwen?"

"Yes. How did you know?"

"I've heard him say that name a dozen times in his sleep since he came back from Kansas. On his mind, maybe. On his conscience. . . ."

"It ought to be," the stranger said. He stood there looking at her. No—studying her. Then he said:

"He's a fool. He ought to know better. To leave a fine woman like you mean mad and hurt—but it's more than that. You're a full-blooded woman, aren't you, ma'am?"

"What the devil do you mean?" Hannah said sharply.

"Blondes sometimes are, even though they don't look it. And, on you, it shows. . . ."

"What shows?" Hannah asked, tightening her throat against the quaver, and thereby, to her pained astonishment achieving a velvety purr halfway between an invitation and a caress. So she tried it again, letting the cord-quiver, throat-scrape shrillness through: "What shows, Mr. Pilgrim?"

"The lonesomeness," the man said. "When I see Roak, I'll tell him he'd better be getting along home. . . ."

He bent over the lamp, still smiling at her. Then he blew just once, entered into darkness, and was gone.

Roak sat in the *taberna* with the mug of *pulque* cupped between his hands. Anybody who could drink *pulque,* a kind of Aztec beer made from the juice of the *maguey* plant, needed the stomach of a goat. But he could. Maybe because to do the things he'd done required the stomach of a goat, and a goat's conscience as well.

He was waiting for Belén to finish her marketing so he could take her home. He had brought enough silver dollars with him to last a long time; and here, on the Mexican side of the river, it looked like they were going to last three or four times longer than he had figured on. He didn't talk to any of the men in the *taberna,* although he could have now, because Belén had labored to drive the minimum essentials of Spanish into his head. He could have talked about the weather and the crops and the next fiesta in the slow and simple sentences of a backward ten-year-old child. Only he knew better than to try to talk to any of them because he had broken the first rule for getting along with people who talk Spanish, which is to let their women alone. They would have accepted him grudgingly had he turned Catholic and married Belén; but the Martínez' house servants had told everybody he was already married, so what he was doing right now had no pardon on earth or under it. He couldn't explain to the people of the pueblo that he couldn't go back home because his gringo fellow ranchers were bent on hanging him, and he couldn't even find out whether it was safe for him to go back because since Juan Nepomuceno Cortina, brigadier general of the Line of the Bravo, Army of the Republic of México, had turned rustling the Texans' cattle into the number one industry of the northern border districts, no decent Mexican even dared cross the river any more, because the Texans had taken to shooting anybody who even looked like he had one Mexican great-grandmother.

So he sat there drinking his *pulque* and thinking about his child who surely must have been born months ago, and wondering why Hannah hadn't figured he'd head south and tried to get some word to him. Which meant that the situation was just the same as before, or maybe worse, or that Hannah was sick, or had maybe even died giving birth, as women slim as she sometimes did.

He didn't like to think about that, so he got up from the table, rang a coin on it, and walked out into the sunlight through the loud hand-clapping of all the village women who, as usual, were making the paper-thin flat cakes of cornmeal they called *tacos* out of a lump of dough they slapped between their hands until they got it thin enough, and afterwards baked on a slab of sheet iron over the fire. When Belén came home, she'd do the same thing, and then maybe wrap those cornmeal pancakes around shredded chicken and green peppers and onions and garlic with a red pepper sauce called *mole* hotter than the hinges of hell poured over the whole thing to make *enchiladas de pollo*. Or she'd wrap them around a mashed-up mess of pinto beans named *frijoles* that looked like they'd make a body heave if he put them in his mouth, but turned out to be delicious once he did. Or around a green mush that looked even worse that she said was *guacamole*, and that tasted even better. Just thinking about Belén's cooking made him hungry, so he walked faster, and then he came around the corner and saw her standing in front of the town's *albergué*, its inn, and with her a man who was blocking her path and making her face go sick with fear.

Roak came walking up to them. He didn't have so much as a toothpick in his hands, and this man was a *pistolero*. He had on an enormous sombrero with silver embroidery work woven into its brim and crown. He was very dark, and his mustache was enormous. Twin cartridge belts looped over his shoulders and crossed each other over his chest. He wore two six-guns with pearl handles, both of them hung low and tied down. And he had a Spencer repeating carbine in a scabbard by his saddle. A belt knife, bowie style, hung between the six-guns, close to his belt buckle. Small leather Mexican *armitas* protected his legs instead of full-sized chaps. He was plenty big for a Mexican, and there was competence written all over him. Texans could joke all they wanted about a "Mexican stand-off," by which they meant to run like hell; but Roak knew that, as riders, nobody except maybe a Comanche came anywhere close to them, and in battle they were never beaten because of anything so simple and uncomplicated as cowardice, but mostly by the stupidity and incompetence of their leaders, aristocratic fatheads passed, because of their connections, over men with plenty of brains, guts and savvy, who merely happened to be of humble birth.

The rider sat there on his horse, looking at Belén. He didn't say anything. He just sat there looking at her.

Roak came up to them.

"What can I do for you, friend?" he said.

The rider spat into the street.

"Die," he said.

"What is this of dying?" Belén said. "Who are you? By what right—"

The rider spat again.

"I am a Mexican," he said, "and that is my right. That I am also a friend of thy brother Ramón has no importance. Nor that thou hast become *una inmodesta, impúdica, ilícita, deshonesta, deshonrada, inmoral, licenciosa* thing of bad milk. What is important is that all the bad things thou art, thou has not the right to flaunt thy shamelessness before all the world because even this thou dost can be done quietly and discreetly. And most of all thou canst not live openly with a pig of a gringo, throwing this thing of a bad smell in the face of all the people in the full sight of the Holy Church. Therefore I promised Ramón that when I rode this way I would kill this gringo for him, since he is hurt and cannot do it himself. Is this not entirely clear, *putita mía?*"

Roak didn't understand all the *pistolero* said; but he understood enough. He understood that this Mexican was going to kill him, maybe because Ramón had sent him to do it, but mostly because he had broken that number one rule. And he understood that the fact that he was entirely unarmed would mean very little to one of Juan Cortína's *bandoleros,* which this one surely was.

"You'll give me a chance to get my gun, friend?" he said.

The rider smiled.

"I am not your *amigo,* gringo," he said; "and I came not to participate in a duel, but to perform an execution. The difference is immense. How would you prefer to die, *cerdito?* I will allow you to turn your back and even a minute to say your prayers—that is, if you heretics pray. . . ."

On the edge of his field of vision, Roak saw Belén edging toward the rider. The rider saw her, too. His grin broadened.

"No, little whore," he said; "do not force me to shoot thee as well, for I mean to make full use of thee when I have done with thy gringo pig. This, of course, was not discussed between thy brother and me; but surely he will understand that one does not kill a man without recompense. . . ."

Roak tightened all over, waiting. He knew very acutely and perfectly and finally that the Mex would have let daylight through him five or six times before he could cross that intervening space; but something in him, that pride that clawed bone-deep, soul-deep, maybe, wasn't going to let him die with his back to his murderer or even standing still. He was going for this man barehanded, in the considered belief that dying was a thing you did only once and you never got another chance to make up for it if you didn't do it well. And if his life had been an ugly business maybe he could lend it some dignity and even some meaning and consequence by the way he took leave of it. So he had already bent his knees into the beginning of a crouch, set to spring, when he heard that sound that could never be mistaken for another, the snickering cluck-aluck snap of somebody levering a shell into the chamber of a Henry rifle. The sound came from above and behind him, where the *albergué* jutted out over the street. He didn't turn to look. He didn't have to.

He heard the rasping intake of Belén's breath, saw the Mexican reach, clumsily, slowly; and above his head, disembodied and soundless, the chuckle floated, raising his hackles with sudden cold.

"Wouldn't do that, if I was you, Greaser," the voice above him said. "Only safe thing for you to do is to grab yourself two handfuls of sky."

Slowly the Mexican raised his hands above his head.

"Now," the voice said, "you put down your left hand, and unfasten that there gunbelt. . . ."

Roak saw the heavy gunbelt slide down from the rider's hips. But the holsters didn't fall away because the rider had tied them down to his thighs so that they wouldn't swivel when he had to draw fast and smooth.

"Your knife," the voice said; "cut 'em loose with your knife. . . ."

The rider reached out and took his knife from where it hung on the sagging gunbelt. He cut the thongs holding the tips of the holsters to his thighs. Then very smoothly, beautifully, perfectly, like a great cat, he came off that horse in a leap that brought him across the space separating him and Roak, before the man in the window above could even caress that trigger, the knife up and back and downward striking, and Roak clutching his wrist and rolling with him and Belén tearing the very fabric of sound with her scream; and above them, Fritz Heindrichs sighting down the rifle, but lowering it at once seeing that he had no chance at all of firing with any surety of which one he'd hit.

Roak doubled his knees, kicked, and the Mexican flew out and away from him. And Fritz Heindrichs, who in some ways was entirely too much of a sportsman, called out pleasantly, "Here, Roak, catch!" and Roak, putting up his hands, felt the double scabbard with his twin throwing knives in it smack into them, heard Fritz say: "Plumb forgot to give 'em back afore you left Abilene. . . ." But that was all he had time to hear, for then the Mexican sprang.

Roak danced away from him, jerked off his coat, and wrapped it about his left arm. Then he came on in.

"Wait!" the Mexican said; and Roak stopped. Calmly, slowly, the Mexican turned his back, unslung the poncho from behind his saddle, and wrapped it around his arm, just as Roak had done.

"Now, *caballero*," he grinned; "shall we continue the waltz?"

Belén tried to turn her face away, but she couldn't. She wasn't afraid of the sight of blood. She had seen too many bullfights for that. But there is nothing harder to watch than a knife fight. A gun battle is mild in comparison. She hung there, leaning against the wall of the inn and watched the flickering lightning of those blades, watched that footwork, swift shuffling, dancing, the left arms, cloth-wrapped, catching the thrusts, turning them aside, while the knife hands drove in to be met by the clash and clangor of a parry, by the glittering of sparks, maybe, then the backward leap, and in again, upward stabbing, ripping for the gut.

Fritz leaned his Henry against the windowsill and watched it. He saw something very clearly: Roak wasn't trying to kill the *pistolero*. If he had wanted to do that, he could have done it a dozen times over by now. The Mexican fighter had been away from the hunger of his native village too long; banditry was a profitable business; he had put on fat. He was tiring visibly now. The sweat poured out of him. He gave, gave—

And Roak went in like a ballet dancer, like the fencer he was, thrust wide, and cleanly, and the Mexican's knife clattered to the ground. Roak put the point of his own against his opponent's throat, and held it there.

"Kill him!" Belén said. "For if you do not do it now, you will only have to do it later. Or else he will kill you—"

"No," Roak said; "no, Belén, that is not my way. Unload his guns. You know how." He stood there holding that blade pressed a little into the Mexican's flesh while Belén spilled all the cartridges out of the guns.

He heard Fritz's flesh-creeping chuckle, and turned. Fritz stood directly behind him. And none of the three of them had seen or heard him come down from the window of the upper room.

"Don't never learn, do you, Roak?" he said. "Safer to kill a feller outright so you don't have to worry 'bout him no more. . . ."

"No," Roak said; "I don't hold with killing—not even with scarifying no more." He took the knife away from the Mexican's throat. Then he said, speaking very slowly and clearly in his bad Spanish:

"You go tell Ramón not to send others to do a thing he is himself incapable of, *entiende*? And that I do not dirty my hands with the blood of hirelings. Now, go!"

The Mexican stood there, looking at him. Then he smiled and put out his hand. Slowly, Roak took it.

"Of verity thou art much man, little gringo," the *pistolero* said. "I shall not again seek thy life. . . ."

Watching him riding away, Belén stood by Roak, her head resting against his shoulder.

"Come," she whispered, "let us go home that I may prepare food for thee and for this thy friend, for the having of too much fear has put a sickness in me."

"Mighty pretty," Fritz Heindrichs said; "mighty, mighty pretty. You always did have good taste, Roak—though it most generally runs to blondes. Ma'am, my compliments—"

"Thank you," Belén said. She looked at him a long time, staring into that wreck of a face without shuddering, or any apparent distaste at all.

"Belén," Roak said warningly.

"Let her look," Fritz said; "don't 'pear to scare her none. That's right, ain't it, ma'am? You ain't scared of my face?"

"Not at all," Belén said; "should I be?"

"Nope," Fritz drawled; "you less'n anybody on God's green earth. But don't it even make you sick to your stummick? It does most fillies. . . ."

"No," Belén said; "but then I am accustomed to looking behind faces. Beyond the fact that you have saved Roak's life, I see what you are in your eyes. . . ."

"And what am I?" Fritz said.

"A man. A true man. One who has suffered much; and has been twisted by that suffering. But one who is basically kind. A man any woman could like very much if she is not fool enough to be *repugnada* by mere *cicatrices*—I mean—repelled by—scars. . . ."

"Baby," Roak said, "you want me to whittle him up some more?"

"You mean—" Belén whispered, "that you—that you did *that?* Oh, Roak, I love thee; but truly, thou art a swine!"

Sitting by the fire, Belén could see the tension between the two men, feel it between them like a presence. And what lay behind it was more than just another knife fight, more than the matter of scars. Her head ached dully; she felt listless, sick. She often felt like that now, and the worst of it was she knew why. Only she couldn't tell Roak; she didn't know how to tell him, how to put it in words. And then, seeing Roak had stood up, was going outside to get, maybe, another log to put on the fire, the man with the scarred face leaned swiftly close.

"Why don't you go lay down, Miss Bel-laine, ma'am?" he said; "you sure do look mighty peaked."

Belén stared at him.

"I—I'm all right," she said.

"How long d'you calculate it's been?" Fritz said.

"Oh!" Belén said. *"Dios mío*—you mean that you— that you can tell?"

"Yes'm," Fritz said. "You see, I was married oncet. . . ."

"And your wife?" Belén said.

"Dead. Her and the child. It was born dead. And a couple of years after that, my wife run away. 'Twasn't 'til three months ago I got word she'd passed on."

"Why did she run away, Don Fritz?" Belén asked.

"Well, now," Fritz said, "that there's kind of ancient history, ma'am. . . ."

Belén stared at him.

"Because of your face," she said; "because of what Roak did to your face. And yet, you saved his life. *Madre de Dios,* but you are rare!"

"No'm," Fritz said; "I ain't rare—I'm smart. You ever read the Bible, ma'am?"

"No," Belén said. "I don't know why, but we Catholics almost never do. It's not forbidden; we can read it if we want to; but somehow we don't. We read the catechism, the missal, the lives of the saints; but *la Sagrada Bíblia,* no. And yet, it seems you heretics—I mean you *protestantes*—always do. Why?"

"Nothing else to read, I reckon. But if you get a chance to, read it. There's a verse in it about heaping coals

of fire on a feller's head that makes a mighty heap o' sense
to me—"

"What the devil are you two talking about?" Roak said
from the doorway. Belén could hear the edge in his tone.
Fritz's eyes rested on his face a long time. A very long
time. Belén wondered if he was even going to bother
himself to answer.

"Heaping coals of fire on folks's heads," he drawled.
"To be more exact, on your head, Roak. . . ."

"You're doing mighty damn well right now," Roak
said flatly.

Fritz stood up.

"But I aim to do better," he said, "a mighty heap better.
Be seeing y'all. . . ."

"But where are you going, Don Fritz?" Belén asked.

"Damned if I see how that's any of your business, baby,"
Roak said; but Fritz ignored him.

"Got a errand to run, Miss Bel-laine," he said, "a mighty
important errand. I'll let you know how it comes out."

"Her, but not me?" Roak said.

"Oh, you'll know afore she does," Fritz Heindrichs said.

Fritz drew up the team that was pulling the buckboard.
Then he passed the reins over to Hannah. Beside her, on
the other side of the seat, in an enormous basket, little
Jessica slept.

"This is where I get off," Fritz said. "Don't want to
be mixed up in this no more than I have to. So now you
go right on, ma'am. You know where she lives?"

"Yes," Hannah whispered; "at the end of the street.
I've been here before—on much the same sort of errand.
Only hope I have better luck this time. . . ."

Fritz chuckled softly.

"Ma'am, you're holding all the cards," he said. "What
you've got there in that there basket is purely a royal
flush!"

He went around behind the buckboard and untied his roan.

"Be seeing you, ma'am," he said. "In fact, you can dance at my wedding, since I wasn't around to dance at yourn. . . ."

Belén was sitting in the doorway when she saw the buckboard coming up the street, saw the sunlight fall on Hannah's pale hair and blaze. She glanced quickly to where Roak lay on the bed, staring at the ceiling. He had heard nothing. Quietly she closed the door and went out to meet Hannah. It was something that had to be faced. She had known that all along. But she had put off even thinking about it because it wasn't a thing that thinking about did any good.

She had her people's profoundly tragic view of life; but she also had their intense capacity for hope. She had in her blood, her flesh, her nerves their unequaled tranquillity, their childlike, God-given ability to say *mañana* and leave for tomorrow what thinking about today wouldn't help, and for another tomorrow when the first one had become today without any change of circumstances or any new reasons for believing they would change. But now, all her tomorrows had run out on her, so she walked toward Hannah very quietly, wrapped almost visibly in the immense dignity of her people, in that pride which has earned them the black envy of richer races, who, confronted with that unbending pride, that shattering dignity in a people bare of foot and ragged, wonder furiously and aloud. "What the hell have *they* got to be proud of?" Not counting, being out of the very pragmatism of their natures unable to count, that bottomless treasury of sanctity and heroism and mysticism and—yes, even these, maybe even especially these—fanaticism and bigotry, and that absolute contempt for death that risks life grandly and with style not only over great issues, but even over issues of little importance or none whatsoever such as the ritual murder of a bull.

And Hannah, seeing Belén coming toward her, saw her not alone but at the head of a procession, accompanied invisibly by warriors and heroes and saints and *penitentes* with bloody backs who even in the act of contrition couldn't be humble, making of remorse and repentance a public spectacle, of defeat an object of pride.

"Yes?" Belén said. "Yes, Doña 'Annah? What is it that the señora desires?"

"My husband," Hannah said flatly; "will you go and call him, please?"

Belén's inclination of her head measured the limits of dignity to a hair's breadth.

"Very well," she said; "I shall call him. But that he should come back to you is, of course, his own decision—which is quite another thing. . . ."

She half-turned; but Hannah's voice arrested the motion, speaking calmly, flatly, and with a pride to match her own.

"Wait, Belén," Hannah said. "The last time we met, you asked me to show you Roak's love. Will you have the goodness to look into this basket, please?"

Belén came toward the buckboard, bent and looked down at the sleeping child. For a long time she did not move. She stood there looking down at that pink and white and golden mite, sleeping in the basket, and not a tremor showed in the line of her body, nothing showed except that awful tautness, that petrified sculpturing of the lineaments of despair—naked and as pure as nakedness, as lonely, as defenseless. She lifted her face and met Hannah's gaze, not even trying to hide the slow brimming, the spill, the luminous tracery, making of her grief and its acknowledging a thing of pride also, and said:

"Yes. I will call him now."

And stood there watching it all, unmoving, carved of brown granite and not even crying now as Roak lifted his firstborn, his face going slacksoft unsettled, raising his eyes to hers involuntarily so that for a long moment she saw the mingled joy tenderness wonder in them, before the awareness of her presence, the recognition that she was even there came flooding back and his eyes going sick with shame remorse grief at this one more dirty trick life was playing on them both. That. Which was enough. But then she saw added to it insupportably the sudden emasculating slash of pity, the unwillingness to hurt, the inability even to say what must be said. So, with a hundred centuries of racial memory to instruct her, knowing one must never violate manhood personal pride dignity not even for compassion's sake; with her cuirassed and befeathered ancestors both insisting in her veins that cruelty itself better became a man than what she saw in Roak's eyes now, she said it for him:

"Go, Roak. Go with my blessing. And with God's."

Then she went into the house and closed the door behind her very quietly, taking great pains not to let it slam.

When they had gone, when the last crunching whisper of the wheels, the last slow clipclopping of the team and of Roak's grulla pony had died out of time and mind, Belén opened that door and came out again, walking not down the street between the shade of the houses but away from the village out upon the desert itself. She carried nothing in her hands, no bundle of food, no canteen of water, no weapon, and her head was uncovered to the sun. She went on walking steadily, slowly, under a sky that was white golden, even the blue washed out, and the sun like a brazen disk above her. She walked like that for two hours, three, until the village dwarfed and dimmed out of existence, merged with the shimmering heat waves and was gone.

She realized that she was stronger than she had thought, that she was going to be able to go on walking until the night came down with its coolness, and looking up she saw that the circling of the buzzards was still aimless, that nothing had yet told them death moved below them steady and slow into the badlands, climbing the lava ridges, descending into the arroyos, skirting the chaparral, cactuses, yucca, Joshua trees.

She was not even thinking. She knew that this slow, tormented dying was no less a mortal sin than the quicker, more merciful laying of violent hands upon herself; but the aching feel of guilt in her—combined, maybe, with that inborn love of cruelty for its own sake which spares the sinful self as little or less than it does the offending heretic, shaped and conditioned by a lifetime of watching each year's repetition of the unspeakably barbaric spectacle of Holy Week; and, even as a watcher participating in it, all her blood and nerves throbbing in time with the drum slow cadenced beat of men marching bent under heavy crosses that wore their shoulders raw, clanking the chains around their ankles, dyeing the cobblestones with the blood of their shredded knees as crawling they offered their awful God His meet recompense of broken flesh and spattering blood in payment for a few hours or even minutes of stolen joy—told her that a quick and easy ending of her existence would be an offense in the nostrils of her stern Hebraic Iberian Aztec God; that He required the thorns, the lash, the ultimate humiliation of her, before her death, just as he had required them of His Son.

Her act remained, of course, suicide; but she reasoned dimly that God and His Holy Church had outsmarted themselves because eternity remained eternity, and hell, hell, whether one entered them for one sin, two or ten thousand. So, having equated eternal torment with the lesser sin of adultery, they had left her free to do the greater sin of self-murder, to end her sorrows, to spare her unborn child the multiple indignities consequent on being both bastard and half-gringo in a society prepared to accept neither. Which is not to say that she put the matter to herself with such brutal clarity; but that was the way she felt.

She moved on without stopping to rest until night fell. Then she lay down on the bare rock with no covering and let the iron chill of a desert night enter her, for though it was late enough in the spring by then for the heat to lie blindingly upon the land by day, the nights had not yet lost their rawness. She felt the tiredness in her, the ache. But it was not enough. There would still be tomorrow and the day after that and maybe even the day after that one, too. She thought very calmly now about her death and the manner of it; but no matter how she examined it she could find no reason for regretting it or changing her mind. So she lay there very quietly until at last she slept.

The next day went by like the first, but more slowly. By the afternoon of the third day her lips had puffed into blisters then cracked and the blood from the cracks had dried and she had lost twelve pounds by dehydration and was slowly going blind from the glare. Already her sense of direction had failed her and by late afternoon she was much closer to the village than she had been the day before because her path had become circular, almost as circular as that of the vultures scribing black death upon the yellow-white sky above her, and very nearly as purposeful.

Watching her from where he rode, where he had ridden these three days behind her, Fritz Heindrichs shortened the distance between them. He could have caught up with her at any time during those three days, but his icy intelligence, the bone-deep cruelty that both Hannah and Belén would have sworn he didn't have, told him not to. He wasn't playing children's games, or practicing Anglo-Saxon concepts of sportsmanship. He was stalking not so much Belén Benevides as Roak Garfield, closing in now not for the kill but for the destruction of Roak Garfield, living; the slow, step-by-step reduction of his foe out of manhood, the never-ceasing inexorable stripping him one by one of every human creature he loved and everything he gloried in until nothing was left but a beast thing on its knees groveling and crying, begging even to die.

He saw her fall. Reined in his mount, waiting to see if she could get up. Repeated that act with a patience that even a vulture could have envied, even following without haste or pity her helpless crawling antlike across the sands when she couldn't get up any more, staring without compassion at the blackening, instantly drying smears of blood from her hands and knees as her body's instinct to live fought her mind's will to die.

Only when she had ceased to move did he come upon her, dismount, lift her head, pass his bandana wet from his canteen across her cracked and blackened mouth. Repeated it at intervals until her eyes fluttered open, her desperate hands clawed at the canteen, and he, tearing it away from her, said:

"No. Too much'll kill you now, Belén."

And dragging her into the slim shadows of a Joshua tree, fed her the water drop by drop until she could open her mouth, push out upon the choked, parched rustle of her breath the single word:

"Why?"

And he, saying it slowly, gravely, almost tenderly:

"Because I'm a widower, and he ain't. Because the kid'll even look enough like me, seeing as how I'm blond, too. Because I don't reckon the good Lord gives much of a care how we worship Him so I'm willing to get baptized all over ag'in your way if that'll help. Because nobody'll dare point the finger of scorn at you 'n' the kid with a good honest-to-God Catholic husband at your side even if he is a gringo. And because after I learn the lingo and

settle down amongst your folks and take up their ways
I'm betting they'll forget even that. . . ."

She studied him with eyes big with wonder.

"I do not love you, Don Fritz," she said; "you realize
that?"

"I know. And I know I got love enough saved up for
the both of us, and some left over for the kid. Anyhow,
you don't have to answer right now. When you're back at
home, well and rested, you can answer. I'm a mighty patient man, Belén—"

"You mean that you would take me, knowing that I
am cast off, with child by another, and he the man who—"

He smiled at her, then.

"You said I was—rare, didn't you?" he said.

She lay there in his arms, staring up at him.

"No," she whispered; "what you are is—a saint, Don
Fritz. But I cannot do this. I cannot ask you to shame
yourself thus—for I—"

"You," Fritz said, "just shut up for now, Belén. I'll
take you home. We'll talk about this ag'in, next week."

"*Sí*," she whispered, "*la semana próxima, si Dios quiere*
—next week, if God wills. . . ."

But that next week she faced him with eyes grave and
sorrowing and said:

"No, Fritz; I cannot. It is too shameful a thing to put
upon a man. . . ."

And the week after that, and the next, and the next,
until any man on earth but Fritz Heindrichs would have
given it up; but he, being Fritz Heindrichs, didn't give
up; maybe because he was Fritz Heindrichs, because the
same thing that made him leave Roak Garfield alive, believing, even knowing, that death was a nothing, an ir-
relevancy, told him, assured him that time was on his
side in this as it always is on the side of the patient, the

ice-cold, the unloving, who have nothing more to lose, having already lost it all; and nothing to gain even except the assuaging of the itch, the misery, the dull, slow, aching desire for vengeance, and even that reluctantly because when that would be gone, assuaged, appeased, stilled, he would have nothing left, nothing at all.

So he waited. Came finally and stood in the doorway of the house, fanning himself with his Stetson, lounging there like that, utterly at ease, leaning against the door frame, boneless almost, a wisp of broomstraw stuck between his teeth, his back to the light, so that to her he made a shadow, a long, thin curve of blackness between her and the sun. She had the feeling that that darkness would be there always, shutting out the sky; but she waited very quietly until he pointed with his quirt and drawled:

"It shows. Folks can tell now, Belén."

And she coming up from there, her eyes the shape, the description, and the repository of despair, said:

"All right. We will do it now. Today. I have already advised Father José. . . ."

He stood there unmoving, black against the light. Then he threw back his head and laughed aloud. The sound of it washed against the walls, boomed, reverberated—harsh, unlovely, triumphant, deadly.

Belén shivered.

"Why do you laugh like that?" she asked.

Because I've got him now, he thought; because I've robbed him of the woman he really loves and of the kid he'd spread himself all over Texas bragging about, 'specially if it's a boy like I got a feeling it's gonna be. Because that's only a start. Soon as I find out what else it is he cares about, I'll take that away from him, too. . . .

But he didn't say his thought. He looked down at her, his eyes somber, lightless, still.

" 'Cause I'm plumb downright happy, Belén," he said.

Chapter Sixteen

AND THE wind rose and the wind died; the sage purpled the prairie and was gone; winter came in on the howl of the blue northers, melted into the drift and whisper of April; the trail herds pounded north; the riders rounded up the cattle for the spring branding; the heat lay along the *malpaís* like a weight, the sagebrush went brown and the only greenness was the chaparral and the cactuses; the rivers dried and sank; and the cattle tanks were scum-slimed and stinking, until the day came when the wind was a lifting and a hint of coolness and there was a nip of frost in the air. Going like that, the round of seasons circling, the days trailing into weeks, months, years, until—

It was 1875 and Jessica Garfield was six years old, sitting on her father's knee, prattling:

"Why can't I have a baby brother? Ruthie Nevis has got two brothers, and—"

"Things like that, Jess, baby," Roak said solemnly, "you just have to blame on the good Lord."

"Why on Him?" Jessica piped. "Josefina says that if I say my prayers *los reyes magos* will bring me a baby brother. A real live baby brother instead of a *muñeca*. Oh, Papa, I—"

"You," Hannah said cooly, "had better come take your nap, my pet."

"But I'm not tired!" Jessica wailed. "I want to stay with Papa! I want to—"

"Sorry, pet," Hannah said, "but there are some men

outside waiting to see your papa. So you come with me. Your papa is a mighty important man. As president of the Cattlemen's Association, he has to look after everybody; so he doesn't have too much time for the likes of you and me. . . ."

Roak listened deeply for her tone. Searched out its content of mockery, of pain. But he couldn't be sure. He never could any more. She really wasn't poking fun at the very useful Cattlemen's Association he had founded. He suspected she was actually proud of his accomplishments. He wondered if she'd be less proud if she realized, as he did, that the ranchers had only accepted his ideas, made him president, out of shamefaced recognition of the fact that they had wronged him not once, but twice; that they'd come damned close to wronging him forever. Afterwards, of course, they'd seen what a force for good the Association had become, turned enthusiastic, given him all the support he needed; and, what was better, all the respect.

Respect. That was the word. Did Hannah respect him, really? Had she, inside her mind, truly forgiven him, even after all these years? She knew his reasons: "I was shot. Shot bad. I had to go to someone I trusted. . . ."

And he knew her answer, given coolly: "Of course. But after you were cured, did you have to stay with her? Wasn't there anywhere else you could have hidden?"

Was there an answer to that one? An answer that made any sense? Were there any answers to anything in this world? What is truth? Pilate had said.

And more. He, Roak, could ask the questions that had shaped his life: what is guilt? How far does it extend? What are the furthest limits of man's responsibility? He had committed one act out of simple lust, another out of blind rage, neither with premeditation, and in neither case had he known at the time that those acts were going to have consequences that spread out to the rim edges of forever. Only—Fritz had disappeared. Had shown no signs of life for years. Why? In God's name, why? Who knew what went on in the recesses of that twisted brain? And it was precisely not knowing that was the terrible thing.

Maybe, Roak thought, he knows Gwen is all right now. Maybe she wrote him like she wrote me. Maybe he's satisfied because her shop is prospering, happy because she's thinking of being wed, at last. Nice fellow, this Matthews, from what she says. Lord grant he'll be good to her. . . .

Guilt. Hannah now. The way she acts, a body'd think she was the guilty one instead of me. . . . Oh, Lord, I—

He thought about that, about his wife's strangely, disturbingly changed ways. First, after he'd come back, she'd gone religious on him. She'd go all the way to Brownsville on the stage to attend church. Often he'd gone with her. But the preacher's hellfire and damnation bothered him. Too many things the good man of God said seemed aimed directly at his head. Then she'd dropped that. Said, her eyes wide and anguished, "It doesn't help. Maybe Reverend Brownley's not smart enough to help me. Maybe there's nothing in it, anyhow. . . ."

Then she'd turned to books. The damnedest books. Weighty tomes, not books of fashions, cookery, or even romantic novels like a body'd expect a woman to read. No. Greek philosophers. Books on all the outlandish religions of the world. Medical books. Science. Darwin, now. She fairly doted on Darwin. She spent more money on books, sending all the way to New Orleans for them, than most women did on clothes. Only that phase hadn't ended. Her love for reading had become abiding and sure. She even talked like a book now, he thought.

He'd dipped into them himself. But most of them were beyond him. And the ones that weren't bothered him the same way that the preacher had. But what was Hannah searching for? He'd asked her that.

"To save my soul," she'd said; then she'd added, softly, "if it has a salvation, now. . . ."

No good to dig into that, he reckoned. Their lives had fallen into a pattern, tested, accustomed—acceptable. There were reticences they both respected; questions they didn't ask. And if, after seven years, they were something less than ardent young lovers, they were something more than friends. When, out of a sudden need, he turned to her in the night, her response was swift and sure, with nothing of dutifulness about it. Even, upon occasion still, it was she who turned to him, whispering, "Oh, Roak, Roak. . . ."

But their love bore no further fruit. Bart Nevis now had two sons and a daughter. Candy Tyler had five boys. Hank Flynn, two boys. Other men he knew were sending back East for wives; the land was filling up, becoming less lonely. There were occasional barn dances now at which they had to heifer brand only a third of the men. Settlers had come in; traders. There was a little hamlet growing up around the stage station called by common consent Furniss, after Captain Jess. And, Roak thought wryly, it said something about this sweep of earth, about the men on it, that if the first building thrown up in Furniss was a saloon, the second was a church.

Then he went out into that slant of sun where the others waited.

"Roak," Bart Nevis said, "they've hit us again. You worse than anybody. This can't keep up. We don't start to do something, they won't leave us a cow with the hide on, the miserable skinning bastards!"

"Yourn," Canby Tyler drawled, "was skint alive, Roak. And that means something—"

"You got any enemies down south of the river, Roak?" John Farrell asked.

Roak looked at them. Studied their faces. Then he said:

"C'mon up on the veranda and sit a spell, boys, while we dig into this. . . ."

They climbed down, came up on the porch with that curious awkwardness that cowmen have when they are off their horses. Sat. Roak called for Josefina to bring some Mexican beer. They didn't talk for a long time. Then Bart said:

"Hide peelers are the worst breed of rustlers there is. Lot easier to get away with the hide than with the whole cow, but—"

"But mostly they're cowards," Hank Flynn said, "and stupid little rats to boot. Even though, just like Bart says, it's easier to bundle up a green hide, or a stack of them, and load a pack mule with the lot, we always caught peelers quicker than we did regular rustlers before. But now—"

"They get away slick and clean," Canby Tyler said. "There's a thing in the way this particular bunch of Greasers operate that would make a body think a white man's leading them."

"You think Cortina would let a gringo in on his enterprise?" Roak asked.

"I think this one horned in," Canby drawled; "and I think he sure as hell ain't no friend of yourn. . . ."

"Why?" Roak asked.

"Because for every cow we've lost, you've lost two," Bart said. "At first, I thought that operating brush ranges like I do, it was just harder for 'em to spook my steers out of the chaparral. But when I checked with Hank, here, I found out he wasn't losing any more than the rest of us—and the Flying U is mostly open range. So it adds up: somebody who hates your guts. Somebody whose head is really screwed down tight with lots of clockwork in fine shape 'twixt his ears. You got any idea who that could be?"

"No," Roak lied, "not the slightest, Bart."

"Then this beats me," Bart said.

"The Association has spent a mighty heap of money for arms," John Farrell complained; "thirty Winchester repeating rifles and Colt Frontier revolvers for all hands. Latest models, just came out last year. But that doesn't help when none of the boys ever sees a living rustler to shoot at."

"That's a fact," Bart said. "Roak, as head and founder of this Association, you got any ideas?"

"Yep," Roak said. "I vote we send a man—namely me —down into Mexico to look into things. I say me, because I've special connections down there, and because I've learned to twist my tongue around the lingo better than any man here, except maybe Bart. Down there, I'll just take a quiet look at cattle brands; find some altered ones, I ask questions—"

"Hold on, Roak," Canby Tyler said. "That'll work long as the regular rustlers are tied up with the hide peelers. I'm betting they ain't. And tracing hide peelers is just about the hardest job anybody ever heard tell of, I reckon."

"Not if a feller's got a lead," Roak said, "not if he can go down there with a damn fine idea of who to look for—"

"And who'd that be, Roak?" Bart said.

"A Mex," Roak said, "but a special Mex—who's got reasons to hate my guts, just like you said."

"Why?" Bart said.

"Private matter, Bart. And the only part of it that concerns any of you is that it may have brought on the hide peelers. But then, it may not have. Because what this here Greaser's got against me happened a mighty long time ago, and I ain't even wet my pony's feet in the Rio Grande in nearly five years. But it could be that. Some of those pepper guts have got a bad habit of remembering—"

"That's right," John Farrell grinned; "heard tell you

was a great fancier of chili peppers when you first come down here. Them Greasers don't forgive that, easy—"

"Which is neither here nor there," Bart growled. "You men willing for Roak to try it?"

"Won't hurt none, long as he don't get hisself killed," Canby Tyler said.

"All right," Roak said; "I'll ride down there first thing tomorrow."

They stood up then, all of them except Bart. He said:

"You fellers mosey along. I got a few matters to go over with Roak."

They nodded wordlessly. Mounted, rode away from there.

"Well, Bart?" Roak said.

"That one," Bart said; "that little one who was with you at the bullfight—her, ain't it? And some of her folks is hounding you?"

"Could be," Roak said.

"And the last time," Bart went on slowly, "when the boys hereabouts run you off on the charge of pizoning Cap'n Jess, took you a mighty long time to come back, as I remembers. You was down there clean 'til spring. . . ."

"So?" Roak said.

"So I ain't got no right, but I'm saying it anyhow. I got a lifetime of friendship with Hannah to remember. Wasn't for you, she'd of been my missus 'stead of Ruth. Things turned out the way they did, and I ain't complaining. But I sure hope you ain't using this as an excuse to git mixed up with the Benevides gal ag'in. I remember her mighty well, and staying away from her is gonna call for more will power than most bowlegged humans has got; but for Hannah's sake, I hope—"

"Forget it, Bart," Roak said quietly; "that's over and done with. Anything else I can do for you?"

"Yep. I want to have a look at them shorthorn Eastern

critters I told you you couldn't raise. Should of knowed better. When you start out to do a thing, you do it."

"You were damned nigh right that time," Roak said, "you 'n' Hank both. Tick fever took the whole blame herd the first year I brought them in. After I buried the lot of 'em, I found myself left with just three calves. But, as luck would have it, one of the three was a bull. All three of 'em had had tick fever and got over it, so they were immune. But the damnedest part about it is that it looks like they've transmitted that immunity to their calves. I've bred two generations now—and no fever. C'mon, look 'em over. They're a mighty pretty sight."

Bart stood by the fence of the enclosed pasture where Roak's shorthorned Eastern cattle grazed. With half a glance he could see that they ran considerably heavier than any beef animals he had ever seen. But with his second glance he spotted their major natural defect—a defect which, from the very circumstances of the times, was economically fatal. He turned to Roak.

"You aiming to keep them there fancy critters to supply your family and your hands with beef?" he asked. "That so, you done already bred too many of 'em. 'Cause 'til the railroads build down here, you're sure Lord stuck with them. Short-legged cows like them there sure can't walk to Kansas—"

"Thought about that, too," Roak said. "C'mon, let's ride a little further on."

When they got to the second enclosure, Bart sat there, his jaw dropping. Because these cattle were a new breed. Their horns were medium—neither short nor long. Their barrel-shaped bodies showed one of their blood lines clearly; but their legs were thick and powerful, yet almost as long as a longhorn's.

"Garfield Reds," Roak said. "How do you like 'em Bart?"

"Them," Bart said solemnly, "are the goddamnedest

bunch o' cows I ever laid eyes on. You'll get ten dollars above the market for each 'n' every one of 'em when you git 'em to Kansas. Don't reckon you'd be willing to part with a bull 'n' a cow of that line, would you, Roak?"

"Can't be done like that. What I'll do is to lend you my shorthorn seed bull. You service your best longhorn cows with him, and breed the hybrids to each other 'til you've got the strain fixed. But it calls for stout fences and a careful eye. One randy old longhorn loose 'mongst the Reds'll push the whole works right back to the first generation—"

"You mean you'll *lend* me your bull?" Bart said.

"Yep. You and any other member of the Association. And don't think I'm being so damn generous. Only way any of us will be able to keep that Red strain pure on the open range is for all of us to breed these hybrids. They're proof against ticks; they weigh in at almost two hundred pounds more than longhorns, and they can hoof it to Kansas. And since there just ain't any way for us to fence in the whole blame range, I reckon we'd better all standardize on this new breed—and get rich together instead of halfway making it separately. I'll bring it up next meeting, after I've attended to those rustlers."

Bart looked at him.

"Any way you try to trim it, you're still being mighty white, Roak Garfield," he said.

"Hannah," Roak said that night at supper, "I'm going away for two or three days. And I'm going to tell you right now straight out where I'm going, so you can start squawking like a prairie hen and get it over with. I'm going down south to visit Belén."

Hannah looked at him. She didn't say anything at first. But, after stretching the silence out until it cracked, she said in a light, pleasant, conversational tone:

"Might I ask—why, Roak? I'd assume you'd grown

tired of me—if it weren't for—last night. Or am I mistaken? Did I only dream—last night?"

Roak grinned at her wickedly.

"If you did, I hope you keep right on dreaming, baby," he said. "Nope, Han. You know damn well I haven't sunfished 'cross the border since the time you came down there with Jessie in her basket to fetch me home; that's one thing. For another, if I was planning anything what wouldn't stand the light of day, I'd hardly tell you about it, would I?"

"You might," Hannah said tartly. "Best cover-up in the world. Do a thing openly, telling everybody where you're going, whom you're aiming to see, so that folks will say: 'He wouldn't dare—not right out in daylight like that.' Only I know you; know you would dare. Anybody who'd trust you as far as they could throw you is a fool, Roak Garfield. And I don't think I'm a fool!"

"Han," Roak said, "are you going to listen to me? Or do I have to ride down there without explaining anything at all?"

"I'll listen," Hannah said, "but whether I'll believe you or not is another matter!"

"All right," Roak said. "The hide peelers. They're killing and skinning two of my cows to every one they take from anyone else. And I'm not the closest rancher to the river. Bart is. And Canby Tyler is as close as Bart. What does that look like to you, Han?"

"An enemy. Go on."

"An enemy from south of the border. Who down there has any reason for hating me? And because of—whom?"

"Ramón Benevides. Because of Belén. Only that's too easy, Roak. I won't buy that one—"

"Why not?"

"You haven't been down there in almost five years. So far I know you're telling the truth. Therefore Ramón has waited one heck of a long time to start. Doesn't add

up, doesn't figure. Mexicans are a hot-blooded people.
When you get them riled, they hit at once; they don't wait
and brood over it. That's—Nordic, Roak. That's even
more than Nordic; that's special. Only one man I know is
capable of it: Fritz Heindrichs, the man whose face you
butchered. In a knife fight, wasn't it? Over his sister—
Gwendolyn. I do have her name right, don't I? Tell me,
darling: just how many poor innocents *have* you ruined?"

Roak stared at her.

"So," he said dryly, "Ruth couldn't keep her mouth
shut after all—"

Hannah smiled, softly, sweetly.

"Ruth didn't tell me that, Roak," she said.

"She didn't? Then who the living hell—"

"Fritz," Hannah said, her tone velvety, warm as a
caress, "Fritz Heindrichs himself—"

Roak stood up. His knuckles, gripping the table, went
white.

"Fritz . . ." he whispered, "Fritz was *here?*"

"Yes," Hannah said. "He paid me a very pleasant visit
one night. You weren't here. You were in hiding—from
men who no longer had anything against you. But I'm
not being fair, am I? You didn't know that. No matter.
Knowing or not, you were so busy putting in a crop in a
field that didn't belong to you that you—had no time to
keep your own fences mended, shall we say?"

"You lie!" Roak said. And his voice was pain. The
thing itself, not the sound of it. "His face—no woman on
earth could stand—"

"Is that what you thought when you scarred him?" Hannah said. "Well, you were wrong. I found his face strong
—and kind. I had pity on his scars. . . ."

"You mean—you mean—" Roak hunted the words
through a long labyrinth of breath strangle, gutsickness,
gathering black, encountered them, found them unuttera-

ble, hurled them back; and, substituting for them a clumsy half-evasion of his thought, he pushed it out upon the slow stretch of tension, through the tearing of the fabric of the silence that would lie forever between them now:

"Goddamit, Han! You can't mean that he—that you— Damn it, you purely can't!"

"I can't mean—what you're thinking?" Hannah said. "Perhaps not. But then, I don't really know what you're thinking, do I?"

Roak crossed to her. His fingers bit into her shoulders.

"Han," he said, "if you're trying to say that you—"

"Have betrayed you?" she said bleakly. "No, Roak. Not with my body, anyhow. Maybe not even in my mind—"

"Maybe?" Roak said. He'd caught the aching emphasis she'd put upon that word.

"I—I don't know!" she whispered. "If I knew that— really knew, one way or another, I could perhaps be peaceful in my mind again. You see, I am not an adulteress; but only by Fritz Heindrichs's own exquisite courtesy. Because, darling, he didn't want me. While I. . . ."

"While you?" Roak got out.

"While I—offered myself to him. Wait! He had Jessica in his arms! He—he was threatening to kill her because you'd cost him a child. So I—I thought of that. To —to distract him. To make him stop. Or so I thought—"

"But now you think differently?" Roak said quietly.

"Dear God!" Hannah said. "Must I tell you this? Why'd I start it anyhow?"

"You were trying to torment me," Roak said; "getting even because of Belén. Only it looks like your shot backfired. Anyhow, finish it. You've got to, now."

"All right," Hannah said, her voice dark anguished. "I've wondered ever since—why. Why didn't I just throw myself on him like a wildcat, and tear Jessie from his arms? Why didn't I try to kill him? Why, in God's holy name, did I—offer—that?"

"Don't you know?" Roak said.

"No. I've prayed over it. Cried over it. Come close to going out of my mind over it. Roak, do you think it's possible that I—that I—*wanted* that terrible man?"

Roak looked at her. But he didn't say anything. Nor to that were there any answers, or anything to be said.

She turned away from him. Her voice came out slow, toneless, dull.

"He refused me. And told me why. That he was only concerned about taking from you what you truly care about. Not a cast-off wife. Not even a deserted child. So, not Ramón, Roak—Fritz. And you're going to the right place. Because that's where you'll find him—where your heart is, and your treasure. I'm sure of that. His mind works that way. His perfectly fiendish mind. He'll take Belén—or more likely, he has taken Belén—that will be, or is now, one half of his vengeance—"

"And the other half?" Roak said.

Hannah looked at him. Slowly, sadly, she smiled.

"He's already had. Funny, I only realized that, right now. For him, subtle as he is, that would be enough—"

"What would be enough?" Roak said.

"To leave you knowing that—that you're married to —to a woman he doesn't even want. Like a dog guarding his putrid scrap of meat from an indifferent world—a world much better fed. Which is why he is invincible. He has to be. With a mind like that, he has to be. . . ."

She stopped then, looking at Roak. Her eyes went far away. Came back again.

"I shouldn't have told you that, should I, Roak?" she said. "Now it will never be the same between us again, will it?"

Roak got up then; walked to the door. In it, he did not even turn. He stood there very still, until she saw the stretching of the fibers of his neck, his face moving into profile, still not facing her.

"No," he said; and was gone.

The first thing he saw as he rode the pinto up to Belén's house was the child. A boy. Four years old, about. With hair like all God's sunlight, above a tiny face burnt coppery by the desert glare. But the child's eyes weren't the blue he expected them to be. They were black. Like a night sky, Roak thought; but a night sky filled with stars. . . .

He climbed down, enwrapped in that luminous gaze, that duplication of what had been one of the precious things in his life. What had been, what was still; what always would be. He took the boy's tiny hand.

"Howdy, partner," he said; "your mama at home?"

The little boy stood there staring at him, those eyes velvety, phosphorescent. Roak tried it again.

"Your mama," he began; but the dry sound of that chuckle stopped him.

"He don't speak English," Fritz Heindrichs said; "never did get around to learning him. . . ." He turned to the boy. "Roakie," he chuckled, *"di buenos días al señor."*

"Buenos días, señor," the child piped.

Roak stood there.

"Roakie," he whispered; "you—you called him—Roakie. . . ."

"Named the little maverick after you," Fritz said. "My idea. Belén wouldn't hear of it at first. But I convinced her. Seemed to me no more than fair, seeing as how he could be yourn—"

"Could be?" Roak said.

"Yep. He come a mite early after the wedding. But then the first ones sometimes do, so I can't be rightly sure. Come on in. The missus'll be mighty proud to wrastle you up some grub—after so long."

Roak could feel the breath in his throat like a thickness, a choking.

"No," he said; then again, louder still, "No!"

Then the door opened, and Belén was there. She had grown a little heavier, but it became her. She was softer, rounder, more woman. If that were possible. Roak doubted it. Nobody could ever be more woman than Belén already was.

"*Hola,* Roak," she said.

Roak stood there with all the sky spreading out above him, sweeping out beyond the edge of the world, beyond the rim of the universe, and he caught at the center of that vastness, at point zero of all silence, at the nadir of his existence; staring at the lineaments of loss, the shape and coloring of anguish, spoke not the words of fire of his rage, nor the torn and bloody syllables of his hurt, because now this thing was beyond the irrelevance of speech; beyond—and this way he defeated Fritz Heindrichs for the moment—even the tears that Fritz was waiting for, being unable to see them where they ran like brine and ice and fire through the darkness of his heart. No. He was a doer, and words were not his business. They never are of men. For they arrange nothing, help nothing—certainly not this quiet kind of dying, impaled upon Fritz Heindrich's malevolence like a crippled hawk upon the spires of the chaparral. No. Never in this world.

He turned like a sleepwalker. Went back to his paint. Mounted. Sat there, towering above them; black against the yellow wash of the sky.

"No. Not '*hola,*' Belén—*adiós,*" he said; and turned the pinto's head away from there. And it was then that he heard her scream. The sound of it was a shrillness, a vibration.

"No, Ramón!" she cried. "For the love of God, no!"

And turning, Roak looked into the muzzle of the Winchester that Ramón Benevides was aiming at his back.

He pulled the paint up and sat there, seeing Ramón heavily mustached now, tall, a man, sighting down that barrel, and Fritz Heindrichs saying, "No, I told you I didn't want him dead, Ramón," so easily, smoothly, perfectly, that it wasn't until afterwards that Roak realized he had said it in Spanish; and Ramón snarling: *"Me cargo en tu padre, Fritz! No me importa* what you want; *I* want him dead and in hell and with no prayers for his miserable soul!"

And he, Roak, not even reaching for the six-gun he didn't have, nor under his coat for the knives he did, nor forward and downward for that sawed-off shotgun in his saddle scabbard, sat there while Ramón's finger tightened upon the trigger, and Fritz waiting until the last measurable fraction of a second before slamming the Winchester's barrel up with the palm of his hand so that the ball was a screaming whistle, arcing skyward through the flamesplat, the sodden bark; and then in the choking silence, Fritz's voice flat calm cold, saying:

"Look, you fool; can't you see you'd be doing him a favor?"

And Belén crying very softly and endlessly and hopelessly, and the child clinging to her skirts and beginning to shriek; and Ramón saying:

"Sí, you have much right, *cuñado mío;* but all the same—"

Then Roak touched the paint with his knees and got out of there, riding without haste, his back bar rigid against not the actuality but the memory of her cry.

So he had to put his mission down as a failure, giving it the rating he had already given his life. He rode up to the house at first dark, pushed open the door; and little Jessica flew to him as usual, shrilling: "Papa! Papa!" And he lifting her, swinging her ceilingward in a counterfeit, a mockery of the game he played with her each time he came

home; knowing, as he did, that all games go sour, flat,
after the loss of joy, forcing himself to laugh, to say:

"How's my kitten tonight? Tell me what—"

And little Jessica staring into his eyes and going very
quiet then, her high piping treble dropping into almost an
alto, saying:

"Put me down, Papa. . . ."

He held her above his head, his hands gripping her
slender arms too hard; his voice becoming a rasp, a sand-
storm rising, as he said:

"Why?"

And she: "Papa—Papa—you're hurting me!"

And Hannah's voice behind him, measuring out the
cool rustle of her words:

"Put her down, Roak. Can't you see she's—afraid of
you now?"

That. And some hours later, one more thing:

He was sitting in his study looking out the window
at the sky. It was very late, hours after he usually went to
bed. He wasn't doing anything so precise as thinking;
rather he was cramming his mind with irrelevancies, re-
minding himself of tomorrow's chores, searching the
shrinking circumference of his world for materials useful
in stilling thought, when he heard, unturning, the whisper
of her step, became aware of the perfume she had used
upon their honeymoon, and rarely, if ever, since.

"Roak," she whispered, making, unexpectedly, a flute
note of his name. He sat like stone and would not turn.
So she said his name again, rushed on breathlessly into
what she had planned to say, revised carefully, got by rote:
"I know you—didn't. I know what you found down there
was bad—that you—that you're hurt. It was written all
over your face so clear that even the child could tell. So
now. . . ."

"So now what, Han?" he said, still without looking

back, feeling the wash, the glitter, and the sting in his eyes now, and not wanting her to see.

"So now you are alone," Hannah said, "truly. After all these years. As alone as I've always been, and maybe even as lonely. So perhaps now I can have you for my own, for my very own—the way I want you—"

"Do you?" he said. "Me—and not Fritz Heindrichs?"

"Roak," she said, "turn around and—and look at me. . . ."

He turned very slowly. She stood by the other window, the one the moonlight was pouring into. She was wearing the silken nightgown he had brought her back from St. Louis—out of contrition? Out of shame?—and through it he could see she was as sliver-slim as the day he'd met her, as outthrusting, high-lifting, inhollowed, sweet-curving, unedged and rounded. Then she put out her arms to him, white-blazed by the moonlight, and said:

"Come."

But just before morning, something—that instinct that had kept him alive during four years of slaughter, that awareness he had of danger that was neither visual nor olfactory but beyond them both—brought him upright in his bed beside her. He swung his feet down upon the floor, groped for his clothes. Then he heard it, the sound that had maybe awakened him: the belling of cattle far off and faint, the sound drowned in the sweep of space, lost in the immensity of air. He dressed quickly, glancing at Hannah from time to time as he did so. But there was no danger of her awakening. Not after last night. He was grimly, even proudly sure of that.

He moved out behind the house and saddled the paint. There were no hands around. But with the double-barreled sawed-off riot gun across his saddle and his pocketful of shells loaded buck and ball, a fistful of buckshot in each one and musket ball on top of that over a double charge of black powder, he reckoned he didn't need any of the hands getting in his way, anyhow. Because what Fritz Heindrichs had left in him, only killing would ease now. He rode out to where he had heard that sound. Reached it. Sat there looking at the empty enclosure in which he'd kept his hybrid cattle, the ones he'd christened Garfield Reds.

Then he turned his pinto's head and started for the river on a long slant that he knew would bring him there before them because they damned sure couldn't drive a herd of cows as fast as he could ride. Got there and found that he was wrong, that those magnificent beasts he'd bred could be driven as fast as a herd of mustangs, that they had got there before him, or that at least part of them had, because the lead steers with the two men he recognized at once as Ramón Benevides and Fritz Heindrichs riding point were already past the trail fork where he'd figured on intercepting them; and he, realizing it was too late to head them off, clapped spurs to his paint and bore down upon the flank riders and the swings, going in close, lifting that hand cannon, not even aiming, firing now, turning the night hideous with the screams of down and thrashing horses, the moans of gutshot men, reloading as he swept past them and hitting the drags, blasting at the wink and splatting of their revolvers, one shot of the sawed-off shotgun being enough to empty half the saddles of the drag riders, and the next the rest, and he turning to take on Fritz Heindrichs to finish this thing between them once and for all to rid his life of horror, saw what he should have seen before, what he should have thought of: that squat physical embodiment of bloody murder he was using had been enough and more than enough to spook the herd.

Garfield Reds. Heavier than longhorns. Stronger. Loping in now, a tight-packed mass of steerflesh, their horns popping against one another like gunfire, their hooves drumming thunder, their eyes fire coals flaming even in that darkness. He dug spurs into the paint, quirted him cruelly, pounding out and away from there, trying to sweep past that brawling broil of wild-eyed cattle before they crowded him into the river, would have swept past, would have made it, but Ramón Benevides sighted along the barrel of his Winchester, touched the trigger, and the paint somersaulted, cartwheeling the earth and the sky; and he, Roak, fighting his way back out of the red fire and the utter dark, leaped to his feet or tried to, going down again and turning over, staring at the white sliver of his thighbone where it had punched through the flesh, through the cloth of his levis, white, so white, lance-splintered, there amid the rough blue cloth, and now the sudden, thickred torrent before the pain came and the black onrushing dark drowned even the hoof thunder and the cattle brawl.

He felt hands clawing under his armpits, lifting powerfully. He fought his eyes open, but they wouldn't stay. He was aware of the bunching of horse flesh under him; the stabbing jar of each stride, the iron grip that held him, kept him from falling, the ghost shape under the black sombrero rising and falling rhythmically under the graying sky.

Then in an interval of no time, the sequence unbroken, the gap in his continuity healed without a scar, he was lying in his own bed, his leg stretched out, heavy with its splints, swathed in bandages, and Hannah was bending over him calling: "Roak, Roak!"

"Yes, Han?" he said.

"Oh, thank God!" she wept. "You don't know how scared I was! You just don't know—"

"A busted leg's nothing to take on over," he said tiredly. "Who doctored me? Benito?"

"Yes," she said; "I knew you'd want him. I hid all the liquor on the place 'til he got through, though. You—you've been out for days. No wonder. If you'd seen that leg when Fritz brought you in—"

Then she saw his eyes.

"Roak, don't!" she pleaded. "I don't know why he does those things! I don't know why he saved you. I only know he did—and that I'm grateful to him. Don't look at me like that! Haven't I got enough with you like this now and—"

His voice was dust, sifting through the silence.

"Like what now?" he said.

She looked at him, and her eyes gathered the light, blurred it, ejected it in white traceries falling slowly.

"Crippled," she said; "what good is it to try to hide it? Not very much, but enough. That leg is going to be a little shorter than the other, which we can fix with a built-up boot. But Benito says that your knee won't bend any more. You'll walk stiff-legged; and you—you'll never ride again. And you rode so beautifully! I—I never saw anybody who—could ride like you!"

Roak said: "Don't cry, Han; I'll be all right. . . ."

She turned away from him, staring out the window. She was so still he couldn't see her breathe. Then her voice came over to him, far-faint, quiet, not even quavering.

"All right? Is anybody ever all right in this world, Roak? We go on burying ourselves by bits and pieces: the you that made music and wild poetry, and even a kind of grandeur out of the simple act of forking a mustang; me the girl who believed in life and love and that her chevalier had come a-riding! Now look at us—just look. . . ."

"I'm looking," Roak said; "me, a cripple—"

"And I worse maimed," Hannah said. "I've had hoping and believing hacked out of me and the doctor left his choloroform at home—"

"So you figure Fritz has won?" Roak said.

"No. I figure that the cards are stacked, the game brace-dealt—and that nobody ever wins. Certainly not Fritz, because what he's aiming at is too little in the first place. Getting even isn't a thing a body can fail at respectably."

"What is?" Roak said.

"Many things. Like trying to live your days out in absolute verity, whether you believe or not, whether there's anybody up there watching or not. Like existing in decency, dignity and self-respect whether those qualities are rewarded or not, or whether they mean anything or not or even granting that they are meaningless—I know, I know, it sounds crazy to you; but since we're all foredoomed to failure, at least let us fail grandly and with style, trying to make the condition of being human, of being man and woman together linked and through Jessica continued, not wholly wanting in significance, having some small importance, if only to ourselves, if only for this brief flickering in the dark we call our lives. . . ."

Roak lay there, looking at her.

"You haven't failed then, Han," he said; "by these your lights, if such they be, you haven't failed at all. . . ."

Chapter Seventeen

LYING THERE waiting for his leg to heal, learning to walk again with the aid of a stout cane, Roak had plenty of time for thinking. And what he thought was this: that the world just wasn't big enough any more for him and Fritz Heindrichs both.

He thought that very sorrowfully and without anger. He was against killing on principle; but equally on principle he was even more against living like a mouse between a cat's claws, released again and again to run, only to be caught and maimed a little more each time. What he'd done to Fritz had been done without thought, and had had consequences beyond his expectations. But by now he'd paid for both his acts and their consequences over and over again.

So now he was going to Fritz Heindrichs—or after him. The choice of the word depended upon Fritz. Because he was going in peace, but armed. He was going to try to hold a parley, call off the war between them forever. Failing that, he was going to kill Fritz Heindrichs or die trying. But living under the circumstances Fritz had forced upon him was the one thing he wasn't going to do. Not now. Not any more.

Leaving Hannah sleeping very peacefully, he got up and dressed. He wasn't worried about her waking up, or about her asking questions if she did. She was accustomed to his getting up before dawn. He had always been a light and fitful sleeper, and the awkward business of turning over in bed with a knee which wouldn't bend sufficiently

made him remain too long in one position until his whole
body ached and that woke him up. So he took his cane and
limped out of there, remarking with satisfaction that his
limp really wasn't too bad.

He waited while Angelo harnessed his snow-white pair
to the buckboard—for Benito had been right, his leg remained too stiff for him to ride a horse. Then he put his
sawed-off shotgun—loaded buck and ball this time, because if it came to a fight, he wasn't going to be playing
children's games—into the special scabbard he'd had made
for it, just forward of the footboards, slanting upward
along the dash. Then, with Angelo helping him, he climbed
in and took the reins.

He could see the Mexican cowboy looking at him curiously, but he didn't offer any information as to where
he was going. He figured it wasn't anybody's business except his and Fritz Heindrichs's.

"Adiós, patrón!" Angelo said.

"Adios," he said gruffly, and flapping the reins across
the snowy backs of his team, he moved off, heading south.

He wondered if there weren't maybe an omen in Angelo's
saying *"Adiós!"* to him. Because *adiós* meant "to God,"
and was a final way of saying farewell. What Angelo
should have said, what, in fact, he usually said, was *hasta
luego,* or *hasta la vista,* or *hasta mañana,* which meant
"until a little while," "until I see you again," and "until
tomorrow," respectively. You only said *adiós* to a man you
thought was going to be gone a long time. Maybe even
forever.

Then he forgot about all that. One of the reasons he'd
been a good soldier in the War was that he could shut off
his imagination whenever it threatened to get in the way
of what he had to do. Because the minute you started imagining all the things that could happen to you in a big war
like the last one or even in a private war between men
facing each other under a desert sun, you were finished.

Added to all the other burdens a man had to carry around with him anyhow, fear was too much. Was too much, didn't help anything, and fouled everything up dirtily. So he couldn't afford it.

He had seen all the ways that a man could die violently in battle, and all the most horrible ones involved high explosives, grapeshot or shrapnel except sabering and bayoneting. Therefore all the really bad ways to kill were beyond either his capacities or Fritz's. For that reason he didn't have to worry about the manner of his dying, if he had to die that day. As for the thing itself, it didn't matter at all. The only questions about a man's death that made any sense were how and when. And the when was even more irrelevant than the how. It wasn't a thing you could get out of, so when it happened made very little difference. Men died. Some late, some soon, but they died. All of them. Done well and with dignity, it was an acceptable thing. What wasn't acceptable was living like a rat. For that was to surrender everything that made life worth living: manhood, and dignity, and pride.

It was still very early when he came up to the little blue house at the end of the street where he had known happiness of a kind and to a degree that he couldn't bear remembering any more; and also pain to an extent that he couldn't bear to remember either, except that, the human mind being what it is, he couldn't help remembering it. He sat there in the buckboard watching the morning sunlight slant along that street, seeing the desert out beyond it, sand glare, rocks, cholla cactus, Joshua trees—seeing all that, the street silent and empty, the various-colored houses with their tiled roofs, the white wisps of smoke rising from the chimneys into a sky empty, too, all blue with no cloud in it anywhere, with nothing in it anywhere except the tiny black specks of the buzzards so high up that at first he hadn't seen them, but which were always there, because death was always present even on days like this one. He saw all that, fixing it in his mind with the almost conscious thought that this was maybe the last time he was going to see these things or, for that matter, anything at all. Then, very stiffly, he climbed down. He didn't go to the door to knock on it. He called out, his voice stabbing the soundless street long through the silence:

"Fritz!"

The door opened almost at once, and Fritz came out. He grinned.

"Why, howdy, Roak," he said; "what brings you down here so early?"

"I came to settle things, Fritz," Roak said. He spoke quietly, evenly, without haste. "I've stood for enough. Suffered enough, if that's what you want, to suit even you. You willing to shake hands and call off the war now, Fritz?"

Fritz's grin widened.

"No," he said.

"Then, mighty sorrowfully, I'm going to kill you," Roak said. "Go get your gun, boy. I'll wait."

Fritz's grin didn't even waver.

"No," he said again.

"Then I'll kill you without it," Roak said tiredly.

"You won't," Fritz said. "You just haven't got it in you."

"I wouldn't bet on that," Roak said, and drew the shotgun out of its scabbard.

Fritz didn't move. He stood there nerveless and cold, waiting.

Roak could feel himself trembling on the inside. Feel the green taste of nausea rising to his throat.

"God damn you, Fritz, I—" he began; but Belén came out of the house with the little boy in her arms. In her right hand she held Fritz's revolver. She handed it to him, butt first.

"Here," she said; "take it, my husband, and settle this, like a man."

Fritz stood there staring at her. Then he put out his hand and took the gun.

"You're right," he muttered. "It had to be settled like this, someday. . . ."

"Now," Belén said serenely, "I shall count for you. Neither is to fire before the count of three. *De acuerdo, caballeros*?"

"Belén!" Roak said, his voice a scrape, a hoarseness. "Take that kid back into the house! You don't want to see —you don't want him to see—"

"The man who truly is his father murdering the man who has protected him, supported him, been *eternamente* kind? Or vice-versa? Why not, Roak? Since life is like that, a thing of sickening barbarity, of endless cruelty, with neither justice nor mercy nor even pity in it, why should he not learn it, now?"

"Mama!" little Roak wept. *"Tengo miedo*! I have fear, Mama! Much, much fear!"

"Oh, Jesus!" Roak whispered.

"Are you ready, gentlemen? One!"

"No," Roak said; "no. You win, Belén. I can't. Like this, I can't. . . ."

But Fritz flashed his wolfish grin.

"I can," he chuckled; "now I can! Seeing your face right now, boy, is enough. Now I can finish it."

"Two!" Belén said. And waited.

"Come on!" Fritz laughed. "Come on, *bebé*! Count that three!"

"One moment," Belén said, her voice filled with that matchless serenity that Roak had never heard equaled, and never would; "I shall continue counting in a moment, Fritz. But first, I think that you should know that if you kill Roak, now or ever, I shall leave you and take the child with me. You cannot prevent this. The only thing you will have to decide is whether to open the door and let us go, or close it—and bury us. Both of us."

"Lord God!" Fritz said.

"And you, Roak," she went on quietly, "if you kill Fritz, I shall erase your memory from my mind, teach your son that he is fatherless. Now I am ready. Three!"

The walls of the houses threw back the echoes of her voice. There was no other sound.

Roak stood there, his weapon pointed at the ground, looking at Fritz. Slowly Fritz pocketed his gun.

"Thank you," Belén said. "Thank you, both. Roak, will you have coffee with us now?"

"Coffee?" Roak said; "coffee!" Then he turned so fast that his bad leg gave under him so that he had to clutch the side of the buckboard to keep from falling. He dragged himself upright, feeling at the last her hand on his arm, helping him, and he, looking at her, saw that her black eyes were swimming, flooded, blind, and snarled:

"Don't pity me!"

"No," she said, "it is myself I pity for having lost thee, Roak. This of thy leg is nothing. It reduces thee not. Nothing exterior to his own heart can diminish the stature of a man."

Roak climbed up then, sat there in the buckboard looking down at them. At all three of them.

"Well," he said, "looks like the war's over, in spite of us, Fritz."

Fritz grinned at him; said:

"Maybe so, Roak—and maybe not. I won't kill you. Not now, not ever. But if one day you get tired of living, Belén can't rightly blame me, now, can she?"

"You'll have yourself one long wait, boy," Roak said, and turned his team around.

"Adios, Belén," he said.

But she didn't say "adios" to him. What she said was a stranger thing:

"*Hasta siempre,* Roak!" she whispered.

Until forever. He wondered what the devil she meant by that. He was going to go on wondering that. All the rest of his life, maybe.

Chapter Eighteen

AND THE rains came and the waters were upgathered and all the rivers ran thunderously, stream and branch and rivulet overwashing their banks, and here and there a tributary cut across a neck of land to rejoin the mainstream; and now and again desperate men and women threw up a wall to prevent such a juncture.

Which was precisely what Hannah Garfield did or tried to do, willing into being dikes to enforce a separation essentially artificial, impermanent, unlasting as all divisions between branch and river always are, serving only in flood time to swirl the waters deeper, higher, louder raging, until they burst her puny walls as inevitably they would: for her dikes were but her jealousy, her love, her fear; and the torrent she opposed—was time.

Roak wasn't there when the telegram came. He was out riding, as usual, with Jessica. Riding in that splendid buggy with its curved dash cut down so that his leg could stick straight out, unbending, drawn by those two extravagantly showy, snow-white horses—stage props, symbols, not of what was but of what he ferociously desired; imposing by sheer insistence, by never deviating a hair's breadth from the role he had written for himself, until other men came to believe it, too: that image of gruff Captain Garfield, draped in imported broadcloth, a gold watch chain as thick as a man's thumb sweeping across his embroidered waistcoat, his black, low-crowned Stetson set unslanting on his head, his boots handmade, the left one built up with a four-inch-thick sole, the whole of him broadened, thickened by his enforced lack of exercise, squaring off into a dignity that curiously included his rolling, lurching gait, so that when his Mexican *vaqueros* said *"el cojo"*—"the lame one"—they said it with pride.

So it was that Hannah had all the time in the world to stare at that slip of paper, then upward at the dust-grimed face of the rider, who came only from Furniss now instead of all the way from Brownsville because almost single-handed Roak had rammed through a petition to the State legislature, signed by all his neighbors, to extend the telegraph line that far in anticipation of the Southern Pacific's arrival, although in that year, 1880, the railroad was still west of El Paso and building eastward so slowly that it would be another two years before it got to where they were.

"But," she said, "we don't know anybody in St. Joseph, Missouri—"

"You mean *you* don't, ma'am, begging your pardon," the rider said, "but this here telegram is addressed to Mr. Garfield, and it 'pears to me I heard tell he come from up there somewheres. . . ."

"He came from Ohio," Hannah said; "but all the same —thank you very much. . . ."

She took the telegram and went into the house with it. She sat down by the table, holding it in her hand. She figured she hadn't any right to go into Roak's mail; but a telegram was a thing a body sent when matters were worse than urgent, maybe even desperate, so she tore it open and read:

AM IN BAD TROUBLE. PLEASE COME. GWEN.

She didn't move. Her hand holding the paper didn't even shake. Her mind moved off—edgewise it seemed to her—upon one of those odd speculations that had become characteristic of it: she wondered with curious detachment if it were true that time moved in only one direction; if, in fact, the conception of past, present and future made any more sense than most of the ideas that mankind clung to with such maniacal tenacity; if time weren't amorphous, formless, omnidirectional, so that at any moment the gray slime of the past couldn't creep over and absorb the present, drowning it, along with all the illusory risings and settings of a relatively motionless sun men call the future. Or if time didn't exist in layers like geologic faults, which would split asunder when acted upon by subterranean pressure, letting the past (what was the past? Did such a thing exist? Is the moral continuity of an action so definitely broken that we can call it past? Do not the sins of the fathers back unto the third and fourth generations weigh still upon our hearts?) scream through to impinge upon the present, arrogantly warping it out of any recognizable shape—

Like now.

She had known all along that Roak's lingering in St. Louis a week longer than Bart Nevis and the rest at the end of the trail drive of 1869 (eleven years ago, dear Lord! So long as that? So very long?) had meant something. She had seen him come back, sunk fathoms deep in silence, with that bad sadness in his eyes. And she had made the obvious guess: a woman. Roak wasn't built for monkhood or sanctity either one. But now (why wouldn't the goddamned past stay the hell where it belonged? The language of her thought no longer shocked her; her days were lined with suppressed fury like a splendid cloak with scarlet velvet) she saw that the incident had been graver than she'd thought: not *a* woman, *that* woman; perhaps even *the* woman, instead of Belén as she had believed. And time had become hydra-headed, entwined, serpentine, its tendrils so intricately linked that there was no separating them into their nonsense names of present, future, past. Gwen, now. Gwen, then. Gwen forevermore. Gwen whom Roak had loved, now would/will love, had left, returned to, betrayed, cherished, slashed Fritz Heindrichs into hideousness over—emerging from the amorphous mass, blasting volcanically upward out of the geological fault, entwining two or more heads of the hydra to—

No! By heaven and hell, no! She was already running blindly, head down, toward the door.

"But why do they cut our bobwire fences, Papa?" Jessica said.

"Barbed wire," Roak corrected her automatically. "Because they just haven't caught up with the times, baby. They're trying to hang onto a thing that's dead. The open range was fine back in 1870. Clean up 'til '75 it was still all right. But now it makes no sense at all."

"Why not, Papa?" Jessica said. She didn't really care, of course; fences, barbed or not, aren't subjects of overwhelming interest to the feminine mind, not even to the eleven-year-old feminine mind. What interested her was what chiefly interests female minds at all ages: the man at her side. She would have discussed hay baling or tick fever to keep her beloved papa talking; unconsciously she was using him to practice techniques she was not even really aware of yet—a very new sidelong glance, a swift flutter of golden lashes, a slow and tender smile.

"Because," Roak said slowly, minding his grammar as he always did when he talked to his daughter, "the open range was necessary back then. Now it isn't. In those days we had to drive our cows to Kansas—to Abilene, Elsworth, Dodge City—in order to load 'em on a railroad car. But nowadays the railroads are reaching almost everywhere. By next year we won't have to hoof it any further than El Paso. A year after that, the line will pass through Furniss on the way to San Antone. So we won't have to cross other folks' territory, which means every man can get legal title to the ranges he's working just like I've done. And with the cows fenced in, we can breed true to type, improve the strain constantly, breed beef instead of two yards of useless horn, and sixteen hands of tough, stringy leg. And with the railroads right at our front door, we'll—"

He stopped short. He leaned forward swiftly, reaching for the sawed-off double-barrel shotgun which nestled in a sheath under the dashboard. It was the only weapon he carried now. But the rider, a big man under an enormous sombrero, made no motion toward his six-gun. Instead he made a swift sidewise motion with his head; and Roak saw for the first time the old Indian, mounted on a burro equally old, who accompanied him.

"*Hola,* Don Roak," he said. "*Vengo pacíficamente*— I come in peace. In fact, I come as a supplicant. . . ."

"*Diga,*" Roak said gruffly. "Speak. What is it that you wish?"

"A job," the big Mexican said; "I have lived upon that gut robber, pride, too long. And, as the last of my line, I must take care of *abuelito,* here. Though it may not seem so from the looks of him, he also eats—"

"I wasn't quite sure he even breathed," Roak said, staring at the old man, who sat there on his burro like a statue of brown granite, only the one eagle feather he had stuck in his white hair moving; "how old do you figure he really is?"

"*Hola, abuelito!*" the Mexican laughed. "*Cuantos años tienes*? How many years do you have?"

"*Ciento cincuenta,*" the old Comanche said.

"A hundred and fifty!" Jessica said. "Oh, Papa, he's the oldest man in the world!"

"At the risk of disillusioning the señorita," the big Mexican said with a grin, "my *abuelito,* my little grand-father, does not know how many years he has. But my *abuelita,* my little grandmother, who died last week, had ninety-two years when she died; and she always said that *abuelo* had two more years than she. My grandmother was a woman of the most honorable, so—"

"You mean he's fibbing?" Jessica said.

"I mean that he is very old, and that he forgets," the Mexican said.

Roak stared at him.

"I've seen you somewhere before," he muttered.

The big Mexican laughed.

"You and I exchanged knife slashes in the street for a merry half an hour, Don Roak. And when you had your blade at my throat, you gave me back my life. Which is why I sought you out. You are that rarity—a man with a heart. Could not you use one more *vaquero*?"

"Rustling business *that* bad?" Roak said.

"Worse than bad. Since '77; when our brave and noble leader was arrested by General Servando Canales and condemned to death—"

"Don't tell me they actually blasted Cortina!" Roak said.

"No. Our illustrious *Presidente, su Excelencia* Don Porfirio Diaz, was generous. He commuted the sentence to life-long confinement to *la Ciudad de México*. But the effect was the same: our repossession of *abuelita's* cattle—"

"Don't hand me that one," Roak snapped; "nobody knows who stole whose cows first. Mexicans and gringos have been raiding each other's herds for over a hundred years, and even your little old grandmother wasn't born then—"

"I know," the Mexican smiled; "it is just a figure of speech. To put it another way, without Brigadier General Cortina's leadership, our widespread importation of foreign cattle ceased to be either easy or profitable, especially since both the United States Army and the Texas Rangers have stopped respecting the border while pursuing the —eh—importers. To make matters worse, our illustrious *Presidente* seems bent upon making *México* into a law-abiding country. His *rurales* have orders to shoot rustlers on sight. So as I have always had the ambition to live as long as this, my ancient Comanche Indian of a grandfather, claims he has, or even as long as he really has, I bethought myself that a man kind enough not to cut my throat when he could have, might be equally unwilling to let me starve."

"Papa," Jessica said gaily, "give him the job! I like him!"

The big sombrero came off in a grand sweep.

"And thou, *señorita mía,*" the Mexican said, "hast a servant for life!"

"Very well," Jessica said in the language she had spoken before English, since Josefina had nursed her, "see that you comply with my orders. First, how do you call yourself?"

"Severo," The Mexican grinned; "which is a ridiculous name and fits me ill, but thus my good *padre,* whom I have in glory, called me. Severo González, at your service, señorita . . ."

"Now, wait a minute, both of you!" Roak said. "Severo, before I give you this job, you'd better give me some mighty straight answers to some straight questions: if you're so badly off, why didn't your good friend Ramón Benevides give you work? Heard he's doing mighty handsomely down there with that herd of red cattle he started from the bunch he rustled from me. And you and he were thick as thieves back then when you tried to carve me up—"

"But, like thieves, we fell out, Don Roak," Severo said blandly. "You see, he runs the vast and prospering Benevides Hacienda in partnership with his brother-in-law, Don Fritz Heindrichs, who does not approve of me. That is one thing. The other is that Doña María de Belén Benevides Camargo de Heindrichs repeated to her brother some unfortunate remarks I happened to have made in her presence upon the occasion of my unsuccessful duel with you, Don Roak. She did not have to repeat them to

her husband, as he overheard them. So, I believe, did
you—"

"Seems to me you did hold forth at some length on the
subject of what you intended to do to Belén after you got
finished with me," Roak said dryly.

Jessica gazed at Severo with vast and wondering eyes.

"And just what did you intend to do to her, Severo?"
she demanded.

"Now, just a minute, pet!" Roak began; but Severo
lifted a hand.

"Bite her," he said gravely; "just one tiny, tiny little
mordisco, señorita—because she was so pretty and sweet
that I was sure she would taste good, too!"

"Did she?" Jessica said.

"Alas!" Severo sighed; "I never got my little, little bite!
Your so gallant father intervened and beat me up. . . ."

"I must say you deserved it," Jessica said primly, "going around biting girls!"

"Well, seeing as how you can tell the truth occasionally," Roak said, "reckon I'll give you a trial. That you can
handle cattle, I know. Think you can get used to using a
real, legal brand instead of drawing fancy pictures on a
cow's hide with a running iron?"

"*Sí,* señor!" Severo said gaily. "You will find me *com-
pletamente honrado* and—"

"All right," Roak said. "You ride down to the bunkhouse and report to Old Will. There's a 'dobe house on
the east range you can put your grandfather in, but looking after him is up to you. Tell Will I said that, too. Tell
him to put you on that scrub mustang roundup. And don't
give him any lip if you value your hide. Get going,
now. . . ."

"*Sí,* señor!" Severo said.

Jessica snuggled up cosily next to Roak.

"He's nice," she giggled; "loco, but nice. Papa—"

"Yes, pet?"

"Couldn't we ride down to Uncle Bart's place? I haven't seen Tim and Richie and Ruthie in so long . . ."

Roak grinned a little wryly. He could deny Jessica nothing, and already she knew it. Despite all his longing for a son—at least for a son he could call his own—she had wrapped her childish fingers around his heart and put her brand upon him better than any running-iron artist in this world.

"All right, pet," he said.

But as he pulled that snowy team around, he heard his name called. Turning, he saw Hank Flynn riding toward them. And with Hank was a slim, dark boy who sat in the saddle as though he had been born there. Roak drew back on the reins and waited. Hank and the boy came up to them. Roak heard the sharp intake of his daughter's breath, and looking at the boy with Hank, he knew why. The boy was strikingly, even spectacularly handsome. Many a woman, including, Roak suspected grimly, Hannah, would have given her sacred honor to achieve waves like those this kid—fifteen or so—had in his dark hair. His eyes were dark, too, large and brooding under heavy brows; and the only place Roak had seen a nose as perfect as this one was on a statue in a museum he'd gone to with Fanny in New York, mainly because museums didn't cost anything. Beside that, the boy had a good mouth and strong cleft chin. In fact, Roak, giving way to a common masculine prejudice, decided at once that any boy this good-looking couldn't be worth much of a damn.

"Roak," Hank said, "I want you to meet Rod Cameron."

"But," Roak protested, "old Rod was a sight too old even fifteen years or so back to—"

The boy smiled. He had a good smile. Roak felt his prejudice lessening under its candor.

"He was my grandfather, Mr. Garfield," the boy said. "My father, Rod II, didn't like ranching, so he ran away, went back East, and married an actress. So my grandfather disowned him, cut him off in his will—"

"Howdy, son," Roak said, and put out his hand. The boy's grip was firm and pleasant as the rest of him. "This here's my daughter, Jessica."

"Delighted to make your acquaintance, Miss Garfield," the boy said.

Jessica didn't answer him. She just sat there, staring.

"Haven't you any manners at all, pet?" Roak said.

"Oh, Papa!" Jessica breathed. "Isn't he just too handsome for words!"

Hank laughed.

"You could do worse, boy," he chuckled, "a whole lot worse. Li'l Miss Garfield is the richest heiress in West Texas. . . ."

"I don't care about that, sir," the boy said. "When I marry I'll find myself a girl who is both pretty and good, just as my father did. The money isn't important. I intend to make my own—"

"Oh!" Jessica said plaintively.

"And Miss Garfield is pretty," the boy said gravely, "very, very pretty. But I don't know if she's good. Is she, Mr. Garfield?"

"Well, now," Roak said, "I wouldn't like to have to take my Bible oath—"

"Oh, Papa! You're mean!" Jessica wailed.

"Roak, I come looking for you on purpose," Hank said. "I already have seen Bart. I need both of you for witnesses—"

"Witnesses for what?" Roak said.

"To sign the adoption papers. I'm adopting this boy," Hank said.

Roak stared at him.

"Yep, I got kids of my own, maybe even enough kids," Hank said heavily; "but I'm trying to do the square thing, Roak—"

"Maybe you better spell that one out for me," Roak said.

"Simple. Long before he died, old Rod disinherited this kid's pa. So legally Rod III, here, ain't got a leg to stand on when it comes to the Flying U. It's mine. The old man willed it to me, and the circuit judge probated the will. Only—"

"Only you're a white man," Roak said quietly, "and you know that what's legal ain't always just—that's it, Hank?"

"That's it. Rod here's a orphan, now. When his ma died a month back, he made his way out here to keep 'em from putting him in a home. And he's a good kid—"

"And you're dead, damned right," Roak said. "When's the signing?"

"Tomorrow, at the Justice o' Peace office in Furniss, if you can make it."

"I can make it," Roak said. "Fact, it'll be a pleasure."

"Papa," Jessica said, "Rod can call on me, can't he? Tomorrow, maybe?"

"Why, you forward little minx!" Roak said. "How do you know he even wants to?"

"I do, very much," Rod said, smiling; "may I, sir?"

"Well—I reckon so," Roak said. "But not tomorrow. We've got to get you adopted proper and legal tomorrow, son—"

"Friday evening, then, sir?" the boy asked.

"Friday it is," Roak said. "Had yourself some mighty fine home training, didn't you, son?"

"My mother," the boy said softly, "had the idea that bad manners were about the worst thing on earth. Well— Father," he added to Hank, "we mustn't detain Mr. Garfield any more—"

"Right," Hank said. "Be seeing y'all, Roak, missy—"

"Be seeing you—Rod," Jessica said.

But even after that they never reached the Nevis place. Halfway there, Bart Nevis met them.

"Roak," he said, "I hate like hell to make you climb down with that there gimpy leg; but you 'n' I've got talking to do what ain't rightly fitten for this precious li'l kitten's ears—"

"Now, Uncle Bart!" Jessica protested. "I'm quite grown up, and—"

"No, you ain't, kitten," Bart said solemnly, " 'cause the day you are, you'll know it. You'll be all dressed in white and standing up before the preacher with my Tim. I got my claim staked on you for my first daughter-in-law, right now. . . ."

"Oh, fudge!" Jessica said. "Tim's too little! He's a whole year younger than I am, and—"

"Late as yesterday," Roak said dryly, "that didn't seem to matter to you, pet. You don't mean to tell me that just because this—"

"Oh, Papa! Please be quiet!" Jessica said.

"Tim'll catch up mighty fast," Bart said. "Roak—"

"Give me a hand, then, Bart," Roak said.

They moved away from the buggy, Roak limping heavily, leaning on his stout walking stick.

"Roak," Bart said when they were far enough, "I'd appreciate it if you sort of put off visiting us 'til another day. Fact is, I reckon you ought to mosey on back home mighty fast—"

"Now, what the hell have I done to hurt Ruth's touchy feelings?" Roak said.

"Nothing. Nothing new, that is. Only, womanlike, Ruth's blaming you. If you hadn't brung that filly to St. Jo, it never could of happened. So far she's right—you have to admit that—"

"Right about what, Bart?" Roak said.

"You bringing the Heindrichs woman there from Abilene. You see, boy, we just got a telegram from St. Jo's chief o' police. Seems like Gwen Heindrichs kilt Ruth's old man."

Roak stood there. A long time. A very long time.

"Why?" he said.

"Damned if I know," Bart said. "Folks don't do much explaining in telegrams."

"They don't have to," Roak said tiredly; "I wrote Gwen old Wilson was there—a point that Ruth's forgetting, Bart: that you and she brought that shivering old polecat there, just like I brought Gwen, so the blame has to be divided at least—and that maybe she'd better sell out and move on, since, knowing her past as he did, he sure as hell could make trouble for her. But she wouldn't. Said she wasn't afraid of him. Now, you tell me one thing, Bart: how'd Harry Wilson make out with his store?"

"Lost it inside of six months," Bart said disgustedly.

"And what's he been living on since?" Roak asked. "You?"

"You've called it, partner," Bart said; "leastwise up 'til a year ago. Then he wrote he'd hit a streak o' luck on one of them big deals he's always talking about, and since then he hasn't asked for a red copper. . . . Funny thing, ain't it?"

"Funny?" Roak said. "I call it sad, Bart. Because you've already put your finger on the answer, if you'd ever bothered to think about it. Gwen started a lady's dress shop with the grubstake I left her. She's got taste and style, so she made a go of it. I happen to know she was earning money. Also, as of last year, there was a right decent widower fellow, fiftyish, walking out with her. She used to write me once in a while to a post office box in town. So there's the picture, Bart: the woman whose life I ruint had made another start. Was living like the lady she was born to be. With some hopes for future happiness and peace. Now, you tell me—just what nigger can you fit into that particular woodpile?"

"Goddamn!" Bart said feelingly. "He would, wouldn't he? Be just like the old son of a bitch!"

"Only he must have crowded her a sight too far, I reckon," Roak said; "and sure dumped one hell of a stew into my lap. What the blazes can I tell Han that'll convince her a crippled-up old wreck like me has got some real business in St. Jo?"

"Not a damn thing," Bart said. "In fact, if you don't git home mighty blamed fast, you're gonna have some tall explaining to do yourself. That there rider told me he'd left another telegram for you!"

Roak whirled then, started lurching toward the buggy. When he was close enough for Jessica to see his face, she let out a shriek.

"Papa!" she said; "Oh, Papa, what's wrong?"

"Nothing," he said quietly; "nothing at all, pet. Only we'd better be getting along home."

Hannah sat in the salon of the new *casa grande,* looking at Belén. Even under the circumstances, she couldn't repress a feeling of pure joy at the sight of the two or three gray hairs visible in Belén's black hair; and that, at thirty-two, Belén's figure, which would have caused any Mexican whatever to chant hosannas, was a sight too plump by gringo standards. So time existed after all, if only in its visible tracery upon human flesh. And if her own pale blondeness tended to hide any gray hairs she had, certainly the saddle-leather weathering of her face, the crowfeet around her eyes, the neck tightening into stringiness had fared less well than Belén's serene loveliness. She sighed.

"Fritz will not be long," Belén said. "He is with Ramón, supervising the branding. I have sent a rider after him. Would you like some tea—or even some brandy?"

"Brandy," Hannah said. "Your new house is lovely, Señora Heindrichs. . . ."

Belén pulled the bell cord. A stiffly starched maid-servant appeared as if she had been conjured up from the earth.

"*El cognac viejo,*" Belén said; "*el bueno,* Pili. *En segui-da si puedes por una vez en tu vida.* . . ."

Then she turned back to Hannah, smiling a little.

"Cannot we be friends even now, Doña Hannah?" she said. "You used to call me Belén."

Friends? Hannah thought wildly; what does the word mean? By definition one who withholds the knife from your back at least half an hour before driving it home. Enemies are perhaps kinder. . . .

She looked at Belén.

"No," she said slowly; "I do not mean to offend you, but I don't see how it is possible for us to be friends. I look at you and I am reminded of a thousand, thousand hateful things, that, until I see you, I manage most of the time to forget. I'm sure it must be the same for you—isn't it?"

"Yes," Belén said softly; "and you are right. It is bet-ter that we try not to be *hipócritas,* no? Still, it saddens me sometimes. Because we could have been friends had it not been—"

"For life and fate and a man named Roak Garfield," Hannah finished for her dryly. "Ah, the brandy! You can-not imagine how much I need it. . . ."

Belén's gaze was suddenly direct.

"Among us," she said, "it is considered ill-bred to ask a visitor *el motivo* for her visit unless she volunteers the information. Still—"

"Still," Hannah said, putting the brandy down untasted, "if we cannot be friends, we at least now have no further reasons for being enemies. Upon that basis, Belén, and so far as I know it, the truth: I have news of your husband's sister. The one who was the cause of all the trouble be-tween Fritz and Roak—"

"Gwendolyn," Belén said. "I know the story. And?"

"She's in trouble. Dreadful trouble. I can't tell you what that trouble is, because I don't know. This morning a rider brought this telegram."

She put her hand out toward Belén, with the paper in it. Belén took it, read it, looked at Hannah.

"And Don Roak, of course, has not seen this message?" Hannah's smile was wintry.

"I don't think I even look like a fool," she said. "You —you've been in love—notably, with my husband—"

"Only with your husband," Belén corrected her, quietly; "go on."

"You're honest," Hannah said. "You've been in love with Roak. You have now a husband who represents, if nothing else, a great deal more ease and comfort than you've ever known. So you must understand. Even if it meant leaving this poor, stupid woman to get out of whatever she's got into as best she can, or suffer the consequences, I wouldn't show Roak that telegram. But, fortunately for my conscience, the woman in question has a brother who is as well equipped as Roak is to aid her. And who can do it without hurting anybody, or endangering his marriage, or—"

Belén got up then, crossed over to Hannah, gave her back the telegram.

"You have much right," she said, "as far as you go. Fritz can fly to the aid of his sister with my entire approbation and my consent. In fact, I should even go with him, if he wants me to. But how seldom is life so delightfully simple, Hannah. Even the explanation of what I think now is long and wearisome and complicated. Let me put it in a phrase, leaving the complications and the explanations to your quickness of wit: I—out of, let us say, certain memories, certain good memories, I have of Roak—would not show that wire to Fritz. For the same reasons, and even better ones, I don't think you should, either. . . ."

Hannah felt her throat quiver with sudden panic.

"You mean that Fritz—that Fritz would blame Roak for this, too? That he—he might even—kill him?"

Belén bowed her head. Then she looked up again.

"I don't *know* any of these things," she said; "but I think so, yes. Except for this of the killing. That I know Fritz would not do. He thinks that killing is a childish and primitive method of taking vengeance—and that pain, physical pain, even when it amounts to prolonged torture, is only a little less so. There is a thing he says: 'The only proper death for an enemy is suicide; and even then, if that was Roak Garfield, I'd sure as hell try and stop him, so he could go on squirming a sight longer—' "

"But—but," Hannah protested, "he has done nothing in all these years except to twice save Roak's life—"

"Which was part of it," Belén said; "the negative part, *quizás*. He is a very complicated man, my husband. . . ."

"And the positive part of his vengeance," Hannah said, "what is it, Belén? I confess I don't see—"

"I know you don't," Belén said, and turned to the bell cord. When the maidservant appeared, she said quietly: "*Tráigame el niño aquí,* Pili," and waited, her black eyes suddenly cruel, something about her smile oddly reminiscent of Fritz Heindrichs's own. She said pleasantly: "Another brandy?"

"No," Hannah said, "no, thank you; I—"

But that was all she had time for, because the maidservant came back through the archway leading the child. A boy, nine or ten years old. She guessed that, because he had to be. He looked younger. He was small for his age as —as his father had been, was still. And Fritz was right, so right as Belén's not unskillful adoption of his methods was demonstrating now, proving beyond all questioning or any doubt. There were things the dead couldn't do, like contracting their lungs into a solid mass bearing simultaneously the contradictory attributes of ice and fire, like reducing their stomachs into one long slow quiver a pouchful of field mice or bats maybe yes surely bats because that gut-flutter had the feel of obscene wings. Like hearing somewhere in the mind's own utter dark in the dead still arrested stopped unmoving no longer beating red cavern of unspeakable pain that was her heart the long long bloody tearing of a scream and if according to Keats unheard melodies were sweeter than heard the evidence was all in now and conclusive that an unvoiced shriek was more anguished bitter than mere sound.

"Mama," Roak's image in miniature, except for the added cruelty of Belén's nightshade eyes, piped, *"quién es esta señora? Es muy guapa—tiene pelo como lo de Papa y el mío, verdad?"*

And she, Hannah putting out her arms in the direction of the sound, because by then she couldn't even see him any more, and saying:

"Ven, hijo, ven aquí—come, son, come here. I am glad that I am pretty in thine eyes. Yes, I have hair like thine and thy father's. Tell me, how art thou called?"

The boy came to her without shyness.

She bent and kissed him in a perfect agony of tenderness.

"How art thou called?" she said again.

"Roak," the boy said; *"me llamo Roak."* Then, staring at her in wonder: *"Porqué tu lloras, señora? Te he dicho algo que te has hecho llorar?"*

"No," Hannah whispered; "no—Roak. Thou hast done nothing, said nothing to make me cry. It is just that thou are—so handsome—and I have prayed so long for a son like thee. . . ."

"Thou hast no children, then?" the boy said gravely.

"Sí," Hannah said; "I have a daughter. But I wanted also to have a son. . . ." And looking up, she met Belén's pitying eyes.

"And Don Roak?" Belén said. "Has he not likewise a desire for an *hijo?"*

"Terribly," Hannah said dryly, "as you know well."

"Yes, I know it," Belén said. "And so does Fritz. I think you begin to comprehend the extent of his vengeance. You see how much he has robbed your husband of?"

"You mean he—he knew?" Hannah said.

"Of course. I think sometimes he only married me to obtain possession of Roak's child—"

"No," Hannah said bitterly, "to take you away from Roak as well—"

"And the red cattle," Belén said, her tone as acrid as Hannah's own, "other owned creatures dear to Roak's heart. And this of keeping him alive after his leg was broken that he might enjoy in his own peculiar way the spectacle of Roak lurching through life with a gait that is ugliness's self, Roak who was all grace like a *bailerín*, a dancer, or even a *torero*—"

"And putting him in a buggy like an old man," Hannah whispered, "he who was a part of his mount as though they were one flesh. Yes, now I see. And I think that there is no one on earth colder or crueler than your husband, Belén. . . ."

"Or more patient," Belén sighed. "You see now why this of the *telegrama* must be hidden?"

"Yes," Hannah said, "I see that now—" Then she stiffened. "That rider! The one you sent to—"

Belén smiled.

"How innocent are you *nórdicas*, you blonde ones! I sent no rider at all," she said.

It was dusk by the time Hannah got home again. She pushed open the door, and saw Roak standing by the mantel, leaning on his cane. He put his right hand out toward her, palm up.

"Give it to me," he said.

She stared at him, sparring for time.

"Give what to you, Roak?" she said.

"My telegram," he said quietly, "the one I got from Gwen."

Her eyes went darting, wild.

"There wasn't any—" she began.

"Give it to me, Hannah," he said.

She put her hand into the pocket of her riding habit, came out with the folded piece of paper, gave it to him. He neither opened it nor looked at it. He simply stood there holding it in his hand and looking at her.

"Where did you go?" he said.

"Down there," she whispered; "I thought that—that since she's his sister, Fritz—"

"You fool," he said, not even raising his voice. "Fritz hasn't spoken to her in years." Then he paused long enough to read the message. His face didn't change. "What did he say?" he said.

"I didn't see him," Hannah got out; "Belén thought. . . ."

"Go on," Roak said; "what did Belén think?"

"That it—it wasn't wise," Hannah said, "that it wouldn't help anything to get Fritz riled up again. He—he's calmed down now, it seems. He's willing to let bygones—"

"Be bygones? In a pig's eye he is," Roak grunted. "The only thing possible to do with Fritz Heindrichs would be to kill him. Only I can't do that for a good many reasons, besides the fact that I promised Belén I wouldn't deprive her of a husband who's been mighty good to her. So there he is, down there; sitting there waiting and watching—"

"And occasionally saving your life," Hannah said dryly.

"And occasionally saving my life," Roak repeated. "When it suits him to—when he's afraid I'm going to be able to lie down peacefully in my grave and stop thinking about all the things he's taken away from me. . . ."

"Belén," Hannah said; "your son—what else?"

"Any real security I might have for the future, how it's going to turn out, I mean," Roak said; "that, too. You got any idea what it's like to have to worry about what he's gonna figure next? To wake up in the night in an ice-cold sweat for fear that one day it'll occur to him really how to get to me?"

"Jessica!" Hannah said suddenly. "That's it, isn't it, Roak?"

He looked at her. He went on looking at her until the interior trembling quivering her nerves became exterior and uncontrolled.

"Don't even say it out loud," he said, and started to stump out of there.

"Roak," Hannah's voice was jagged, a splintering, "you —you're going to her! To Gwen!"

He turned, and his eyes thawed a little.

"No—not to her. To help her, yes. There's a difference."

"Why?" Hannah said.

" 'Cause I've got to. 'Cause if it wasn't for me, she wouldn't be where she is right now. 'Cause I owe her that much. And maybe because of those things you said— verity, whether or not, dignity and decency, meaningless or not in God's name, whether He's up there or has taken a permanent vacation from mankind and all its works, as He damn well should have by now considering what we cook up for Him daily. But not for love, Han. That's over with, now—"

"Over with," Hannah whispered; "over with for her, for me—for Belén, too, Roak?"

"Maybe," he said. "I don't know. But it doesn't make any difference, one way or another. I'm here with you. She's down there—"

"With him," Hannah said.

"With him. Better like that. You and I suit each other—"

"Thank you, my lord," Hannah raged, "for these many favors and gracious compliments!"

He looked at her.

"Verity. The truth," he said. "The only thing that really counts, and is somehow kind of beautiful. All right. Take it—and cherish it, Han. I don't get a choke in my throat and my pulse running wild like a stampeding herd when I look at you. But then, I never did—"

"Dear God!" Hannah said. "Will you please, please shut up, Roak Garfield?"

"No. The truth, whether or not you even want it. Because it's valuable all by itself. And the truth is I feel some things for you I never felt for Gwen, for Belén, or for no other woman born. And those are the lasting things, Han. They go on after the wrestling and the panting and the bed tumbling are over and done with. So here they are: I like you, which 'twixt a man and a woman is a hell of a lot rarer and harder to get to than love. We can love people we can't rightly stand, baby—like I loved Fanny, a gal you never even heard of, and never will hear of again. The next thing is that I admire you, 'cause you're damned sure worthy of any man's admiration: you've got brains running out both your ears, and guts enough to rope a steer with. Besides, you're good, the real thing, the first-class, twenty-four-carat article, with no base metal in you anywheres. You're the best damn wife and the finest mother for his kids any fellow could have prayed to the good Lord for. I don't deserve you. And I'm grateful to you for all the things you've put up with for my sake, for all the things you've given me—completely, finally, and very humbly grateful, Han. . . ."

She didn't say anything; but he could see she was smiling and crying at the same time. Then she said, very slowly and softly and sweetly:

"You sawed-off, runty, gimpy-legged little Philadelphia lawyer. Get out of here. Go get packed. I'll drive you to Furniss in the morning to catch the stage."

He stared at her in wonder.

"You mean . . . ?" he said.

"Yes. That you can go save your old sweetheart. If she can be saved. Because after a declaration of love and affection like that one—in what the orators call 'your own inimitable style'—I can't say no. Because, Roak Garfield, you fork-tongued little sidewinder, this time you—you were even—maybe—telling the truth. Though God knows I've had to wait long enough to hear it from you! So go. I —I'll even go with you, if you want me to—"

"No, Han; but only because it's going to be mighty rough," he said.

It was. And one month from that day, when he stumped back in the door again, she could see how rough it had really been. She sat there listening to him, happy that he could tell it, even knowing as she did that he was talking less to her than merely talking it out, ridding his heart of the weight and ugliness of it.

"Old Wilson had been bleeding her white. You see, he had clippings from the Abilene paper about the time that Fritz killed Prince Parker and saved my life. And those papers were mighty outspoken. But she would have gone on paying at least 'til she could marry Mr. Matthews —a real decent fellow, Han; stuck by her even after it all come out in the wash—and move away from St. Jo. But one night the old coot got drunk and tried to take his payment in kind instead of specie—"

"You mean what I think you mean?" Hannah asked.

"Yep. Old as he was. Useless as he likely was, too. Gwen wasn't having any of that. So she got out her little derringer to scare him, she says, and I believe her, but he tried to take it away from her and it went off—"

"On that basis they should have acquitted her," Hannah said.

"They would have. Wasn't a dry eye in the house when she got through with her testimony. Only that hypocritical old bastard had joined the Episcopal Church—reckon he thought it would give him tone—and being a mealymouthed old faker, before long they'd made him a lay elder or something like that. Nope, vestryman. That was it. Head vestryman. So when that smart crook of a district attorney got up and rung in half a dozen witnesses from Abilene to prove poor Gwen had been a cabaret dancer and—"

"Your mistress," Hannah said tartly. "Oh, darling, I'm sorry, I—"

"And my mistress," Roak said quietly; "all right—and eight or ten more to prove she'd been a whore in St. Louis before that, and stood there pointing his finger at her and a-sneering and saying, 'I ask you, gentlemen of the jury, how can you believe this woman's accusations against that poor, forlorn Christian gentleman, a pillar of the Church, a sober, hard-working, lonely old man of seventy? Attempting to rape her—*her?* The one completely and demonstrably rape-proof woman in St. Jo? Gentlemen, I ask you!' "

"And?" Hannah whispered.

"They gave her life. And that only because there was one or two fellows on the jury who were squeamish about stringing up a woman. So they changed that 'guilty' to 'guilty with recommendation for mercy,' and the Judge had to hand down on that basis. Damn nigh killed him. He was for hanging her out of hand."

"Roak," Hannah whispered.

"Yep, Han?"

"Put your head on my shoulder. There—like a good boy. . . ."

He looked up at her from where he rested wearily against her.

"Now what?" he said. "This here's a mighty silly position for a grown man. . . ."

"Now—cry," Hannah said gently; "cry it all out. Or don't you trust me that much?"

His eyes were old granite, blue-weathered.

"I trust you, only I can't," he said.

Chapter Nineteen

THE FIRST drought came in 1886. Or rather the drying up of a land already so dry that nobody in his right mind would have believed further dehydration possible began that year. And it went on and on until all of them believed there wasn't going to be any end to it. Of course there were drizzles, sprinkles, even a thunderstorm or two. But they didn't matter. They only prolonged the agony. Because they were not enough—not nearly enough in that land where the stink of death came into every window.

The sky belonged to the buzzards now. The sky and the earth beneath. The air was always black with them, always thick with the stench of putrefaction. Around the dried-up water tanks, the cattle died. And the sorrowing hands came out and skinned them. The hides were worth money. But they left the carcasses to the buzzards. There was nothing else to do with them.

"Roak," Hannah said, "we're just about ruined, aren't we?"

"Nope," Roak said. "We've managed to build up a mighty handsome grubstake over the years. But I'd give every penny of it for three good rainy months—"

"Papa," Jessica said; "why don't you dig a well?"

Roak looked at his daughter. At seventeen, Jessica was something. Very like Hannah had been when he'd first met her. But with an indefinable extra added. A certain verve she'd got from him, maybe.

"Now, why didn't I think of that?" he said.

"Because it's too simple, I reckon," Jessica said; then she saw the grin lifting the corners of the thick red mustache he'd grown for his forty-fifth birthday and kept ever since. "Oh, fudge!" she said. "You're teasing again! You mean you *have* dug a well, Papa?"

"A dozen," Roak said wearily. "If there's any water under this here stretch, pet, I'll be blessed if I can find it. . . ."

"That's because you're not going at it right," Jessica said.

"And how do you propose to go at it, missy?" Hannah asked. "Go on, we're waiting. Give us another demonstration of how much smarter you are than your elders!"

"Oh, Mama," Jessica wailed, "don't you ever get tired of picking on me?"

"That's because she's jealous," Roak said. "You're younger and prettier. But seriously, pet, I'd listen to a locoed mustang right now. Tell me, what is the right way to go about it?"

"Well," Jessica said, eying her mother defiantly, "first you ask Severo's grandfather where the water ought to be—"

"That old Indian!" Hannah hooted. "Why, he can't find his way back home, much less water. He's almost too old to move, and—"

"But he *knows* where there's water," Jessica said stubbornly.

"Which," Hannah said, "he's abundantly proved to you by means of . . . ?"

Oh, hell, Roak thought, why can't wimmenfolks get along with one another? Even when they're mother and daughter, they—

"He hasn't proved it," Jessica said; "but I believe him. That's the difference between you and me, Mama: I trust people—"

"Commendable trait," Hannah said, "but it can be over-done. Roak! Where are you going?"

"To look for an Indian," Roak said solemnly, "an old, old Indian who doesn't even know his way home. Coming pet?"

"Of course, Papa!" Jessica said.

"I think you're both positively outrageous," Hannah snapped.

"And we think you're mighty sweet, don't we, pet?" Roak said.

"Yes, Papa," Jessica said. But it was clear from her tone that she didn't think anything of the kind.

They had to ride a long way to find Severo, because the Bar F, too, had grown with the years. The invention of barbed wire had changed everything, together with the fact that in 1883 the Southern Pacific reached both San Antonio and Houston in its slow west-to-east crawl, crept on past them to link with New Orleans. So Roak's gamble with effete shorthorn cattle paid off—more than paid off. He quit grieving over the herd of red hybrids that Fritz Heindrichs had relieved him of. Even those Garfield Reds, heavier than longhorns, yet retaining enough of the ornery old breed's ranginess to hoof it to Kansas, weren't neces-sary any more. Nobody in that part of Texas had to drive a herd any farther than Furniss to ship their cows to mar-ket. So all the ranges were filling up with downright comical-looking critters with no horns to speak of, bodies like barrels, and legs so short their bellies fair dragged on the ground. But beef, every ridiculous pound of them.

So the pattern of ranching changed. Men acquired legal title to the ranges they had worked, strung barbed wire fences to enclose stretches bigger in some cases than the State of Rhode Island. The line rider disappeared to be replaced by the fence rider, just about the same job, really, but meaner. Because a fence rider for the Bar F

could be thirty-two miles from the house and still be on
the ranch's ranges, deeded, titled, and certified as such
in the big books at the State Capitol. Worse, being that
far away, he'd still have to fight a single-handed war,
against squatters, who cut the fences to drive their thirsty
steers to the tanks they'd been fenced away from. Or
against rustlers. Or against good, honest neighbors who
didn't cotton to any surveyor's opinion of where the fence
ought to run. But those mean, twisted strands of hide-
ripping wire made scientific breeding possible. Roak had
two dozen different "cow camps" on his spread, each
carefully segregated from each other, and all of them
guarded against rampaging old longhorn bulls—gone wild
now, who could, and did upon occasion, ruin in a single
night a strain it had taken five generations to breed pure,
accomplishing that ruination by busting through the barbed
wire fence, knocking the fat and helpless shorthorn sultan
sprawling with the first rush, trampling him within an inch
of his life, and sometimes even beyond that inch on the
second; and then taking good care of the fallen sultan's
harem for the rest of the night.

That was where Severo González was now. Out at one
of the farthest of the cow camps, likely enough plunking
at a guitar on the doorstep of his adobe hut, while his
graven image of a grandfather, the man time had forgot
about, death overlooked, sat there listening or not listening—no man could tell.

They drove with their bandanas over their mouths and
noses, which effectively stopped all attempts at conversation, but made the stench only barely bearable. Passing
through that sunstricken hell, Roak saw one thing: his
fancy shorthorns couldn't take it. The few remaining heads
of longhorns he'd kept out of pure sentimentality were
gaunt and miserable enough, but they were alive. The
easternbreds weren't. Not many of them, anyhow. If he
didn't find water damned soon. . . .

He didn't finish his thought. There was no point to finishing it. The completion of anything lay far out of his hands now.

He heard Jessica's voice, muffled by her kerchief, saying his name with sudden urgency, making a small double-breath explosion of the two syllables: "Pa-pa!"

And he, looking up, saw the rider sitting there looking at him, man and horse alike black against the light, gathering, it seemed to Roak, about them all the darkness left in a world heat-killed, sunstricken, brazen with glare, but pooling that darkness, concentrating it into an absolute: a one-man, one-horse reservation for nightshade, out of which that slow, dry, almost soundless chuckle emanated, stole, spreading its irresistible counterfeit of hoarfrost, of bleak winter, over the convincing replica of hell's bottom pit through which they rode.

"Come to gloat, Fritz?" Roak said.

"Nope," Fritz Heindrichs said. "The dry-up's right pert bad down our way, too. Who's the li'l lady? Your daughter? Heard tell you had one—"

"Yes," Roak said.

"Howdy, missy," Fritz said. "Your pa 'n' me are old friends—or old enemies. Sometimes I ain't rightly sure which."

"Howdy," Jessica whispered.

"Aren't you?" Roak said.

"Nope," Fritz Heindrichs said. "Funny. . . ."

"What's funny?" Roak said.

"How things turn out," Fritz said. "Spent more'n twenty years camping on your trail, living in your shadow, kind of. Figgering out ways to make you suffer—and you ain't; not enough, leastwise. But that ain't the curious part. What's plumb downright loco 'bout the whole thing is that getting even, robbing you—I made my own life. I got me the sweetest, best woman what ever drew breath, and a son, all of sixteen years old now, what any man could be proud of. Got me a nice li'l rancho, too—"

"Rancho," Roak snorted; "hell, you've got yourself a hacienda, Fritz."

"Yep—you could call it that without stretching the truth too far," Fritz said. "The point is, I'm happy. Done lost track of Gwen; but last time I heard from her she was doing all right, getting set to git hitched to a feller called Matthews."

Roak's face tightened. So you don't know, he thought. Figured you didn't. Or else—

But Fritz was laughing now—a flat-toned, ugly sound.

"Yep," he said; "figgered she was gonna grieve for you forever, didn't you?"

"No," Roak said; "I didn't figure that, Fritz."

"No matter. Twenty-two years is a long time to keep a thing up, even for me. Like Belén says, life goes on and things change. Even my face."

"Looks the same to me," Roak said.

"Yep. Only the effect of it ain't the same no more. Done quit being a door locked 'n' barred 'twixt me and being happy. Folks down there have plumb forgot to pay it no special attention, 'cepting a occasional stranger what wanders into town. And since it 'pears to me that Gwen is most likely all right—"

He leaned forward suddenly, put out his hand.

"War's over, Roak," he said peacefully; "I'm calling it quits. You wanted that once. Still of the same opinion, boy?"

Roak stared at that outstretched hand. At the heart's core of living there was always this uneasy business of deciding things, of making up your mind. And mostly you had to make your decisions before all the evidence was in—like Fritz was doing now. Wanting peace, calling the war off on the basis—at least partly on the basis—that Gwen was all right, had lived beyond Roak Garfield and the slow poison he had injected into her life twenty-three years before. And now, he, Roak, had to make up his mind, had to decide whether it was best to accept an armistice on that basis, whether peace and Fritz Heindrichs's pardon should or could be maintained on the shaky foundation of this one more lie. He was dog-tired, and now Fritz had seen Jessica grown up, had seen her and sure as hell had guessed what she meant to him. It was maybe dirty stinking rotten to make what was essentially a coward's peace, letting Fritz believe that Gwen was safe and happy while the actual fact was that she was doing life in the woman's branch of the Missouri State Penitentiary; but the risks involved in telling the truth were too great, the prospect of being able to let his guard down even a little was too inviting.

He took Fritz Heindrichs's hand.

"Papa," Jessica whispered after Fritz had loped away, taking with him that private segment of winter that accompanied him forever, iron-frost and chill, "who was that awful man?"

"Don't worry your pretty head over him none a-tall, pet," Roak said. "C'mon, let's go find the old water witch."

Severo was playing the guitar. And his grandfather was sitting on the doorstep, listening or not listening, just as Roak had expected.

"*Hola, patrón!*" Severo said. "What brings you and the señorita queen of all men's hearts way out here?"

"Oh, you!" Jessica said; but it was plain she liked the compliment.

"Your grandpa," Roak said; "he ain't deaf, is he?"

"Now that, señor," Severo grinned, "is a matter I have been trying to decide for years. Let us say that if so, it is a deafness of enormous selectivity. Suppose we try him today."

He turned to the statue of weathered sandstone that

didn't even convincingly look alive and said: *"Dime, abuelito; eres sordo hoy o no?"*

"No," the old man said; "today I hear very well, *nieto.*"

"Good!" Roak said. "I have been told, Grandfather, that you know how to find water. . . ."

The old Indian let his faded gray-brown eyes rest upon Roak's face.

"No," he said; "I do not know how."

"Oh, hell!" Roak said feelingly. "We came way out here just to—"

"But," the old Indian said, "I do know where."

"Oh, Papa!" Jessica squealed. "Didn't I tell you!"

"You don't know how, but you do know where," Roak said. "There's a difference, Grandfather?"

"Yes," the old man said.

"Mind explaining it to me?" Roak said patiently.

"To know how, a man must be a worker of the dark medicines and the bright," the old man said. "To know where, he needs merely to have been shown."

"And you have been shown?" Roak said.

"Yes," the old man said.

"Will you show me?" Roak said.

"Yes," the old man said, and that was almost, but not quite, that.

The reason it wasn't quite was a thing he had some trouble explaining to himself. Maybe he never would have explained it if he hadn't said to Hannah:

"Damned if I can understand it, Han. Here I've got everything all set up, the boys digging like crazy at that well. And at twenty-five feet we hit mud. That's a good sign. Only we're down to eighty feet now, and still mud. Looks like if we dig clean through to China we won't find anything a cow can drink."

She looked at him then, smiled, searched inside her mind and came up with one of those phrases that came out of all of those big books she was always reading, or out of her own weird little brain maybe; or what she herself and life had done to her way of thinking since the night of Fritz Heindrichs's visit.

"Life has its own way of operating, Roak," she said, "and there isn't a blessed thing we can do about it."

"You mean that things don't ever come out quite right, Han?" he said.

But she didn't answer that, not directly. She very often didn't answer a question now, but went on extending it obliquely in another direction. The direction of the plane on which she lived now, the tangent whose point of contact with life and living as he understood them, was to him disturbingly tenuous.

She said: "If they did, Roak, if they ever did, we wouldn't need any more priests or poets. . . . Ever thought about it that way?"

He said: "No, Han," and looked at her in the way he did when she moved out beyond him, which, as she grew older, was a thing that happened almost daily. And she:

"The pattern makers, darling, the givers of shape. Because we just can't understand or endure formlessness —it goes against the grain, somehow."

He retreated into the world as he understood it, the solid, the comprehensible.

"Mud," he muttered. "Eighty feet down and nothing but goddamned mud."

But she wouldn't let him stay there.

"Exactly," she said. "Mud. Thick, oozing, without pattern, shape, form or beauty, so—"

"So what, Han?" he said. "Blamed if I can follow you half the time—"

"I know." Smiling now, her blue eyes the color of the horizons he had been searching for all his life and had never quite got to—he, nor any other man; which, as she had once told him, was what horizons were for. "Don't try. Just listen. We have to preserve our sanity, Roak. So we have to go on believing in the face of all the contrary evidence that life has form. That it is not just—mud. That there's meaning in it, dignity, sense. That things happen for a reason: droughts are God's punishment for our sins; the cattle die of thirst because of your frequent committing of adultery, or because I was once maybe tempted to; we're being destroyed because you ruined Fritz Heindrichs's sister, and afterwards scarred his face—oh, consummation devoutly to be wished!"

He stared at her.

"You mean you want us to be punished, Han?"

And she: "Yes. Isn't that better than being ignored? Wouldn't you rather your well, your beautiful eighty-foot-deep well produced nothing but mud because God cared enough about you to chastise you, Roak? That the stink of rotting cow carcasses getting into everything, the curtains, the bedclothes, was an awful warning to mend your ways? Wouldn't even those things be better than—silence, than prayers that rise no higher than the roof, and ring in your ears like a mockery, because He's forgotten us, forgotten He ever created the world maybe, simply doesn't care, or—"

"Or maybe isn't even there," Roak said. "Go on, Han; you started this. So take it all the way. Have the guts to say what you really think. You're a big girl now—with a patch or two of gray in your hair, crowfeet 'round your eyes, a scrawny neck, and a grown daughter. So finish it. Say it for yourself—"

"Or—maybe isn't even there," Hannah whispered. "Oh, Roak, how terrible!"

And he: "Yep. I'm going to miss Him. He was mighty comforting to have around. . . ."

"Roak, no!" Hannah said. "We can't believe that! You can't—I can't—"

"No," Roak said quietly, "we can't, can we? Sure

does cut us down to size if we do, doesn't it, Han? Little crawling things to be stepped on, or burnt up 'cause we wandered too far out of the mesquite to where there wasn't any shade. So, like Job in the Good Book, I'm going to give Him another chance. Go ring that cowbell, honey. And when Pepe gets here, tell him to bring my buggy around. Meantime I'm going upstairs to pack—"

"Pack!" Hannah said. "Where on earth are you going now?"

"Pennsylvania. Heap of companies up there what specialize in drilling equipment. Oil drilling, which means boring deep. Passed through that country once before the War and they were pumping oil up from as far down as 700 feet. Course, I could hire me a fellow to drill me a deep well at a dollar a foot, and that's cheap enough. But that would be playing it small, demonstrating mighty little faith. I'm going to buy me a drilling rig and keep on boring 'til I find water or punch a Chinaman in the behind. And just before I begin I'm going to send up a mighty powerful prayer. After that, it's up to Him."

Hannah stared at him. When she smiled, her eyes remained still and sad.

"Amazing," she said, "after all these thousands of years. . . ."

"After all these thousands of years, what?" Roak said.

But she didn't answer him. Instead she went on, moving out beyond him again:

"Maybe you're right. Maybe He can be bargained with. Maybe He does prefer Abel's charred goat meat to Cain's stinking vegetables. Perhaps He does have that much of humanity about Him—perhaps He was really backward enough, primitive enough to lift mankind's sins at the price of a rather barbaric lynching. Or maybe we have to recreate Him every day in our images; and maybe He's even accommodating enough to take the likeness we dream up for Him."

"Han, sometimes—"

"You think I'm crazy. I know. But it's a good thought, Roak. Maybe He'll grant you your miracle of water from the rock—even though you're nobody's Moses, and who knows where Horeb is? Maybe He *is* kind enough to pass a convincing imitation of miracles for people desperate enough, hopeless enough to need miracles. And when our Mexican friends drag chains around their feet and carry heavy crosses or even wear their knees bloody against the stones by crawling on them for miles in fulfillment of a vow, maybe He's big enough not to be insulted by His retarded children's dim and mistaken apprehension of His qualities. Maybe He looks upon them —upon us, more pitiful still, since we don't even enjoy our sins—with tenderness, and occasionally even grants us what we want, knowing we meant no harm by putting Him in the position of a huckster who can be bargained with, but only promised Him our candles, abstinences, self-flagellations and bloody knees because we were—so very thirsty—and our cattle were dying. . . ."

"So?" Roak said.

"So, go to Pennsylvania! Buy your rig! And say your prayer. Most of all, don't forget that."

"Han, look at me!"

She turned to him, slowly.

"Yes, I'm crying," she said simply. "Sometimes, darling, you make me so very sad. . . ."

He went—perhaps understanding what she had meant and perhaps not. In any event, one month and a half later, she got the following letter from him:

Dear Han,

I bought the rig two weeks ago, so it ought to be there by the time you get this. It and a fellow to operate it. Cost me $30,000—the rig, I mean. The fellow's going to cost me $35 a week in salary plus his board and his railroad fare both ways. Anyhow you see that he drills in all the places Severo's grandpappy shows him. Don't know why but I got faith in that old cuss. And see that Pepe and Angelo and some of the others learn to run the rig, 'cause we'll be using it right along.

I'm telling you all this because I can't come home right now. Got to thinking about what you said about sin, so I took myself a detour by the Missouri State Woman's Prison to visit Gwen. I bought her some books and a Gramophone with records. Only I was damned nigh too late.

Because she wasn't in her cell no more. They'd carted her off to the prison hospital. After I'd done some tall arguing, they finally let me see her. All I could do was sit there, hold her hand, and try not to cry. She was down to skin and bones. Looks like she's sixty-five years old instead of the forty-two I happen to know she really is. Hair snow white. Skin wrinkled. And the kind of a cough that I knew what it meant right away because I used to cough like that myself before Benito cured me.

Only nobody can cure Gwen now. It's too late. I went all the way to the Governor of the State to try to get her out of there on the basis that she's suffered enough. The Governor was mighty white about it. Let me bring in the fanciest dang lung specialist in the Midwest to examine her. German fellow from Chicago. Studied at Heidelberg. Can't even understand him when he talks English, and *Deutsch* I've clean forgot. Anyhow, my own special-

ist crossed me up. Handed down the opinion that
it would kill Gwen to move her.

So now she's got to die in jail. Only she's not going to die alone. I owe her that much. And my
specialist comes every day to treat her and won't
take my money, telling me to send my check to a
T.B. sanatorium he's interested in. Says they need
it; he doesn't.

Gwen looks some better now. Keeps telling me
to go back home to you. And I keep telling her she
doesn't know what an angel you are. That you'd
want me to do this. That you'd never forgive me if
I didn't.

Only one thing worries me. I gave 'em Fritz's
address as her next of kin to be notified when she
passes on. Seemed to me the only decent thing to
do. So you better have some of the boys keep an
eye out for him in case he goes wild and blames me
for this, too.

Reckon that's all. Kiss my pet for me, and tell
her not to pay too much attention to young Cameron
—at least not yet. Both him and my pet's still a
mite too young.

                                        Love,
                                        Roak.

She put the letter down. Stared at her daughter without really seeing her. Thought:

No. You give me too much credit. I don't want you
to do it. I haven't that much charity, Christian or otherwise, in me. I want you home—with me. But you're right.
You should do it. You must. You do owe her that much,
maybe you even owe God this milder version of bloody
knees and a lash-striped back. Maybe since the only
things we don't share with the other animals is our
ability to weep, to suffer pain that isn't physical, you

owe Gwen and yourself and God this measure of anguish, and maybe expiation is worth something after all if it only makes you feel better—because pardoning one's self and living with the knowledge of all the dirty rotten stinking things we've done or even thought is a lot harder than obtaining God's forgiveness or some padre's assurance that He does forgive and has in this instance done so. So, *ave Maria,* Roak! Or *ave atque vale.* Or *ave Caesar*—we who are about to die, salute thee!

"Mama," Jessica said, "what has Papa got against Rod Cameron?"

The image of lionlike old Rod Cameron, dead now, rest his soul, came to Hannah's mind; and after that, young Rod II, his son, whom she hardly remembered, because he had fled to the East his delicate temperament required; and, last of all, Rod III, his son, whom Hank Flynn had adopted, thereby, perhaps, equating legal with moral justice, at least in Roak's opinion, and to whom, doubtless, Jessica referred.

"Nothing," she said. "Your papa thinks that you're both too young to be thinking about marriage. . . ."

"Mama, how old were you when you married Papa?"

"Nineteen, pet. Why?"

"Two whole years to wait," Jessica wailed. "Oh, Mama, I'll die!"

"No, you won't, pet," Hannah said gently. "In fact, you'll be surprised at the number of things a body can survive. . . ."

The drilling rig came, together with a Mr. Henry Thompson, bachelor of science, who informed her at once that he was an engineer. And who refused to drill where the old Indian indicated, holding it beneath his dignity to be bound by such unscientific nonsense, until Hannah told him flatly to get off the place, rig and all, unless he was willing to obey orders; whereupon, reluctantly, he fired up the boiler of his little steam engine that worked a walking beam which lifted and dropped the cable-supported bit assembly in the hole. He informed Hannah that this was the percussion method of drilling, which, coupled with a sand pump, also steam-operated, to suck the loosened cuttings out, would get down to at least a hundred feet in a hurry. When Hannah pointed out that Roak and the hands had already dug eighty feet by hand, he allowed that he had an ace up his sleeve: that the rig could also handle a boring auger with extensible handles, capable of boring all the way to China if necessary.

"Start with that—you'll need it," Hannah said.

So the bachelor of science started in with Pepe and Enrique to help him, got down to all of 244 feet without finding water before Roak came back home.

Which, once he started out, didn't take Roak long now; because you could go from St. Louis to New Orleans by train now, change to the Southern Pacific there, and get off in Furniss itself. And that, when a body remembered the Brownsville stage, seemed nothing short of a miracle. So, three days after he left Missouri, Roak was home again. Being himself, he stopped off at the would-be well before going up to he house.

"I tell you, sir," Henry Thompson said, "we're drilling at the wrong place! Just because that old fool Indian says—"

"Just you keep right on drilling, friend," Roak said.

Then he turned the nag and the rickety buckboard he'd rented at the livery stable in Furniss toward the house, riding heavily, grumpily, his stiff leg resting too high on the dashboard for comfort, his blue eyes red-streaked and tired from the glare, maybe, his nose reacting to the lessening stench of rotting cattle, because the buzzards had got their job pretty well polished off by then, and damned nigh all of his herds were already dead, picked clean, and bleaching on the prairie.

But he wasn't thinking about that. He was thinking about Gwen who had died very quietly and without saying anything, which had grieved him more than anything, because he had been hoping for her explicit, spoken pardon, until Doctor Paul Hoffmann explained to him that deathbed speeches existed only in novels, because dying required too much attention to leave either the desire or the breath for talking, and maybe the brain itself had gone out like a gutted candle long before the body gave up its ferocious, dumb-beast, instinctive struggle to gain one more second, one more feeble breath. So Roak reckoned he'd have to go back a week for her farewell, and cherish that as best he could. She'd taken his hand and pressed it to her cold mouth and said so low he had to lean forward to hear her:

"Kind of . . . lucky. I was."

"Now, Gwen," he protested, "don't tire yourself—"

"Tired now. Too tired. But must say—"

"What, baby?"

"Lucky. To have . . . known you. In spite of everything. I wouldn't—"

"Gwen, baby, please!"

"—have missed it, for all . . . the world."

And I, he thought now, was lucky to have known her, too. Maybe lucky even to have done her dirt because the evil and the sinning and the suffering went into me and made me what I am. A man. A real, honest-to-God, grown-up man. Knowing that suffering is what a body most in generally can count on; and that hanging on, facing up to it without ever whining and crying is about all that can be expected of anybody. That, and going out quietly when the time comes, and until then treating his fellow sufferers with the pity that's their due —allowing for them and forgiving them without ever asking that they allow for and forgive him. Which reminds me. I guess I'd better go visit Fritz, leaving my artillery at home. Surely by now he won't take this wrong, because if he was willing to call it quits a few months back, by now, he—

But he had come up to the house by then, and Hannah stood on the veranda very still and did not even come down the steps to greet him. Instead she waited while he stumped up those steps with his cane. Turned her head a little so that his kiss fell on the corner of her mouth.

"What ails you, Han?" he asked. Then: "Gwen's gone, poor thing. So if that's what's worrying—"

"No," she said; "I—I'm just out of sorts."

Then, very slowly, she smiled. Put her two hands alongside his face and looked at him straight in the eyes. Her mouth trembled a little. Her eyes went misty.

"So now you're back home," she whispered. "Really back home this time, aren't you, Roak? For good. And I've got you, if only by default. . . ."

"You've always had me, Han," he rumbled. "Took me a heck of a long time to find that out; but once I did, the idea went down smooth and easy. Anyhow—"

She kissed him then, meaning it. Swung back against his encircling arm; said:

"Welcome home, darling!"

"Home," he said, "where a man's heart is, and his treasure. My treasure, my two treasures. By the way, where the devil is she?"

"Out riding somewhere," Hannah said.

"Didn't you get my telegram?" Roak said. "I wired I was coming today."

"Yes," Hannah said.

"And Jessica didn't stay home to greet me? That's mighty odd."

"No," Hannah said. "You see, as usual, yesterday we

had a terrible fuss. And, also as usual, about the same thing: why she can't marry young Cameron right now instead of waiting 'til she's nineteen. So she's in a mood. She—she rode off this morning before I got up. . . ."

"I see," Roak said. "I'll gentle her down a bit when she comes home. Lord, I'm tired! Trains are faster and smoother than stages, but they wear you out just the same. . . ."

But when, two hours later, bathed, shaved, rested, even having slept a bit, he came down to his midday meal, Jessica still hadn't come home.

He sat there, staring at Hannah.

"Must have been some fuss!" he growled.

Hannah turned to him, her eyes wide, her mouth trembling.

"Roak I—I—I—lied to you. She—"

He searched her eyes, waited with all his breath stopped for what he was afraid she was going to say.

"She—she's been gone since yesterday! And she said she was going to run off with the Cameron boy the first chance she got!" Hannah wailed.

Roak sat there, relief washing over him in waves. Because, since a man's deciding always had to be between evils, this particular evil was one he damned well could take in his stride. At best, Jessica had run off and got married too young, which, with him and Han around to give her advice, could surely work out all right; and at worst, she had run off without getting married, which was a thing he could fix mighty handily with a shotgun and a quirt. But he doubted that. The Cameron boy struck him as being a mighty decent youngster. And, either way, all it meant was that he'd be a grandpa before he was fifty, which was a thing he was looking forward to, anyhow.

"Could have done worse," he said mildly. Then: "Call Angelo to hitch up my rig, Han."

"Then you aren't—you won't—"

"No, I'm not mad, and I won't be too harsh with the youngsters, Han. How can I? Didn't you and I do exactly the same thing? Doesn't leave me much of a leg to stand on, does it?"

But it wasn't that. Rod Cameron III was helping Hank Flynn mend fences, and his candid young face showed no evidences of guilt or even of doubt and confusion no matter how Roak searched his eyes.

"You mean to tell me that you haven't even seen Jessica since last Friday?" Roak said.

"Word of honor, Mr. Garfield," Rod said.

Roak stared at Hank.

"The boy's telling the truth, Roak," Hank said.

"I know he is," Roak whispered; "but God in glory, how I wish he wasn't!"

Then he turned the buggy with those two extravagantly showy white horses south.

Toward the river.

When he came up to Fritz Heindrichs's *casa grande,* he had the sawed-off riot gun in his hands. But no one opposed him, no one stopped him. He came up to the house in the midst of an echoing silence that crawled along his nerves like a living thing. He pushed open the door, entered the dim hallway, the shotgun cocked and ready. Went on, kicking open doors, staring into rooms richly furnished but empty of life. No one. Just as there had been no one in the courtyard, no one at the gate, no one in all the two long miles he had driven up their entrance before reaching the house.

Which was—strange. The house brooded there, deserted. No one. Neither *patrón,* nor mistress, nor servants. No horses. No dogs. Nothing.

He kept on doggedly. Every door. Mustn't miss one. Here. Another one. Open it, too—

Then he was inside, the shotgun shoulder-high and aiming.

"Put your hands up," he snarled; "don't reach, damn you, or—"

But the boy turned, and he was staring into those luminous dark eyes, into that face that was his own face, but refined by the other strain it bore into a beauty his face had never had, retaining that beauty through the mass of cuts and bruises he saw now with a deepening of his rage into both comprehension and pity it had been beaten into; then the boy was saying, gravely:

"I have no arms, señor. . . ."

And he, Roak, lowering the shotgun, and saying:

"Still can't speak English—son?"

And the boy:

"A little. What I could pick up."

And behind him that deep animal groan; and the boy turning, his voice woman-gentle, murmuring:

"No, Uncle, for God! Your wound is very grave, and—"

Roak put down the gun. Came to the bed. Bent and looked into Ramón Benevides's face.

"Ramón," he said, "you—"

"I am shot," Ramón said between set teeth; "I am shot by my brother-in-law, and my children will be fatherless because I opposed him in this—in this—"

"Don't talk!" young Roak said.

"—in this of thy daughter," Ramón said; "he—"

"You opposed him because of Jessica?" Roak said. "Why? I always thought you hated my guts—"

"I did," Ramón whispered; "but one grows beyond hate, Roak. And I remain a Benevides. We do not war upon women and children nor stoop to strike at an enemy through them. I—I have daughters now; and this obscenity Fritz proposed to do was—too much. . . . I have much fondness for Fritz, but I do not comprehend him. When the telegram came, he—"

"Let me tell it, then," the boy said in Spanish; "for the señor speaks our language, does he not?"

"*Sí*," Roak said. "Speak, I'm listening."

"When the telegram came with this of the death of *mi tía*, my aunt, whom I did not even know I had, Papa had, it seems, an *ataque de locura,* an onslaught of madness. It seems she died—badly. And in—"

"Prison. Of lung sickness," Roak said. "I know. I was with her when she died. Go on."

"So," the boy whispered, "my Papa decided to revenge himself upon you, señor, by taking the señorita, your daughter, *alal,* but she is pretty!—and selling her to—to a filthy old man who operates a house—a house—"

"*Una casa de putas,* Roak," Ramón said sardonically.

"Silence, *tío!*" the boy said sternly. "You are not to talk, my Uncle! Who operates a house for old and dirty men who think it is possible to buy love. In *la Ciudad de México.* So Papa rode to your hacienda and came back with her across his saddle, bound and gagged. *Mi tío Ramón*, here, opposed him, so Papa shot *mi pobre tío*—"

"And thy mother?" Roak said.

"Likewise opposed him. So he beat her until her face was all blood, and pistol-whipped me when I came to her defense. The peons, seeing these hateful things, all left. Which is why we are alone now."

"Where has he taken Jessica," Roak said, "to Mexico City?"

"No. He has not taken her anywhere. He wired the filthy one who came from *Ciudad Victoria*, and took her away in a carriage, early this morning. After that, Papa rode away in a different direction, I know not where. Then Mama took the Winchester of *tío* Ramón, and rode away after the carriage, making me swear before *la Virgen Santísima* that I would stay and care for *tío*

Ramón. But all the same it is a shameful thing! It is I who should have ridden after the filthy one in order to save the señorita, your daughter, and Mama who should have stayed to nurse *mi tío. Perdóneme, tío!* I love thee much; but this is not a thing of men!"

"She—she didn't want him to—to oppose the man he—he considers his father," Ramón said heavily, in English; then: "May the Holy Mother of God preserve her, because she has not come back. . . ."

Roak was already turning, hobbling for the door; but Ramón cried out:

"Roak, have pity, *por Dios!* See if you cannot at least stop the bleeding! My Rosita has four infants now and a fifth on the way. I—I cannot die. . . . I cannot even afford to—"

Roak hung there. When you gave up the notion of God, you gave up cause and effect, the punishment for sins, and the reward for good. But Ramón Benevides had found him in the *malpaís* choking to death on his own blood. Had saved his life; and maybe there was cause and effect, good and evil, sin and sanctity after all. Maybe if he left Belén's brother to die the effect would follow the cause, and the punishment, the sin. Maybe God would take into consideration a meritorious action, and keep Jessica—and Belén—safe until he came. And maybe if he let Ramón die, there would be no saving them either, which was all, his mind told him, god-damned nonsense, and there was no time, no time. . . .

Then he slumped, said wearily to his son:

"Roakie, go put some water on to boil—" and seeing from the boy's blank look he hadn't understood, rasped out: *"Agua herviendo, chico! Y pronto, por Dios!"*

And then, afterwards, the boy, white to the lips, holding his Uncle while Roak dug and probed for that ball with a hunting knife he'd sterilized, found it at last, packed the wound with clean lint, bandaged it with an expertness born of having watched the same thing being done to him so many times. Ramón, he could see, was out of danger now. Perhaps he had never really been in danger. The ball had gone into his side, low down, missing the ribs, and from the looks of things, it had missed the big gut, too. A couple of weeks in bed and Ramón would be good as new.

"Guard him well, my son," Roak said, and got out of there.

He knew the Victoria Road, the beginning of it, anyhow. He did not whip up his team, but rode on at a pace that he knew they could keep up for days without killing themselves. The sun came up over the mountains and blazed. He kept on through the heat of midafternoon, then he slowed the horses, stopped them, gave them to drink from the water keg the boy had warned him to take, drank himself, and started out again.

It was still hours before nightfall. The sun was a bronze disk in a yellow-white sky. Even the cholla cactus and the Joshua trees were brown. He saw a rattlesnake in the shade of a thorn bush, too heatstricken to move. And then, looking up, he saw the buzzards.

Which could mean anything, or nothing. A locoed steer down in the wasteland. A mule. A goat. A calf. Or—

He turned off the road, headed toward the place they were circling above. Got there. Sat under the canopy of his buggy looking at—

That overturned carriage, splintered; one horse still in the traces, dead; the other broken free and gone. At that obscene mass of fat that had been a man once—the filthy one, Roak guessed, the one Fritz had sold Jessica to—already turning black and swelling, his mouth open, frozen into his last scream of anguish, his hands clutching his belly where the bullets had gone in, and the pearl-handled Colt lying at his feet. But beyond that, nothing. No trace of Jessica, no trace of—

He got down, stiff-legged, bent, sniffing the earth like a hound. That black splotch, sunbaked. Another a little farther off. Another. Beyond that one, finally, the Winchester, too hot to touch, dust-covered in the sun. Another splotch, bigger now. Then, full length in the dirt, the imprint of a body. Of a woman's body. He could tell that because that wide sweep in the sand had been made by a skirt, not trousers. The deep-clawed traces of hands, of knees, getting up, fighting to get up. Here, another fall. Then again the earth clawed, the bloodstains, and beyond that, the hoof marks.

He got back into the buckboard. Followed them. Went on following them, becoming aware at last that they had doubled back toward the river, were, in fact, paralleling the road. He drove on, not thinking, achieving, living the suspension of thought because he dared not think. He didn't know precisely when it was that he realized beyond all questioning and doubt that he was being followed in his turn. The rider kept a prudent distance behind him. Looking back, he could see the white dust, slow and steady rising. He took the shotgun out of its scabbard, placed it across his knees, looked back again at the dust cloud closer now—at the two dust clouds, separate and distinct. Two of them, by God! Well, he was a match for any two or any ten with that hand cannon cocked and ready. He drove on, still looking back, his attention so taken by the riders behind him that he would have passed the horse standing head down and riderless in the desert except that something came over to him faintly, a husk of a voice a whisper so sand-dry that somehow it carried:

"Papa! Papa! Oh, thank God!"

And he was down from that buggy stumping toward her, holding her in his arms, then stiffening, saying:

"Go to the buggy, pet. There's water in the back—don't drink too much or it'll make you sick. . . ."

And she:

"Papa—Papa—what about her? She was so brave—so brave. . . . Papa, oh, Papa, I—"

And he, quietly: "Go on, pet," and kneeling there gathering Belén or what was left of Belén into his arms and thinking it, saying it aloud:

"For me. Even this. Dear God, I—"

Then he couldn't see her any more. Couldn't see her, knowing she was there only by the weight of her, the looseness, the sag, the give; and he, straightening up, started walking toward the buggy or toward where he thought the buggy was because by then he couldn't see that either, the brine and spill and flooding making red mud out of the dust on his face so that he seemed to be crying blood which maybe he even was.

And Jessica crying out. "Papa! Papa! Look out! He—"

And Fritz Heindrichs saying:

"Now I've seen what I wanted to see, Roak: you crying. Only it's too late, too late, because what it took to make you cry was too much, too goddamned much and I— Here, give her to me! You heard me, Roak! Give her to me—she—she's mine, mine and I—"

And he, Roak, moved by some obscure impulse, some surrender of will, the fight gone out of him, everything gone out of him, let what remained of Belén Benevides down gently into her husband's arms, and stood there, seeing, because by then he could see again, even tears failing him now, Fritz doubling, sinking to his knees, and his butchered face twisting into a caricature of grief that was all the more horrible for being real.

Saw that his foe-friend, his adversary, his brother in pain, his twin in sorrow, his enemy who had loved him with the love that was the reverse of the coin of hate, was crying in a way that even he could not cry for Belén, could not so terribly mourn his love, his loss, and he, in this, at least, defeated by Fritz Heindrichs utterly, stood there hearing those hoarse animal stranglings of a pain beyond both belief and bearing, so that even listening to it was a gutripping, a tearing of his insides, a disembowelment that left him hollowed out and pure agony rushing in to fill the bloody sack, ballooning in him, swelling, his lungs collapsed by it, his heart squeezed dry, and there being no answer to the way he felt, no surcease for that absolutely unendurable anguish, he turned away his face and saw—

The other horseman, the second rider he, Roak, had forgot about, sitting there on his horse, pressing one hand against his side where the black-red splotch of his blood showed dark against his shirt front, and drawing his revolver very slowly—

And he, Roak, crying:

"No, Ramón! No!"

But his voice was lost in the shrilling of Jessica's scream, in the flame splat, smoke puff, board-breaking sound. He saw Fritz Heindrichs's leaning forward very slowly until he lay across Belén's body, the two of them very small and dark in that vastness, very still under that sun.

He said: "Why, Ramón? It wasn't necessary and he couldn't harm her any more nor you nor me nor anybody so why?"

"A kindness," Ramón whispered; "I did it as a kindness. As I told you I—was fond of him. . . ."

First in the morning, Roak Garfield rode into the gates of the Bar F with Jessica sleeping against him and young Roak sitting very tall and erect at his side. The white horses moved tiredly, stiffly along the road that led to the house. And the light came stealing over the land, creeping out to the rim edges of forever, and there, suddenly, in the midst of the light, was a column of silver standing up like God's pillar of cloud. And Roak staring at it uncomprehendingly until he heard Angelo's and Pepe's voices yipping:

"*Patrón! El Cojo* has come! *Mira*, señor! Look, señor, the water! The blessed water sent of God!"

And he sitting there staring at that fountain, at that geyser sprung silver and tall, laughing with spray, blinding with mists, from the bowels of the earth, knew, even before he heard Jessica's awed whisper, "Oh, Papa!" and his son's *"Que hermosa!"* what it was.

But he didn't tell them. To put a name to a benediction was to spoil it, maybe.

"Come on, let's go find your mama," he said.